ASPECTS

ALSO BY JOHN M. FORD

JOHN M. FORD

ASPECTS

TOR

A TOM DOHERTY ASSOCIATES BOOK

NEW YORK

ASPECTS

Copyright © 2022 by The Estate of John M. Ford

Introduction copyright © 2022 by Neil Gaiman

A Tor Book
Published by Tom Doherty Associates
120 Broadway
New York, NY 10271

www.tor-forge.com

Tor® is a registered trademark of Macmillan Publishing Group, LLC.

Library of Congress Cataloging-in-Publication Data

Names: Ford, John M., author.
Title: Aspects / John M. Ford.
Description: First edition. | New York : Tor, 2022. | "A Tom Doherty
    Associates book." |
Identifiers: LCCN 2021041773 (print) | LCCN 2021041774 (ebook) |
    ISBN 9781250269034 (hardcover) | ISBN 9781250269041 (ebook)
Subjects: LCGFT: Fantasy fiction. | Novels.
Classification: LCC PS3556.O712 A96 2022 (print) | LCC PS3556.O712
    (ebook) | DDC 813'.54—dc23/eng/20211014
LC record available at https://lccn.loc.gov/2021041773
LC ebook record available at https://lccn.loc.gov/2021041774

Our books may be purchased in bulk for promotional, educational,
or business use. Please contact your local bookseller or the Macmillan
Corporate and Premium Sales Department at 1-800-221-7945, extension
5442, or by email at MacmillanSpecialMarkets@macmillan.com.

First Edition: 2022

Printed in the United States of America

0 9 8 7 6 5 4 3 2 1

An Introduction

I

With the close of day there comes an end to screaming
And a calmness in the dying of the fire.
Holding tight to breath has worn your fingers ragged
And the earth comes up to meet you in a kiss.
You will waken on another day of never;
There is nothing that can hear you, in the dark.

John M. Ford wrote that. It's the last stanza of a sestina, a form of poem in which the words that end the six lines repeat through each of six verses. He wrote the entire thing, inspired by something I had once put into *Sandman,* a tossed-off jewel in an email about something else entirely.

II

John M. Ford was Mike to his friends, and I was fortunate enough to be able to count myself as one of his friends.

Mike Ford looked gentle and amused. As the years went by his eyebrows grew out, like insectile antennae, putting him in touch with the infinite. He was mild-mannered, a description that normally is only applied to reporters who are secretly Superman, which seems appropriate, as all of Mike's friends suspected him of secretly being, well, if not a Superman, then a different kind of human, one vastly smarter and wiser than the normal manner of person.

Mike died alone, taken by a sudden heart attack, in 2006, and it was devastating. He was forty-nine when he died, and it felt like he was only getting started.

He had been giving me *Aspects,* a few chapters at a time, for years: whenever we saw each other he would have another section printed out, or he would apologise for his slowness (his excuses were valid: he had, for example, had a kidney transplant) and he would promise one next time.

Mike has been dead fourteen years, as I write this, and I would do anything to put off writing this introduction, because writing it means that I have to acknowledge two things that, on a very fundamental level, I do not wish to believe:

They are, that Mike is actually, really, irrevocably dead; and that *Aspects,* his final novel, will never quite be finished.

It's magical thinking, I know, but it's still real: the belief, amounting to a certainty, that as long as I don't finish this introduction, as long as *Aspects* in this form is not published, it could all be a mistake.

I know, deep in my soul, with the same conviction with which I know that the sun will rise tomorrow, that pretty soon I'll do a signing at DreamHaven Books in Dinkytown in Minneapolis, and Mike will casually turn up about half an hour before the end, browse the shelves, talk to people, and then, when it's all done, I'll drive us both somewhere for some food, probably sushi, and we will talk, and Mike will do most of the talking (for which I will be grateful) and at the end of the meal Mike will produce the final chapters of *Aspects* from deep inside a coat pocket and I will take them gratefully, and then I will drive him back to his place, an office that was a living space that was his life, with the model train set that runs all around the room.

During the meal I will learn things. I have learned always to ask questions, because when I do, Mike will explain something to me that I did not know. Mike's conversation is always erudite, and travels smoothly from high culture to low. He can modulate from movie and TV trivia to Marlowe and Shake-speare with a side trip into quantum physics or obscure economics in the same thought. Perhaps during the meal Mike will let slip some unlikely jewel of personal history, and I will learn more about the intelligence communities' attempts to recruit him as a boy genius. . . .

He talks only about the parts of his life he felt comfortable letting you know about. Other bits are shadowed and brushed away.

But DreamHaven Books has moved away from Dinkytown, and I don't really do those signings anymore, and as I type this COVID has closed the world down—which means I worry, irrationally, about Mike Ford, whose health was always precarious and would need to isolate (*He's dead,* I remind myself, *he doesn't need to isolate himself, he won't be catching anything from anyone.* . . . And still I persist in worrying.)

I'm honestly not that irrational about any of my other friends who have died. I'm sad, or resigned, or just used to it. I'm frustrated I can't talk to them any longer, but they don't feel so *there.* Mike feels like he stepped out of the room mid-sentence, and I will never stop expecting him to come back.

Physicist and writer Carlo Rovelli relates that Einstein wrote to the wife of a colleague who had recently died to reassure her that her husband had not ceased to be—her husband was still present and working, but in the past, a place she could not go. (The past is truly a foreign country, as L. P. Hartley told us. Just one to which we can no longer travel. The inhabitants aren't dead—they are there, in their country, and they cannot leave and join us. The borders are closed.)

Sometimes I go back and read Mike's emails to me. I don't do that with anyone else. Then again, nobody else I knew was likely to take a typo in an invitation I'd written to come to a bonfire party and turn it into a small play in verse, and then, as an afterthought, round up a small bunch of talented people actually to perform it. Mike did.

There. I stopped writing this introduction to reread all the surviving emails from Mike, which sent me off on a small You-Tube trip to watch the final two minutes of *The Prisoner* TV series, inspired by Mike's commentary on it. He said something I wanted to reply to, and I needed to check my own memory. . . .

And then I remembered, once again, as I always remember, that I couldn't ever reply to him. I found a sestina, though, that he sent me, inspired by something I had once written in *Sandman,* and the final stanza felt like it fitted the beginning of this introduction. So there's that.

III

When I was a teenager, I dreamed of being a Young Novelist. The kind who would write the first of a lifetime's worth of great novels as they enter their twenties. I wasn't one, which is, in retrospect, a good thing: I wouldn't have had anything to say.

Mike was, and he did. He broke into print, with short stories and poems, when he was seventeen. His first novel was published when he was twenty-two. It's called *Web of Angels,* and it's a proto-cyberpunk novel, with an honest-to-goodness cyberspace Web in it, and it came out in 1980, four years before William Gibson's *Neuromancer.*

I met Mike Ford—the M was for Milo, not Michael—in Birmingham in 1984, at a convention. He was funny in the way writers usually aren't funny, in that he would come up with the perfect riposte, line, or comment at the perfect moment for it, and not (as is the case with me) two weeks later, but he would say it quietly, as an aside, never to put people down or to dominate the conversation, although his comedic delivery was world class. We became friends. He was just about to win the 1984 World Fantasy Award for his alternate history novel *The Dragon Waiting.* (It contains no dragons, or rather, the dragon of the title is Wales.)

Whenever he would come to the UK—he would come in August, sometimes, for the Fairport's Cropredy Convention—we would get together and eat, and talk, and I would learn.

We became correspondents, too, back in those days when that involved typewriters and postage and airmail. Somewhere I have a letter from Mike written to teach me how to write a sestina. It was in the form of a sestina.

He wrote brilliantly for people who were, he assumed, as brilliant as he was.

Mike followed *The Dragon Waiting* with two *Star Trek* novels— one a First Contact novel about the Klingons, *The Final Reflection,* and the other, *How Much for Just the Planet?,* a slapstick musical comedy in science fictional form. I am there, under an anagrammatic pseudonym, and my character sings, I fancy, the finest of all of the songs in the book.

When I moved to the U.S., Mike's being in Minneapolis was one of the deciding factors of where I went.

He was my best reader. Every writer has one, or hopes they will find one. The person you know will read your story and understand it for what it was, see what you were trying for, identify the places you fell short, and tell you, succinctly and correctly, how to remedy them.

IV

I first read *Aspects,* as I have mentioned, as Mike was writing it, in chunks. They were always handed over in person, in passing, with a comment from Mike about my not ever actually having to read it, and another comment about something obscurely wrong in the text that Mike hoped I wouldn't find too alarming. I never noticed the wrong things, if they were indeed there.

I loved the book, though.

It began with a duel, and I thought myself, as I read the first chapter 150 years ago in Europe, in the kind of imaginary place and time that Avram Davidson had once written about, and then I realised, as I read, that it was something else entirely, not that at all.

It felt like he was building something quite new in Fantasy, a place where nothing is ever new: it was what *A Game of Thrones* might have been, if the author had been fascinated by trains, and set in a place that wasn't nineteenth-century Europe, just as Westeros isn't fifteenth-century Britain, and it was about—I thought—communication and politics, magic, redemption, and the forms that love can take. It was shaped only like itself, as Mark Antony said of the crocodile, and the tears of it were wet.

The world of *Aspects* feels like that of a classic movie—in black and white perhaps, shot by Howard Hawks or John Ford (Mike loved to begin his books with quotes from John Ford movies).

I had so many questions for him about what I was reading—about the characters, about the setting, about the way the people were and were not us. There is science fiction hidden here, alternate world-building aplenty, in this story about love and life, trains, government, and death.

I thought, back then, *I'll put off the questions until he gives me the final chapter, and I've read the whole thing.*

I should have learned, I realised, when the final chapter never came, to have simply asked the questions when they occurred to me. He always took so much pleasure in answering them.

V

Mike died fourteen years ago. I originally agreed to write this introduction eleven years ago, and I should have given it to its editor a year ago.

I begin to write it, but then shy, like a skittish pony, and I back away, do something else. Often the something else I do has to do with *Aspects*—I reread old emails from Mike Ford, or I reread the book. We have almost all of it, after all. Endings, and the books that would have followed, can be imagined. . . .

Perhaps what delays me is the conviction that if I can only write this introduction well enough, it won't be needed. We'll jump the rails, find ourselves clattering along on another track, one in which Mike finished this book and wrote the other *Aspects* books he planned.

But no. I write it as best I can, and Mike stays dead, and remains in his own country, which is the past, and this book is what he left us.

Neil Gaiman
April 2021

ASPECTS

I

AUTUMN GAMES

Leaves fall, and lie forgotten on the ground,
Until a footstep rustles them again:
A letter brought my thought once more around,
Crisp deckled pages, fine-veined from your pen.
Most loves choose other seasons. Many hold
Forever fogblind spring, or summer's sweat,
Or silent winter's deep respectful cold;
Most chase them all, and have not caught them yet.
But we keep to our thoughts, and letters sent:
We play our autumn games, and are content.
I entertained an autumn thought of you,
An unexpected warmth with summer gone;
It colored deep, as leaves in autumn do,
And I allowed the wind to blow it on

CHAPTER 1

THE CITY AND SOLITUDE

I t has been said that, if a person is going to die, he should do it in the morning: when the day is new and clean and full of unanswerable questions, when the sun has just risen to cast an afterglow on the things that have been done by night. It has also been said that, if a person is going to die, the circumstances are irrelevant.

On this Paleday morning in Lystourel, capital city of the Republic of Lescoray, the twenty-fifth day of Shepherd's month, three days before the Equinoctial holiday and six until the autumn Equinox itself, a legal duel was scheduled for seven o'clock in the morning: by seven thirty at the latest, a man whose beliefs ran one way about death and morning was going to kill one of the other persuasion.

It was a foul morning anyway, cold a month too early, the wind off the Grand Estuary hard as a slap across the cheek. The sky was lumpy and curdled, and sooty as well, because the weather had forced fires lit before the flues had been properly cleaned: there was creosote in the air, there would be chimney fires tonight, and the price of dusted coal on the City Exchange was over two gold marks the wagonload for the first time in years.

The gilded dome of the Lystourel Cathedral looked dull and sullen as old copper; the copper dome of the National Gallery looked green and moldy; the glass sheds of the Grand Ironway Terminus were clouded, vapors thick beneath them, like infected blisters. It was the kind of day that made people in the streets long for a King over Lescoray, to heal the aerial sickness, blow away miasma with a royal word. None of the people in the streets was old enough to remember when Lescoray actually had a King over it, which made the longings perfect.

The time was now twelve minimi before seven, and the duel was organizing itself in Willowpark Square, in the western part of Lystourel, just south of the fashionable Silverthread District. The square was four rows of high houses, including the Consulate of a tiny island republic, facing on a small green plot surrounded by an iron fence. There were drooping willow trees, just turning yellow, miscellaneous bushes and benches, a neglected rose arbor. On the outside of the fence were the uninvited spectators: some coatless boys with schoolbooks, some curious tradesmen. The residents were discreetly in their upstairs windows. Inside the fence was the crowd for the matter at hand.

It took rather a lot of people to conduct a legal duel. There were the two duelists' seconds, young women with their hair tucked under their tall hats and long winter capes over their morning coats; one was in blue, one in green. They were looking rather sadly at one another, but did not speak. The one in the blue coat carried a long, narrow leather case and had a black cheroot between her teeth, chewing more than smoking it. The dueling proctor wore a dark green belted coat, with a silver chain of office crookedly over his shoulders, and a white weeper tied around his silk hat. It fluttered dismally in the wet wind. He tapped an ivory-hilted cane on the ground, looking bored, or impatient, or both. At his side was a boy in a jacket and cap, with a badge pinned to his chest and a wooden box under his arm.

Behind the proctor was a bailiff in the uniform red-and-silver livery, silver buttons on his jacket and black leather cap and boots, silver rope over one shoulder balancing the sling of the magazine carbine on the other. Everyone looked with distaste at the bailiff's rifle, and the bailiff returned the looks in kind.

A little distance away, leaning against a tree, was the surgeon, in a wine-red, swallow-tailed morning coat and crimson cravat, a white fur hat rakishly on her head. Dangling from her waistcoat pocket was a golden sunburst watch fob, indicating that she was also an accredited sorcerer. It had become fashionable for the observing magicians at affairs like this to fade into the background. The sorcerers' guild had created the fashion, trying to discourage the idea that a sorcerer would help anyone cheat in the first place.

There were two reporters, rather less well dressed than the rest, one in a short wool coat, cotton cravat, and round-crowned hat, the other in a leather engine driver's jacket and cap, a soiled silk scarf around his neck, and no cravat at all. One was from the *Evening Observer*, the one in the jacket from the *Northern Star*. The *Star* man would be hitching a ride on the next freight train home with his story as soon as the duel was over, saving the cost of magnostyle and the indignity of having his words rewritten at the office. He had a hip flask of whisky out and open, and was sharing it with his comrade of the press. This was not the usual duel, which they could write up beforehand and insert the names in the appropriate spots after; one of the parties was a Coron in Parliament, and if he died, it would be actual news, at least in the North where his Coronage was.

The duelists were the last to arrive, as was customary. One, a young cavalry officer named Chase, was crossing the square, whirling his cloak off as he shoved through the gate; he tossed the cloak to his second and stretched, his tied-back brown hair bouncing as he moved. The wind fluttered the linen ruffles of his white shirt.

The other man, the Coron Varic, took a step away from one

of the willows. He was rather tall, dark haired, severely thin, in a steel-blue frock coat and gray trousers. He took off the coat, folding it lengthwise and over, and handed it to his second; he adjusted his braces slightly, loosened his dark blue cravat but did not remove it.

The breeze rose slightly, shaking the willow trees. The Goddess Coris, it was said, must have been in a terrible melancholy when She made willows. From a few blocks away, a tower clock began striking seven.

The dueling proctor said, "There is still time, honoreds, to conclude these differences without violence, or to lessen their extremity. I remind you both that the insult has been deemed mortal, yet lesser strokes have satisfied greater men. Will you accede?" The law required that the proctor say the words; it could not demand any feeling or concern in them.

Lieutenant Chase said, "The insult remains, honored: no pretense that it is less can make it any less. I do not accede."

Varic nodded without speaking.

The proctor said, "Then I am required to remind you that the matter, being so begun, may only be so concluded." He waved to his assistant. The boy held up the wooden case, and the proctor took from it a large, heavy pistol, an antique, firing a single shot with a cap and hand-tamped powder. There was no legal requirement that he use such a thing. "I am the instrument of conclusion," he said, as prescribed.

The duelists looked at the proctor, then at each other. Varic said suddenly, "How many people have you killed, Lieutenant? I've killed two, under just these circumstances. A young man in Trumpeters' Park, and a very pretty young woman by the Estuary. She was a cavalry lieutenant as well."

"Then I have more honor than my own to redeem," Chase said.

"She's dead," Varic said, "and won't ever notice."

"You don't begin to frighten me," Chase said, thin patches showing in his voice. "I don't care how red your lance may be." He looked, expectantly, into Varic's face.

The Coron's expression did not change at all. "Frightening you was not my intention. I just thought you should know that this is an old business with me. I have no particular interest in killing you, Lieutenant."

"Then you, honored, are at the disadvantage." It was not a challenge, just a flat statement.

Varic said, "Just so. As the . . . injured party, you have choice of weapons." He motioned toward his second, who rolled the cigar to a corner of her mouth and opened the long leather case. Four swords gleamed dully on velvet inside. "Sabers or rapiers, Lieutenant?" There was no mention of pistols. They were all gentlefolk here, except possibly for the reporters, and the well aspected did not shoot one another over honorable disputes. The proctor's gun was another business entirely.

Chase inspected the swords. "These are excellent weapons, Coron." Varic nodded meaninglessly. "Rapiers, then," Chase said, and selected a sword, with a straight thin blade and a plain cross hilt, not ornamented at all. Chase tested the sword's balance, then stepped back as Varic took out the matching weapon.

Varic said to his second, "If it goes against, you're to report directly to Brook." The woman nodded, closed the case, dropped the stub of her cigar, and ground it under her boot.

The proctor held up his cane. Varic and Chase took up positions to either side, crossing their points above the stick.

The cane fell. The swords, the duelists, the whole square held still in the cold, bad air for a few instanti, half a heartbeat, and then steel flashed down like a thunderclap.

They stayed close for the first minima or so, Lieutenant Chase parrying brilliantly, thrusting very near his opponent, stepping lightly from side to side. Varic stood nearly still, moving his blade in simple straight lines, easy for the eye to follow, for the hand to predict. Click, ring, step, scrape, the two of them matching moves as if this were an open-air production of *King Zargo*. Wherever Varic put his sword, Chase's blade was there first.

And then, suddenly, it was not. The very tip of Varic's sword was in the meat of Chase's upper left arm, and there was blood on the white linen. Varic pulled out, held his sword at high guard. Chase did the same. They fell to again, both walking now, stepping off the narrow garden path as they circled one another, steel whipping across the space between. The lieutenant was not content to fence now, he was fighting, trying to find an opening in his enemy's guard, cut a way into Varic's flesh. He leaped to the top of a stone bench, slashed, leaped down again.

Varic recoiled, executed a circular disengaging parry, seemed to stumble. Chase lunged into the gap, with a perfect deadly geometry. Steel cut air, whistling.

And then there was a sharp, bright note as Chase's rapier hit the pavement. There was a gash the width of his right arm, a sheet of blood running from it. Varic was standing entirely away from Chase; if not for the blood dripping from his sword, he might have had nothing at all to do with the wound.

Chase looked at Varic, at Varic's sword, at his own on the ground. He took an uncertain step, his boot squeaking in his own blood. Varic simply waited.

The lieutenant turned and ran.

The dueling proctor leveled his pistol at the fleeing man's back. Varic took a long step, and his sword flicked out, knocking the barrel of the gun upward even as it snapped and fired; the bullet rustled the boughs of a willow, and there was an explosion of sparrows.

"Your pardon, honored," Varic said softly. "I've spoiled your aim."

"No matter," the proctor said, examining his pistol for damage. "I believe the affair is now concluded?"

"To my satisfaction, certainly."

"Indeed." The proctor's assistant held out the gun case; the proctor put away the weapon, adjusted his cloak and white-sashed hat. "You will of course excuse me, ladies, gentlemen. I have another of these matters to attend at eight. Find Goddess in your ways."

"In your way," the others said—though Varic only nodded, and the leather-jacketed reporter was already running to find his train—and the proctor left Willowpark Square, his assistant and the bailiff following behind him. The surgeon stood still for a moment more, then tipped her hat and departed after them.

Varic was sitting on a park bench, cleaning the sword blades with a lemon and a cloth. Lieutenant Chase's second said to him, "Well and fairly done, honored." Her face was a bit flushed, perhaps with the cold. Varic said, "Thank you," and the woman went away.

The *Observer* man came up, his notebook and fountain pen out. "That was quite a fight, milord, quite a fight. Tell me, Coron, were you ever in the army?"

"No," Varic said, wiping a rapier and replacing it in the case. "I've spent most of my career in Parliament." He looked at the reporter, smiled faintly. "That's a sort of fencing practice, you know."

It took the man a moment to get the joke. Then he laughed, said, "Oh, yes! Very good, milord, very good indeed. Thank you." He scribbled in his book and departed.

Varic's second had lit a fresh cigar. She said, "Why did you say that, milord Varic?"

Varic put the other sword away, closed the case. The woman

was only an acquaintance of his, a retired foot soldier; Brook had suggested her for this morning's duty. "Because he's a reporter," Varic said pleasantly, "and he wanted something to report. I gave him a line he can use, and now he won't have to make something up." He sat back, feeling the sweat on his shirt go cold, and looked at the park fence: the spectators, perhaps twenty of them, were starting to drift away from the iron bars. A small blond boy kept staring. Varic gave him a small salute, and the boy turned and ran away. "What's the time?"

The woman checked her pocket watch. "Twenty-five past seven."

"Ninety-five minimi to the session bell. . . . Best see if you can find a cab for me. And, Rose?"

"Milord Coron?"

"If I ever have to do this again, I'd be pleased to have you as second. But I hope we never have to."

"Of course, honored," she said, sounding somewhat puzzled.

Varic thought, though there was no way to explain it to Rose, that this probably would be his last duel. Those responsible had now failed three times; time to try something new.

Rose had probably been in duels, at least seconded often, since Brook had recommended her. But she was a soldier of Lescoray and therefore had no personal experience of war.

She hailed a two-wheeler with military authority. Carrying his coat over his arm, Varic thanked her again; she would take the swords back to Varic's house in Healstone Court. After that, barring a fourth duel, they would meet only at sociable functions, Infantry Balls, and charity teas. They would smile at one another, and say, "Yes, we've met," sharing the secret: and let the world confound itself trying to guess at it.

"Parliament House," Varic told the cab driver as he stepped aboard. He sat down, added through the trapdoor, "West entrance." The driver nodded, snapped his whip once smartly, and they were off through the gray and hazy streets.

They turned south, out of the residence blocks, and soon were in the heavy morning traffic along the Fresh, the smaller river that branched to the west from the Grand. A bit of Varic's mind registered the route, making sure the cabby stayed direct, while his main thoughts ticked over the schedule of motions before the Lords today. There were seven on the calendar. Things had piled up, as they always did before a recess. It had the small advantage of shortening the debates.

Four days to the Equinox, he thought. Four days and he would be forty marches away from the City, a guest at Strange House surrounded by friends and fellow guests, a long way from Parliaments and political duels and polluted air. They would play games and argue philosophy and take tea in the autumn twilight—and Varic would spend the whole time with one ear listening for the click of the magnostyle, and when finally the train brought him back to the Grand Terminus, he would feel an inexplicable relief.

The cab turned right, crossing the Fresh on the New Castle Bridge, an ironwork only a few years old; its bright green paint was beginning to turn dingy, and Varic supposed that next spring there would be a motion to repaint it. He filed a thought to check the price for red lead. Just to the right was the Old Bridge, now closed to all but foot traffic. On it, people were strolling or admiring the view, poor as it was today. A coal barge was passing under the central stone arch. The arches were sound after five hundred years. The pilings had been laid by the Quercians, six centuries earlier still. Varic wondered if the New Bridge would be anything more than rust in a century. Even with the red lead.

He looked out the left-side window. Receding behind them,

on the point of land where the Fresh branched from the Grand River, was the Castle, a confused but certainly impressive jumble of towers, subfortresses, arches, and buttresses, ringed by the remnants of three different wall systems. Its foundations were Quercian, too, as was the innermost wall. Every ruler since the Empire departed had considered it a personal duty to build something onto the Castle, and usually to tear something else down. Quercia was like that: dismantled, overbuilt, plowed up, quarried, exploded, still the Luminous Empire ended up under your feet, in the walls around you.

The cab reached the South Corner, a fringe of parkland and middle-cost houses around the water, holding back the sprawl of industries farther south. They turned smartly east around Greengage Circle and crossed the Grand River on a stone-and-iron bridge high enough to pass a sloop's topmast. The haze was lifting a bit, and away to the south a forest of masts and rigging was just visible, lining the Estuary. The road came down again into the measured and formal street grid of the East Bank.

Measured and formal when it was laid out, at least. Now the streets were full of flower carts, beer wagons, two-wheel cabs, and four-wheel coaches—Varic heard his driver snort, and saw where some idiot had tried to take a four-horse rig down a side street, blocking it hopelessly—vendors of groundnuts and fresh fish and sausage rolls and eel pies, jaunty signboard-men and tired prostitutes, doctors on rounds and fiddlers playing for copper aces, dawn-service priests tipping their hats to highday-service priests, those who had worked all night passing those who would work all day passing those who were too wealthy to work at all and were exhausted with their efforts. The streets smelled of starch and urine, mountain flowers and fried pork and cheap beer; they sounded of trade calls and children's verses, outraged horses and human pain. They were all walled in with many-windowed building fronts, roofed over with coal smoke and magnostyle wires, and packed so solid you could cut slices from the mass.

How could human beings live in this place, Varic thought; how could anyone feel entirely alive until he had lived here?

The streets broadened. Trees appeared, and geometric plots of grass, unbelievably green against the gray City. The cab passed the Park of the Clarity Kings, still hung with fog that made its monuments look sepulchral. To the other side, fronting on Vineyard Avenue (where the last live grape had grown six hundred years ago; now there were iron vines climbing the streetlamps) was Parliament House, twenty columns on its south face, forty broad marble steps down to the avenue. When there was sun, it was very white, and quite beautiful.

The cab passed it by, as instructed, and stopped at the western side, where there was a small walled courtyard and a modest door.

"Fare?" Varic said, gathering his coat and his thoughts.

"Three plates four, honored."

Varic gave him four silver plates, said, "No change." The cabby saluted with his whip and drove on. Varic went through the garden, which was empty, pulled the bell cord at the door. The porter admitted him, with only a slight off glance at his shirt and undone cravat. The foyer within was simply decorated, the walls painted a cool pastel green meant to be soothing to redrimmed eyes. The glass-cased clock showed six minima to eight. He should have given the cabby a larger tip, Varic thought, or at least taken his license number. He went two floors up the oak stairway, to the floor of offices one below his own. From behind the other doors along the corridor there were small sounds, of teacups rattling, newspapers rustling, the crunch of toasted muffins.

He knocked on a door. "Yes," came the answer. Varic went in.

The Chief Parliamentarian's office was large, three ordinary members' offices combined, but crowded. The walls of the front room were completely covered with plaques, scrolls, awards, an enormous globe standing next to an enormous desk. The library was visible through a door at the rear, and the door to the conference room. They had spent a lot of time in the conference room, around the green table, taking apart Lescoray's wheezing patchwork Constitution like surgeons over a dying patient, trying to stitch together something that would heal, be strong, stand on its own. Surgeons, of course, could summon, or themselves be, sorcerers, thought-work a raddled blood stew back into organs and whole bones. Laws and articles broke more easily and mended harder.

Brook was sitting on a green plush davenport by the window, in the pale north light, reading a book. A cart with the remnants of a breakfast and all the morning papers stood a little way from him.

Brook's hair was gray with a touch of silver, swept immaculately from his high forehead and temples; he had long and feathery mustaches and a neatly pointed beard. Steel-rimmed reading glasses sat low on his broad nose. His morning coat was of a gray just less than black, his trousers dove gray. A linen napkin rested on one knee, and half a buttered muffin on the napkin.

He closed the book and considered the muffin. "You look like you've spent the evening in a joy house."

"It would have been pleasanter," Varic said.

"So you killed the lieutenant?"

"No. I cut him, and he ran."

"Then the proctor . . ."

"Missed. I must change my shirt."

"There's time. Have some tea. And one of those." He ate some more of his own muffin.

Varic looked at the breakfast service and was instantly hungry; he had drunk a cup of strong black tea before the fight, but that was all. He poured tea, not commenting that there was a second clean cup, and lifted a silver cover. There were two kippers underneath it. Brook hated kippers. But he knew about duels; he had fought his share once.

Brook said, "You never told me why this young man wanted so particularly to kill you."

The salt fish stung Varic's mouth; he swallowed some tea, said, "The speech I gave on the eighteenth, about the value of cavalry. Civilian idler impugning the honor of the service, and so on."

"Ah. Of course. Honor of the service."

Varic raised an eyebrow. Surely Brook didn't believe that.

Brook said, "Your friend Winterhill brought me a copy of a letter last night, concerning Lieutenant Chase and a large gambling debt. Honor of the service, you know." He looked over his glasses at Varic. "I'd ask you how Winterhill comes by such things, but I'm afraid you'd tell me."

"Just as well Chase *is* a cavalryman," Varic said. "I doubt he'd ever seen so much blood in one place before. If he'd been a real fencer, like the others, I'd have had to kill him."

Brook said, "I have not known many souls who could keep weighing the need to kill a man after the swordplay had begun." He finished the muffin, put the book aside, stood up. Brook was a large man, taller than Varic and half again as broad. "And I know this is useless, but you might be more careful in public speaking of the Lescorial Forces of Defense."

"I've shown you the papers on Sarmanjai; you were there when I spoke," Varic said. "The Imperial Horse were the equal of anyone's—certainly ours, who haven't seen a fight in ninety years—and in one charge against a rather ordinary bunch of emplaced riflemen, they lost seven in ten dead and the rest too badly hit to reach the enemy." He put his cup down. "It's nothing to do with bravery. War isn't, not these days. I can't help it if the word hasn't reached here."

"Well, hurrah for peace," Brook said quietly.

Varic paused and chuckled.

Brook said, "So your humor lived through it as well. Good. Good."

Varic said, "I don't suppose the gambling letter mentions any interesting names."

"No. Did you expect it to?"

"Chase made a joke about 'reddening my lance.' I don't think it was original with him."

"Ah," Brook said thoughtfully. Two centuries earlier, when the Parliament was new, the Coron Redlance had been the driving wheel within it. Brook was occasionally called *the second Redlance,* a title he detested. Whoever had bought Lieutenant Chase's debts had probably given him the comment to deliver as well. But of course there was nothing provable in that, and Brook said so.

Then he said, "Speaking of the letter, Winterhill brought it to me because you were out last night. *Were* you in Cold Street?"

"No. I was at home. But I'd sent Midden home early, and I must not have heard the bell."

"Winterhill thought you'd gone to Cold Street."

"Winterhill has a fascination with Cold Street. Something to do with his name, I imagine."

"When were you there last?"

"Some weeks, I think."

Brook said, "Some months, I think."

"As you say. I must change my shirt before the session."

"They ask about you. They like you, Varic."

"I pay my bills on time."

"I said," Brook said, very softly and firmly, "they *like* you."

"I'm pleased. I haven't felt the need."

"Congratulations."

"Brook, as you very well know, we've had six major votes in that time, a seventh today, and another in three weeks. Are you suggesting that my intimate activities are an essential part of our strategy?" He smiled again. "If you are, I shan't disagree, of course."

"We are a long way from completing the Revision," Brook said. "We have a battle today, and then a hundred more, small and great. And you will be no use at all if you're so intent on the battles that you forget to breathe."

"One doesn't go to Cold Street to breathe. At least, I don't."

Brook said, "You are going to Strange House for the Equinoctial?"

"Certainly. My train is tomorrow."

"Very well." He sorted papers on his desk. "And you'd better get to your office. You really do need a clean shirt."

Varic went out and up a flight to his own floor. They had not spoken of the day's schedule. It was not necessary.

He went into his office: one room with a large closet and a lavatory alcove. He rang for the porter, pulled off his cravat and shirt, poured water into the basin, and began washing up, untying, smoothing, and retying his hair at the back, pausing to soak his eyes. He took a fresh white shirt from the closet drawer, had it on but unbuttoned when the knock came.

Leyva, the third-floor day porter (since the Quercians, the saying went), was there with her brass cart and her long white coat. She didn't even blink to see him with his braces down and his undershirt showing. "Good day, milord."

"Good morning, Leyva." He handed her the used shirt. "Wash and light starch, please?" One could get meals here, washing and mending, have a bed rolled in, bathe or shower down the hall. The office wing was everything a hotel was, except comfortable.

"Of course, milord."

There was a firm click of heels from down the hall. "Porter, what's the time?" a woman's voice said. "How long until the Assembly?" The voice had a touch of Western throatiness. It was vaguely familiar.

Varic leaned out the door. The woman was wearing a black velvet tunic brocaded with silver, a sword-and-sunset emblem on the left breast, riding trousers tucked into boots. There was early white in her black hair, which was held back with a silver mesh band. The costume was only, Varic guessed, a hundred and twenty years behind City fashion. Her face was a bit flat, her nose a bit broken, but quite pleasing, he thought. "Nine minimi," he said. "There's a single bell at three before. Plenty of time to reach the Chamber."

She looked hard at him, at his open shirt, then said, "Thank you."

"Of course. You're Lady Longlight, correct? From the Far West."

"I'm glad to see someone here knows me."

"Now, you'll hurt Leyva's feelings," Varic said, buttoning up. "I'm sure she recalls you."

The porter said, "The lady Coron was last here on the tenth day of the Spear, just after the last Evenday. She had number 319 then, as well, and salt beef and eggs for breakfast, as she did this morning." Leyva smiled fit to break one's heart.

"You see," Varic said, "The Coron of the Third Floor remembers you very well. You're here with a private motion, I believe. Number seven on the calendar."

Longlight said coolly, "I'm here with the same motion you've ignored five times now, thank you very much."

That turned the page in Varic's memory. "Longlight, daughter of the Palion Chesdonay, Coron of the Great Rogue Hills. You have an outlaw problem."

"Ay—yes," she said, startled. Far Western dialect, yes, Varic thought. She said, "And you are—"

"Varic, Coron of Corvaric." He bowed slightly as he fastened his cuffs. He was weighing the situation. She had inherited the Coronage three years ago. The Assembly had voted down her motion for assistance against the outlaws five times since then. There was no more support for it today. And he had Motion Five to deal with.

Longlight said, not too harshly, "If you know I have a problem, do you propose to do anything about it?"

Perhaps Motion Five was already safely dealt with—was on rails, as Winterhill liked to say. Well. He would know by highday. "There's no time to discuss it now, if I'm to make Assembly fully clothed. Would you—tentatively—be pleased to talk it over at lunch?"

"Certainly," she said.

"Then I'll speak with you at the highday break. Good morning, Coron."

"Good morning . . . Coron."

Varic shut the door and began tying on a cravat. He had just buttoned his waistcoat and was shrugging into his blue coat when the first bell rang.

He made it, as he had said, in plenty of time and was pleased to see as he looked around the Chamber that Longlight had as well.

The Chamber of Lords had four hundred seats in eight tiers, forming slightly more than half a circle around the speaker's platform and the President's bench. High at the back was a visitors' gallery, with two bailiffs in red and silver at the corners. They carried maces and had never in memory had to use them for more than traffic control. At least the House had managed to keep the Justiciar from giving them guns.

The room had light-colored, golden-veined marble walls, only a little sooted from the two gas chandeliers; the tier seats were of dark oak and wrought iron, and around the walls were armorial banners, from the wonderful old days when Palions on horseback beat each other's brains out for glory's sake, and the national flag of West Mountain silver quartered with Grand River blue. It had taken twenty years after the Abdication to move the royal banner from the Chamber to the National Gallery, where every day, Varic knew, people went to sigh their hearts out over its lonely exile.

The nine o'clock bell rang. The chaplain asked Goddess in all Her aspects to bless the Assembly, and the President—this year it was Saltworthy, one of the Lords Sorcerous—proclaimed the session begun. Then it fell to Brook, as Chief Parliamentarian, to read the calendar of motions.

The Chamber was nearly half full, Varic saw. That was an excellent attendance. There were, according to the roster, two hundred seventy-eight Coronage seats (the Lords Temporal), another eighty for the Lords Sorcerous, and thirty-six Lords Spiritual. Of that, only about a third were usually present. That is, someone was present: the Corons and magicians were allowed to send proxies to observe, argue, and vote for them, and most did. Not that the proxies always troubled to appear for sessions.

Over the years, the size of a voting quorum had been steadily reduced, until now it stood at seventy Corons, twenty sorcerers, and no priests at all. Even that number were only required for binding votes. There had been a memorable session, just after the winter recess two years ago, that had opened with Brook, Varic, the current President, six other Corons, two sorcerers, and a priest present at the bell. They thought for a bit about what to do, and then decided to work.

The following morning, a quorum was seated, unsteadily, and found that fifty-three motions were through debate and ready to be voted on. Attendance had been poor on occasions since then, but never again so destitute.

Varic's count was just over two hundred fifty present. There were only a dozen priests; there had been a Church election two days ago, and they would be returning from the four Imageries. Varic knew the new Archimage well. He would be seeing him at Strange House in two days more.

And all but a dozen of the magicians or their proxies were here. The news of Motion Five had spread. Well.

Varic looked for the Coron Bowenshield. Present. That could only mean one thing. Varic looked at the visitors' balcony. There, seated behind one of the bailiffs, with an extra next to him for good measure, sat Cable, Chief Justiciar of Lescoray, in a bloodred coat with a silver shoulder sash. Cable was a little past forty, still hawkishly handsome, though the hawk had eaten a few too many mice for his figure.

The Constitution, in one of its rare clear articles, forbade the Justiciar from speaking or presenting motions before Parliament. So Cable could not, but Bowenshield could. Together they had gotten through the motion allowing Cable to give his bailiffs rifles. After all, the bailiffs were provided for explicitly in the Constitution, Article Twelve, Section Three. The army itself had no such mandate to exist. And the town bosses and merchants in the Commons thought it was a wonderful idea.

Cable was smiling today. So was Bowenshield. Something about Bowenshield's face made a smile look ugly there. And seven-eighths of the Lords Sorcerous were present and voting.

Motion Five might be on rails, Varic thought, but trains did jump the tracks. He looked at Brook, who was composed as always in the Chamber. Brook would have registered the situation, would have seen Bowenshield, the crowd of magicians, could hardly help but see Cable in the front of the gallery.

The first motion came up, presented by one of the priests. It was a request for an official day of recognition for the retiring Archimage of Capel Storrow, one of the four principal priests of the country, the one Shadowday's election was replacing. There was no debate; it was immediately seconded and passed unopposed by acclamation vote. A messenger ran it to the Commons Chamber for approval.

Motions Two and Three had come up from Commons. They were both requests from the town of Coombe Strait to demolish historical structures. The first was a five-century-old bridge that was a crumbling menace to navigation, but the other was a Quercian building, a noble's house above the town. Varic suspected that the house's "wreckage"—ornamental stonework, pottery, and iron, perhaps even some sculpture or frescoes or an inlaid floor—was worth considerably more than the property it was so rudely occupying. But there really wasn't anything to be done. If the motion failed, the town would present it again, less politely. Or there would be a terrible incident of vandalism that would never be solved.

Parliament could Preserve property for the state. They did it with forests, and parks, and the Ironway trackbeds. But Preserved land produced no taxes. And it was seizure, no matter how lawful. Motions to Preserve were to be kept for the most important cases. At least, Varic thought, they did have the law requiring approval to demolish.

Both motions passed, the bridge by acclamation, the house by a voice vote, three to one.

It was ten thirty. The President called a quarter-hour recess. Varic went into the hall; the Chamberlain had tea and biscuits out. Varic gathered two cups and returned to the Chamber, handing one of the teas to Brook.

"I just had a word with Whetstone," Brook said. "He said he would like to meet you. You've not met?"

Lord Sorcerer Whetstone was returning to his seat in the front tier of the sorcerers' section, a hairless, heavyset, wrinkled man, wearing a dark blue suit and an ascot with a sunburst stickpin. He had an addled look, which was illusory. Whetstone was the best-respected sorcerer in Lescoray, six times Master of the National Guild. He was rarely in Parliament, and erratically so: his presence did not of itself mean that something important was on the calendar. Though today it did.

"No, that's true, never formally," Varic said. "Of course I'd be delighted to meet the Guildmaster. But at some more appropriate time, don't you think?"

Pitched so that to anyone else it would sound like idle conversation, Brook said, "What in the name of dear Mother Wolf have you done, my lord Coron?"

"I hope I haven't done anything at all," Varic said. "As you haven't done anything but put a motion on the calendar." He looked up at the gallery; Cable and his personal guard had gone out. "It's all up to what other people do, and when they do it."

"Yes," Brook said distantly. "Thank you for the tea."

Varic went back to his seat. There was no difficulty—at least, none with Brook. They could not work together on every detail of every plan; for many details it was much better that they did not.

Last night, Varic had spent an interesting and somewhat tense evening with three society sorcerers. Midway through he developed a headache, which he ignored until he was fairly certain the thoughts he wanted to communicate were gotten across. Then he went home, dismissed his butler, and stared at the wall, so intent that he hadn't heard Winterhill's ring.

But the headache was gone, Whetstone was here, and Brook had spoken to him in front of two hundred members. It was on rails.

The recess ended. Motion Four was a petition, read by one of the middle-plains Corons, for a grant of Household to one of the merchants in his holding. It was an old form, older than Coronage. A Householder could fortify his property and arm his servants. Since there had been no new Coronages created in a hundred and fifty years (and under the Revised Constitution, there never would be any more), it was a popular petition among the newly wealthy. And since the Householder paid taxes on the fortifications, guards, and weapons, it was popular in Parliament as well.

The Coron spoke for a few minimi about what a nice, unwarlike chap this fellow who wanted guns and revetments was, and the motion passed by acclamation. The Commons might well kill it, Varic thought. They had a rather clearer idea than the Lords about potential Householders' character, and those who had grants of their own didn't want to see the honor handed to just any Smith or Midwife with a friend in Lystourel.

It was eight minimi past eleven. Brook passed the calendar to the President, who made the announcement of Motion Five, since Brook would be presenting it.

Motion Five was a test case. In Brook's Revised Constitution, it would be a full Article. It said that "as Sorcery is given to be an Art practiced by Willing Artisans, knowing its Limits and Risks, so shall all fruits of that Art be considered Willful Acts of the Artisan, and subject to all the Rights and Liabilities as shall appertain to such Acts under the Law."

It meant that if a sorcerer made it rain on your dry fields, you could not deny payment by claiming that the rain fell by Goddess's will. The Lords Sorcerous could be expected to like that. It also meant that if the rain drowned livestock or washed the crops away—and the nature of magic made that entirely likely—the magician could be dragged into court for damages, and the sorcerers could be expected not to like that at all.

No, they did not. They murmured until the President tapped his rod, and then one of them stood to request the floor. The man's name was Deriano. He was a thin man of middling height, with thin dark mustaches and a neat square beard. His long coat was black, plain but of expensive stuff, his waistcoat embroidered with golden sunbursts, and there were matching thumbnail-sized rubies on his watch chain and his ring. He was, down to his assumed Quercian name, the perfect newspaper-engraving image of a society sorcerer. He was a little pale this morning, a little gray below the eyes; he would have been up late last night.

Varic knew he had been up late, because it had been late when Varic left Deriano's assistant and his companions, and it would have taken the assistant at least half an hour by cab to reach his master and tell him what the sick-drunk Coron had said.

Brook yielded the floor to Deriano. The magician thanked him, giving him a look somewhat sad and somewhat malicious, and faced the Assembly.

Deriano said, "I begin by saying that I appreciate, I admire, the Coron Brook's impulse toward justice. Are there any of us here who do not share that impulse? I think not." He looked up, at Cable in the gallery. Cable smiled.

Varic didn't smile, but he was pleased. Acknowledging Cable in front of the House was a bad move. It implied that the Justiciar had some kind of authority here, which would offend even Bowenshield (perhaps especially Bowenshield). And everyone with any experience of Cable knew that his impulse, his passion, was for the law. Cable didn't give a rat's turd for justice. Deriano, an absentee member, didn't know any of that. He had only heard that Cable was opposed to Motion Five, and to Brook. So he played to Cable and Cable's faction.

"But justice," Deriano went on, completely unaware of what he was doing, "is not simply a matter of drawing a line and measuring all humanity against it. Some of us grow up tall, and some of us grow up short. And some of us grow up with the sorcerer's talent.

"You are all intelligent, educated people. You know that we do not choose to have the talent; it chooses us. And, just as with any other art, it does not always do what we wish it to do. But do we prosecute a singer for being off-key? Do we fine a painter for an ugly picture?"

Cable was interested now, the hawk looking hungry. That was, Varic knew, *exactly* what the Justiciar wanted to do. It was why he opposed Brook's law: it put sorcery's effects into a legal framework; it was not a system for regulating the act of magic itself.

Deriano went on in that vein for a little longer. He was an easy, informal speaker, well rehearsed, the centerpiece of any social event. His Archanum, the method that organized his magic, was in the cut stones he wore, and he glittered. Winding down, he gave a direct look to Bowenshield, who adjusted his coat to rise for the floor.

Whetstone stood up.

"Will the Lord Deriano yield to the Lord Whetstone?" the President said with a note in his voice that said he knew it was a silly question.

Brook looked carefully at several people, including Whetstone, Varic, and the President. Varic did not move. He knew entirely well that people were watching, noting, where Brook's gaze went and what happened there. No one was looking at Deriano.

"Gladly," Deriano said, and took his seat.

Whetstone walked to the podium. "I thank my colleague for yielding," he said, "and I will not speak long. I merely wish to raise my voice in approval of this intelligent, important, and, may I say it, long-overdue measure."

The other sorcerers were silent, of course, but some of them looked startled, some angry, some quite pleased. The proxy voters just stared at Whetstone blankly, as apprentices ought to look on masters. Deriano pressed his fingertips together and looked rapt.

Whetstone took no formal notice of any of them. He continued, "For entirely too many years, this nation has treated the practitioners of my ancient Art as children, less than responsible for our actions. Perhaps worse, a few less-than-competent, less-than-scrupulous workers have hidden their own faults behind this legal convenience."

After that, it was on rails, greased, downhill, with the wind at its back. Bowenshield rose after all, to say something elaborate and meaningless about justice and freedom and self-control, fulsome as a month-old bouquet. There were only thirteen votes against, though more than forty abstentions. A passage was, however, a passage.

The President called the highday recess. Longlight came over to Varic's seat. Varic looked at Brook: the Parliamentarian was giving him an intense look, difficult for even Varic to interpret. Then Brook turned away. Varic and Longlight left the Chamber.

They went to lunch at the Golden Sconce, a small restaurant a block from Parliament. The sky had lifted slightly, but the outdoor terrace was closed against the cold; they sat near a high arched window with a view of Clarity Park. Varic had chicken and thin pancakes, with cream and mushroom sauce; Longlight had a large rare steak.

"What does *Varic* mean?" she said.

"'A difficult place to land.' My home country has a very inhospitable coast."

"Alch mine," she said, delight bringing the West back into her voice. "We call it the Rogue's Teeth."

There was a pause, and they ate. She looked around at the other diners, most of them in frock coats and trousers, said, "I dress oddly, don't I? I don't think about Lystourel when I'm not here, and we never hear about your fashions."

"By the time you had, they would have changed. They know you're from the frontiers, and they may look a bit long at you, but it's only curiosity. The City doesn't think about the rest of the country, either."

"You seem to do so."

"As I say, I'm from the edges myself." Which was literally true, though he had not entered his Coronage in years. She was trying to make social conversation, not understanding that the essence of City social conversation was that it should mean nothing.

Varic said, "You know that you have the last motion scheduled for today."

"Yes."

"I wonder if you'd consider postponing it until tomorrow. It doesn't require a formal vote, only a request, a second, and an acclamation vote. I can assure you of a second, and almost assure you of the acclamation. After six motions today, a postponement will probably be unanimous."

"That would put me first tomorrow?"

"No, last again. But there are only three motions on tomorrow's calendar. Four, with yours. It's the last day of sessions before the holiday, and there'll probably be an early adjournment as soon as they're read and voted."

"I had planned to start for home tomorrow."

"There's an evening train west. I'll be on it myself." She gave him the hard look again, and he added, "With friends. We're holidaying together." He knew that the sleeping cars would probably be booked full by now, but this wasn't the moment to offer her his compartment.

"I have a very long trip home. Eighty hours on the train, and then another twenty on horseback. The Ironways don't reach very far into my country."

"Then would you consider giving your motion today for a vote tomorrow? You don't have to be present. We could magnostyle the results ahead of your train."

"Why? Do I genuinely have a better chance of winning a vote tomorrow than today?"

"I believe you might. Certainly no worse chance."

"Would you tell me why?"

"Because most of the members will be gone. Just as you plan to be. There will be fewer votes to balance against votes. There will probably be barely a quorum."

"What if there isn't a quorum?"

"Then there will be no vote," he said automatically. There was no use in fencing with her: if she wanted to be direct, he could be direct. "That would not, however, necessarily be a bad thing. Look. You have no faction. No support. It takes time and effort to assemble those things."

"I'm not interested in City politics."

"I know that," he said evenly. "But what if those politics are the only way to get the votes you want?"

"Allsen the Demons gobble the Parliament whole-breathed," she said, and slashed a piece from her bleeding steak.

"There is a possibility," Varic said. "Not secure at all, but here it is. Did you notice the reactions while milord Brook's motion was being debated? When they discussed law and justice?"

"Yes. And the ferrety Coron got the last word."

Varic couldn't help grinning. "Bowenshield. Yes. May it do him good. All right. The Assembly is thinking about law and order. The ferrety one in particular. You have to get your problem across to them in those terms, that these are outlaws, criminals, not a lot of noble Blackwood Jacks defending the oppressed, or romantics in lace who kiss all the pretty boys and never shoot anybody for real. Understand?"

"You're telling me they're ignorant fools," she said, staring at him.

We should stand you for President of the House, Varic came to within a hairsbreadth of saying aloud. What he did say was, "It's not the worst strategy to treat them that way. But without letting on, please." He checked his pocket watch. "We just have time for tea, if you'd like."

"If you won't think it rude, I would like to go back to my office. Think for a few minutes before the Assembly begins again."

"Of course. I believe I'll stay for a cup. Will you allow me to pay?"

"No. I feel I should pay you, for your advice."

"My colleague Brook has a saying: advice only costs after it's taken."

She laughed and bowed, left him her share of the bill, and went out. He ordered his tea with Northern whisky, watched Long-light through the arched window, framed against the Park.

There were three things a Coron could do in the modern world. One could stay on the holding and send a proxy to Parliament, as more than half of them did. One could leave the holding in the hands of a manager and move to Lystourel, as Brook and Varic had. Or one could pretend that nothing had changed in two hundred years: live at home and rule as one pleased, and when times were dire, ride to the Royal Court with one's petition to the Crown.

Two hundred years ago, Redlance had built a Parliament; eighty years ago Queen Beryl the Fourteenth had abdicated; but the word just did not seem to have reached everyone.

The Assembly resumed, exactly as before except that Cable was gone from the Gallery and Deriano from the floor.

The sixth motion, from one of the priests, was to borrow a moderate quantity of coal from the Naval Reserve to heat the National Hospitals. It was an easy pass, with the recommendation added from the floor that a committee study the allocation of state coal stockpiles.

It had been, of course, more complicated than that. The original thought had been to force the emergency purchase of commercial coal at an artificial low rate. The mine-owning Corons threatened to tie such a motion up forever. The Superintendent of Hospitals (who told Brook he was "breathing fog in his office of mornings") was aimed toward Coron Deerleap, the strongest advocate for rails in the House, with the suggestion that the coal would have to be borrowed from the Ironways. Deerleap's interests were too well known for him to propose the navy transfer, but he had no difficulty persuading the Reverend Intercessor Essence to move the idea.

Brook introduced the seventh and last motion of the day. Longlight came down to the platform.

"You all know who I am, I think, unless your memories are very short. And you should all remember why I'm here, since I was here for it six months ago, and six before that, and in all five times in the last three years for the same reason. Well, here I am again.

"My Coronage, in case you've forgotten, is on the west coast, in the mountains. We have a bandit problem. Going to sleep already?" She was looking at the Reverend Mother Orchard, which was unfair, since Orchard always looked seven-eighths asleep, and poorly done, since Orchard had no enemies in the Chamber.

Longlight said, "Well, yes, this is old news, old before I was born. The Great Rogue Hills, as their name implies, have always had bandits, and up to now we've managed them ourselves. But up to now they haven't had repeating rifles or Ironway coaches to attack."

That got Coron Deerleap's interest, Varic noticed. Deerleap took attacks on the Ironways personally. That would be useful.

"We're not large, I grant you. We don't have any great cities, or trade roads, and only the one Ironway." Deerleap still looked interested. "But we're as much a part of Lescoray as this city is, and I'm telling you that without some kind of help we're not going to be a part of it much longer—we're going to be a bandit kingdom."

Stop now, Varic thought. Don't say anything more, this isn't a feudal court any longer.

But she did go on, exactly as he was afraid she would. "And if that's what my family's land is going to become, then I suppose I'll have to go along with it."

There was a ripple of talk from the Corons. Deerleap looked bewildered, Bowenshield appalled. At least Cable was gone.

The President tapped his baton for quiet. Longlight looked around the Chamber. She seemed to understand, now, what she had done. It was no shortage of intelligence, Varic thought; she couldn't help believing what all her ancestors had believed.

He weighed the possibilities. Deerleap was not going to speak. This was of no importance to the magicians, and the priests wouldn't enter the debate. There had been no time to win over the frontier Corons' representatives, and even those that might sympathize could hardly be expected to second a threat of rebellion.

What Varic could do was move for a delay of vote, until tomorrow—if they were lucky, there would be no quorum tomorrow, and the vote would come after the holiday. With a little time, the case could be made that the bandits were the real rebels against the state. That was a magnet for a coalition. The hopeless cavalry might even be sent on an expedition, and they would forget all about their grudge with Varic.

He stood up. Bowenshield was standing as well.

The President said, "Milady, other members are requesting the floor. To whom will you pass it?"

Varic could read Longlight's thoughts. Assuming that she trusted Varic, should she let him speak next? Or would it be better to let him have the last word? In her position, he wouldn't know the answer either. What Longlight didn't know was that the debate was already over.

What she did was what Varic supposed he might have done, not knowing better. She turned to the Parliamentarian and spoke to him directly, too quietly for the Chamber to hear.

She was, Varic knew perfectly well, only asking him the correct procedure. To prevent what was about to happen, Brook should have announced that to the House: though he did not have the floor, no one would have protested the technicality. But Brook, the master proceduralist, would of course not do that.

And—as Brook would know—if she went from a private conference with Brook to pass the platform to Brook's chief associate, the whole thing would stink of collusion, and she was finished. There was only one thing to do. Varic sat down, leaving Bowenshield uncontested for the floor.

Bowenshield got it. He asked for an immediate vote on Motion Seven. He got that.

Longlight's Motion was defeated one hundred sixty-two votes

to one hundred two, which was far from a disaster. But still a defeat.

All calendar business being completed, President Saltworthy asked for opposition to adjournment. There was none, and the session officially ended at twenty-two minimi past fifteen. The Lords began leaving the Chamber. Varic watched as Longlight went down the tiers to Brook's seat. Brook was talking to her, making calm gestures. Then Brook turned to look at Varic, waved his hand. Varic went down.

Longlight said, "Milord Brook has been explaining things to me. I seem to have done almost everything wrong."

"No, no," Brook said kindly, "you didn't do anything wrong. It's simply the nature of politics that they tend to become *about* politics, rather than issues. Varic, the Coron says she's leaving tomorrow. We ought to give her some pleasant experience of the City. You're not yet accompanied for the Embassy cotillion to-night, are you?"

Longlight said, "Which Embassy?"

Brook said lightly, "Oh, never ask which Embassy. People might think it made a difference to you. It could lead to war."

Varic said, "It's at the Ferangarder Embassy. Their new Ambassador has just arrived. And of course I'd be delighted to accompany you."

Longlight said, "But this will be formal dress, won't it?" She swept her hands down her tunic. "Whatever formal is in Lystourel, I'm sure this isn't it."

Brook said, "Varic. Have the porter find you a cab, and get the lady to Ivory's, before the evening traffic starts. And for Shyira's sake, have them fit you, too: you've worn that blue coat to the last four parties. Go on now, and I'll see you there."

As they left the Chamber, Longlight said, "I have some things in my office. . . ."

"Papers? The porter will have them sent along. If Leyva can't be trusted with it, none of humanity can. And if they're clothes, forget them. We're going to Ivory's."

Ivory, Ivory & Co. was in Watercourse Street, some twenty blocks south of Parliament House. It was too near the Estuary Docks to still be an exclusive address; the clothiers did not care and would not move. As the eldest living Ivory put it, "Anyone who says that Ivory's is unfashionably located knows neither Ivory's nor fashion."

The company covered three glass-and-iron shop fronts. On the right was the Accessories Shop, selling cravats, collars, stockings, and other ready-mades. (Not that they could and did not make such things to order, but that was considered a bit above and beyond.) On the left was the Seamstry Hall; through the high front windows strollers could watch twenty or more employees cutting, pinning, stitching. One could touch fingertips to the glass and sense the whir of the sewing machines, or raise a hand and feel the draft of exhausted air.

The doorman tipped his high hat and ushered Varic and Longlight through the center door, into a long high-ceilinged hall lined with boxes, bolts of fabric, mirrors, valet racks, and hatstands. In an alcove were the armorial patents of the last six monarchs of Lescoray. Longlight paused at the display. "My grandmother was created Palion by the last Beryl," she said, "and my great-grandfather by Lionstone."

"Indeed?" said a voice from behind them. It was March, the youngest working Ivory, in shirt and pockets-vest stuffed with scissors, pincushions, tapes and notions. "Milord Coron. It's been some time."

"So I've been told," Varic said pleasantly. He introduced Longlight and explained the situation. "The difficulty is that the ball starts at nineteen tonight. A little less than three hours."

"One hour is a difficulty," March Ivory said, the tape already in her hands. "Three is merely a challenge. And we'll be dressing yourself as well, Lord Varic? Please say yourself as well."

"Myself as well."

Longlight and Ivory began a discussion of styles—they would be fitting an existing outfit for her, as even Ivory's could not do a full custom construction in three hours—and disappeared into a consultation room. Another fitter checked Varic's measurements against those on file, asking if his habits had changed since the last record: Did he carry a stick now? That called for adjustments to the sleeve length. Or should they cut room for a revolver? Varic demurred with a little unease, and asked if that was becoming popular. The fitter smiled and said, "I wouldn't know that, honored," which meant that it was not. Ivorys never gossiped, but they would not deny a fashion, either.

Varic was shown the book of garments available for alteration. He selected a tailcoat in blue-gray broadcloth with black satin facings, a shirt of silver-shot silk. The fitter approved. Varic knew very well that, while unfailingly polite, Ivory's employees would not do work they did not approve of. The coat was brought out, and Varic put it on, standing entirely still while the fitter chalked it for alterations.

The marked coat went to Seamstry Hall. Varic followed. All twenty machines were in use: the holiday rush was on, celebratory clothes due tomorrow for the Equinoctials. The workers, in shirtsleeves and canvas aprons, hair netted or tied back, all with the silver or golden scissors badge of the Needlecrafters' Guild, were slashing and stitching their way through stretch after stretch of silks and satins and velvets in pale greens and golds and mad autumn reds.

From each machine, a leather belt half a span wide went up to the ceiling, where two drive shafts ran the length of the hall.

Wooden fans mounted on the shafts pulled hot air out to the street. The ceiling was skylighted, but dim with the persistent clouds; the workspaces below were brightly lit by flickerless gas-mantles.

At the back of the hall, behind a wall with double glass windows, was the stationary steam engine that spun the drive shafts. Brass fittings and gauges gleamed in half darkness, and an iron flywheel twice a man's height interrupted the light from beyond. There was a muffled squeal and a rain of sparks as the machinist ground needles and scissors back to sharpness.

As Varic walked along the double rank of machines, he could hear that most of them were humming, none loud enough to be heard by the next in line, all different tunes but all in the rhythm of the driveshafts, "Love's a Labor" merging into "Whisky, No Water" into "Silver Over Gold."

"Milord Coron," said the fitter, and led him out again to try the coat pinned into shape before stitching it. It fit perfectly, at least as far as Varic could tell.

When the coat had gone again into the hall for work, Longlight reappeared. With a promise to Ivory to be back by eighteen exactly, they went a few doors up the street for a light supper. "Don't stint," Varic said. "For embassy banquets, you're best off not eating for two days beforehand, but for cotillions there seems to be an attempt to produce the smallest savories possible. And Ferangarder punches—"

"Ferangarder punches have a reputation even on my coast," Longlight said. "But do they actually serve Beast-Slayer or Old Skull Blast? At an Embassy ball?"

"Yes," Varic said, lightly but meaning it. "And when the War Government is in power, they even use those names." He turned to the puzzled-looking waiter and ordered an omelet with spinach and bacon. Longlight asked about the rabbit stew, but caught Varic's look and asked instead for braised lamb kidneys. When the waiter had gone, Varic said, "Never order rabbit stew in the City unless you've seen the rabbit. And made sure that it *is* a rabbit."

"Oh, you're joking."

"Mind you, I've seen rabbits in Clarity Park. But these days most of them are carrying revolvers."

"You *are* joking."

"Always, just a little, I hope," Varic said, and wished at once he had not said it, and that he had some excuse to look somewhere, anywhere, but at Longlight. She looked back, questioning. He didn't have any answer. And it had been a horribly long day.

Why had Brook done this to him?

"We mustn't be late," he said, to shift her mind, and his own, from conversation to food. "Or at eighteen and five instanti, Ivory will be at the door to drag us back."

They ate, and did not talk, and returned on time. Ivory sent them to their separate fitting rooms.

Varic was met by his fitter and an apprentice, and a large mustached fellow with little hands who brushed and retied Varic's hair, and did what little he could with Varic's chewed nails. Varic put on his shirt and narrow cravat, a black waistcoat with his watch chain correctly hung, then the tailcoat; the fitter adjusted the silk ruffs at Varic's chest and cuffs. March Ivory came in: she was comfortable with the look, and Varic was comfortable with the fit—"So that's that, I think," Varic said.

"Well, then," Ivory said, and Longlight came out of the back. Ivory had dressed her in a long, narrow-waisted coat of lozenge-quilted black velvet, sewn with little white crystals at the intersections. The collar was deeply cut, the lapels very broad, and a wide black cravat wrapped her bare throat. They had buffed the silver headband, and shone her boots to black glass, and done something with makeup that made her planar face seem gentler but no less strong. Varic wanted very much to know how they had done that.

"One minima," Ivory said, and went into the Accessories Shop. Longlight looked at Varic with an expression of radiant bewilderment.

Ivory returned with a black kidskin sabretache on a fine silver chain. She displayed the bag to Longlight: it had her Coronage armorial, a horizontal sword above a setting sun. Ivory hung it on Longlight's shoulder, adjusting it like someone hanging a picture.

"Yes," Ivory said finally, "I think that *is* that. And you have twenty-four minimi yet. I love challenges." She turned to Varic. "Milord will, I suppose, want his old clothes sent home?"

"Milord will," Varic said. "And would you have the runner tell my butler that he won't be needed any further tonight, and the best of the holiday?" He took out a five-plate coin. "And the same to the runner."

Ivory accepted the coin with a nod. "And the lady Coron?"

"My hotel is the Bronze Door," Longlight said, rather hurriedly.

"Of course," Ivory said, and stepped back to survey her work again. "Oh, dear, the chill, I'd forgotten," she said, and had cloaks brought out, draping Longlight's herself.

The doorman summoned a cab, and Longlight and Varic headed north and west.

As they crossed the Grand River, the sun was going down behind the Castle, turning it amber and gold, rippling down one side with light bounced from the Fresh. Longlight watched the beautiful, confused building from the cab window, her face warm in the light, her eyes golden, like opals.

Or agates, Varic thought, for a variety of reasons, not all pleasant. He did not want to think about Agate just now; he would see her in just a few days, but she was not here. She would never be here. Not in the City. "Have you ever been in the Castle?" he asked Longlight, who was here, in the City, now.

"No. My grandmother told me stories. She was the Palion Moraine, have I said?" She turned toward him. "Your holding is . . . Corvaric?"

"On the north coast. Beyond Bryna Kóly."

"And your family . . ."

"We never dwelt much on history. I think one of my grandfathers was a sorcerer, and died of it. My parents were killed when I was sixteen. In a bandit attack."

"*Oh*," she said. "And I've talked about nothing but bandits since I met you. As if no one else knew anything about them."

"We only met this morning," he said, and that suddenly seemed a very meaningful statement. "And as for knowledge, that's a perfectly correct attitude, for what you came here to do. I can't really say I 'know' anything. I was half the country away when it happened, visiting . . . friends." He hoped she would let it lie there. There had never been any good explanation of what had happened on the Coast Road. Suspicions—hinderknowns aplenty, as they would say in the North—but no answers. He supposed, when he thought about it at all, that such an answer would require that he take some kind of action, some sort of revenge. Varic understood that vengeance, like religion, could give a life shape and direction. He had to pay attention to anything that powerful. But his life already had a shape and a direction.

"When you next visit, and have a little time," he said, "you should see the Castle. The University has charge of it. Do you have any particular period of interest? The Middle Reigns? The Preregnum? The Quercians?"

"The Middle."

"You should talk with Preceptor Falconer, then. Spend a day just walking around the place with him. I guarantee you'll learn a hundred things you didn't know and several you won't believe."

"That sounds wonderful."

"Yes, just that," Varic said, and stopped for a moment. "Send me word of your next visit, and I'll arrange it."

"You're interested in the Midreigns, too, then?"

"I'm interested in everything," he said vaguely. The usual Middle history, a catalog of Palions and tournaments and greedy illiterate kings, bored him, though Falconer's accounts of towns forming, roads being built, the granary system, never did.

He was not being fair to her. He was assuming that the heraldry and armored noise, her Palion grandmother's stories, were what interested Longlight. He was always too ready to assume that, as if Falconer had never taught him anything. Longlight was a Coron, a resident and successful one, which of necessity meant successful at more than holding entertaining courts and sitting on a horse properly: she would have to have experience of the complexities, the mine production and high road maintenance and flood control that Varic himself had left to others ever since he'd inherited the blasted title. He looked closely at her, wondering if she could guess how much he wanted to take her home, and sit alone over tea, and talk about dry grain storage.

"You don't really want to go to this party, do you?" she said abruptly.

"I hadn't planned to go," he said honestly, and thought hard about what to say next. *I don't mind, now* wasn't adequate. How, precisely and politely, did he tell her about the turns his attitude had taken in the last few hours? From a mild annoyance at Brook for sending him to another Demon-damned diplomatic dance, to a greater annoyance that he would have to lose Longlight's company and conversation to the empty social forms—to this sudden outrageous pleasure that he was accompanying her to this unworthy event, exactly because it was unworthy, and someone might be forced to notice the fact—

His head hurt.

"These things have their pleasures," he said finally. "Sometimes I lose track of that. You will promise me that if you get bored, you'll tell me so?"

"If you'll promise me the same." She smiled. "Mutual defense policy."

He laughed out loud, wondering why he had doubted Brook's perception.

The Ferangarder Embassy was on the east edge of the Silverthread District, not very far from the site of the duel that morning. The building, three stories high in white cut stone, had been designed to resemble a frontier lord's defensible manor (from an era not quite so far in Ferangard's past as in Lescoray's) while in fact incorporating large windows, sun porches, and other more peaceable developments. The façade, shining with candles and gaslight in the early dark, was set some distance back from an immense stone-and-iron fence that, while not unattractive, was definitely there for defense.

The cab pulled through the gates, joining a line of cabs and coaches in the driveway. Varic looked at Longlight in the glow from the house. "You're not worried," he said.

She put her hands to the pinch waist of her coat. "They stitched this very quickly."

"Nothing to fear on that account. You're wearing a family's reputation. If anything embarrassing happened, March would take dull scissors to her wrist. And then come back to spook whoever had done such an unfashionable job on her shroud."

He wanted her smiling when they went in; he wanted her luminous. If he could not reflect the glow, at least he could hide in it.

They went through the arched, ironbound front doors, into a long copper-tiled hall hung with swords and portraits. The weapons were all heavily draped and knotted with the gold and green of the Ferangarder Peace Government's flag. Another set of doors was opened, and they stood at the head of the sweeping staircase down to the floor of the two-story ballroom, behind a white-coated butler who cracked his rod on the floor and announced them. He knew Longlight's name and full titles without prompting; Varic saw Brook's hand in that.

There were perhaps a hundred people in the ballroom, making it seem practically empty. Some of them turned at the announcement of new guests, and of those, most kept looking. Varic knew they were not looking at him. He smiled within.

Then he saw Brook, standing at the bottom of the stairs, dressed in his usual deep grays, with a violet shoulder sash. He looked positively huge, like a heroic statue someone had carelessly invited to dinner. As they descended, Varic saw that Brook's sash carried a large medal, of iron and gold set with small gems and an enameled boss. It was the Ferangarder War Government's Order of the Ringed Citadel, given to him three shifts of regime ago. Varic wasn't sure which was the greater gesture: wearing it to meet the Peace Ambassador, or wearing it in Lescoray at all.

Standing next to Brook was a woman in a white military tunic and blue trousers with gold stripes; her coat had a gold shoulder rope and several iron decorations, and the triple rank bars of a decenion. A short, straight infantry sword hung at her side. Her hair was short, straight, and dark; she looked small next to Brook, but only because she was next to Brook. On her sleeve was a silk flash of gold and black, the War Government's colors.

Brook said, "Ah, Longlight, splendid to see you. I would have you meet Tephar Diante, decenion commanding the Second Citadel Guards Regiment, and Ambassador to Lescoray of the Ferangarder War Government. Varic, you know the decenion, of course."

"Of course," Varic said, and there was an exchange of bows. Brook made excuses and moved off to meet someone else. Tephar Diante said, "Your presence, Varic, is a sight to gladden. The both of you, most glad to see. This evening for me, I do fear, won't come smooth."

"They don't plan to recall you?" Varic said, not loudly.

"Oh, little enough do I eat. And the Ironway fare they'll save when I do go home, think of that." She turned to Longlight, said in a much lighter voice, "You have a military problem, Brook tells. Mountain warfare is in my knowledge, and to talk it over with you would delight." A pause. "If it is no interference."

"That might be very interesting," Longlight said.

"Then we must so arrange. Corons, until later, your pardon?"

Tephar Diante moved away. Longlight looked around, said quietly, "Was that a serious offer?"

"Offer of what?" Varic said, making sure they were adequately isolated. He thought that she did understand, however; this, she might understand better than Brook did.

"She's from *Ferangard*," Longlight said. "In the *army*! I can't make a plan of defense with a Ferangarder officer."

"No, that's right, you can't," Varic said offhandedly. "There might still be an act somewhere making it treason. But don't misunderstand. Tephar Diante was sincere enough, she has reason enough. Did you catch the wind of her comment about saving railcoach fare?"

Longlight thought a moment. "Going as freight," she said. "In a coffin."

"Exactly. The Peace Government doesn't want the commander

of the Second Guards anywhere near the Second Guards just now—though she's here, where she can be found if needed. They've decapitated most of their elite units the same way. Tightly led military units often vote as blocs, you see."

"But I didn't think they needed a War Government to go to war."

"They've been separate functions for a long time. 'Peace' and 'War' are just factional names now. No, this is purely politics, not military policy."

Longlight said, "I should say it's not."

Varic showed her a small grin, then looked at a hunting mural, spears and boars and dogs. "If we wanted to have a war with Ferangard, this would probably be an excellent time for it. That's a secret, of course."

"What about Bryna Kóly? Don't they control all the passes between here and there?"

"That's no secret. Would you give me some technical advice?"

"What?"

"How do you defend a mountain pass? Against an army that wants to just march through."

"It's not hard. You barricade the path and attack from the heights. It's like shooting staked goats."

Varic nodded, chewed his lip. "That sounds somehow very familiar. Who else attacks like that?"

"Mountain—" She stopped, the light breaking through, and said slowly and softly, "Mountain bandits."

"You see," Varic said, "why a lot of people would like a general solution to the problem."

He looked at her, reading her mind, and knew too well what he had done: he had led her, much too suddenly, away from the hearth fire, introduced her to the outer darkness.

He hated himself for it, but that was nothing new.

They turned back to the crowd, a hundred fifty or so now,

Corons, members in Commons, the Grand Terminus Manager, several prominent sorcerers (though not Master Whetstone). A fat, merry-eyed man with side whiskers was Pinner, publisher of the *Lystourel Morning Clarion;* none of his reporters were here, of course, though the lucivitor in the corner, juggling his glass plates and flash powder, was probably Pinner's doing. There were at least two dozen other Ambassadors and Consuls, their frock coats weighed down with extravagant decorations from each other's governments.

A couple approached Varic and Longlight. The man was young, not tall, in a long brown coat with elaborate frogging and cuffs, a rapier on a gold silk sash. He had curly brown hair, carefully tied with gold ribbon, and his eyes were almost feverishly bright. The woman was about the same height, considerably older, her gray hair in a green lace caul. She wore a fan-skirted gown of sea-green satin foamed with white lace, and carried a cane she certainly did not need for support.

"Varic!" the man said. "You've finally done it, brother. You have finally *nearly* outdone me in companions."

"That's an amazing statement," said the woman, then to Longlight, "You'll forgive him, my dear? Even if it is a bone-bald lie?"

Longlight said, "Well, of course—I mean—hello."

Varic said, "Milady, this is Winterhill, a friend and associate. Winterhill, please meet Longlight, Coron of the Great Rogue Hills."

"Delighted," Winterhill said. "This must be a very formal occasion; Varic's sheathed his wit. Else he'd never have been able to resist introducing me as a Great Rogue."

Varic said, "I'm chastened."

"And I should be, but it's much too early. Would you both please meet Malis Ainee, the Dowager Duchess of Davesque Isle? My dear Malis, these are Varic and Longlight, both landed Lords of Lescoray. And I think that's enough alliteration for one evening." There was a screech of strings from the center of the room. "They're tuning, if that's what you want to call it. Shall we dance?"

"Oh, Goddess," the Duchess said, "it's a linearegia. Couldn't they have waited until we'd had a few drinks?"

"Best time to play it," Winterhill said, taking her arm. "When we're all sober and strong. Could be hazardous, later."

The linearegia was a group dance that dated from the Preregnum centuries ago. While rigidly formal in its steps and movements, it steadily increased in tempo until dancers were shifting and whirling past one another like gears in an overwound clockwork. It was impossible to keep track of where one's original partner had gone, difficult enough to remember one's own place in the shuffle. Finally there was a drumroll and cymbal crash, and the dance stopped, this time as usual only instanti short of an overall collision.

Varic found Longlight as quickly as he could; Winterhill and the Duchess Malis found them.

"You both do that absurd dance very well," the Duchess said.

Longlight said, "My mother taught me. She said it was invented for the old Lords of Tarse, so they could have a look at every eligible person in the hall without anyone's companion getting suspicious."

"Really?" the Duchess said, laughing.

"In Tarse," Longlight went on, "if you hold your hand so during the crossing step"—she held her left palm out, tips of the fingers bent slightly—"it means, 'No, thank you, I'm staying with the person I came in with.'"

"I see I must visit Tarse someday," the Duchess said.

Winterhill said, "I must unburden the latest gossip upon Varic now. We'll return bearing drinks." He bowed; Varic did the same, a little less certainly, and followed him.

"Gossip?" Varic said.

"You'll never guess who died this highday," Winterhill said, almost merrily.

"No, I won't. You'll just have to tell me."

"Fellow named Chase. Lieutenant of cavalry. He was run down by a coach in Cutsail Lane. Positively mangled, by reports."

"Cutsail . . . by the Estuary?"

"Not nearly so noble a place to die as Willowpark Square, I grant you." He paused. "Willowpark's where the Duchess's Embassy is. She saw the duel this morning—but don't mention it to her, it's one of the very few things I think might embarrass the lady."

"I take it this has something to do with how you met her."

"The Embassy, yes. But it was some time ago. And I found out later the shotgun wasn't even loaded. . . . Ah. This looks like dangerous stuff." He began filling stemmed glasses with sparkling pink punch. "Would you pick me up two or three of those chocolate whatever-they-are, brother? I haven't had any dinner."

When they returned, Malis and Longlight were on a settee, the Duchess gesturing as she spoke: ". . . but my third husband, the Forty-Seventh Duke, *was* a pirate. He had a letter of marque from Lescoray, of course, and two or three from Alinsea—they've always been very generous about that sort of thing. I couldn't let him go on with it, of course, even though he always insisted he had nothing to do with the demise of the Forty-Sixth Duke." She sighed. "But Forty-Seven was never entirely happy. He took to sailing model ships in the Ducal Residence duck pond." She turned. "Here are the young men now. Milord Varic, do you know when this magnificent new Ambassador is to appear? Or have I missed him already? I'm terrible about Ambassadors, you know. If they don't show up demanding something or wanting to start a war, I tend not to notice them at all."

"I would expect him at twenty, honored. Another ten minimi."

They clicked punch glasses, Winterhill balancing his against a plateful of pastry. After sips all around—the pink stuff *was* potent—Longlight said, "What's the group over there?"

"I don't know," Varic said. "Shall we look?" They left Winterhill and the Duchess on the couch, and crossed the ballroom. A small crowd was gathered around a table.

At the table, an Archreader had the Book spread out, in a layout Varic had not seen before, an arc of seven cards above a triangle of three. No one sat across from the sorcerer. Two or three of the onlookers had Books of their own out, packs discreetly palmed, and were drawing doubles, examining the two cards and then slipping them back.

Varic looked at the cards, assuming the three below must represent the subject of the reading: they were the Six of Stones (this one showing a six-arched viaduct), the Sky reversed, and Justice. Above were the City, Ace of Springs, the Gateway reversed, Five of Steels reversed, Prince of Springs, King of Staves, and Solitude reversed. Without a knowledge of the layout, he could make very little of it, except that there were a lot of power signs displayed.

One of the Embassy guards, accompanied by an underbutler, had moved to the side of the Archreader. The guard wore a decorative gold gorget and a long sword, nothing very dramatic, and said quite calmly and politely, and even in Lescorial syntax, "Honored, pardon, but I am required to ask if you bear a license to practice sorcery in Ferangarder territories."

The Reader showed his sunburst medallion. "I'm an accredited member of the Lystourel Guild."

"Yes, honored. But this building is not Lescorial ground. I must ask you to display a license, or cease your practice."

The Archreader tapped his hand lightly on the Book, then said pleasantly, "Of course. No harm was intended."

"Surely not, honored."

The sorcerer gathered and squared the cards, slipped the Book into an enameled gold case. He said to the guard, still pleasantly, "You'll personally express my regrets to the Ambassador, when he arrives?"

The guard paused a moment, turned to the butler next to him. The butler said, "Honored, by our honor, done."

The Archreader looked at them both, as if about to press the point, but did not. He stood up, and walked up the staircase, out of the room.

"This should be interesting," Varic said to Longlight, "but from a little distance." They returned to the corner of the room.

The Duchess of Davesque Isle was saying, ". . . but the ducks weren't laughing, as they say. We invested the Forty-Eighth Duke that day, before the wedding, and had the pond turned into a Hanasish garden." She looked up. "You're back. Is another dance starting?"

"In a manner of speaking," Varic said, and described the incident. They watched as five more sorcerers made polite little scenes and left the cotillion.

Winterhill said to Varic, "Want to find Brook?"

"Brook will have noticed. And he won't say anything. Not here—"

Two butlers and four guards appeared at the top of the curved staircase.

"—and certainly not now," Varic finished.

A butler, somewhat mellower-voiced than the first, announced, "His Honor from the sovereign state of Ferangard under Peace rule, to the Republic of Lescoray Ambassador, Rocha Serestor."

The Ambassador appeared, in a sparely cut dark green suit with gold embroidery slashed on the sleeves and trousers. Rocha Serestor was a big man who moved in a crouch, coiled as if he were about to leap. His hair was dark, a little wavy, and his face was fiercely intense. There was polite applause as he came down the stairs.

He reached the floor, said, "Guests most in our esteem." His voice was smooth and well projected without being beautiful. "That you have come to greet my arrival tonight, to me is joy and gratification. And I am sure that many of you, persons in your country grave and dear, questions grave and dear wait me to ask: What policies his? What attitudes? Most plainly, who this man is, and what wants he, this is to be known?

"Time will be—many years, I hope—for the difficult discussions. Let me herewith say that to speak for Peace is my cause, a message all of you are pleased to hear certainly. Now—a party in being, stand still allow us no more."

The musicians began a standanza, slow, comfortable rhythm, and the guests formed into eights to dance it. Afterward, Longlight drifted off with the Duchess, who was starting to describe the demise of the Forty-Eighth Duke, and Varic found Brook.

"Are you enjoying yourself, Varic? In spite of yourself?"

"It's been pleasant."

"Well, perhaps you can do even better. If you try a bit. You're not attending the Assembly tomorrow, are you?"

"Is that a question?"

"So far."

"My train isn't until eighteen."

"All the more reason to get adequate sleep. Can you actually sleep in those little rolling closets? I certainly can't." He crouched his broad shoulders in pantomime discomfort.

Varic said, "There are three motions on the calendar."

"A petition of Household the Commons won't pass, a permission to demolish a Midreign grain bin that's pitfalled four cows and nearly a child, and the Proclamation of Equinoctial, which I believe will arrive whether we ratify it or not. Sleep late, Varic."

"Brook—"

"Do come to the office when you are up, though. I'll be closing for the recess, and we'll have lunch before you go."

Varic realized that he was not pursuing an arguable point. "Tomorrow about highday, then."

"Good night, Varic. And I mean *good* night."

When he got back to her, Longlight said, "If you're going to travel in a fog, you should ring bells."

"I'm . . . sorry." It wasn't fog, he thought, it was a spinning compass. He looked at her, absolutely poised in her dazzling dress, and felt himself about to say something he might seriously come to regret in a day, or a month, or never.

The louder butler banged his staff for attention. "Guests all: the Ambassador's wish it is to announce an interesting and amusing demonstration of art and science, in the South Garden about to begin. If you will follow me?"

"Sounds like a spectacle show," Varic said. "Do you like the specs, my lady Coron?" He offered his arm.

She took it, whispered, "Do you think there'll be clowns?"

Overhead, a Paleday gibbous moon struggled with the clouds. There were lanterns all over the garden, not all of them placed with concern for the plants. A light rope blocked off an area around a stone-flagged walkway. At one end of the path, on a table, was a breech-loading repeating rifle; at the other, perhaps thirty stretches away, was a big concentric target, more like a mark for archers than riflemen.

The butler said, "Honoreds, lords and ladies, the Centurion Ardel Tenati!" An infantry officer in full dress uniform stepped out of the shadows. He bowed, removed his coat, stretched his braces. Varic sighed. Had it only been this morning?

Ardel Tenati picked up the rifle, checked its breech, then aimed at the target and fired. He hit the center ring, with a puff of pulverized straw. The audience applauded, having no idea what else to do.

Ardel Tenati pumped the ring-lever on the bottom of the rifle and fired again. Another palpable hit. He pumped, fired again.

Then he began jacking the lever and firing rapidly, a solid fifteen rounds a minima, one long ripple of thunder. Smoke wrapped him.

"I'd never have him in my guard," Longlight whispered to Varic.

Varic said, "It's not his accuracy we're here to see."

She looked again. Ardel Tenati was still pumping out bullets like a machine. Then she understood. "Where are they *coming* from?"

After fifty shots, the Centurion stopped, spun the rifle to shoulder arms, saluted. Varic saw him wince as the hot breech stung his shoulder, but he didn't flinch.

"Honored guests," said the butler, pointing across the audience, "the scientific part of tonight's entertainment is now displayed. The Art herewith: Master Emed Erekel."

A tubby, plain man stepped out of the crowd. Varic doubted that anyone had noticed his presence even before the shooting started. He wore a brown coat, a maladjusted cravat, droopy trousers, and a leather shoulder bag. He reached into the bag, produced a box of fifty rifle cartridges. Emed Erekel pulled one of the bullets from the box, made a snapping hand gesture; light blinked between his fingers.

Across the garden, Ardel Tenati brought his rifle back to ready and fired.

Applause.

Varic looked carefully at Emed Erekel. The magician's shoulder bag was very finely worked. His buttons were of knotted leather as well, and braided bands showed from his cuffs. He would be an Archovane, then, structuring his spells through leatherwork. Would this particular magic be in the cartridge bag, Varic wondered, or a bracelet, or elsewhere?

Varic had just turned back toward Ardel Tenati, intending to examine the sling on the rifleman's weapon, when the air shook.

A thunderbolt struck at the far end of the garden, light and furious sound. Guards quick-marched, and everyone turned, except Varic, who saw the sorcerer stare at his hands, and the Centurion nearly throw his rifle. Both of them recovered nicely. A moment later, the guard captain returned with the announcement that all was well, it was apparently a juvenile prank.

"Are there insufficient prisons?" Pinner the publisher muttered—though he was grinning through his side whiskers—and the guests began moving inside, suddenly remembering that it was cold out.

"I think that's probably the high point of the evening's entertainment," Varic said. "Would you like another dance?"

"Yes, I'd very much like another dance," she said, and her tone made his palms damp.

The musicians finally played a single-partner dance, wave-like music for a ricolette, couples revolving elegantly around the floor. As it concluded, Longlight said, "When does it become polite to leave one of these things?"

"Depends on whether you're a magician or not," Varic said, or rather felt the punch saying, and caught himself firmly. "Come with me."

They found the Ferangarder Ambassador with Brook, talking amiably enough, though there was something intimidating about the two big men facing one another, and Rocha Serestor kept glancing at the opposition party's medal on Brook's chest.

". . . but many of the things indispensable in the population's naming," Rocha Serestor was saying, "are actually only things they are used to having. Live without them for a while and why they were ever considered necessary is forgotten." Varic noticed that the Ambassador's speech had become markedly more Lescorial in style.

"Communion is an important ritual," Brook said.

"Divisive, though. Confusing. The priests say it is an appearance of Deity, but could they be wrong?"

"Naturally, I don't condemn your government's actions. You have your ways. But I'm forced, if only for your information, to say that banning Communion will not be popular with Lescorials, at least not in your life or mine."

"Yet you banned Crown Communion, which was a clear danger to policy."

"We did not ban Goddess possessing our Kings. We eliminated Kings." Brook turned as if cued. "Ah. Varic." He made introductions.

Rocha Serestor said to Varic, "I knew your father somewhat. We hunted together a few times. I think you must have been away—at school?"

"Very likely, Your Honor."

"We must converse soon. And perhaps hunt. The hunting on your lands is very good. Though, forgive me, not as good as in our Wyrowne Woods."

"I'll be pleased to visit you." Varic had always heard that the hunting in Corvaric was terrible, but apart from a few rides after tethered deer before he was ten, he had never hunted and really didn't know.

The Ambassador said, "And a Coron from the Far West. We have a great admiration for your people. You have the strength that bends not."

Varic said, "You must excuse us both, but my lady Coron has an early train tomorrow, and I should see her back to her hotel."

"Of course," the Ambassador said. "Good night to both of you, and do visit me. Here to meet and serve I ever am."

"Good night," Brook said, and twisted the tip of his mustache in what Varic seriously hoped was a meaningless gesture.

They made a few more farewells around the floor—the Duchess gave Longlight a head-turning hug—retrieved their cloaks, and boarded a cab.

As Varic leaned up to give the driver instructions, Longlight said, "Which is closer, my hotel or your house?"

"My house, considerably. But—"

"And where's your house?"

"Healstone Court."

"Driver," she called through the trap, "Healstone Court." She sat back, pointed out the windows, at the streetlamps bouncing by. "You know the City. Tell me what we're passing, I want to know."

So he did, naming the lanes, the parks, Butterbread Square and Hobnail Row, Crossways Park and Heighday Street, the river bridges and the monuments, the Quercian survivals and the steam-driven factories.

She interrupted him once, to say, "The excessively dashing young man with the Duchess—Winters?"

"Winterhill."

"He called you 'brother.' He isn't, is he?"

"No. He finds it funny. I suppose I do, too. But my family's gone. All gone."

And then they stopped, right in front of Varic's town house, and he knew that it was over. He put his hand on the door handle. "Good night, my lady Coron."

She stared at him. "Is that what you want to say?"

"I believe it's what is said."

"Birdlime."

"Pardon?"

"Crowcrap willat say up hills"—she stopped, recovered her City speech—"but you had me in a polite mood. Are you going to leave me here? Are you actually, honestly going to do that? You're not married; I asked Brook that. You're not even involved, he said. Or was he wrong?"

"No," Varic said, "not wrong," and that was true, because Agate was something else again. "And you?"

"There's a wonderful young Palion. We like each other, and it's very pleasant, and it'll die in a year or so, from lack of sunlight." She inclined her head. "He wouldn't respect you for this. He'd call you an idiot. I certainly make no claims, but I trust his judgment."

It was too perfect: so spontaneous and authentic that it froze his blood, so honest that he knew nothing but evil could come of it. Varic had a sudden, breath-stopping desire for her, so entirely physical that it rallied his senses and saved the moment from itself.

"In fact, honored," he said, no air in his lungs, "I cannot think of a single reason why we should not have one another's entertainment tonight. And because there is always at least one contrary reason to everything, I must perforce be missing what this one is: and that doubt prevents me."

"You said you were sure I'd never been terrified," she said. "I think now—"

"Milady Coron," he said, knowing that any instanta now he

would agree to what he wanted, "in Lystourel nothing worth knowing is secret. No one cares what is done on Cold Street, because that after all is what those establishments are for. But if you come into my rooms, it will be known. And it will be remembered the next time you speak to the Parliament. Some of them will think that I influenced you, some that you influenced me, most that we conspired together—and I cannot say that this would entirely harm your cause. I don't, honestly, know *what* effect it might have in the Chamber. But you must make your decision knowing that it *does* mean something beyond the hour."

"If I had not thought it would mean more than the hour," Longlight said with maddening calm, "I would not have proposed the hour at all. But your point is well taken. . . ." She laughed, and Varic caught the joke and laughed, too, and the tension was gone.

Longlight said, "I haven't had a night like this in . . . No. I've never had a night like this. Thank you, Varic."

"Thank you, Longlight."

He got down from the cab, watched it drive on, just caught the driver's glance back and headshake. Varic shook his own head and unlocked his door, turned up the gas to light the hall.

There was a ribbon-tied package on the hall table. It was a small summer fruitcake, smelling of plump sultanas and oat flour, an Equinoctial gift from his butler's wife. Midden's wife was a splendid cook, who made the meals the one or two times a year Varic had guests. The cake was just the right size for two. But there weren't two people in the house.

Varic overwrapped it in brown paper and tucked it into his larger satchel, packed and waiting in the hall for tomorrow. Agate would enjoy the fruitcake. He would share it with Agate, and be happy that he had come home alone tonight.

No, he thought, as he went upstairs to bed. Agate would be

pleased to see him, and he would be happy at that. But tonight had been something else entirely.

❧

The doorbell woke Varic from cloudy dreams at a little past ten. He pulled on a dressing gown and stumbled down the stairs, light hurting his eyes. The door opened on what seemed pure and intolerable whiteness, though in fact the sky had closed in gray again, the sun shrouded invisible.

"You look a splendid fright," Winterhill said softly, slipping inside. "Trust you earned those stripes under your eyes?" He glanced toward the stairway.

"This is the second morning running that people have told me I look slept under," Varic said sourly. "Forgive me if I misremember, but I recall dissipation as being more fun than this."

"You mean, she's not—she left? Or did you send her away?"

"We came to an agreement, not that it's any of your business, and she went home as any weary soul might. What is all this sudden concern with my bedroom habits?"

"I *told* Brook. Never with another Coron. Not if she'd been Communed with Shyira Herself."

"I am going to make some tea now, Winterhill. Perhaps after I've had a strong cup or two you'll begin to make some sense."

"My dear brilliant idiot friend, haven't you noticed that the Lord Chief Parliamentarian has been trying to keep you accompanied, last night and this morning?"

Varic pushed through the kitchen door. The indispensable Midden had laid out the tea preparations the night before; Varic could have found them by touch alone. "If Brook has decided to turn procurer, he can certainly—" Varic stopped short. He put his hands on the tea table, leaned hard on them. "Chase," he said.

"Comes the dawn," Winterhill said. "You see, the prime movers in the recent business don't care that much about killing you. All we had to do was make it inconvenient for a while, and they'd lose interest. Certainly they wouldn't risk an incident at a foreign embassy, or while you had a guest of some consequence. I wouldn't count, a rental companion might be bribed, but a Coron, ah." He sighed. "I suppose we should be happy that they were even less determined than we'd thought."

"I see," Varic said.

"Don't sound so blessed disappointed, brother." Winterhill yawned elaborately. "Are you still going to make that tea? I m'self was very thoroughly occupied last night, and now I'm caught between utter exhaustion and the feeling I could kill tigers with a butter knife." He snatched a butter knife from the sideboard and illustrated.

"The Duchess. . . . Oh, you didn't. And if you did, I don't want to hear about it."

"No one ever wants to hear my best stories," Winterhill said wistfully. He took a small paper sack from his coat pocket. "Here, have a biscuit." He accepted a cup of tea in return, then said, "Oh, and there's this." He dove in the pocket again, handed Varic a small, shiny, cold object. It was a brass-cased rifle cartridge.

"Mirit Oprana .30 caliber," Winterhill said.

"Yes?"

"That's what the magical marksman was using last night."

Varic looked closely at the cartridge. It seemed very ordinary. "And where did you get this one?"

"From the courtyard bushes, a little past where the Centurion was standing. On a line, in fact, from the sorcerer and past the shooter."

"So they missed a few."

"Several. I got three in the couple of instanti I had. From what

I saw, I'd guess at least one in four appeared somewhere other than in the rifle breech."

"The noise was yours?"

Winterhill smiled, held out his empty hand, and snapped his fingers. Another of the rifle shells appeared between them. "The luciver sold me a handful of flash powder."

Varic put the bullet down, drank tea, and chewed a biscuit. "One in four doesn't seem so bad."

"Depends on the circumstances. But there's something else. Did you notice the Embassy guards?"

"Only the one who insulted the Archreader. . . ." He thought a moment. "But that's the way the Peace side is toward magicians."

"Not what I meant. The outside guards usually carry carbines. But not last night. Now, it could be that the Peace Government is conducting a program of disarmament—"

"Thank you, Winterhill."

"—or it could be that Emed Erekel's Craft Archain can't tell one gun breech from another. In the heat of battle, that could be very awkward."

Varic contemplated the cartridge. "So was it all just a stage performance? Or were we supposed to take it for one?"

"Oh, no, brother," Winterhill said, "the depths are not for my sounding. Especially since the *Feranpactar* are, as you say, *that way* toward sorcery. You and the Parliamentarian decide what it means—only do me one favor: If it means a war with Ferangard, give me some notice? Davesque Isle needs a Fiftieth Duke."

"And just how—"

"You said you didn't want to hear that story. I *can* tell you that it involves draining a duck pond."

"All right, all right. When will I see you at Strange House?"

"I'll likely be a day late. My apologies and best to everyone."

"Of course. What's the time?"

"Just before eleven."

"Then I'd better get dressed and moving. We'll see you on Shineday."

"If Her humor holds," Winterhill said, tucked away his bag of biscuits, and went out, whistling.

Varic shaved (cautiously), dressed, examined the weather. It was still cool, but the sky had begun to crack blue, and the north wind was clean. He selected a hat, a light topcoat, and a stick—not his swordstick, but nicely weighted—and began walking the two milae to Parliament House.

It was half past highday when he arrived. The building was nearly deserted, the short session concluded. Brook was in his office.

"Varic. Good to see you. You look well."

"Yes. I'm well."

"You'll have to excuse me for a few moments longer. It was a very hurried morning—of course everyone wanted to have business finished before highday recess, and we did, but, well, my. Shall I ring for some tea?"

"Brook, has Ferangard actually outlawed Communion?"

Brook put down the papers he was holding, looked over his reading glasses. His mustaches were drooping slightly. "As a formal, public ceremony, yes."

"You don't find that significant?"

"I shall be interested to see how well they enforce the law."

"I'm sure Cable will be, too."

"You can't think that Cable has anything to do with Rocha Serestor."

"No, of course not," Varic said. "He couldn't. If there's a saving grace to Cable at all, it's that he can't treat anyone as an equal." Varic smiled a little. "The Ambassador won't like him at all."

Brook sat back, nodded. "Yes. That's exactly right."

"Cable isn't the point. If the Peace faction can pass something like this—"

"Varic," Brook said calmly, firmly, "have you ever been present when an Archimage bore Communion? Here, never mind Ferangard?"

"No."

"No. You can only be called an Anticonist because 'Atheist' is still a legal slander. And your father was far from a pious man. Varic, Communion is Goddess possessing the Archimage's body—"

"I know that. Birch is just about to be *made* Archimage of Capel—"

"—*possessing the priest's body,* literally. Magic is done there, prayers are answered, on the spot, in Her own voice. Do you know what people do, when She descends? They bring handfuls of desiccated earth and ask that it be made to bloom. They bring their deformed children and their mad aunts and their barren wives and say, 'Please, Goddess, mend thy handiwork.' They bring the dead on carts, Varic, and ask for them back." He leaned over the desk. "And sometimes . . . they *come* back. And it is *not* a blessing."

Brook put his hands on the papers, the draft laws, the Revised Constitution in eggshell. "They can't legislate it out of existence. I think they're fools even to try. It's bound to end up in repression and disaster. But I don't see how I can fault them for wanting some kind of control." He waved a hand. "Rocha Serestor was right about Crown Communion. Even when the ruler survived the process, it was drastic for policy."

"Very well," Varic said. "And the insult to the sorcerers?"

"You're under a strange cloud this morning," Brook said. "You don't believe in Goddess and you've no use for magic, and here you are wanting to interfere with a friendly government over both of them."

"I don't want to interfere," Varic said slowly, "and I'm not certain how friendly the government is."

"Well, *finally*. Sit down, Varic."

He did. Brook reached under the half-scattered papers, handed over a heavy paper folder. Varic knew what file the folder was destined for, and it was not kept in Parliament House. The name on the label was enciphered, as were the notes within. Varic said, "Whose?"

"Rocha Serestor's. You see, I'm not so old and blind as you think. I do not like the Ambassador either; like our own much-maligned Justiciar, he's blind and calls it clear-sightedness."

Varic flipped through the pages. He had the cipher key memorized, but he could not read the file without going through the decoding process. "What do we have?"

"Not a great deal. Real fanatics are hard to blackmail, unlike hypocrites. However, whatever we think of the Ambassador, he is the lawful representative of a sovereign nation, as old and civilized as our own. And what happens in Ferangard, as long as it stays inside Ferangard, is not our business . . . *except* as it provides examples, good or evil, for the reform of our own country's Constitutional document." His tone was even, never scolding: a teacher's, not a lecturer's.

When he was done, Varic nodded.

"Is that all you give me? A placid nod?"

"Did you want an argument?"

"I want to hear what you have to say."

"I haven't anything to say. You're right. I'm sorry."

"Varic. . . ." Brook stood up, walked around the desk, his hands locked together. "Yesterday, the maneuver with Master Whetstone—how on earth did you make it happen, while staying so completely out of it?"

"There's a lot of leverage in the relationship between apprentices and masters," Varic said, trying to make it a joke.

Brook said, not smiling, "I should thank you for it. And I do." He spread his hands. "Varic, the Revision is the most important thing I shall ever do. It is also the *last* important thing I shall ever do." He paused for a moment, said, "Anyone else would have answered that with, 'But, honored, you must live forever.' Not you, of course."

"Are you sorry?"

"Let's say that your constancy is reassuring. Just as I am sure in the knowledge that when I am gone, you will claim no particle of credit for the Revision, not even your considerable proper share. Not because you're modest—that you might hope to outgrow—but because it isn't wholly and entirely yours. And so, eventually, you'll have to make something that *is*."

Varic said, "Possibly. But as you said yesterday, we have a long distance to cover. I haven't time to consider it now."

"And you won't do when you have the time. It's your flaw, Varic. You're not selfish, and I have never met a soul to whom greed meant less, but you can't share."

"Well."

"Now *you're* missing the point. You've put your reputation and fortune and body on the block for this project that isn't yours." He paused, watching Varic, then said much more quietly, "You see the difficulty, don't you? Anyone else—an ordinary clerk, blast it, never mind a landed Lord—would be calling me an ingrate now, at least with his eyes, with his mind. But you're content."

"Do you want me not to be content?"

"I might be more comfortable. And you know that's not my meaning. I'm telling you that someday you'll be standing where I am, watching your life's work come to its peak, and looking at the person who helped you reach that point. And, because

Goddess makes only one snowflake of a kind, that person, un-like you, will want a piece of the glory, and will have earned it. And you won't give it up."

There was another silence. Varic knew what the next ques-tion in logical sequence was: he should ask if Brook was actually afraid of this in Varic's hypothetical future or his own imme-diate one. Fortunately, Brook also knew that this was the next question, and they both also knew the answer (such as it was), and thus all the difficulty of speaking either was avoided.

Varic said, again trying for humor, again not quite succeed-ing, "This great thing of my very own—you're not afraid it will be a war with Ferangard?"

"No," Brook said. "You're not mad. You're hiding an awful rage, hiding it even from yourself, I think. But you're sane, and calm, and wise for your age. And I have listened to your stories of cavalry charges in distant lands: you have a good idea of what war means these days. You won't start a war."

Both of them lived on the margin between what people said they would do and what they actually did, like merchants on a percentage; and in time, as with the merchants, one grew un-able to see anything without that margin framing it.

And they understood each other so well that Brook's next words were an awful shock. "Not like this, Varic," he said, as if he were bleeding. "Don't go away on a note like this."

Varic could not find his voice for perhaps half a minima. "I'm only visiting the House for holidays," he said finally. "Two Pale-days and I'll be back. And Strange has a magnostyle, you know that."

"Of course I know that."

"It's Equinoctials, Brook. See a play, or a concert . . . or you could always come to the House. How long has it been since you've seen Strange?"

"Much too long," Brook said, and his tone was a relief. "And please tell Strange that I hope it will not be much longer. But not this trip." He looked up, as if a haze were lifting. "Tell him to keep me a room for the Solstice. And to uncase the cards and lock up his money."

"I'll tell him. I think he'll be delighted."

"As will I. Now. Shall we have some late lunch, before your train?"

CHAPTER 2

THE ROAD AND THE SKY

Brook led Varic out of the Parliament building and across Clarity Park. Brook strolled energetically, tipping his high hat to people who knew him and people who didn't, flipping a silver plate to a ragged but competent juggler, who caught it, whirled it round her cascade of cloth beanbags, and vanished it away.

Varic said, "It is pleasant to see you in a good mood."

"It's pleasant to be in a good mood. And to be out of the charnel house of laws for a few days." He looked straight at Varic. "And also to hear you express a pleasure." He turned at once, stepped up on the low marble ring around a fountain, walked heel-and-toe halfway around it before hopping down with a thud and a suppressed groan. Varic took a few brisk steps to catch up.

"Thank you, kind sir," Brook said as Varic drew close, "but my parents taught me never to speak to strangers, especially near a government building." He looked past Varic, across the park. "Though if you'd take me to see that fellow over there, I might make an exception."

Varic turned. Some distance away, a fingersmith was performing for a crowd of perhaps a dozen. Brightly colored silk scarves floated above him, and shiny bits of glass and metal flashed through the clear, still air. It was difficult to see the worker himself, but he seemed to be wearing a long robe of dark velvet, gilded with the skysign symbols. It was known in the South as the Sheath of Night, or the Starmantle, and several other exalted and portentous names. Among themselves the sleighters called it *the Black Rag,* and prized its power to blend into a shadow when a bailiff was too close behind.

"I want to see the miraclist," Brook said with deliberate childishness. "Once one found a coin in my nose and the prettiest green marble in my ear." With a mock pout, he added, "I suppose you're going to tell me it was just a trick."

"Where did you plan to have lunch?" Varic said very calmly. "I mustn't miss my train."

Brook touched Varic's sleeve. "Yes, of course," he said, his voice immediately adult again. "Just down this way; you know the spot." They turned away and walked east.

Larkrise Street, on the park's east edge, was clotted solid with holiday traffic. Varic and Brook wove between horses and high-spoked wheels. A delivery wagon dripped steadily as the ice cooling its cargo melted down; an ubicarriage was piled with luggage and packed with complaining passengers. The driver, safely outside the riders' compartment, had the reins wrapped loosely around his wrist and was riffling intently through the Book.

Varic knew their destination now. He followed Brook down a dire-looking side street, dim and cutthroat-crooked, to a building just by an even narrower alley. The corner door was open. A lamp hung above it, curved glass petals, the deep blue of a winter sky, enclosing the mantle. A broad street-side window, gold-leafed in sweeping curves, showed only a few soft glows from within.

Brook stepped through the doorway, removing his hat. Varic followed.

It was dim inside, the high ceiling in almost total gloom;

stained-glass table lamps made little puddles of brightness on table covers of heavy figured damask. Scents of tea and cinnamon drifted through the warm, still air. The whole space was L-shaped, tables and chairs in the larger space, a glass case of pastries in the smaller limb, which led to the kitchen.

A thin man, slightly taller than Varic, appeared from behind an ornately carved wooden screen. He wore a kitchen-stained white apron over a white shirt. "Brook, so pleased. And, Varic, good to see you. Lunch, I should hope?"

Brook said, "Good day, Linnet. Lunch, please. No cards. Surprise us."

"Find a seat, then. I won't be long." Linnet gestured with both hands, inclined his head, and turned toward the kitchen. Fine blond hair trailed down his spine, almost to his waist; the queue was wrapped in net and white ribbon.

Two of the ten tables were occupied; a couple here, three there. Someone looked up briefly and smiled, but no one paid them serious attention. Brook sat down at a table right on the point between the main room and the case alcove; Varic adjusted his chair so that its back was to the wall and his view of the entrance was clear, and sat down.

There was a tall, narrow vase, holding four blue blossoms, in the center of the table. Varic shifted it to the edge.

Brook said, "There's room. Or was that a symbolic gesture?"

"You will allow me my unromantic boredom with the idle symbols of romance," Varic said without heat.

"Blue roses are rare and delicate."

"Scarcity is relative, and delicacy's a virtue of situations. In the North, they sprout and die with insane determination. The farmers who send them down here consider it money for weeds. Of course, they do take the money, and don't expunge the weeds."

"How long has it been since you were north, Varic? To Corvaric, I mean."

"Six years . . . no, seven. It was just after the Bridges and Roads Act. You thought I should vacate for a while, remember? So I decided to see the old family crypt."

"I had supposed you would visit Strange."

"I value Strange's hosting too much to abuse it."

Brook protested with his look, but didn't speak.

Varic said, "And I thought Agate might visit. I wasn't in a fit state to see her."

Brook said, very quietly, "Now I think you do abuse Strange's hospitality, to assume he could not deal with that."

"Brook, I am sorry."

Brook shook his head, said, still quiet, "I cannot ask you not to speak of her. I regret few things in my life so much as the hurt I caused her."

"Yet there is in Agate's hurt none of grudge nor rancor, and your regret would bring her naught save grief."

Brook said, "Is it my talk of the North or something else that puts the accent back into your voice?"

Linnet came out of the kitchen with a covered plate in each hand, a basket of bread caught in his left elbow. He set them on the table. "I think you'll find these pleasant. Promise me this, though: my lord Brook, that you'll taste it before salting it, and, my lord Varic, that you'll taste it at all while you're eating it too fast."

They agreed to this, and Linnet took away the fogged glass covers. "I'll have your tea in a moment." He disappeared again toward the kitchen; Varic watched Brook watching him go.

Varic had been given thin strips of redfish, grilled and seasoned with herbs, on a nest of superfine noodles lightly coated with cream. Brook had an omelet with chicken; the chicken was almost as red as the redfish, and Varic could taste the pepper sauce from across the table. Brook sliced out a large piece and chewed it. Sweat appeared on his forehead. He smiled.

Varic said, "And you won't eat smoked fish."

"I appreciate the pungent, not the acrid. Oh, my." He picked up his water goblet and drank off a third of it, followed by a piece of Linnet's herb-and-cheese bread.

Linnet brought the tea, and a large crystal water pitcher to refill Brook's glass. "Well?"

Brook said, "That warning about salt was a bit much, Linnet."

"No, it wasn't."

"Very well, it wasn't. And it is, of course, excellent."

Linnet nodded and looked at Varic, who said, "Very good, thank you, Linnet. Isn't it early in the season for redfish?"

"I thought you would know that. Those were brought in by an Alinsea trader. A steam-power ship, weeks ahead of the sail fleet. Now, have I told you something you did not know?"

"Yes," Varic said, "thank you."

Linnet bowed and went back to the kitchen.

Brook was holding his knife and fork delicately poised, in thumbs and forefingers, their points just pricking the omelet. His eyebrows were elevated, and his whiskers twitched like a curious rabbit's.

"No, Brook," Varic said, "I am not going to begin a discussion of engine-powered shipping. It is the holiday recess."

Brook's face relaxed and he returned to his lunch.

There was a small commotion at the street door. Varic turned as a plump little man came in. He held a brown leather portfolio tightly to his chest; his stare wandered urgently around the room. He took several uncertain steps toward Brook.

"Oh! My lord Parliamentarian—Leyva was good enough to say you might be here."

"As indeed we are, Hawken."

Hawken was short and slumped, broad and curiously proportioned, with a head and arms that appeared to belong to a much larger man. His feet seemed more of an impediment to than the means of walking.

He was the member in Commons for Mark Pinegirt, a town of moderate size but no great ambition; its Coronage was Black Vale, just southeast of and touching Varic's own lands of Corvaric.

"I'm sorry to interrupt you, milord Coron—"

"Nonsense, honored member," Brook said. "Would you care to join us?"

"The redfish is very fine today," Varic said, so that they were both welcoming him.

"Oh! I can't. Truly. I'm supposed to be home for the 'Nocts, and there's a three-twelve train—at any rate, I've only just acquired the Coal Exchange figures for Bowenshield, Deerleap, and Thunders, and the decline is—"

"Thank you, Hawken," Brook said.

Oblivious, Hawken put the portfolio on the table, began to open it. "Page eight, lines sixteen through forty indicate a serious—"

"I shall pay the most careful attention to those lines, once I am in a better light for reading."

Hawken finally got the idea. "Ah. Yes. Of course." He shut the folder. "I am sure," he said, loudly enough to bring Linnet out of the back, "that the figures will speak for themselves." He shook Brook's hand and nodded deeply to Varic, then bought a bag of popovers from Linnet and went out. Through the gilded window, Varic saw him pull one of the hot pastries out of the bag and wander off chewing contentedly.

Brook had tucked the portfolio under his chair, without any fuss. Now his expression was placid and amused.

Varic said, "Yes?"

Brook said, "Every time you see that dear little man, you look as if you wish you had a weapon to hand."

"I'm sorry it's so obvious."

"Are you telling me you . . . *mistrust* him?"

"My ancestors spent considerable effort trying to conquer his ancestors, or at least kill them and pick up what their dead hands let drop. Blood melts down much time, North, Brook."

"The Northern accent fascinates me. So softly spoken, for such hard people."

Varic said, in an even heavier Northesse, "An thou taste on blood, drink deep, and cease not till the cup be dry. For it will surely sour and turn to poison."

"Quercian," Brook said. "Quercian survives most in Northesse and Westrene. The South had more contact with more of the world, because of the ocean, and its language diluted more completely with others. And the Empire never controlled the East."

"Silvern's told me of gravestones. 'Beneath this monument lie the best of the Seventeenth Legion. This stone be their curse on these stony people.' The Estra leave the markers alone, of course."

"You are statesmanlike when you're angry, Varic."

"Am I angry?"

"The more dangerous a Northerner is feeling, the softer he speaks, and you were almost to a murmur. I'm sure you wanted to be at the rump session this morning. But it truly didn't matter. And a few of the Lords Sorcerous had little suns in their eyes for you; they found out who their novices had been drinking with. Give them the recess to forget."

"Or else lay this batch up to age with all the other grievances."

"I see why you don't trust Hawken."

"I trust Hawken. I also think him capable of more than his appearance might indicate."

Brook ate a few bites more, doused the fire. He sipped his tea thoughtfully and said, "Assess Hawken for me. As a type, I mean. Why is he here and not running a mine or a mill?"

"Because his family isn't the sort that operates mere trade," Varic said. "Not an uncommon Northern type: a first child looks unlikely to carry your hopes on, displays no Talent Archain, and the Church has become *so* particular . . . so you find him a nice seat in Parliament."

"Can you think of a better place for him?"

"Of course."

"Which university?"

"Coron Black Vale."

Brook laughed.

"What can be said for that paperweight Snowbed except that she's better than the creature born to the job? What can be said for Coron in Residence Fledger except that he sent Snowbed to the City and keeps himself home, where they know to keep little girls out of his reach?"

Brook turned his head slowly, and Varic knew he was looking over the other patrons for signs of interest, and also silently telling Varic to mind his comments. But no one else had stirred. And nothing had been said that was secret.

Nothing could be said that would change anything, and wasn't that the pity.

Brook said, "Perhaps that can be your great project, after I'm gone: the selection of Corons on merit."

That effectively ended the discussion, and they returned to their lunches, which were certainly too good to let go cold.

Linnet appeared now and again to refresh drinks, bring desserts for the other patrons, clear their tables. Eventually only Varic and Brook remained in the restaurant. Varic said, "May I ask you again to come with us to the House?" He almost added, *And be forgiven by Agate,* but did not.

"You may ask. I will say thank you, no."

Linnet came out, swung a chair around, and straddled it, his arms folded on the chair back. "I was planning to close early today," he said, "and there are some things that will just spoil. So I'm having a small party for the regulars. I hope you can stay?"

Varic said, "I have a train. I am sorry."

Brook tapped his fingertips on the table. "I should be delighted to help you save an innocent pastry from doom."

"Excellent, Brook. And, milord Varic—Ironway food? Let me send something with you. A jam linka, perhaps; that won't get crushed too easily in transit. Don't say *no*."

"Yes, then."

"Apple, cherry, or Ruesberry?"

Brook laughed. Varic said, "Cherry, please. And thank you, Linnet."

When Linnet had slipped back to the kitchen, Varic said, "Silvern will appreciate it. Though I'd better not mention that swipe at the Ironways. Edaire, contrariwise, would laugh, that's the odd thing."

"You don't know much about husbands and wives, Varic."

"And you do? Beside which, they're not husband and wife, they're conseil." Varic managed to smile slightly. "And I know nothing at all about *that* condition."

"Nor I, nor I, nor I." Brook looked toward the kitchen door, the glass case full of sweets and savories. "Do you think that if Lescoray had suffered a Great Flood, or a Plague, or a Fire, a thousand years ago, instead of a Great Famine, we'd constantly be giving each other boats, or medicine, or buckets of water? Well."

Varic looked at his watch. "It's nearly one thirty. I must go, Brook."

"Is there such a hurry? Linnet can signal a cab—"

"You saw the streets as well as I did. I can walk faster; I can probably walk it on the roofs of cabs." He stood up. "Thank you for a lovely lunch, Brook. The pleasantest of holidays to you."

"But no wish of finding Goddess? Wait. Come here." Brook plucked a blue rose from the vase, snapped its stem, tucked it in Varic's lapel. "Now you're disguised as a romantic, and no one will recognize you. Fair parting, Varic, fair return. Remember me to Strange."

"I will."

Varic tucked the bag under his arm, picked up his stick. He paused in the doorway, looked back. Linnet was standing by the table, holding Brook's hand carefully in both of his own. That was good, Varic thought as he went through the door. Brook would at least not be alone.

Now Varic had to cross Lystourel. When he got to Larkrise Street, it was difficult to tell if any motion at all had taken place during his lunch; the ubic' seemed perhaps half a block farther along, but the passengers were still complaining, the driver still ignoring them and dealing his Book.

There really seemed to be no hope for the City's traffic. A proposal to widen the streets around Clarity and Highgate Parks, trimming several spans in from their edges, was presented and vetoed every year. From time to time, someone had the idea to stack iron-framed causeways (or, if the inventor was in a monumental mood, stone viaducts) on top of the existing main thoroughfares. The latest variation on that theme called for the bridges to carry Ironway tracks. None of these exercises in cat-belling explained how to get light and air to the ground level, what to do about rust and drainage on the upper, or how to deal with sparks and cinders, metal dust and ash from motives and carriages grinding by overhead.

Cinders. Fire above. That was another issue Parliament had not even begun to consider. There were iron-fronted dwellings ten and twelve floors high in Lystourel; Varic could look up right now and see one, a dark mass of stone veneer and dark hooded windows looming beyond the parkside shop fronts. How could firefighters reach the top of such a thing, let alone pump water to it?

His mind could see people jumping from those impossible upper windows, amid flame and smoke, as if a volcano had suddenly appeared within the City, and the dark aspect of Goddess demanded sacrifices—

He noticed that his steps had quickened. He was beginning to hate Lystourel, to want out and away from the ancient and beautiful City. It would not do, he thought, it really would not do to leave angry, slamming a mental door on the way out. There was no Parliament anywhere else. There was no place for him, none that really mattered, anywhere else.

Strange House was a sweet distraction, a good and friendly and perhaps even necessary refuge from the hard world. But that was *exactly* what it was, a refuge, far away, and not the world.

Some of the other guests thought that Strange meant for Varic to inherit the House. Varic himself found the idea too distant to consider, too flattering to take seriously. Supposing Strange did die, ten or twenty or fifty years from now. Edaire might be ready to retire by then, or Birch. Edaire would be the best choice, Varic thought: the sanest of them, the most understanding. Even Birch, who would in a few days be fourth priest in the nation, would have agreed about her understanding.

There was a clatter; Varic stepped aside as a two-wheeled cab put one iron-rimmed wheel on the walkway, trying to pass a slow coal wagon. Varic muttered something unpleasant, snatched a pencil from his pocket, and wrote the cab's number on the wrapper of Linnet's pastry.

Traffic again. Shelter Bay was experimenting with electrical trams that did not scatter sparks among sails and rigging, did not puff soot on cargoes of tea and silk and rice. The motive units were not very powerful, and the electric fluid could not be sent a long distance from the dynamo house. It might not work beyond the limited needs and space of the central docks. Still they ran, and the dockers who had begun by making ward-signs against the sparking motive, daring each other to ride behind it, now accepted the equipment, posed with it for lucives, seemed proud of it. Lystourel would surely have one soon; City pride would demand it.

He turned down an alley too narrow for wheeled traffic; it was lined with bookshops and stationers, almost the entire wall surface to either side shouting signs for inks and papers, nibs and pencils, job printing, No Job Too Large or Small, Read *Collected Essays from the Star* by "Waspish," APIARIA'S FABU-LAND ROMANCE SERIES: New Numbers Weekly Price Only ⅔ in Sturdy Glued Bindings, Root's Shaving Soap (what was that doing here?). . . .

It was quiet in the alley; most of the stationers would have closed for the holiday. Varic emerged, turned the corner, and the Terminus rose before him, across a sea of cement and flagstones bobbing with humanity.

The front of the Terminus was an inward curve of gray gran-ite, as long as two ordinary blocks and four floors high, fronted with half columns and a central spill of stairs. Carved along the upper coping was a frieze representing Transportation, pedes-trians trudging behind carts chasing horsemen hot after Quer-cian chariots in pursuit of six-horse rigs trying vainly to overtake the earliest steam motive hard on the rear buffer of *Lescorial Maj-esty,* winner of the Blackslope Power Trials.

The space within the building's curve was simply full of people, and luggage, and pigeons, all in constant motion. Only the news vendors were idle, here in the low spot between early and late papers; the evening sheets would be out in an hour or so, plus however long it took the wagons to actually get here. A few bailiffs urged along anyone else who stood still, presumably, Varic thought, to keep the confused and weary from impeding the labor of pickpockets and baggage fishers.

Varic went up the steps neither slowly nor hurriedly, narrowly avoiding half a dozen collisions. He went through the doors and into the Great Hall.

The Hall stretched for two full blocks, curving back to his left and right. It was almost twenty steps across, its ceiling vault the full four storeys above. Dividing its length were thirteen arches, separating the twelve gates leading to the tracks. They were open about two-thirds of the way up, in double arches, the point-topped arches of the Midreigns. Above and to either side of the openings the stone was elaborately carved, and at the upper trackside corner was a picture in colored glass. Sun came through windows on the track side in angled, dusty shafts, and echoed voices and footsteps made the whole Hall boom.

He looked up at the nearest arch-panel. They were designed in the ratio of the square's side to its diagonal, the absolute rectangle of the Quercians. The space below the arch was a perfect square, which made the panel above the opening another absolute rectangle, and the square of stained glass at the top generated another. The corners of the smaller frames were connected by an arc of fluted stone that curved from the trackside apex to the street-side floor. That curve was known as the generative spiral, and it was echoed in flowers and snails' shells. It was sacred to Shyira, for those who cared.

The architect's original vision for the Hall had been of the fanned Book, each panel a gigantic card on end. The Readers'

Guilds were flattered but furious: just *which* cards did this amateur propose to make the reading for the Capital Terminus? Because that (they said) was what it amounted to.

Coron Deerleap, younger then than Varic was now, had come up with the solution. He proposed that each of the panels should represent, and be the gift of, a particular city (Lystourel had the two centermost, flanking the doors): so the carvings displayed fish and sea freighters for Shelter Bay, coal and timber for Black Vale, sheep and college spires—some saw a joke in that—for Ascorel. Somehow Deerleap had persuaded the towns to compete for generosity and beauty rather than blank-faced pride and power. The wily old hart had even gotten the Archreaders to contribute to the general building fund, on the ground that the spread of panels would put travelers in mind of a reading—if not any particular reading.

The entrance side of the Hall was all shops at ground level; food (Linnet was not the only soul to mistrust Ironway cooking), newsagents, hats and gloves and umbrellas for the forgetful or the sudden change of weather. Signs announced with discreet pride that accessories from Ivory, Ivory & Co. and Canemaker's and Felton, Spline were sold here, along with less exalted names. A level up were sit-down restaurants, grooming salons, a pleasant and surprisingly quiet tavern called the End Carriage, and a Book parlor—which might have proven something about sympathetic sorcery.

The floors above that housed the offices of the Ironway administration. At almost top center was the Directors' Dining Room, with a splendid view of the City. Varic had dined there twice, with Edaire. Both times the meals had been catered from elsewhere.

Varic decided he ought to have something for Strange; something that wasn't food. A few doors along he found a small-goods shop, a long display counter of wood and glass tended by a thin girl with straight broomcorn hair.

It only took a moment to find what he wanted: a plump fountain pen, its barrel a black false marble trimmed with silver. A fine silver chain attached it to a castelline brooch.

The attendant was clearly a bit lonely, and when she spoke, the North was plain in her voice. "That's a marvelous practical thing, honored," she said. "I tris, myself at first could not see the use, but one's always forgetting, eh? Or knocking the good pen to the hard floor. So—well, you do see?" She drew a much plainer pen from her own pocket, displaying its cord and castelline, and wrote up the bill of sale. "Is't for yourself, honored, or a gift?"

"A gift."

"Oh, then, if you would have something more elaborate, I have a brooch with a lapis inlay. It's very beautiful. And this chain is but plate—full silver is available. I can do the work right quickly."

"No, I think not."

"Do allow me to wrap it? Won't be long in doing, and no charge."

"I would thank you. And time's light yet." As she cut the paper and spanned the cord, he said, "You would be from . . . Pineshadow? Woods Arch?"

"Pineshadow, yes," she said delightedly. "And you?"

"Corvaric."

"Oh, the Hard Coast," she said, nothing showing in her voice, but for an instant she cupped her right hand, Shyira-Guarding-Seed. Varic ignored the sign and said, "My train home goes through Pineshadow."

"Yes, through the Palisade. That is the great forest, north and west."

Which kept my ancestors from burning your ancestors' houses, Varic thought. "I do confess I am a town boy," he said, watching her wrap and seal the package, dress it in gold cord. The work was perfect and human at once: warm geometry. He began to wish he had asked for the new chain, just to watch her attach it.

"I suppose I am, too, now," she said, her voice at once all City. "Will you need a card?"

"No. I thank you."

He paid, tucked the parcel into a coat pocket, tipped his hat, and went out. From the very corner of his eye, he saw the attendant settle back onto a high stool and draw a glueback novel from her apron.

She would live in one of the stacked flats south of the Grand, he thought, or perhaps share a town house with several other shop folk far from their birthfields, their *cors coris*.

He went back to the center of the Hall, looked up at the announcement board, a black wooden grille of small windows displaying train destinations, times, and track numbers. As he watched, more information appeared; behind the board was a team of youths on ladders, slipping cards into windows, right side up Or Else. Varic's train would be at Gate 8, Track 16, and the lads had not yet dropped the LATE card.

A train for Vining, in the East, was boarding through Gate 6; the high doors were open, and Varic could see dimly through them to the train shed beyond, the curved glass roof above the concrete jetties, the varnished coaches.

Each gate led to a jetty, each jetty had a track to each side; twenty-four tracks twisted into an iron braid and then fanned out across all the country.

Varic had grown up without Ironways. His father had been noisily contemptuous of bringing rails anywhere near the Castle; fortresses, he said, were *supposed* to be difficult to approach.

So the tracks went to Corvaric, but the main Northern line terminated at Harktown, barely five stades into the Coronage.

From there a slow (if scenic) branch wound on to a fishing town called Annets Point. A straighter, faster line would have better served the cod and salmon and sea skate, packed in ice and salt for the inland markets. But that would require two handfuls of negotiations with the Householders and townspeople on and off the present line or the new one. No one but the fishermen—who would see nothing but improvement, whose land would not be graded over or steamed through—really seemed to want it, and none of the inlanders seemed interested in doing anything for the fishermen.

He took a step toward Gate 8 and stopped still.

He would never be certain why he had noticed her, in the crowd, in the hurry, his mind on other things and expecting her long gone; but there she was, sitting on the end of a bench with a leather bag at her elbow and a canvas one with Ivory's mark behind her feet, a book tight in her hands.

"Hello," Varic said.

Coron Longlight looked up, her face tight as a fist. Then it softened. "Oh. Hello."

"I thought you would be gone by now."

"The cab got stuck. I was late. I can't get back to the hotel either, even if there *were* a room, and there's one more train west—on which I've been promised the very second seat someone cancels."

"You'd be going . . ." He angled his head, looked past the arch at the great mural map of the Ironway system. ". . . to Great Gate?"

"I would, and will, if there's a seat."

"Will you trust me to stay here—*exactly* here—for exactly fifteen minimi?"

"Yes."

"Then I have to see about something."

"Wait. What do you have to see about?"

"If a man with no magic can pull coins from his nose," he said, and left her.

Silvern was at Gate 8, not difficult at all to find. He stood almost a full head above the crowd, and they flowed around him like the Estuary dividing around the Castle. He was standing with a long leather satchel over one shoulder and a carpetbag between his boots; he might have been a monument, the Traveler as Hero.

He was wearing a hunter's jacket of sueded leather, dark gray, with shell loops and game pockets; his trousers were forest-green moleskin. His cravat was pleated white silk, without a pin.

Silvern's hair had once been dark chestnut brown, but decades of Craftwork had bleached it to a gray with veins of red, a kind of granite with quartz. His face was quite dark and somewhat battered. Along his left cheekbone was the trace of a scar; some people thought it looked romantic. Varic remembered the wound, the six seasons of bandages and sorcery.

Silvern's eyes were the color of graphite: a deep metallic gray with a strange and evanescent shine. He had been named for his eyes. As had Agate—

As Varic thought of her, a hand seemed to finger over his heart. It could, possibly, be magic; he did not know where Agate was, if not at the House. If it *were* sorcery, there was nothing he could do without more information; and the present time pressed.

"Glad to see you made it," Silvern said. His voice was deep and slightly scratchy, with the grinding consonants of the East. He held out his left hand, palm up, showing a ring: a broad band of gold and black enamel that wound twice around the third finger. Varic put his hand upon Silvern's.

Silvern said, "I don't think we can board for at least a quarter. Some tea? And what's in the paper?"

Varic said, "I need your assistance in a complot."

Silvern grinned hugely. "Aha! And will there be bold actions, hearts in peril, escape by the mourn of our fingernails?"

"All of those, I think," Varic said, a bit absently, and Silvern's eyes widened to match his smile. "Well, then," the Palion said, "more to a blue rose than fancy, *aiga*?"

"You have a double compartment, correct? But Edaire won't be joining you."

"Yes, and I believe not."

Varic nodded. "Leap one fence at a time. . . . All right. Stand *right here,* and if I lose track of you despite that, do not you lose me."

"To the storming of the heights, my captain."

Varic almost threw his hands in the air, but he still had the linka under his arm. "Hold this," he said, and gave it to Silvern, who accepted it in both hands, with a small bow. Varic dodged through the crowd again, to Longlight again. She looked up.

"Honored lady," he said, "a compartment has been located to your use." He held up a hand to stop her reply. "Your own exclusive use. I can guarantee it only as far as Leith Meadows, but there is a good chance it will be available to the end of line, and if not, I personally guarantee transport will be arranged for you. Are these all your bags?"

She laughed aloud, then stopped it with a hand to her mouth. "There's a trunk in the baggage room. A small one."

"Then we should hurry. This way." He picked up the Ivory's canvas and led her to Gate 8.

"Silvern," he said quickly, "I would present the Lady Longlight, Coron of the Great Rogue Hills, and at present in need of passage space homeward. My lady, this in turn is the Palion Silvern, Armiger of the First Degree, Military Liaison to Bryna Kóly. Silvern: give me your tickets. And you, my lady."

Silvern produced an envelope at once; Longlight extracted hers from a pocket of her leather satchel. Varic took them, said, "Once again: if I lose you, lose me not." Then he set down Longlight's bag and was gone again, leaving Silvern and Longlight a tiny, calm eddy in the crowd.

After a moment, Longlight said, "Palion—and Armiger—"

"My name is Silvern, my lady Coron," he said easily.

"And mine is Longlight."

Silvern nodded. "It will be most pleasant to have a new guest at the House."

"A what? I—Do you know what he means to do?"

"I thought I did. You're not coming to Strange House with us?"

Longlight explained her situation. Silvern said, "Now I think I do understand. May I suggest a cup of tea to clear both our heads, and I'll try to answer your question?"

"We won't lose Varic."

"Between your hunter's sense and my perch?"

Longlight said sharply, "What scry you—" She stopped, pressed her lips tight, and said more quietly, "Hunter's sense sees hunter's sense. . . ."

"Of course," Silvern said, his tone a shrug, and she nodded and followed him.

They walked only a little way, to a tea cart, and found a bit of wall to stand against with their bags safely warded and hot paper cups in their hands.

Silvern said, "Now. I have a double compartment, with no companion. Varic would have had a single. I should think he has gone to swap us around."

"Oh," she said, "oh. I see." She smiled.

"What a smile is that," Silvern said.

"He was careful to say the compartment would be exclusively mine."

Silvern said, "In that case, it will be. And he will be sharing with me—and pop goes your smile."

"This won't be an imposition for you."

"None."

"And he—this is the sort of problem that pleases him, is't not?"

"*Aigashté.* A salute to your perception."

"Was that word Kólyan?"

"It was."

"I don't believe I've ever heard it spoken. Other side of the world from me."

"*Tré shin ye baród.*"

"And that means?"

"'I praise the person my friend loves.' The Kólyan habit is never to speak in abstracts. They would not, for example, say that you were beautiful. They might say, instead, '*Keshtine tseyt, knórowa kneyt sha.*' 'Your gaze has caused the falcons to preen in envy.'"

She laughed, then said in a smaller voice, "Do you think I am the person your friend loves?"

"I see that which he could not help but find desirable. Beyond that, I have no place to speak." He held up his left hand, showing the ring.

"That's—you're conseil."

"Correct. Look at the band." He spread his palm. Circling the braided ring were interlocking circles and straight lines.

"They're swords and buckler shields," she said.

"Yes. And also motive wheels and side rods. Edaire, my conseil, is with the Ironways."

"Edaire," she said. The word meant both "a surprise" and "a miracle." Longlight looked closely at the ring. "I see how it's both images. Was it your design, or—uhm, Edaire is—"

"Edaire is a woman. The design is Varic's, and the rings were his gift."

She drank some tea. "I should like," she said with audible bitterness, "to have known him." She told Silvern about the motion before Parliament, how she had overstated her case and ruined her chances.

Silvern said, "People solve problems according to their natures. To the heart: if Varic were of another nature, he would have had another carriage attached to the train, just for the three of us."

"He could have done that?"

"He *could* have."

"Dwillsey, Peritepalion—"

Silvern waved a finger through the steam rising from his tea-cup.

Longlight nodded, said, "Silvern. Who *is* he?"

"Someone who will leave Lescoray a better place, if he can only find the time. My often distant but always very good friend. Do I think he loves you, Longlight? Ask me if I think you love him. But ask it quickly: here he comes."

Varic held out ticket envelopes to Longlight and Silvern. "Your ticket to Leith Meadows," he said, "Compartment One, first cabin carriage. Your trunk should be waiting for you there. While you, old friend, get my company and baggage."

"And glad of them both," Silvern said, his voice oddly flat. "Would you like a tea, Varic?"

"Let me buy the first cup of the voyage." He pointed at the paper parcel atop Silvern's carpetbag. "Something to go with it as well. Now I think we ought to move toward the gate."

They joined the queue forming before the door, showed their tickets to the guard, passed onto the jetty. Under the glass triple vault of the train shed, the echo of voices and footsteps was shorter, hollower, with an overtone of humming iron. To their left, Track 15 was occupied only by an open carriage piled with restaurant supplies. On 16, they passed the parlor, its tail roofed and sided with glass, then a sleeper. The carriage sides were the deep maroon color of the Ironway Western lines, with tracings of gold leaf around the windows; the wheels were almost out of sight, below the level of the concrete platform.

At the forward end of the sleeper, where it connected with the next, a woman in a brass-trimmed uniform was carefully checking a piece of equipment on the forward car's end. Varic stopped short and looked long and straight at her.

Longlight said, "Varic? Are you all right?"

Varic turned away. "I'm sorry," he said. "For a moment she looked like Edaire."

"Not a bad guess," Silvern said, "but I'm harder to fool about some things."

Longlight said, "Your wi—conseil works for the Ironways, you said."

"No," Varic said, "she is not a carriage mechanic."

"Mostly," Silvern added.

Longlight waited for an explanation.

"This is our carriage," Varic said. "Yours is one closer to the motive, and the restaurant will be one farther still. The last car is the cabin passengers' parlor. Shall we meet there, say, just after the captain has checked tickets?"

"Agreed," Longlight said.

The two men entered the car, turned left down the narrow corridor, went through a door about halfway along. Silvern clicked the electrical lights to life.

The compartment was a little more than two steps wide, three times that long. There were two upholstered chairs, a wide bed at the rear, and at the front a toilet cubicle and an alcove desk. The ceiling glasslamps were softened and diffused by a half tube of fluted and frosted glass.

A sturdy trunk, Silvern's, was against the inboard wall, and next to it Varic's traveling desk and old leather Linkman bag. Varic bent to examine his equipment, and looked at the carpet, which had a fussy pattern of colored dots. He said, "I thought Edaire objected to these carpets."

"Indeed. Drop anything smaller than a shoe and you'll never find it again. But apparently the passengers object to plain carpets; they want the sense of something expensive to go with their cabin tickets."

"Yes," Varic said distractedly. "I suppose they are expensive."

"You could ask Edaire."

"Hm. Brook's got shelves full of handifactors' sales books—no one in Lords knows the price of a step of carpet or a spool of lampwick, and if it comes up, they'll suggest you wade down to Commons and ask. This is considered a great jest."

"I'm sure," Silvern said.

"Leyva—you recall her? The third-floor caretaker, Eastern?"

"I do."

"Brook lets her come in on her idle time, and she reads those swatch and show books as if they were fabulands."

"How Craft bends the soul," Silvern said, almost laughing. He sat down on the edge of the bed. "Three people, and compartments for three. Craft bends the soul."

"I asked Brook to come, and he said no. If I had power, would I have used it?"

"Still denying your talent."

"For what? Making women late for their trains?"

"I hadn't thought of it in those terms. Now that you say it, however . . ." Silvern curled the fingers of his right hand. His face set, and there was a flash of blue lightning from his eyes, a streak of fluid light through his hand. When the afterimage cleared, he was holding a dagger, its grip square and plain, the blade a stubby triangle, the whole apparently carved out of a solid block of blued steel.

"The blade's a bit short," Varic said dryly.

"No one here I wanted to kill." Silvern relaxed his grip, tilted his head, and the knife shattered into streaks of light; they faded to specks, a wavering in the air, and then nothing. Silvern said, "Talent, *hazhna*. Compared to what you're talking about, this hardly seems worth the effort."

Varic sat on the chair nearest the window, looked out. The next track was empty; on the Gate 9 jetty, passengers were boarding another train, painted in the deep green of the Northern lines. One of the people, by shape and gait, appeared to be Hawken. Varic silently wished him joy of the North.

There was a bump, a long screech, and Varic's train began to move. Varic looked at his watch: the hour mark had just touched three. He looked at Silvern; the other man was flat on the bed, apparently asleep.

They slipped out of the Terminus shed, into full daylight. The wheels clacked and banged over the complicated intersections of the distributing tracks. Switchmen in bright red coats were moving quickly but not hurriedly from throw bar to throw bar, piloting the rails.

Through an iron arch hung with signal lights, then another, and they were on the City through-tracks. Their speed built. Varic could see into back gardens and yards of middle-class houses, see their washing hung to dry, their rosebushes, their children flicker past. A park opened up between houses, a football ground with a scatter of scrumming players. All of it was well back from the tracks, separated by grass and gravel, walls and fences, and back alleys.

Then the houses closed in. This was Midlington, the zone of laborers' dwelling blocks that edged the City north and west. There were no yards, no green spaces, and it would be mad to hang clean clothes here against the motive's plume. There *were* children playing, on the very slope of the track embankment; they were a blur as they passed, but if Varic twitched his eyes to follow he could stop a face for a moment, see it grimy and open and jeering. The train ran faster.

The house backs here were plain stone and black brick, with a few crooked stairways of iron or wood, a few small windows. They seemed to waver toward and away from the train, and here and again there were gaps between walls, opening on more walls; Midlington streets followed a pattern from the Midreigns, twisting deliberately to confuse and disorder any hostile forces—foreign invader or domestic rebel—marching against the City proper.

The train plunged like a steel bolt through the arcs and winds of Midlington. It was possible to live in a jetty house almost over the tracks, smoked and cindered every time a motive passed by. Landlords argued in Commons that it was no worse than living above a blacksmith's or a tannery, and people had done that for ages before Ironways. And besides, Cinder Hall was always clearly advertised as such, and the rents were accordingly cheap. No one was *compelled* to live there, and if no one voluntarily did so, the rooms would be promptly pulled down to spare upkeep.

Indeed, the same voice said, and a shoeblack who raises his prices is a waster of polish and an idler; chalking portraits on the sidewalk ought be taxed as an unfair use of city pavement; medicine for those who could not afford it merely prolonged the suffering of the weak and extended their threat to the healthy. Indeed and truly, keep the streets crooked in the workers' districts, lest ease of movement ease revolt.

In the coal regions of the Midlands and North, there were underground fires that had been burning for generations, mine disasters that hung on and on. Now and again they burst out, sulfurous fumaroles that might consume a grove or a house.

These tenements, black and grainy as a coal face, dark and

winding as a mine gallery, made Varic think of those buried slow fires. He turned away. In a moment they would be into the mill district, where those laborers went to work, and whatever his interest in the means of production he was in no mood just now to see them.

There was a knock at the compartment door. Silvern was on his feet in an instanta, and admitted the train captain, who examined and punched their tickets, asked if the baggage was in order, touched the visor of his cap, and moved on.

Silvern said, "Tea in the parlor?"

"Right after you."

The open parlor was almost twenty steps long. It was set with stuffed chairs covered in cloth of a deep wine color, trimmed with gold braid; there were tables with heavy iron bases and rosewood tops circled by small brass rails. A larger table, suitable for cards or reading the Book, was near the forward end. Low bookshelves and racks of the day's newspapers were mounted along the long walls. At the rear, the walls were all glass from waist height upward to nearly the roof peak. The panorama windows were rigged with roller blinds that could block direct sunlight from any angle—at least, when set by the purser; few passengers could master the system of pulleys and cords.

The carpet was woven in a strong, sweeping figure of black and gold, orange and red, more pleasing to Varic's eye than the fussy compartment rugs. In the parlor it was permissible to suggest power and motion, rather than coziness. The carriage ceiling was of blond wood, highly lacquered. Four brass candelabra frames held shaded glasswicks, and smaller, brighter lamps arched above the tables.

Electrical lights were much safer in the carriages than anything with a flame. This was not universally believed. Now and then a squib went off in the roughsheet press about ACID!! FLESH-BURNING "BATTERY FLUID" KEPT MERE SPANS FROM SLEEPING PASSENGERS!! Being burnt by lamp oil, or rent by a gas explosion, was a commonplace of life, but the serial novel and the stage shocker kept one mindful of the horrors of acid.

Longlight was standing at the rear, watching the mills and smokestacks pass the glass. As Varic approached her, the last breaker's yard went by and was gone, and they were in the open country of Lystourel West.

"Trees," Longlight said, as if she had never expected to see another one. Varic felt himself lighten inside; partly the landscape, hills, and copses, partly the pleasure in her voice.

He said, "Have you ordered tea?"

"It should be here right away," she said, and looked at the package in his hands. "Now what *is* that?"

He put it on a table. "Have you a pocketknife? Silvern, would you ask the steward for some table service? Quite a bit of it, I think." He took Longlight's knife, unclasped it, and slit the paper open. He started to cut out the corner with the errant cab's number, then let it go. A forgiveness for the holiday.

Within the open paper, the linka was red and golden, a long braid of thin-layered pastry, sparkling with big crystals of sugar, the vivid red of cherries and jam showing through the slits. It made Varic think of Linnet's braid, the golden hair woven over and under down his back.

Longlight said, "But what's this?"

Silvern appeared, holding a stack of plates. "A good old custom: tea for the voyage. Give the lady back her slicer, Varic; we may insult the Ironway's food, but none can fault their tableware."

Varic stepped back; Silvern cut slices from the pastry and passed them onto plates held by Longlight, while the parlor steward distributed forks. The thick porcelain and the heavy silver bore the curving National Ironways emblem. Silvern kept up a steady patter as he cut and served: "One for you, happy holiday. . . . This one's a bit bruised, is that well, honored? . . . Goddess in your way also. . . . You're welcome, young friend, and please thank my generous friend there. . . . And Goddess in yours . . . Oh, come now, don't you think Goddess forgives what is eaten in Her respect?"

When all were seated with tea and dessert, Silvern said, "What shall we talk about now?"

"I think you were about to let me in on the joke," Longlight said, "about Silvern's conseil, and platform attendants."

"Edaire is a Chief-Inspector-at-Large of the Lescorial National Ironways," Silvern said with real but unexaggerated gravity. "That means she is answerable only to the Inspector-General—except for the season in each two years she serves *as* the Inspector-General. As part of the tasks of the Inspectorate—"

"Keeping the sinews of Republic limbered."

"Thank you, Varic. How *is* Deerleap, by the way? *Valahsh,* she is liable to appear in any uniform, or any other character, to see how the employees behave when they think no one is watching. My lady, the shapeshifter."

Longlight said, "Not *really*," and Varic noticed her left hand weave fingers into Wyss's Catch.

"No," Silvern said. "Skill, not Craft; material talent." He finished his slice of linka, drained his teacup, and said, "If you will both pardon me, I believe I shall nap before dinner. Shall I expect to see you there?"

"I cannot imagine why not," Varic said rather firmly.

Silvern stood, bowed, and went out. Varic looked at Longlight, and with her look back a heaviness overtook him; he knew perfectly well what it was.

He pointed out the window, and she obligingly turned away.

"That's the Western Barbican," he said, "the farthest outpost of the City during the Midreigns. Second Kestrel built it, on a Quercian foundation—you can see how squared it is, not round like true Middle castles."

So they talked about fortifications for a while; Longlight described her family castle, a rambling accumulation of rectangular keeps, able to be besieged, or just snowed in, for months at a time. Varic told her about Castle Corvaric, on a rock three hundred steps away from shore, accessible only by an easily blocked or destroyed causeway.

She said, "It sounds . . . You had happy times, I'm sure."

"Of course. And you?"

She leaned back in her chair. "I loved to hunt, when I was younger—oh, still do, but now it's the Coron's Hunt, all very proper. Then I went alone, mostly, after deer, or sometimes mountain cat. I'd cache my shoes and my heavy stuff somewhere. . . ."

He could see that at once, see her silken and leathered in a glade crystalline with rain and alive with track-scent, a living aspect of Coris, the Goddess he refused to believe existed. In the thought, she was bare limbs stalking golden-pelted (and being stalked in turn), bare paws on black stone in a dark ravine of his mind.

An idea crystallized around the image. He excused himself and went back to the compartment.

Silvern was awake as soon as Varic entered. Varic said, "Another idea to waste some of your time."

"You have a bad habit of saying 'waste' when you mean 'invest.'"

"Whichever. I was thinking about hunting."

Silvern's "Yes?" dripped meanings.

Varic said, "It was, curiously enough, the new Ferangarder Ambassador who provided the idea."

"Wait. My mind won't turn that corner. The Ferangarder Ambassador suggested *what*?"

"He made some pleasantry to me about hunting—in Corvaric, of all places. But there *is* good hunting in the Great Rogue Hills."

"True," Silvern said patiently.

"It would be a fine place to build a hunting lodge, would it not?"

"From what I know of it, among the finest."

"If you stood a step back from a survey to best site a hunting lodge, could you tell it apart from a general military survey?"

Light broke in Silvern's face. "Not for a long while, if ever."

Varic nodded. He sat down in one of the chairs and was instantly sleepy. His head tipped forward.

In what seemed like a moment, he was on the bed, his clothing loosened and his boots off, and Silvern was in the chair, reading. The lights were on and the window was dark. "*Kes'baród,*" he said.

"*Barchei,*" Silvern said, "and your Kólyan still has an awful accent. I had thought to swap rooms with the lady down the corridor, but—well, I don't know why I didn't, unless I just didn't want to miss dinner with the two of you. Dress now, and let's dine as well as the rails can serve."

"While I'm getting presentable, will you call on Longlight?"

Silvern seemed about to say something, but he only nodded and went out.

The restaurant car was lit by electric candles on tables draped in white linen. The dinner was, in fact, acceptable if not spectacular; there was a lamb roast, beef in brown gravy, two good wines. Longlight recommended a sparkling water from her Coronage; it had a salt-and-ginger taste, and Varic stopped after one glass but made a note of it for Brook.

The steward brought berry flans and strong tea, and a brandy for Silvern, and the three of them sat and talked for most of an hour about remembered or half-remembered meals and drinks.

Silvern said, "I think, once again, I shall leave you and retire. Good night, honored friends."

"Wait," Varic said. "No sense in my waking you up."

"I appreciate your consideration," Silvern said with a dismissive wave, but Varic was already standing. He held out a hand to Longlight, said, "Until tomorrow, then, my lady? It has been quite a day."

"Yes," she said, touching fingers with him, "It has been quite a day."

And Varic followed Silvern back to the compartment. Varic sat down, heavily, in the window-side chair, worked at the buttons of his waistcoat.

Silvern leaned against the wall, folded his arms. "Are you actually going to go on with this unnecessary and uncomfortable business?"

"In two nights I'm going to see Agate."

"I was thinking of Agate. What good will tension do you then?"

Varic just sat. Silvern pointed a finger at Varic's hands; Varic looked down and saw that his fingers were knotted white.

Silvern said, "There's a chair in your compartment, too. If you really want to make a full battalia with bandsmen of it, I could lend you a sword, and you could stand right vigil." He paused, said more gently, "And I'll be right here. If she makes a desperate sally, call and we'll hold the pass together."

"What is the use?" Varic said to the wall.

"None, when power bends you."

"I was born without Talent Archain. As aside from the claim that I was not born at all, but manufactured. Or simply unearthed."

"That wasn't necessary, Varic."

"Not to you, perhaps," he said, staring out the window. "But an aspect of the reality, nonetheless. Say true that I am not like others; well, is anyone really like anyone else?" He turned back, looked directly at Silvern. "You and Edaire are not alike. But there is a marvelous jointness to your differences."

"As you with Agate," Silvern said, quiet as a Northerner.

"Does it really appear so?"

Silvern's voice rose slightly, but remained infinitely patient. "If it is no more than an appearance, then it is an appearance of Goddess." He folded his left hand, the thumb between the second and third fingers, so the pad of his rather long thumb was caught firmly against the swords-and-wheels ring. He looked straight ahead, somewhere past Varic's shoulder, past the compartment wall, past the world; Varic could see his pupils dilate, black opals set in steel. Silvern's lips moved; the unspoken words might have been "And you." Then he blinked, breathed deeply and easily, and said, "Edaire's train is passing through Little Oxbow. She is having a patcake—chicken salad in dark wheat, I think—and a pot of cider." He clasped his bare hand around the ringed one. "How can you stand to be alone, Varic? How is it you can bear to go among all the loose souls in the world without one voice waiting for you?"

Varic thought for a moment about things to say; he knew that Silvern would receive any of them, even the bitterest, with calmness and grace. And without even closing his eyes, Varic could see Longlight's face, eclipsed by her dark, dark hair. He stood up, picked up his Linkman bag. "Good night, friend," he said, "and same to the friend you love."

"And fair return to our friends."

Low-power glasslamps lit the lacquered wood of the corridor a deep honey color. In the apse between carriages, the train captain was having a smoke with a passenger; the window was open, letting in the cool night air and the beat of wheels on rails.

The passenger was a small, trim woman with a long, white pipe. As Varic passed, she reached into her pocket and held out a cheroot. There was too much noise and draft for a reasonable conversation, so Varic just shook his head and went on through the next carriage door.

That put him right outside the compartment. He knocked lightly.

"Yes?"

"Varic. Good evening."

The door opened. "Good, ay minden so," she said, her speech all Westrene now. "Dwillsey come ere?"

He almost answered her in Quercian, as a joke, but it would have been the wrong joke. She had not dropped her City speech to tease him or be coy. Just the opposite. He went in, turned to shut the door, and set the latch without thinking.

"So you have me now secure," she said. He turned sharply, almost banging his shoulder against the narrow wardrobe.

She was wearing a long, sleeveless shift of soft black wool, a tube of cloth that cowled her head and fell in gentle arcs to her bare ankles. Behind her, the bed was made down, white linens with the Ironways emblem embroidered at the neat corners. She took a half step backward and sat down on the edge of the bed, crossing her arms in her lap.

Varic bumped a knee against the chair and sat down, setting his bag to one side with perhaps too much care.

"Why," she said, "since you're here, are you over there?"

"So we both can talk, and think about what we're saying."

"I know full well what I'm saying. We've both turned lights in forenow. I'm sure we may both lie fallow when we choose: my mother taught me Wyss's Cares when I was ten years old . . . bandits, dwillknow?" She spoke as if dreaming. "Tryan, my father had been teaching me how to deal with bandits, faith, years already."

"I think, physically, there is no question of what we both want," he said, wondering if he was making her understand at all. "I'm trying not to think only physically."

In clear City form, she said, "Do you still feel that this is wrong? That we're still compromised?"

"Less, perhaps, than . . ." He shook his head. "You did say there was someone else."

"Who will not be hurt by this. Wella know, no supposing." She paused. "And you?"

"No one who will be hurt," he said as carefully as he could. "Certain this is, and neither wishful only."

"I like it when you speak Northesse. It's very beautiful. So . . . gentle."

"I don't think you know enough about me."

"Then tell me what I need to know. Am I"—she spoke more lightly—"not playing the game as you wish? Must you argue me into your point of view? Or stalk me into surrender?" She pulled the cowl back, letting the cloth fall around her throat, shook out her hair. Her eyes flashed at him, darkly feral above a grin that might have been only playful.

"You recall my friend Brook. The Parliamentarian."

"Certainly."

"I was most unkind to him, earlier today, over something that wasn't at all his fault. If I could do that, to Brook—"

"If you are unkind to me, I am thorough able to toss you into the corridor, latched door or no. And supposing I believe you were causeless hard to Brook, what does that say? I was verra sharp with Silvern, a minima after meeting him, for no good cause either."

Varic said, "Yes?"

"Do I tell first?"

"Perhaps you should. Silvern didn't speak of it."

"And may Brook wouldn't either. But. He said I was a hunter, before I'd told him; and for a moment I thought he'd pried my mind with magic. He'd not, of course, it was just knowesway."

"Silvern would never—"

"I know. Enough of that for now," she said. "Your go: How were you hard to Lord Brook?"

"We were crossing the park, and there was a conjuror performing. Brook proposed we stop and watch him awhile, and I—there's no excuse for how I behaved."

"I did not ask for an excuse. I asked what and why."

"When I was small, a conjuror visited the town closest to our castle. He was, I gather, quite boastful even for the trade, one of those who liked people to believe he had real magic and not just tricks. One of his tricks was the Miser's Dream, as they call it; pulling coins out of the air. That always goes over very well with adults. Children are pleased with glass and silks, but grown-ups . . . well.

"My father invited him out to the estate for a performance, which he gave. He found coins, and he bragged too much. At the end of the evening, he was shown to his room—and the door was locked behind him. He was told that when exactly a hundred coins had been pushed under the door, he would be fed; and not until."

"I've heard this story."

"Yes. My father was not a creative soul. In the old tale, the King slowly fills the room with sand, to provide raw material for the miraclist and urge the process along; but that was too difficult to actually arrange. Since then I've always . . . turned away from fingersmiths. I know some; there's one I hope to see at the House. So there, too, I am inconsistent."

"Aside that. Does Brook know that story?"

"I think he . . . Do you know, I don't remember. I keep thinking that he must, but when I try to recall just that story . . . That only makes it worse, doesn't it?"

"If you say it does," she said, tiredly, flatly. "No bad but leads to worse with you, is there?"

Varic fought the automatic impulse to nod and agree, even as a joke, perhaps especially as a joke. He said, "May I moot the issue?"

"Coris raise tide! Now he'll call for a vote before he strips my shift! Please, *please,* Varic—if we're to talk away the night, by all means let us do so, but if not—well. Dwilla hear a tale from me? An old hurt, like yours, and then we won't be lonely at least in that?"

"Tell me."

"I told you about my hunting. When I was—younger but old enough to know things, I went out for a horseback chase with one of the guards. He was no more than two years older than I—a trainee, really, a real guard's son. We rode half a day onto the woods, but saw no game worth the stopping for. We had lunch in a small clearing, by water. I remember the stream. It was a pretty day, just after the end of summer." She turned her face to the window for a moment. "Like this. . . . We sat for a while, after we ate, and then he asked me to play the couple game. I knew the Cares, and he said he did as well; there was water to wash—I think he was as new as I was."

She turned her head. Her hands tightened against the edge of the bed. "I told him what game I would have first. I would chase him, on foot, without a bow. This is an old tale, too: Coris and the deer."

"I know," Varic said.

"If I took him, he was my prize; if he could turn on me, the stag on the hunter, and gore me with his horn—well."

"Yes."

"I pulled his hands behind him, tied them with a spare bow-string, cut away his shirt. He wasn't expecting that. Deer can't climb trees, I said. His face when I did that—" Bitterly: "What was he to ask such a thing?"

"Go on."

> *"She gave him a lead of a hundred count*
> *She followed his track without arrow or mount*
> *All light-foot she chased him through dapple and down*
> *And ere the sun slanted she brought the stag down."*

She looked Varic in the eyes. "It wasn't fair. I could run those woods all day, with shoes or without, naked if I'd pleased; I might have caught him had he *been* a stag. A cavalry colt didn't have a chance.

"When I decided to catch him, he was in a clearing, leaning against a great round stone, out of breath. I don't think he heard me coming, so I made some noise, and he turned. I think he was going to stand back against the rock, try to look cornered and dangerous. Or perhaps pinned and fetching. Whatever, he fell, faceup with his hands beneath him, and he *was* pinned then.

"I looked down at him; he was scratched, bloody. He looked up at me, and his eyes were bright: he was my prey and he knew it, his eyes said just how he knew it."

Varic put a hand out to touch hers. He knew what came next; it was deep in what they were. "And you killed him."

"He groaned once when I cut his throat. I hung him head down to drain—it was no different, then, from any other hunt—found the horses and took him home."

"Did you know what would happen then?"

"I had seen Coronal Courts. But never really *thought* about it. So when the court was called, it was like moving through a dream, knowing what would happen a moment before it did, with no power to shift or stop. The Suren-draw—that's the sorcerer—"

"In the north we say Vericate. It's the same. Go on."

"She was our healer. I told you about her."

"You did so."

"Though of course I told the truth. Did he consent? Yes, to the game. Did he agree to be bound, even playing? No, I forced that. Then they asked, did he protest? And I said, no, he did not. So in the end they paid his mother the pound of gold."

"And his father paid half back," Varic said quietly.

Longlight nodded slowly, a tightness around her eyes that Varic knew was long experience of not weeping. "It's not a Cityer story," she said, "but I thought you may'd seil it."

"That was the real cause you were afraid of Silvern. When you thought he'd looked in your mind."

"Yes. Now to a vote: Do you want me?"

"Aye."

"Carried by acclamation."

She moved to clutch and encircle him, her bare leg cool-then-warm against his calf, his body suddenly in an agony of confinement. His head ached with the pressure of blood, and his eyes hurt; he grasped her wrist and pressed the hand to his mouth, kissing her fingers hard as her other hand worked to free him. He let her go, put the heels of his hands against his temples and pressed, hearing her moan as through a waterfall, trying to work the beat of pain out of his skull through her pleasure, preconsciously afraid of spreading the ache by touch and symparchy. Her swordplayer's fingers circled his wrists then, pressing gently on the rocketing pulses; she guided his blind hands to the hem of her soft woolen gown, drawing it up to her knees, and from there he stroked, raised, revealed.

He wanted to be tender, and he could not, he hurt too much;

he wanted to pleasure her artistically, philosophically, admiring her response, keeping control—and she would not let him, drawing a breath into a breath, a groan for a groan, *turning lights in,* as the Westrene said.

The pain drowned in blood and water. Salt dried it. Sweetness balmed the mutual wound.

⊗⊶

"Look at this," Varic said, and turned in the bed so that Longlight could see out the compartment window.

Outside, rolling green farmland was under a thick cover of white fog. The mist glowed pearlescent, and stone walls and slate roofs gleamed with dewfall. In a large enclosure, a herd of black-faced white sheep were standing, as if clumps of the fog had touched down on legs.

Longlight watched it with soft, happy eyes, and kissed Varic. "Where are we?"

"This would be Red Barrow. It should be somewhat after six, perhaps nearly seven. The next Coronage is Cedarrun; we have a stop there, at Three Cedars town. We take on coal and water; it will be a good two hours."

"And is there something wonderful I ought see in Three Cedars?"

"Not that I know of. They cut the original trees years ago, and planted a new set a convenient distance from the principal inn."

"Not truly."

"Verily yea. But my thought was, if you don't trust the breakfast aboard, we could dash off there for something fresh."

"Would Silvern be up for that?"

"In what sense do you ask that? Silvern has been *awake,* I assure you, since before dawn. As for food, if we wish to stay aboard, he will consider it 'relaxed' and approve, and if we choose to go off hunting the wild egg and chop, he will call that 'an adventure' and join in."

She laughed. "How long have you known him?"

"Almost twenty years. Since a little after I came into the Coronage and started visiting the House."

"Strange House."

Varic nodded.

Longlight said, "My grandfather knew a Strange. He spoke very highly of him, as a wise man. Is that an ancestor?"

"The same man. Strange is . . . old. I don't know anyone who knew him young."

"A sorcerer, then."

"No. Strange—I can hardly tell you."

"Very well," she said. "Tell me about Silvern's conseil."

"Edaire is . . . perhaps what you said. The wave and the rock. She's always in motion—and I don't just mean by Ironway. She has seen so very much."

"Are you in love with her?" Longlight said, so abruptly that Varic had to consider an answer. He stroked his thumb over Longlight's broad, rough knuckles, and she made a soft noise and shifted against him. She said, barely above a whisper, "I shouldn't have said that—"

"Don't be sorry. She's one of the particular guests at Strange House. A Player. It's not an easy thing to describe. I do love her, and admire her . . . and the fact that she is sealed to Silvern seems only to clarify that, to eliminate the distractions."

"I like you when you're distracted. But I understand. It seems, an times, things ought be simpler than they are."

"Yes," he said, hoping he did not sound too lost, "things should be simpler than they are."

They idled awhile longer, until Longlight said, "Silvern will wonder what's keeping us."

"He will not. But we ought to give him some company."

They got up, bumping into each other as the train shook. Varic screwed a steel guard to the blade of his razor, braced his shoulder against the corner of the toilet cubicle, and shaved with no loss of blood.

"You needn't do that for my sake," Longlight said when he was finished.

"Maybe tomorrow I won't."

They found Silvern in his compartment and agreed to deboard for breakfast. Not long after, the train heaved to a stop.

The Three Cedars station was of yellow brick, trim painted Western Lines maroon, with a cedar-shingled hip roof. They passed through the building and were on a small crescent, a pair of cabs waiting by the gaslights. They passed them and walked on.

The town was in a small valley. The sky was overcast, but the air had a fine transparency. The land was clear green to the blue horizon, soft hills marked off in hedged fields, stands of cedar and maple, orchards nearing full fruit.

The station crescent led to a curved arcade of shops, most shut with the hour or the holiday. A florist's was open, a boy arranging baskets of blossoms by the door, and a newsagent's, a bundle of the *Banner-Tribune* still tied on the front steps. The arcade in turn opened on an ellipse, three-and four-story buildings around an oval of parkland. The three famous cedars were in the center, suspiciously equilateral in their placement, within a waist-high but impressively spiked iron fence. A horde of sparrows and a few dazzling redwings clustered on their branches.

At the center of one of the ellipse's long sides was the inn, white-painted brick below and (perhaps inevitably) cedar-shaked above, its door flanked by twelve-pane bay windows and crowned by a fake-Quercian lintel.

So the breakfast was leisurely, from porcelain and crystal more delicate than would have served on a train, and nothing rattled. Silvern disposed of four eggs with bacon, Longlight three, Varic one egg and two kippers, along with generous bufferings of mushrooms and muffins and tea.

With Varic carrying a basket of muffins and jam, they went back to the elliptical park. Silvern sat down, rather heavily, on a bench. Squirrels approached him warily.

Varic held out a bit of muffin in his palm, stood entirely still. A sparrow circled him once, then lighted on his thumb, snapped up the food, and flew off.

Longlight's mouth opened. Silvern said softly, "Hunting does not interest him."

She said, "They're tame, surely—they must be fed all the time." She looked at the squirrels. Varic had a small smile; he gave her a half muffin, and she fed it to the eager little beasts.

Silvern burped, and a squirrel and three birds fled. "I think," he said, "I shall return by way of the florist's and find something for my beloved. I will see you aboard."

Longlight said, "How long before the train?"

"Three-quarters of an hour."

"Do you want to go back now?"

"We can. I shouldn't have thought you'd want to, not on a pretty morning."

"I don't. But I asked what you wanted."

Varic put a hand around one of the fence spikes, gripped it hard.

"Dwill tell?" she said.

"I almost said something . . . quite cruel. Again. It is an unforgivable trait."

"You've no power to command me forgive or not. What did you think to say?"

"You have no power to compel my saying."

"Then tell me something about your family. Freewill."

"And have you owe me more of your hurts? Let them be buried."

"Do you think I will not understand? When you so well knew my death's-work?"

Varic said flatly, "My father was a far-province Coron of a particular kind. I can well believe his sort had to exist, once, and I can almost be convinced that it was necessary, once in raw old time. If he had lived, I might have learned how to tolerate and forgive and love him as my father; I am told that most of us do. But day by day I see more clearly that the world is well rid of him. . . .

"Your father," he said suddenly and gently, "was he a good man?"

"I can recall his faults," she said, "but yes, he was good, and kind, and just."

Varic nodded. "I thought it would be so. I just wanted to hear it, before you went back to him."

"Varic, he's dead these many—"

"Milady Coron," he said, "well I know." He crumbled the rest of a muffin, tossed it to the birds and squirrels. "Let's walk and say nothing awhile. Summer hath but hours to live."

That was what they did, walking the straights and arcs of the trim planned streets, saying nothing. When something interesting appeared—a shop display, a fine bit of iron ornament, a spectacular window box—one would point, and the other nod. After a few minimi, they were carrying on a commentary all in gesture. When their circuit brought them around to the station, Longlight was nearly laughing, Varic smiling again.

The rest of the day's travel passed idly. Silvern found an aged cavalry officer in the parlor to trade drinks and lies with. Readers of the Book and arcquet games took turns on the card table. Outside the windows, the vast Lescorial midlands flowed by;

old sprawled towns and neat new planned ones, orchards and farms, roads the Quercians had first laid out. A rain shower passed over, soft drops on the carriage windows, only soothing. Anyone wishing to sleep had plenty of cows to count, or sheep, free choice.

Before dinner, in a quiet corner of the parlor, Longlight said to Varic, "The next time I am like to see you, all your City reasons will rule again. When I bid all good 'den tonight—follow me; set any wait you think proper, but follow."

Which he did.

Very late, Varic had a dream of walking through mud, sinking with each step, driven on both by fear of the depths and some push of need he could not identify. It was dark; there were trees in front of him, which he saw in delirious clarity, and beyond them darkness. The moment he passed a tree, it vanished behind him and another appeared ahead. Any way he turned—and he was sure he was turning without knowing it—it was the same, endless corridors of trees. An owl cried unseen. The bog sucked at him, and his head began to hammer with the effort of motion. He began to rage at the mud and the forest. The anger felt good. It felt as if it might do something, something real.

Deep violet light, blacker than the darkness, burst from him. The trees quaked and the mud heaved. Trunks cracked and branches fell.

He stopped, staring. Needles and broken limbs lay on the ground. Varic took a step, and the brush bore him up; it crunched and shifted beneath his step, but it kept him above the bog.

So the trees would fall to anger, he thought, rage would harden the bog. Very well, then, very well. Anger was easily come by, rage was easily found—

A shout woke him. His face was pressed hard against Longlight's bare shoulder; his arms were tight around her, his legs tangled with hers.

"Is it morning?" she said, though there was only blue moonglow through the window. There was no fear in her voice, no unease at all.

"Not yet. I didn't mean to wake you."

"I think I'm sorry to hear that."

"We've a way to travel yet. Sleep now."

She shut her eyes, and her breathing stilled.

Varic slid out of the bed. He rinsed his face and dressed, then walked back to the parlor car. It was dimly lit by two of the reading lamps, empty except for a dozing purser, who woke enough to ask Varic if there was anything he desired. Varic shook his head, went to the very end of the car, and sat down.

It would be dawn in about an hour. The nearly full moon was very low and cast long, deep shadows, black on silver. The morning was clearer than yesterday's, though clouds of fog crouched in hollows. The train passed through a grove of tall poplars then, making the car very dark; the woods were misty and unreal, like the trees of his dream. He covered his eyes with a hand.

It was, after all, only a dream. He was no Archdreamer, sleeping true; he was no Archanything, had no sorcery at all, no more than he possessed Goddess. He had nothing at all that the quick hand of death or the long arm of distance could not separate from him. Until, perhaps, the Constitution was ratified; and if Brook were right, perhaps that would not do either.

The Talent was well enough if you could heal; there was always a demand for that. Even better was healing livestock: a good, studied horse-mender or cow-save could expect not only a pleasantly supplied life but admiration, even love, more so even than most priests.

Long ago there had been Archirons, but good steel and quality iron required constant high heat, and that was gotten more easily from a machine-drafted furnace than from sorcery.

It was an art in decline, that was the truth. The Ironway replaced the cloud-horse; the talking trance and the Long Mirror were supplanted by the click of the magnostyle. It was not impossible that in a few years some of the Lords Sorcerous would be giving up their seats to Lords Mechanic. That would blur the distinction between Lords and Commons, and after that, who could say? Perhaps the collapse of Parliaments and Republic, the rule of direct vote, all for all, what some called *Poplicate* and others *King Mob*. He thought of what Brook had said about Varic's great work to follow the Revised Constitution. No, he told himself most firmly.

As long as there was work before him, as long as Strange House stood full of life and friendship, he had what he needed.

At approximately the same moment, Silvern was seated, fully dressed, in his compartment, reading. There was a knock at the door.

He admitted Longlight. She said, "I thought Varic might be here."

"No. He must be in the parlor, or the restaurant. Shall we look for him?"

"Soon," she said. "May I sit down?"

Silvern gestured toward a chair.

She sat, hands and feet together, looking unnaturally prim. "You've known him nighan twenty years, he said."

"That's so."

"Does he ever frighten you?"

"Contrary to certain beliefs," Silvern said very slowly, so that the words were like iron breaking gravel, "Palions are not incapable of fear. I think, having known him longer than you, I have been frightened by him as many times more in proportion."

Longlight's hands tightened.

Silvern said kindly, "Hunter's sense sees hunter's sense."

"You say he doesn't hunt," she said, her dark eyes locked directly to his metallic ones, "but he's no prey either."

"Varic is among my dearest friends dear indeed, and there is no aid I would deny him. But some passages must be held by single soldiers."

"I've known souls who were bright as the sun," she said, "and some so black they went all nothing in a shadow. He's bright, but it's cold bright; he's like the moon a thousand times. And he loves not Goddess."

"Then he affects you more than She. No small thing."

She smiled in spite of things. "I'll have that on a blazon. In Quercian, so it will be taken for an ancient wisdom."

Silvern laughed, a merry sound, no bitterness in it. "How he must have had to fight wanting you."

"Am I being flattered?"

"You are. Respectfully so. Look here now, why don't you come to the House? Strange would be delighted to meet you. And Edaire, and everyone there."

"I'm expected . . ."

"Is it something a magnostyle can mend?"

"I have responsibilities."

"Against that there is no appeal," Silvern said, almost seriously. "But allow me to say this: Varic has suggested that I visit your territory. He wants the ground surveyed, for a country property. A hunting lodge, if such would meet with the Coron's approval."

"If I understand you rightly, the Coronage would be much enhanced by such a development."

"Very good. Now, my responsibilities keep me at Strange House for the Equinoctials. But as soon as they end, I shall be available for Varic's commission, and I would be both pleased to escort you home and happy of your advice along the journey."

"If I return accompanied by a Palion," she said thoughtfully, "then I have not come home from Lystourel with nothing."

"I am certain my lady Coron knows her people well."

"They want me to secure the Coronage," she said. "If I won't have heirs, at least take a lover who will. We had nearly a century of that, just after the Middle Kingdoms ended—the age of the Consorts Visitant, an's called. But 'secure' means a few things, and we needn't have 'un all at once."

"Then you will visit."

"Then I will."

"Then we should find our friend and tell him. And by now there should be fresh tea and hot bacon in the restaurant."

Some hours later, on another Ironway train a distance to the south, the train captain encountered a passenger at the fore end of the single sleeper, smoking in the apse. The man wore a green-and-black checked suit, a high-collared white shirt; his dark brown hair was loose and long. His face was thin, fine-boned, almost pretty. He gestured amiably with his white clay pipe.

The captain thought about telling the man not to stand in the apse, but just nodded and went by. Country gentlemen with no sense of fashion tended to be very unpleasant when told the rules. Besides, he had other things on his mind.

The captain went on into the chair carriage. It was a third-class car, fixed wooden bench seats padded with carpet. In the last seat on the right, a frayed brown sack of a man was sitting, his hat on and a scarf around his neck; he was hunched over a small book with a fancy leather binding. The captain stopped for a moment, looking sidelong at the man, who ignored him; then he went to the front end of the car, where one of the pursers was waiting.

"Is that the fellow?" the captain said.

"Been there with his book since Bluehollow Halt," the purser said. "Hasn't stirred except to turn pages. No baggage at all. Didn't take tea."

"Maybe he doesn't like tea. Did you see a ticket?"

"Showed me one from Archways Cross to Coldmere. That's the point of it."

The captain thought. This train had passed through Archways Cross six hours ago, before dawn, and would reach Coldmere in another hour and a half. Bluehollow Halt, where the rumpled man had boarded, was halfway between—and the Halt was not much more than a water tank and a coal bin, an unlikely place for passengers at any time. It all seemed rather irregular. "Anything odd about the ticket?"

"The ink was smudged. Though he's all a bit of a smudge, isn't he? If he's got a plate to his name, I'll count it a wonder." She looked suddenly doubtful. "Unless—he couldn't be one of those eccentric sorcerers, could he? With the old book and all."

"I doubt it. No baggage, you say?"

"Just that book, and whatever's in his pockets."

"Sorcerers generally have some gear. At least a Linkman, or a carpet satchel. Well, no harm in a look."

They went back to the seated man. The captain said, "Your pardon, honored."

"What am I supposed to pardon?" The man's voice was a brassy squeak; the tone might have meant anything.

"May I examine your ticket?"

"She saw it."

"I'd like to."

The man closed his book, tucked it inside his shapeless coat, rummaged around within it for a moment, and produced a crumpled ticket.

"You didn't get on at Archways Cross," the captain said.

"I should think I know that."

"How did you come to board halfway along?"

"It's a tiresome story and I don't choose to tire you with it. Is there something wrong, young man?"

The captain looked closely at the ticket. "This is punched twice."

"She punched it twice. I didn't ask why. Suppose you know what you're doing."

The captain looked at the punches. Train crews' punches had different patterns. But the creased ticket had snagged on something, and a bit was torn away; it could have been the same punch, but—"Did you punch it twice?" the captain said.

"No, cap'n, I didn't. Look how beat up it is. That could've hid the old hole. And he hardly wanted to give it up."

"You hardly wanted to touch it," the old man said with a particularly unpleasant cackle.

"It's a used one, isn't it?" the purser said hotly. "You got it out of a trash bin, or maybe someone's pocket."

"Is that indeed what I did?"

"It seems to me," another voice said from behind the two train crew, "that there was quite a bit of commotion in this carriage just after Bluehollow Halt."

The captain and purser turned. The man in the green checked suit was standing in the doorway, tucking his pipe into a pocket. "Something with the tea cart, I recall."

The captain looked at the purser, who said, "Sandy had a row with one of those kids, opened a packet of sweets he couldn't pay for. I may have looked up, but I didn't double punch."

"Have you compared the punch marks, captain?" the man said. "I think that Purser Lighter, here, employee number one four one six eight, was using a half clover, half square."

There was an abrupt silence in the end of the car. Even the old man looked up, his mouth a small O.

The captain said quietly, "You know a bit about procedure, honored."

"I keep an eye on what's happening, Captain Stones. Number nine two two three. Now, I'd noticed the scholar here, as I was waiting to buy a tea, and I thought I'd offer him the hospitality of a tea in my cabin. If there's a question about his ticket, however . . ."

The captain looked again at the purser, who said, "I . . . could have hit it twice."

"Then I think we'll assume you did," the captain said firmly. "Pleasant trip, honoreds." He handed the ticket back to the old passenger, nodded politely, and walked forward. The purser followed.

"Would you accept my invitation?" the gentleman said, and the old man said, "With the greatest pleasure." They went aft. The man in the checked suit opened the door to a drawing room compartment, ushered the other into the parlor. The bedroom door was shut. "Do sit down," the gentleman said. "I'm afraid I lied. There isn't any tea."

The old man sat down, and said, "I really do not know what to say," in a voice that was not an old man's.

"'Thank you, but I didn't want any tea'?"

"Lix," Inspector of Ironways Edaire said, "this isn't your compartment."

"It was paid for by a hard-goods merchant from somewhere

around Windscapel. We met in the station tavern at Two Blades last night. He wanted to buy some fellow commercial traveler a pint or five, and once he found out I was also in sashes and eaves"—Lix shrugged, palms up—"nothing would do but that we continue the conversation. I don't think he was quite aware we were boarding. Mere minimi after that, he was asleep. I did present his ticket to the cabin-car purser."

"Who didn't check the bedroom?"

"No. The wheel noise just barely covers his snoring, too—do you mark it?"

"I congratulate you on how well you do my job."

"Accepted thankfully."

"I don't suppose that would be one of your friend's suits you're wearing." She raised a hand. "Only borrowed, I know."

"Oh, Edaire, please." Lix opened the wardrobe and displayed two hanging suits, in at least as overstated a pattern as the one he wore, but fully half again as broad. He moved close to Edaire, displayed the fraying at his cuffs, the thin patches at the elbows. "By your grace," he said, and unbuttoned the jacket to show an enormous L-shaped tear in the white linen shirt, neatly stitched up. "Some years ago, the old Coron of Whitewater gave me this, part payment for entertainment at his daughter's eighth birthday party. It is my country gentle's suit; you can tell it would never pass in the City."

Edaire nodded. "That was rude of me, I'm sorry. I know you're no thief."

"I knew you weren't an old man, either," Lix said lightly, "but I didn't go around telling people." He reached inside the checked jacket, brought out a wooden object: a taddelix, the emblem of Lix's trade and the source of his name. It was a polished wood block as long as his hand, with a hinged wooden spoon on each side. This one was in a fine, polished cherrywood, and it had a small brass bell set into one end. Lix shook it; it made no noise. The wooden sounders were fastened by a silk band that must have been crimson once, and a thick felt cylinder held the bell clapper. "All tongues silent, you see."

Edaire said, "How far did you intend to travel?"

He tossed the taddelix in the air with his right hand, made a taffy-pulling gesture with both, then caught the clacker in his left. "As far as would."

"Say to Coldmere, then. That's my destination, and the captain won't be surprised when you vanish."

"A fine town. Not that long a hike from Whitewater Town, either; perhaps I should see if the Coron will have her father's suit mended for a song. And on the subject of clothing—do you have something more like yourself to wear? Or may I bring you a damp towel, to cure your premature age?"

"I've a bag waiting at Coldmere station. And I won't change the other until we're off. It might frighten the purser."

"Yes. What *of* her? Did she really double the ticket?"

"Once before the tea cart fracas, once after. I frayed the hole, and then acted as suspicious as I could manage without irritating another passenger, just to see. You saw, too."

"As the gentles of the road say, most rabbits keep a snare about them."

"I don't think she lied, at first, because I don't think she remembered. But the captain gave her every chance to admit she didn't remember. The word will have to go in." She looked up at him. "You'll get the blame for that."

"Borne as all things, with equanimity."

"Very well. Then until Coldmere, I'm traveling on my valid if misceled ticket, and you're traveling on my pass, and as the compartment is paid for, no one is shorting the service. Just promise me something."

"I know. I promise that I will not take the rails from Cold-mere. As I said, a walk to Whitewater will do me good, on such a fine end-summer's day."

Edaire rummaged in her clothes. "You should have a plate in your pocket. Even nice towns turn out vagrants."

He waved his hand, and a silver coin appeared between his fingers. "For which cause I have a plate in my pocket. This same one, near on thirty years."

She looked at his face. She knew he was at least ten years older than she was; she could make out a hint of makeup on his narrow face, but mostly it was just a refusal to be other than young.

They reached Coldmere within a minima of the schedule. Lix assisted Edaire onto the platform. "Oh, my," he said. "Do you hear that?"

There was a low, whispery hum in the air. It came from no identifiable direction; people looked around nervously as they caught it. It was a sorcerous sound.

"Something's quite wrong," Edaire said.

Lix made a hand gesture that meant *I knew that much,* and said, "There appears to be some difficulty with the women's lavatory."

"Now how do you know that?"

"The manner of that lady's walk toward the inn just up the road." He tilted his head to direct Edaire's look toward the street beyond the station. "You may have to change clothes elsewhere."

Edaire reflected that, when Lix had told the train crew his business was observation, he'd been telling the plain truth. "Let's see."

Inside the station, the head hum was drowned by conversation. A group of people stood in an arc around the door to the women's lavatory; a porter stood by the door, but they were clearly hanging back of their own accord.

Edaire said, in her elderly-scholar voice, "Some difficulty with the plumbing, is it?"

A woman in a straw hat said, "Someone inside's a bit sick, I believe."

A man in a scuttle cap said, "I heard she's got a pistol."

"Oh, go on," someone else said.

Edaire went to the agent's desk. She showed her pass and badge, with a gesture for quiet. "What's happening in there?"

"A woman took terribly ill," the agent said. "I think she may be a sorcerer."

"Did anyone see this?"

"There were two others in there with her, but they both fled and haven't come back. One was screaming. Carter took a glance"—he indicated the porter by the door—"but she come back scared, and I've never known Carter to scare."

"Scared how?"

"Shaking, stark white. She was clutching her chest as if she thought her heart would burst."

Edaire knew then. She could have kicked herself for not see-ing it at once. "I'm going to go in. If you possibly can, get the crowd away; have the arrivals go home and the departures wait on the platform. If nothing else works, tell them the service will stand them a drink—wait. A drink *at the inn down the road.*"

"We have a tavern—"

"I know that. But we need quiet. Now, you're keeping a bag of mine. Would you put it outside the door as soon as you can?" She put a silver cartwheel on the counter. "Tip in advance for Carter. Just have her set it down, don't knock or open the door. Understood?"

"Yes, honored."

Edaire and the agent went back to the arc of the crowd. The agent spoke softly in Carter's ear. She nodded, said loudly and clearly, "Please to come this way, honoreds?"

The only response was more low chatter. Edaire felt the hum rise, thought she saw the lavatory door bow outward. No use to wait; she walked straight to the door and went through.

The women's lavatory was a long, narrow room, finished in dull green paint and brownish tiles like grouted sea-gravel. On the right were three wooden stalls, all empty, on the left two sinks below an iron-framed mirror. Someone had vomited into one of the sinks. There was hissing yellow light from a double gasmantle and a fair amount of day through a diamond-paned window at the far end of the room. Edaire noted automatically that the place was in good repair and had been clean.

A woman was on her knees below the window, leaning against the wall. Her hair was sunbleached in streaks, light brown to gold; a loose blue ribbon had been holding it back at one time. Her hands and face were tanned as a sailor's. She was wearing a blue denim walking jacket over a light blue shirt of fine cambric; below that, a long, comfortably full skirt of puckered cotton, striped blue and white. There was mud on the hem, and a lot of mud on her high-buttoned boots.

Her hands were raised, the fingers locked through the window grate, knuckles bone-white on brown. Something shimmered on the backs of her hands. The lozenge panes were melting out of the leading, and weeping down the woman's arms and shoulders, soft and thick as gelatin, red and green and white. One slid to the floor, landing with a kind of crisp plop among others already there.

Edaire turned a tap to wash the vomit away. The woman on the floor shuddered, and the mirror above the sinks wavered and began to sag. Edaire sprayed the water about with her fingers, then closed the tap. It shrieked brassily, but the woman made no further response.

Then the woman said, "Edaire." The name rang off the tiles, echoed like faraway thunder; Edaire felt something like a scrabbling of fingers behind her breastbone. One of the few panes still in the lozenge window shattered into red dust; Edaire thought of a hard cherry sweet crunched between the teeth.

"I'm here, Agate." Edaire took a step forward.

"Don't . . . touch me."

"I won't. There will be a train here soon. To the House. Is that why you're at this station?"

"Train . . . and you."

"Can you manage the train? What can I do to help?"

"Too much noise. Maybe a little . . . silly."

"Can you keep things down?"

Agate nodded her head toward the sink. "Someone else. Scared her."

"I'll be back, then."

"No one . . . else."

"No. No one else will come in."

Edaire paused for a moment before the door, trying to frame a statement for the crowd. outside. Comforting? Officious? Dismissive?

When she opened the door, no one was there, and her carpetbag was leaning by the jamb. She shoved the bag inside the door and shut it. The crowd had gathered outside, around Lix, who was gleefully busking away, juggling a remarkable assortment of objects: his bowler hat, an apple, his clackers of office, and a walking stick were tumbling in cascade.

Edaire went into the station tavern. The bartender was a pale, plump woman, polishing mugs as ever idle barkeeps did. "How's the sick'un doing?" she said, almost jovially.

"We're on our way to a holiday rest. She'll be fine then."

"Friend of yours, then."

"Yes. I want half a waterglass of Harkamber and a small Clarrez-Foy."

"I shan't ask which is the med'cine. Compliments on your taste, and your friend's." She poured out four generous fingers of the dark Northern whisky, and a precise measure of Alinsea's palest brandy. "Any chaser?"

"Maybe we'll be back," Edaire said, and carried the drinks to the lavatory. Agate had not moved.

Edaire said, "I've brought you a drink. Is that what you were asking for?"

Agate's shoulders moved. With a visible effort she unlocked her fingers from the window grate. Soft glass slid from her, fell hard to the tiles, and broke. "There. Thank you."

Edaire put the large whisky on the floor within Agate's reach, took a step back, waited as Agate closed her hands around the tumbler.

Edaire said, "How about a toast, Agate?"

Agate smiled, though her eyes were pain itself. Her features were beautifully shaped, though air, earth, fire, and water had all worked well on them. "Daren't, love. We'll be . . . House for dinner?"

"Yes."

"Dinner, then. A' sky don't fall." She took a long swallow. "Oh. Fine malt to make madwomen stupid."

Edaire said nothing. The less sound, the better. They drank in silence. Edaire turned, saw herself in the mirror, and shook her head. She set her glass aside, moistened a towel (careful not to let the water thrum or splash) and wiped off the cake-flour makeup that had aged her.

Agate breathed audibly, and Edaire's image wavered and

bulged in the mirror. She turned away, still holding the towel. Her stomach was solidly mounted, but that explained the vomit well enough. She wet another towel, moved close to Agate. "May I?"

"Lightly, I think."

Edaire sponged Agate's forehead. Even without touching the skin, she could feel warmth just short of fever.

"N'more. I'll keep. I'm fresh enough to've come from Blackice Gorge."

"Agate, that's a day's walk."

"A night's. Calmer at night. Don't ask now."

Edaire looked again at the mud caking Agate's shoes.

"Careless," Agate said suddenly, "and you're all a-dust." She put her glass down, tapped it, picked up its note with her voice. She leaned forward, palms on the floor.

Edaire said, "Agate—"

Agate spoke then, and there was Craft in her voice; the air shook with it. The walls shook. Edaire's bones trembled.

> "Don't confuse the cost with cost,
> What I lose is well, well lost."

Edaire was gripped, held, compelled upon position. She knew that Agate was only protecting her from the uncertainty of whatever Craft she intended, its inevitable wildness. And it was, in truth, only a touch; whether Agate intended it so, or stronger, or gentler still, Edaire could, if she really desired it, walk away, right out the door, and scream.

> "As fashion is the scansion of the fabric,
> So tailoring and cleaning are its descants;
> For cloth like verses should be measured clean."

A fresh gale blew through her coat. It whipped at her clothing, though she felt nothing against her skin but the flap of fabric.

> "*The buttons fall like pipe stops to the fingers,*
> *And hem meets hem in a drone chant of stitches,*
> *As fashion is the scansion of the fabric.*
>
> "*The soap may ease the burden of the water,*
> *As stones wear out what was of stones eroded;*
> *For cloth like verses should be measured clean.*"

She understood. Agate was out of tune with the world, full of undirected power. Craft was explosive within her, bleeding out. This little gasp would make it possible for them to go on to the House. To Varic.

> "*We only start to understand the fiber*
> *As we match the pattern, as we drape and dart it,*
> *As fashion is the scansion of the fabric.*
>
> "*The Goddess spins and stretches out our living*
> *For to fit the pattern of Her cloth's designing;*
> *For cloth like verses should be measured clean.*"

Edaire shut her eyes. She could not help it. Magic frightened her. She loved Agate. Silvern she loved more than all things, and the link between them was welded with Craft. Silvern knew this; he could not *not* know it. Perhaps that was how she endured the constant brush of Craft in the world: the knowledge that there were greater powers.

> "*The Spirit and the Flesh shall find a mirror*
> *In the close spare cutting to the sign of bodies;*

> *As fashion is the scansion of the fabric,*
> *For goods like verses should be measured clean."*

Edaire's clothing seemed to explode; eyes still tightly shut, she could feel a cloud of whirling fiber scrape her skin, buttons patter her. Then all stopped.

Her ragged, frayed outfit was now trim and crisp and pressed, fitted neatly to her body, every hole rewoven away, and absolutely clean—as a bandage boiled in carbolic, Edaire supposed.

Agate was standing straight now, her arms outstretched; her outfit was clean as well, her boots unpolished but spotless. There was a ring of soil on the floor around her. Edaire turned: behind her, the direction the Crafted wind had gone, was her own silhouette, hazy in dirt against the tiled wall.

Agate said, "Better now," her voice slurred but not so weak, "but please let's go."

"Do you have any bags?"

"Pen and pad in my pocket."

Edaire picked up her own carpetbag and held the door for Agate, careful not to touch her as she passed. Lix had gone, and the people on the platform seemed barely to notice the two women. The station agent was standing on the platform, looking down the rails for the next train. Edaire quietly handed him another coin. "That one's for the cleaners—there's a bit of mess in there. You'll have to call a glazier as well. Don't worry, none of it's on your hook. You did very well."

"Honored," the agent said, looking no little embarrassed.

Edaire and Agate went to the extreme end of the platform, as far as possible from the other passengers. Edaire could see the train coming.

The motive was a Crowns Works, she could tell that a quarter stade off. Crowns machines had distinctive elliptical boiler-fronts, and pointed golden half coronets to either side of the head-lamp. Their product had come in second at the Blackslope Trials, and they had never since stopped straining for distinction. Steam pulsed from her stack, glimmering in the clear air. Valve gear whirled and air brakes whined. Agate barely seemed to notice; the noise was arrhythmic, and please Goddess the whisky was dulling her sense.

They boarded hurriedly, Edaire using her badge to clear a way past the purser direct to her compartment, a small single.

Edaire said, "You must have the bed."

"I suppose." Agate sat down, slipped off her jacket, and tossed it just short of the chair, clenched her teeth as Edaire unfastened her boots. She tucked in, lay on her back on the Ironway linens.

Edaire picked up the denim jacket, hung it from a brass hook, pulled the chair to the bedside, and sat. "Can you rest now, do you think?"

"Possibly. With your help. I'm very glad of your help, lovely wonder."

"You knew I'd be at the station."

"I read the lines. Iron carries far, veins of society. I tried to reach Varic, but couldn't, of course. Silly."

"Hush. Sleep now. You must be very tired."

"Just a stroll by easy dark. The owls knew me from the other mice." She stared at the lacquered curve of the ceiling. Her gemstone eyes were uncomfortably flat.

The motive blew down steam, preparing to start. The captain's voice called out "Boarding and parting! Boarding and parting, all!"

Agate shuddered. "It won't do, Edaire. I'm still too wound, wound up, tick, tick, oh stop, stop. Please, love."

"You'll wake with a dreadful headache."

"Prob'ly, throbly, could be bad. But click'ty, snick'ty's surely bad." She unbuttoned her shirt collar, pulled it open to show her evenly tanned neck, corded and hollowed. "Needs do, now."

Edaire's hands went slowly, slowly, to Agate's throat, circled it without touching the skin. It was certainly easy to find the pulses. Her thumbs stabbed in.

Agate's blood, prisoned in her fingers, heaved and fought; Edaire felt her own neck go rigid. If this wasn't over quickly—

Agate groaned, and her head rolled to one side. Edaire felt ice thawing in her own body. She covered Agate with a blanket, tucking and smoothing it without conscious thought. The tension around Agate's closed eyes was still visible.

Agate's eyes made Edaire think of Silvern's. A voice, calm and dear, prickled behind her brain. She grasped her ring. "All is well," she said, "all is well. Oh, and you, always and always."

She rang the purser for tea and a patcake. Then she took the leather-bound book from her pocket, set it on the table, and opened her bag—clean or not, she wanted different clothes for arrival. Inside the bag, her fingers found a small paper packet she knew she hadn't packed.

It contained a tiny yarn doll, three strands of green yarn knotted into a figure no bigger than her thumbjoint, and two oatmeal cakes, thick and moist and almost still warm. Lix must have slipped them in somehow.

She tucked the doll into the buttonhole of Agate's jacket, so it sat perched on her lapel.

The purser brought the lunch tray. Edaire sighed at the first bite of the patcake; the salmon salad had been sugared, apparently to conceal the sourness of the sauce. Something else for her report. She drank the tea, which was acceptable, and she ate one of the cookies, wrapping the other tight for Agate.

It was not far now to Leith Meadows, and the coach should

be waiting; perhaps, now that Agate was sleeping, she would sleep until they arrived.

Then it would be Varic's turn.

Edaire put the book in her lap, shut her eyes, and drifted into sleep herself without noticing at all.

CHAPTER 3

THE MAZE AND FORTUNE

"Leith Meadows," the train captain called down the corridor, "change for Derren Valley and the Southwest. Leith Meadows, next station."

Varic braced himself in the vestibule as the train rattled over points. A signal standard flashed past the window, and the platform rolled by. The brakes were applied, and the train ground hissing to a stop.

Leith Meadows was a modest wooden box of a station, hexagonal tiles on its roof with a strip of sharp ornamental iron along the crease. There were four tracks, a glass-covered iron bridge leading to the outer three. The just-afternoon sky was almost completely clear, and the sun was warm, though the still air was cool.

Varic opened the door, reached out to assist Longlight to the platform. Silvern had gone forward to the baggage car. Varic said quietly, "It was a pleasant voyage, wasn't it?"

"Was and is," Longlight said, and Varic nodded. "Will we be met?"

"We are met," Varic said, and took a step toward three people standing together under the eave of the station roof.

There were two women, one tall and slender and pale blond, the other shorter and plumper and darker. The shorter one held the hand of a boy, perhaps seven or eight, with neatly combed short brown hair and wide light brown eyes. All three wore livery coats of soft, dark red leather, with a household emblem on the left shoulder: a gold ellipse, blue moons above and below a red four-towered house.

"Tacker and Roan," Varic said, indicating the tall and short women, "and their son, Hazel. Strange's first coaching crew. Or does Hazel still intend to abandon stables for an Ironway motive?"

"Honored Edaire says I shall if I study," the boy said, and Roan squeezed his hand while Tacker half turned her smile away. "Good day to you, Lord Varic," Hazel said, a little stiffly.

Varic said, "And good day to you, Hazel. This is our new guest Longlight, and you must call her 'Lady,' for she is a great Coron of the West." Everyone exchanged bows, and Varic said to Roan, "Is it only us, or will we be waiting for others?"

Roan said, "No others for a while, milord. Is not our Palion with you?" Her speech had the formal tone of a Northerner, though her accent was definitely Central.

"Up with the baggage."

"I see him," Tacker said. Her voice was calm, crisp, almost military. "Meet you at the coach." She nodded to Varic and Longlight and walked lightly up the platform.

"This way, milady," Roan said. "Hazel, lead you on."

They went through the station hall, which was beginning to fill up with transfer passengers checking their connections and staking claims to seats. They emerged almost alone on the station drive. A four-wheel coach with a splendid four of chestnuts was waiting at the curb. A boy in an Ironway jacket was holding the horses; Varic gave him a plate, he touched his cap and handed the reins, with care approaching ceremony, over to Roan.

Silvern came out, carrying his bag, alongside Tacker, who was pushing a cart with the rest of the luggage. She rolled it to the rear of the coach, tossed the canvas cover aside, and began transferring bags without apparent effort. Roan made a quiet and efficient check of the interior and climbed up onto the driver's box. She took a leather cap and goggles from a chest beside her. "Tacker, how goes the work?"

"Just done now, Roan." Tacker took a seat on the rear platform. There was a short, steel-fitted carbine in a clip beside her.

Roan said, "Then at your convenience, honored guests."

"No convenience like the present," Silvern said.

"Agreed," Varic said. "Longlight?" He gestured to the coach door.

"How far is it?"

"Slightly over eight milae. Is the road fair today, Hazel?"

"Fair and open and broad, honored," the boy said. "We should make fine time."

"Excellent. Then would you help the lady aboard?"

Hazel took up footman's position by the door and step, held out his hand to assist Longlight. "Does my lady prefer to sit facing forward or back?"

"I shall face back, Hazel." She boarded, said, "Thank you, Hazel," and pressed an ace into his palm. He pressed his hands together on it, bowed deeply. Then he turned to face Silvern, bowed, and said, "One arm, Palion? One arm?"

"You're sure you can manage one," Silvern said almost gravely.

"Oh, yes, honored!"

"Very well, then." Silvern extended his left arm horizontally, braced his right against the rear of the coach. Hazel jumped straight up and caught Silvern's extended arm with both hands, swung up just as if the arm had been a tree branch (and it moved no more than a branch would have) and vaulted onto the top of the coach. He sat down on the driver's box, next to Roan. The driver put an arm around her son's shoulders and hugged him.

Varic sat down inside the coach, opposite Longlight. Silvern leaned in at the open door. "I'll sit back with Tacker," he said. "I need some road air."

"Tell me if you want a dust-cutter," Varic said, and Silvern nodded to the two of them and shut the door. Roan clucked to the team and the coach rolled away from the station, between a pair of huge plane trees just edged with autumn gold, and onto a road that was indeed broad and open and fair.

The coach was comfortable, not luxurious, made for trips of an hour or two. Varic could not count the times he had ridden in it, to and from the station, into the apple orchards or around the lake, in the half of his life he had been a guest of Strange's. The feel of its cushions, its smell of wood and leather and iron, the particular bounce of its springs, were part of the welcome, the stay, the farewell.

The seats were upholstered in kid leather, a once-deep red faded now to dark rose. The fittings were white metal, polished non-tarnishing steel with here and there a touch of gilding. At the corners of the compartment, pressed-glass lanterns hung on gimbals; they could be read by, if you held the book close and the letters were not too tiny. Several small books were shelved above Varic's head: Shearer's *Essays,* Bright's *Back Lanes Lescorial,* Fineman's *In Quercian Twilight* (that one, with its minute print, for daylight reading only), an Ironway timetable. Above Longlight, in a fitted cabinet, were three decanters of leather-covered glass—whisky, pale brandy, dark rum—and a stack of silver cups.

Varic was about to ask Longlight if she wanted a drink when she stood up, one hand carefully on the brace handle, and sat down next to him. "I'm tired," she said. "Do you mind?"

"No."

She settled her head against his shoulder. Her hair pressed his cheek. He felt a strong desire to touch her face, but did not. He wondered what Silvern had told her about the House, the guests. If this was how she was choosing to part from him, he did not wish to interfere with the act. He tilted his head just enough to both accommodate her and see out the window, and that was how they stayed for nearly half an hour. Halfway along, he was aware that the panel to the rear slid open, no doubt Silvern wanting a brandy, but no one spoke, and it closed again quietly.

"You can see the House now," Varic said quietly, and Long-light opened her eyes and sat up.

Varic said, "There. Across the lake."

"I hadn't realized it would be so large."

The lake was about half a mila east to west, slightly less north to south. A small, wooded island was in its approximate center. On the far north bank, the columns of the pavilion could be seen, and beyond them the House itself. As the coach followed the road around the lake, slowly turning the angle of view, the House took shape, three-dimensional substance.

The central House was sixty steps square and four storeys high, with tall, narrow windows on all sides of the upper floors. To either side, a long wing reached southward toward the lake. The wings were twenty steps across and eighty long, three floors high; they were connected to the main building by columned breezeways at ground level and enclosed halls on the upper floors. At each end of the long galleries was a square-sided tower, twice as high as the building; the northern pair flanked the main House, the southern two overlooked the lake. From certain angles the House looked like a square-bastioned castle of the Altenreigns, though there were far too many windows and balconies for that kind of defensible place, and nothing of that antiquity could have had the House's array of chimneys and rain gutters. It was surrounded on all sides but the lake with light woods, elms and maples and oaks, green and gold.

"We'll come up alongside the East Wing," Varic said. "That's where guests usually stay."

"Just the East Wing," she said with something between laughter and awe. "It looks as if it could billet an army."

"A small army. There are forty guest rooms, all with cameral plumbing, as well as Strange's apartments and the staff quarters. A small kitchen and buttery in each wing, in case you're hungry in the night, and always someone awake to warm a pie or pull a splinter or fill a hot water bottle." He looked through the trees separating the road from the East Wing, windows flickering between trunks. "It was built for hospitality. And—do you know the fable of the travelers in the hostelry barn?"

"No. It is often said that . . . Westren hosting's thin a'base."

"The same thing is said of the varic coast northish," Varic said, offhand, and then said, "You should have Strange tell you the story. And show you—no, don't ask what I mean by that. You'll see."

The road curved away from the building, into the surrounding woods. Longlight looked over the House, fascinated, wide-eyed. Twice she began to speak, but did not. Finally she said, "How old is it?"

"Two hundred twelve years. We had a party on the two hundredth."

"Then—who built it? If not the Lord Strange . . ."

"Two things," Varic said, gently and carefully. "One, we do not discuss Strange's age. Two, Strange does not like to be addressed as 'Lord,' even though the House and grounds are technically a Coronage."

"I will remember."

"No one will curse you if you forget. We just . . . have our ways, that's all."

The road merged into a paved ellipse before the main house. In the middle of the loop was a stone-edged lily pond, a statue at its center, standing on the water. It was a gaunt woman holding a staff and a shutter lantern, wearing a cloak and a full backpack, her face hooded.

Longlight said, "Coris, of course—but that figure, the lantern, must be Wyss."

Varic said, "Yes."

The coach rounded the circle and stopped before the main house. It was imposing enough from this angle, a massive face of gray stone and black iron and green roof tile; but the windows were unshuttered and bright, and the sun lit it warmly.

The entrance was on the floor above ground, in the usual manorial fashion, with stairways curving down to its left and right. Between the feet of the stairs was a double oak door, and it was this that opened. A strikingly tall woman came out, pushing a man in a wheeled chair.

The woman had very dark skin; her eyes were large and quite black, with an exotic tilt. Her hair was black and straight, cut all around at the level of her chin, like a helmet. She wore a full-sleeved gown of russet satin embroidered in green, belted with braided green leather.

The man in the chair wore a gown of dark red velvet, a scholar's gown with pockets for pens and lenses and paperwork. A broad cap of the same stuff drooped over his ears; a thin fringe of gray hair showed from beneath it. His legs were bundled in a black quilt sewn with gold stars, like a sleighter's black robe. His face was deeply creased, though the skin between the grooves was pink and smooth. His smile was very broad. Muscular hands with prominent veins rested easily on the arms of the chair. He was not a small man, and there was certainly strength enough in his upper body. The chair did not diminish or imprison him.

"Silvern!" the man said, his voice like thunder across still water. "*Sa hashta, bardi.* And Varic, welcome as ever. And you have brought us a new guest. Welcome to our house, honored mistress. My name is Strange. And yours would be?"

"Longlight, honored. Of the sunset regions."

"Then you would be the Lord Blackstone's granddaughter and heir, and welcome for his memory as well as your own." He raised a hand. "I would you meet Dany, my friend of much help."

Longlight bowed. Dany placed a hand across her heart.

Varic was looking away from everyone else. He seemed to be watching ripples in the pond. Then he looked up, toward the House's East Wing. After a prolonged, silent moment, he said, "Agate is already here."

"Yes, she is," Strange said.

"Then I must take my leave of you all. Roan, Tacker, Hazel, thanks for your good care. Silvern, Strange, Dany, well met. And, Longlight . . . I am sure I shall see you at dinner. Expect marvels."

He hurried up the steps and disappeared.

The awkward silence fell again. Then Strange said, quite genially, "Silvern, why don't you and Dany go in? I know you'll be wanting a little combat play, and the arenetto is ready. I'll see that Longlight is settled. We have an old family connection to discuss."

Dany took a step back from Strange's chair. She and Silvern went through the ground-level door.

Strange said, "Which floor do you prefer, middle or upper? Top south end has the best view. Courtyard side, I think. Tacker, you'll see to it?"

"Of course, Strange." She pulled up on the rear step of the coach, and Roan drove it around the corner of the main building, out of sight.

Strange turned his chair toward the house. "Come along, then, Longlight, and see the pile from the inside."

Longlight didn't move. "Who is Agate?" she said.

"Another of our guests. A Player, as the regulars call themselves. I hope you will soon come to consider yourself another such."

"Varic seemed in a great hurry to . . . see . . . her."

"Yes," Strange said, slowly and with a long release of breath. "They are old and particular friends. Please—would you push me in?"

She took the handles of the chair. "Like this?"

"Just so."

They went through the lower door into a stone-floored foyer, lit by two brass lanterns. Cloaks hung on the walls, and rubber overshoes were neatly racked. There were two other doors into the house, and an iron cage lift. Strange pushed the lift door aside. "This way, Longlight."

The cage shut, rumbled, and hummed, and rose a floor. They emerged into a broad room that opened into hallways on three sides. The walls were covered with red satin and hung with gilt mirrors and small gold-framed paintings; there was a marble table in the Quercian style, and a wooden one after the Midreigns, and an inlaid desk of fairly modern design covered with papers and periodicals.

"This is the main floor, where most everyday things happen," Strange said. "The small dining room is just to the south, that way; that's for informal meals, breakfast usually, unless you prefer breakfast in your room. It has a terrace overlooking the garden, and if we're lucky the weather will hold fair enough to dine outside. The main library is just to the left, grand parlor opposite; there are more of both all over. The great hall, where we'll be dining tonight, is just beneath us." He gestured around at the hallway furnishings. "This is not, despite appearances, a museum; if you see anything that catches your interest, you may handle it and examine it and even ask if I remember anything about it. And of course there's the room that your grandfather may have told you about—" He stopped abruptly. "Oh, my, the time. I have a short errand to perform, I'm very afraid, and I must abandon you for it. Down that hall to the west, second door to the right, is the Blue Parlor. Do please await me there; I won't be long. There should be tea. I am happy to have you here, Longlight; I *am* happy."

She stared as he rolled his chair into the lift, shut the cage, waved, and descended. She looked around herself for a minima or two, then, having really nothing else to do, went down the hall to the parlor.

It *was* blue. It had blue damask on the walls and soft furniture, blue velvet curtains, blue crystals in a chandelier glowing golden with glasswicks. A tea cart with a silver service sat beneath the light. A small fire was set in a blue marble fireplace, and a dark-haired woman—not in blue—leaned against the mantel, looking into the fire. Her hair was slightly astray, and she was biting her thumb tip. She turned.

"Hello," she said. "I'm sorry, I was just brooding." She held out her hand, which bore a black-and-gold ring.

"You must be Edaire," Longlight said unsteadily.

"Yes. And whom have I met?"

"My name is Longlight. I . . . came with Varic and Silvern."

"Oh! Welcome, then, welcome. Delighted to meet you. Will you sit? I'm sorry if I look frayed, but Agate and I have had a somewhat rough trip. I'm only glad that Varic arrived when he did."

"Yes. He seemed very concerned about . . . whoever Agate may be."

Edaire looked at Longlight eye to eye. "You don't know," she said quietly. "No, of course. Varic wouldn't have said anything, and Silvern wouldn't have thought to . . . and you were on the road together two nights, from the City. Oh, my honored dear, do sit down."

"Your conseil said," Longlight said firmly, "that you could help me get a train toward my home. I should be very grateful if you could do so. Even part of the way—"

"Will you allow me to tell you some things first?"

"I think I've already *been* told, and quite clearly."

Edaire frowned, tapped a shoe. She said, "I can stop any train passing, and I will do so if you wish it. But there won't be one *to* stop for a while, so you might as well hear what I have to say." She gestured toward a couch by the tea cart, and they sat, facing each other.

Edaire turned suddenly. "And I do need the tea. I'd nearly forgotten it. Do you want a cup, while it's still decently hot?"

"Yes. Thank you."

Edaire poured. "I take it from your state of shock—don't protest, it takes one to know one—that no one even mentioned Agate—or perhaps I should say Varic-and-Agate—until you were through the front door."

"Just outside it," Longlight said.

"And suddenly your traveling companion—and doubtless the man you had thought would be your holiday companion, since he has a way of not interfering with other people's beliefs—runs off to another bedroom, and you're left alone with a houseful of people you've never met."

"I didn't think—that is, Varic didn't know at first that I was coming. Here. To stay. That was your . . . conseil's idea."

"And of course Silvern didn't tell you about Agate."

"No."

"Just as well. As much as I love him—and do not let my tone confuse you about that—he wouldn't honestly know how. Silvern's understanding is great, but in his own elemental aspect.

So: Agate is an Archpoet. Do you know what that means? In these terms?"

"No."

"Have you known any sorcerers well?"

"In what sense?" Longlight said dryly.

"Any sense you please," Edaire said, just as dry.

"Yes. When I was younger. The family healer."

"And was that person . . . sensitive to certain things? When you were sick or hurt, did the healer seem to hurt as well?"

"You've talked to Varic," Longlight said, her tone unpleasant but with a certain humor.

"I haven't even seen him," Edaire said with relentless calm. "To the point again. The Archain are all like that, if they have any ability at all; Silvern can hear a dull sword cry from across a room. Agate's Craft is poetry—rhythm and meter; and there's a lot of bad rhythm in the mortal world. I was lucky to find her when I did, if you believe things like that are luck." She sipped her tea. "Blackberry and dewbell," she said, running her tongue over her lips to taste it again. "Very calming. Do not underestimate your host, Longlight."

Longlight drank some of the tea. "Am I calm enough to hear the rest of this story?"

"Listen, then, and I will try to tell you," Edaire said. "After that, if you still want to leave, I promise you that a train will stop for you."

∞

Varic climbed the last turn of the northwestern staircase and was on the top floor of the West Wing. The hall was a little more than three steps wide, half again that high. The center of the ceiling was elevated, with shallow windows along the sides for illumination. The clerestory windows were of rippled, translucent colored glass, and pastel shafts fell across the hallway. More of the House's endless collection was along the walls, separating the oak apartment doors: armor cabinets, tables from three different eras of design set with lamps and bowls and candlesticks and oddments from a dozen more periods, mirrors and paintings on the walls. In about the center of the eastern wall, to Varic's left, was a particularly good Beadsmith, a view through a wet dawn forest of a Midreign stronghold— either a ruin, or an intact castle partly hidden by the mist.

There were three clocks in the hall, two blocky, ornate table dials and a slim Nockerby tallcase in white birchwood. All—in fact, every clock in the West Wing—had been stopped, their hands set tidily at twelve up, for the duration of Agate's visit.

Varic stopped at the last door on the right. A few steps farther on, the hallway ended in another door, flanked by maid's cabinets; it led to stairs down to the hall kitchen and up to the tower.

Short of that tower, this apartment was as far as one could get from the House's center, the occupied areas. He paused before the door, but did not knock. He pushed it open, slowly, silently, slipped inside, and shut it again without a sound.

Most of the guest chambers were laid out like this one. The hall door opened on a small parlor, with chairs, a secretary table, a fireplace, and an angled skylight. A short hallway led past the bathroom door, to a large, square bedroom with tall windows and a canopy bed. The furnishings varied, by taste and whim and utility. Agate's room was dressed in sea greens and neutral charcoals. The windows were completely hidden by heavy velvet drapes, and the bed was heavily curtained as well. The curtains were open on satin sheets, turned back but unused. A writing desk was open, supplied, ready, but again showed no sign of use. The chandelier, of crystal fitted for electricity, cast a soft yellow light.

Agate was sitting in the center of a green-cushioned cherrywood sofa, space to either side of her. She was wrapped up close in a quilted robe of purple satin printed with silver flowers; a scarf wound up to her chin, and her brown hands lay inert in her lap. Her feet, in white silk bed socks and kidskin slippers, were propped up on a hassock. There was a tea tray in her reach, with a little tea left in a cup and cookie crumbs dusting a plate.

Her hair was loose to her shoulders, gently waved, sunbleached so that its color varied brown to golden. Her large, clear brown eyes—the eyes she had been named for—were open, but surrounded by darkness, and focused far away. Her face was taut, and her head nodded slowly, with a terrible combination of tension and exhaustion.

"Bath and dress and tea we've had," she said, her voice clear and startling as the chime of a clock in a silent room, "how d'you like your lady mad?" The teacup began to spin erratically in its saucer, the splash of liquid inside whirlpooling.

"I see only you," Varic said, and took three steps closer. "Are you mad today, then?"

"Rain come, brain go, kettle boil, I've been half the country's toil. Many those who rode my wake, would have called it Crown Communion; bended me the knee, said, 'Take up the throne and bring us union.'" The crumbs on the plate imploded into a small, perfectly round cookie, half a raisin at its center.

A joke came to Varic's mind, but he repressed it, tried to not even think it. For the next few minimi, they needed silence; each word was a primed charge, and he was not yet set to receive the blast. He simply spread his hands, and she nodded.

Agate was not royal, of course—less so than Varic. Archanum

and kingship had never mixed well in Lescoray; the Talent was just too wild. And where was it wilder than Crown Communion, the population's traces of power focused on the King? Kings were not trained. Agate was a master crafter, and look at her, look at her, candlebellbook at her—

Varic felt himself sway as the power struck him, bouncing like static sparks through his body. "*No,*" Agate cried, and twisted in her wrap. "Here she is metered in marrow and blood, breathing by more than the air inspired; know she would stop it if only she could, know as you must she is terribly—"

"*Weary,*" Varic said, and they both twitched with the pop of released power, felt muscles loosen as energy ebbed.

At once Varic was tired, too. He was ready and entirely able to drop where he stood. But it wouldn't do, for a long while yet.

He covered the last few steps to the sofa, sat down just at her left. He was breathing raggedly. Good; one less rhythm. He pointed to the teacup, and she nodded. He lifted the quilted cozy from the pot and poured, dripped in some lemon—stirring would have been a very bad idea—raised the cup to her lips. She swallowed, relaxed with a visible movement of her shoulders.

"We must get you back to prose, my dear," Varic said. "Tell me what's happened."

She took a breath. "Blackice Gorge . . . smithy and—"

Varic shook his head, just once. Agate did the same and said, "Valley's usually quiet . . . empty. Not this time."

"Someone was there?"

"Bridgers. Pitchers of dirt and ditchers. Flangers and benders and welders and renders. Belting and tressure and bolting and pressure."

Stressed syllables banged on Varic's heart. But he could not stop her now. There was a point in this dance beyond which he had to stop delaying, sidestepping, easing her along; when the cankered energies had to be released. The point was not clearly defined, though, fortunately for them both, there was some latitude about it. Still, if he were wrong enough—

Still. Still. Still was what he had to be now.

Agate said:

> "In the working of the reaping,
> Serving Craft by Crafting service,
> Working Art by bought commission,
> Power shaped by taut volition,
> Leading to this fraught condition,
> Muscle, flesh, and bone all nervous,
> Troubled thought, an end to sleeping."

The chandelier trembled, cracked the dim light into pale rainbows. Agate shut her eyes again, seemed about to weep. He could feel her mind hanging from a precipice, feel her ache and sweat with the grip. His own head was starting to spin.

"All's well, brown maid," Varic said, not really words but only sound to stop the world from her ears; he glided a hand across her shoulders in a caress that made no contact and had no rhythm, fighting the impulse to embrace her.

> "It was not that I did not think of space,
> Or spared myself the eloquence of time;
> But came within my place a belted brace
> And measure-beat a different kind of rhyme.
>
> "Iron coursed and iron beat
> And wood gave splintering in receipt
> Rivets spat hot from the windsuck forge
> And straight sharp iron cut the throat of the gorge."

He understood. She had done a job for a town, somewhere to the east, something to do with the harvest—the details didn't matter. Afterward she had needed to be alone and quiet, and had walked through a valley that should have been empty. But wasn't.

Her dry voice rose, and chimes from nowhere accompanied it. Bubbles of light rose and burst in the room air; Varic shut his eyes for a moment, and the sparks remained.

> *"Iron and fire in close collusion,*
> *Oil and slag and slow pollution,*
> *Steam and shriek in grand confusion,*
> *Gap's elision, speed's illusion."*

He saw the room as if from a great distance. He could see the curtains rippling, the bed breathing, the tea service whirling in space like an orrery of Sun and Planets. He could feel the ends of his ribs burning, and wondered how long it had been since he had breathed.

It was, in a way, easy enough: all he had to do was remain disinterested, let the storm pass him and the lightning go to earth. In another way, this was live working sorcery, and he could easily end up with his knees folded into angle-iron within his rib cage, or turned to iron, heated red and glowing.

"You could die," she had said, years ago, when first Strange had put them together in this ongoing experiment. Yes, well. He hadn't yet, though. Hardly interesting anymore.

One of the drapes came down from the window, and dusty light slashed across the room. Agate looked up, her pupils enormous, eyes just black and white like a doll's, seeing something beyond things. The falling drape folded over the light as if the beam were a valet's forearm, twenty pounds of velvet arched on a streak of sun.

She was thinking on bridges, Varic thought; on suspension. He could hear his ribs creak under load. He could feel the steam hammer in his skull, sinking pilings into his brain. Strap iron laced his girdered fingers. His nerves dangled over the dizzying gap.

She was the motive, he was the rail: together, all they had to do was reach the far side.

When it was this bad, it always broke suddenly; sometimes, when she was less terribly nerved, there was only a gradual calming, but high tension resolved in a high moment.

It came: power sheeting across him like hard driven rain through a suddenly opened door. Like rain, it soaked his skin but went no deeper; it drew warmth from him, but what was that? There was little enough to lose.

He heard the crockery thud to the carpet, the curtain fold up with a groan of trapped air. Agate's head tipped forward, and her shoulders slumped. He did not touch her for a full minima, until the small Craftlights ceased to shift around her eyes and fingernails.

So it was done again. Not so hard after all, nothing really required on his part except to sit still enough, to care little enough. A soul with any decent capacity for affection would have burned up.

There were legends about sorcerers remaining virgin for the sake of their Craft, and of less resolute Archain drinking the—well, whatever—of their lovers. As with most good legends, there was a truth buried there.

He got his arms under her back and knees, carried her to the bed; he placed her on it, then collapsed on the step stool, his head deadweight on the edge of the mattress, until his heart slowed enough to distinguish one beat from the next. His head ached—dully, not the shattering pain he was used to, as if the headache itself were worn and weak.

He stood up, adjusted the pillows around Agate's head, moving hairs away from her eyes and mouth. He pulled her slippers off, set them carefully beside the bed step, and drew the canopy curtains.

He looked at the mess across the room. Worse than usual, but nothing new. He went down the hall, hands braced against the walls, and out of the room.

Bliss, Strange's chief butler, was in the corridor, in his black velvet coat and red satin waistcoat. Bliss was a plump but graceful man, with fine, delicate hands. His face was round, with a large, carefully trimmed black mustache. His eyes were small and brown and bright. He turned away from a hall table, as if he had merely been checking it for dust when Varic happened to emerge. No coincidence in it, of course.

"May I assist you, honored?" Bliss said. "Milord looks a bit pale."

"Milord *feels* pale." Varic tried to reach for the wall, but could not judge the distance. As he staggered, Bliss's hand somehow managed to touch Varic's, steadying him.

"The apartment two doors up and across is clean and untenanted, honored," Bliss said. "As it is rather a long walk to the East Wing."

"An excellent thought, Bliss."

"Thank you, honored." He led the way, all dozen steps, and opened the door. "Strange is anxious to know if mistress Agate is well?"

"Tired. Asleep now. But well."

"Should she be allowed to rest, then?"

"I think it will be all right to wake her for dinner. She would be unhappy to miss the gathering, first night." He stopped in the doorway, looked down the hall from parlor toward bedroom, which seemed to tilt, and shook his head. "I'll ask the same."

"Of course, milord."

"Her room will need tidying. And there's a curtain to be rehung."

"It will be seen to. Is there anything else for you, honored?"

"I'm positive there must be something, but just now . . ." He waved a hand aimlessly.

"Of course, honored. Will you go in now? Do ring for anything."

Varic nodded and went into the parlor, Bliss closing the door silently behind him. At the end of the hall, the bedside lamp was lit, and a tray held decanters of whisky and spring water.

He climbed up onto the bed, got his boots off and let his feet dangle. He sloshed some of the whisky into a glass. As he drank the flourish, he saw that his dinner suit was standing ready on a wooden valet rack at the foot of the bed. *How boringly predictable I've become*, he thought. His arm dropped, apparently of itself; the empty glass seemed to be crawling from his fingers. It got away, he could hardly stop it, as he slowly toppled backward across the bed; he never heard it hit the carpet.

❦

As she had been speaking, Edaire had been watching ripples in her teacup, radiating, crossing, intersecting. From time to time she looked up at the chandelier, its crystals moving in a nonexistent draft, never quite jingling. Now all the small motions stopped. She put the cup down.

Longlight said, "It's over?"

"Yes. As I believe you can sense for yourself."

"I suppose so. It's a new experience."

"What is?" Edaire said, in a very plain voice.

"I do not want to stay—I do not *intend* to stay—in a house where I am not wanted."

"Strange has welcomed you here, has he not?"

"Yes. But he—"

"Has a great many things to do today, yes. All the arrivals, rooms and dinner to consider, dispatching Roan and Tacker efficiently, Birch up in the Bright Room—"

"The *Archimage* Birch?"

"Yes. A guest long before that, though. Before he was a priest at all, actually. You'll meet him tonight. But as I was saying, Strange has made you welcome: therefore, you *are* a guest here, and welcome, and would be so even if there were truly great differences involved. Which—I ask you to believe—there are not."

"Varic could have told me."

"That is undeniably true," Edaire said.

"He just—he acted—"

"How did he behave?" Edaire said.

"I ought not tell you," Longlight said harshly. "I ought make you wonder—and oh, wheran comes this cruelty?"

"From hurt, whence all cruelty comes," Edaire said, "and I can tell you talked with Varic, if you think that doubt could twist me."

"It couldn't," Longlight said with the trace of a challenge.

"That's another thing, to explain another time. I did ask you a question."

"He pleasures a woman well enough. But he didn't—what should I say? Didn't love me. But it was never going to be that, was it?"

"Not by every definition."

"I wanted . . . to know about him. To understand how he could be so hot and so cold. Know what he was hiding. And I wanted him to care alike about me."

"Perhaps you should have told him that."

"You do defend him."

"If you were attacking Varic, I very much imagine I would be defending him. But you are only asking why he is what he is, and I truly don't know that; I doubt that anyone does."

"Varic included?"

"Of course. I care very much for him, which is not always easy. It wouldn't be possible at all if I didn't try to see him as completely as possible, not just a word here or an action there. While there are differences both of degree and kind, the same is true of Silvern."

After a pause, Longlight said, "And Agate—she truly cannot . . . cannot be—"

"You will meet her soon. Ask her yourself. Allow me to say this, however: Is it truly so easy to get near you?"

"Do you suppose he . . ." Her voice wandered, hunting for something more precise than words. ". . . likes that? Knowing, I mean, that with a word, or a touch, he could"—she paused for a heartbeat, then said straightforwardly—"make her suffer?"

There was a flash of something terrible in Edaire's face; Longlight did not flinch.

Edaire wrapped her hand around her ring, shut her eyes, and said, "I have just caused Dany to score an undeserved touch on Silvern. I shall have to apologize to both of them." She looked at Longlight. "To answer your fair and honest question, I believe that Varic has looked quite clearly into the wells of his own darkness. I choose to believe that he knows what he could do, and is happy that he does not do it."

"I said one thing too many, didn't I."

"No. He hurt you—not from wanting to hurt, and not without help from people who should have thought better—but you *were* hurt, and you had every right to ask what he is. What all of us are."

"It's easier for you," Longlight said as a statement of fact, without bitterness. "You're always first in each other's minds."

"Conseil is not a common state, we all know that," Edaire said, "and inevitably misunderstood. There are conseil couples who do not have exclusive relations. We met a pair once who gloried in others; and of course they were both sharing whatever either did. They wanted very much to pair off with us, simultaneously—or perhaps *group* would be a better word."

"That sounds—well. Did you?"

"We couldn't. Our vow *is* exclusive in aspect. Anyway, I think they expected too much. We wouldn't have linked to them."

Longlight said, "Would you have liked to try?"

"It's possible for me to think about it. Just as it's possible for Silvern to respond, deeply, to the sight of a woman who may be nothing like I am, but has those qualities that attract him." She smiled, and Longlight's fingers tightened on her teacup.

The mantel clock chimed four. A few silent minimi later, Strange wheeled his chair into the parlor. "It's quiet down here. Am I interrupting?"

Edaire gave her head an almost imperceptible shake. Longlight said, "No. We were just getting acquainted."

Strange smiled. "No one better to do it with. Longlight, do you really mean to leave us after all?"

"I should like to stay, a night at least. If I may."

"That was never in question. I am most pleased. Then I may say that Dany has asked if you would be up for a match, three points or a concetta? We have all the equipment you might need."

"I'd be pleased."

"Then let us proceed at once. Edaire, dear, will you push?"

She took the handles of Strange's chair, and the three of them started down the hall.

They descended in the lift to the ground-floor hallway, and went through one of the inner doors to the arenetto. It was modestly sized, a room ten steps square with seats and exercise equipment on two sides of a slightly raised wooden square five steps on a side.

Dany and Silvern were at work on the boards. Dany wore a jacket and knee-length skirt of padded rough silk reinforced with broad leather bands. The silk was an autumn gold color, the leather decorated with bronze. It was a beautifully made armor, certainly not Lescorial in design. Below the skirt she wore more typical steel shin guards, and she was working barefoot. She was fighting with an iron-tipped staff as tall as an average man (and up to Dany's shoulder).

Silvern wore a sleeveless shirt and loose trousers of light cotton cloth, pale gray darkened in patches by sweat. He had thin gloves and soft boots, but no armor at all, and his spread hands were empty.

Dany spun the staff as if to sweep at Silvern's unprotected head. Most of the way through the move, she shifted her weight on the ball of a foot, recoiled and thrust with the end of the stick directly at Silvern's breastbone.

There was a circular motion in the air before Silvern's chest, like ripples in water, and the thrust was stopped with an audible bang of metal against metal.

A singlestick grew from Silvern's fingers, a thin rod a little longer than his arm, of a dead black color. He knocked Dany's staff aside with it; the sound this time was like a steel hammer against rock. They sparred a few blows more; then the singlestick flickered and was in Silvern's left hand. The motion made it seem as if he had tossed the rod from one hand to the other, but he had not: it was an Armiger's weapon, made from magic and will. It could not leave his touch.

Edaire turned Strange's chair to the left, silently circling the wood. Longlight stood still, watching the players. She knew singlestick and staff fighting both very well; she had been taught them before any edged weapon. One couldn't count on having an edge to hand, but there was always a stick—a fireplace poker, a branch, a chair leg.

This wasn't that sort of brawl, though neither was it highly formal. Longlight could hardly imagine Dany hurting Silvern, no matter how skilled she might be; his sorcerer's armor appeared as a reflex, faster than thought. This wasn't combat training, or even battle practice. It was mental exercise, honing the already-sharp edge. For her, it had a strange fascination, so much wilder than conventional weapon-play and yet so controlled.

Silvern had two black batons now, and scissored Dany's staff between them. She slipped her weapon free, whirled it on fingertips high above her head, then shifted her grip to the very end and brought it around in a huge swing that grazed the edge of the wooden square and seemed to throw her dangerously off balance. Silvern crouched to one side.

Dany planted the tip of the staff and vaulted up with it, her whole long body tumbling over Silvern's bent back; she landed squarely behind him, and swung the staff upward against Silvern's throat, grabbing the free end with her other hand. Against an ordinary fighter, she could have easily levered back to crush the larynx or snap the neck.

Silvern was, of course, not ordinary. As the staff pulled back, a dark band of protection appeared around his throat. Longlight expected him to throw Dany forward, over his shoulders and onto her back.

Instead, he slashed his right hand sidewise at Dany's right wrist. Longlight had half an instanta to recognize that if the blow connected, it would almost certainly crack Dany's forearm.

But her forearm wasn't there. In that same part'ina, Dany

released her grip, spun to the left—under the staff, twirling it in her left fingers—and came up facing Silvern. He pushed the staff away, separating them by a step or so, and laughed out loud.

Silvern held his left hand in front of Dany's face: the first two fingers were upright, second two folded, thumb extended outward. It was the swordplayer's signal for pause. Dany nodded, turned to look at the spectators. She leaned on her staff and bowed. Then she faced Longlight and held up her right hand, thumb and little finger touching, three fingers spread in a trident. That was the polite request for a match, and Longlight crossed her palms to accept.

Dany turned to Silvern, who was taking long steps off the wooden square. Without looking back, he said, "Oh, yes, Dany, of course I'll proctor. Get Longlight set up, and I'll be ready when you are."

He held his arms forward. Edaire went to him, held his hands discreetly for one moment, then embraced him fully, lifted onto her toes.

"You're all clean," Silvern said. "You'll have to change."

"We're going to dress for dinner, silly." She tilted her head back, and they kissed. Then their lips separated, just by a little fingers-breadth, and something passed between them, silent but perceptible.

Silvern turned to look at Longlight. He said, quietly and plainly, "I am glad you will be staying for the holiday."

"This way," Dany said, and led Longlight across the platform, through a door into a room lined with storage cabinets and exercise equipment. A shower room connected at the back.

Dany opened some cabinets, and quickly found Longlight an athletic breasthalter, a shirt with padded sleeves, a leather vest that buckled to size. Longlight changed her trousers for a loose pair in heavy white cotton, strapped on kneepads, put her own boots on again.

Across the room, Silvern was assembling a pair of splintans, the weapons for swordgame: slightly curved wooden slats held together with leather clips, the edge filled with chalk to mark a touch. The clips were supposed to give way under an excessive blow. It didn't always prevent a cracked bone, but it was considered bad form to snap one's sword. The game was about movement and control, not simple force.

Silvern tried the swords, balanced and swung them, then nodded to himself and chalked the edges.

"Dany's challenge," he said, and offered choice of weapons to Longlight. She took a splintan, went to a corner of the square, and stood at relaxed guard. Dany went to the opposite corner.

Silvern took up a post at the edge of the platform. "Normal rules," he said, "no effect of wounds. Three, two, one . . . *go*."

Both women took a step to the right. Longlight held her sword upright, two-handed; Dany's was horizontal in her right hand, her left close in to her body. They took another step. They were observing the circle, an imaginary pattern on the floor, defined by the length of sword, arm, and stride. In theory, one was safe as long as one kept to the circumference of the circle. In practice, it meant very little in anything but formal swordgame; but one had to start somewhere. The first phase of the game ended when someone broke the formality.

Longlight decided to break it. She took a long, diving step, thrusting at Dany's left hip. Dany sidestepped without effort and crossed swords with Longlight, gently, sending a faint puff of chalk into the air. Longlight returned the stroke. Then they both recovered, stepped back, stepped close again and exchanged serious blows, rattling the splintans. Dany seemed to stumble; Longlight took a wary step forward, felt the swish of air past her shoulder.

Longlight was aware that Dany was drawing her back, one

step and parry at a time. Her family's combat master called it *jugging the hare*. The double object was to analyze your opponent's style, see what response each move brought, and draw the opponent into a position where the learned and logical response would be fatally wrong.

Once you were aware of the strategy, there were two tactics against it. One was to turn wild, fight randomly and furiously for a minima or so, upsetting the opponent's calculations. The other way required a detailed and absolute knowledge of one's own habits and reflexes, the ability to stand above and behind oneself, conscious of what one would do by instinct—then further see what move the opponent was counting on, and alter it into a trap.

Longlight was not in a reflective mood. That settled the issue. She tore in, step-swing, step-thrust, step-dodge-stroke. Abruptly there was a flash of red dust, and a streak of chalk scarred Longlight's left forearm. "Point," she said, and without missing a motion swept Dany's blade aside, scored on her arm, on her shoulder.

"Concetta," Dany said, and let the point of her splintan drop to the boards. They separated, bowed to each other.

There was applause from the sideline. Longlight turned. Another person was sitting with Strange and Edaire: a large, black-haired man, almost as big as Silvern, with a broad smile on his broad, pale face. He wore a black satin waistcoat, a white shirt, and a black cravat. Tucked casually into his waistcoat pocket was a silver rete and quadrant, and a heavy silver ring with a polished onyx was on his left hand.

Strange said, "My dear Longlight, I would have you meet another of our regular companions, the honorable Birch. Birch, my lady Longlight of the Great Rogue Hills."

Birch held out his right hand.

Longlight dropped to both knees. "Supergratio. . . ."

"My lady Coron," Birch said gravely, "most honored. But please rise. In Strange House we do not go about kneeling to one another."

As Longlight rose, Birch said, "I believe we are about to be something like neighbors. Can you tell me how the travel is between your country and Capel Storrow?"

"There are roads," she said, hurrying to think, "and we try to keep them open. No near Ironway, I'm afraid." She glanced at Edaire, who said nothing. "But I hope you will visit us."

Birch spread his hands. "I am your Archimage and would be neglectful if I did not. But I look forward to the pleasure."

Longlight looked at herself, the sweat on her clothes, said, "I must clean up now. . . ."

"Of course I shall see you at dinner."

Longlight, Dany, and Silvern went back to the changing room. Birch said to Strange, "I ought to retire for a bit. At dinner, then?"

Strange nodded, and Birch went out.

From the inner room, the sound of showers could be heard. Quietly, not to be heard above the water, Edaire said, "Sometimes I forget how we can look to a new guest."

Strange said, "I think Longlight will settle in well. She seems to have an independent soul."

"Yes." She drummed her fingers on the arm of his chair. "How much of it did you know, old owl?"

"Most. Her state on arrival, and Varic's. And what happened when Varic left the group to see Agate."

"So you picked me to . . ."

"I set you in her way, I suppose." He shook his head. "I'm sorry for the trouble, and after the day you'd had already. Can I make it right?"

"No need," she said, smiling. "Silvern will say the same thing, a little later. And I'm sure he will."

꧁꧂

Out of the cold shower, Longlight reached for her clothes, but Dany said, "Those are all travel-dusty. No use to put them on again, just to rest and change again for dinner. Here." She was wearing a long, white linen robe and thick-soled canvas slippers, and produced the same for Longlight. "Here, put the hood up, too. Your hair's still damp."

"Thank you, Dany."

"You fight handsome. You mean it when you cut. Next time we should use real singlesticks, do you think?"

"That could be very good. Though I liked watching your staff work. I haven't used a staff in years; do you think we could practice that?"

They talked combat all the way upstairs and into the entry hall, where a voice said, "Excuse me, I seem to be having a vision of Goddess. Double vision, in fact."

The women turned. Winterhill was standing by the secretary desk, dressed in brown riding leathers, his hand on a dispatch bag.

A young woman was with him. She had long, red hair that curved around her narrow face, enclosing it. She wore a thigh-length huntsman's coat of dark red leather, black wool trousers tucked into riding boots. The thumbs of her long-fingered hands were hooked into the coat's belt. She stepped lightly forward, took Dany's hands in hers; they hugged.

Winterhill said, "I am delighted to see you here, milady Coron. I see you've already found an adventure. May I introduce you to another friend? Reccan, the Coron Longlight. My lady Coron, Reccan of the City Lystourel."

Longlight said, "Pleased, Reccan."

Reccan smiled, without opening her mouth, and bowed, pressed Longlight's hand between her palms.

"Can she not speak?" Longlight said to Winterhill.

Reccan flicked a pencil apparently from the air, scribbled on a pad that had appeared just as suddenly in her right hand. She pulled off the top sheet and presented it to Longlight. It said, in precise block writing:

NO. BUT I HEAR YOU WELL ENOUGH.

"My regrets," Longlight said quickly. Reccan gave an elaborate shrug, a dismissive wave of her left hand. Then her left fingers moved in a complicated, rapid set of gestures.

Winterhill's hand twitched in what seemed to be a reply. He said, "Reccan would like to know if you are enjoying your stay here."

Longlight started to reply to Winterhill, then turned to face Reccan and said, "Very much so. My grandfather, as't goes, was a guest here. I wish I had known of it sooner."

Reccan wrote a note: I WISH THE SAME.

"Are you a hunter, Reccan?"

Winterhill tilted his head, with a sly look, but did not speak.

Reccan held out her hands, palms up and empty, then rolled her left hand over. A dark green pencil, unsharpened, poked out beyond her fingertips. Her fingers were long, but the pencil was longer than her whole hand. Then it fanned out into three pencils, red, blue, and green. Her left hand took the fan away, and another grew in its place. Then she crossed the two fans, and they seemed to interpenetrate, weave into a wooden lattice; Reccan tapped it on the desk to show its solidity. Then she tugged at its corners, and it came apart into six straight, solid rods again, which she pressed into Longlight's hand. Longlight looked down: she was holding a single white-painted pencil, with a freshly sharpened point.

"I see," Longlight said. "Varic spoke of you, though not by name."

The short pencil and pad came out again. WINTERHILL SPOKE OF YOU. BUT OF COURSE NO ONE BELIEVES HIS STORIES.

"Ah, I see," Longlight said. Then a breeze caught her legs, and she was abruptly reminded of her casual dress. "Your pardon, but I must get properly dressed."

"Well, I find it quite becoming," Winterhill said. "Call me a Pandekt, but simplicity has great attractions."

Dany folded her arms and pretended to look stern. Winterhill held up his hands in mock defense. "Very well, very well, no Pandekt, just a City boy loose in the woods. Milady Coron, I hope we shall talk later, when you are properly dressed. Dany, I would greet you rightly, but I taste like a horse-path. Until we can be better met, then, I take my leave." He bowed extravagantly and stepped lightly down the hall.

Longlight and Dany looked after him. Dany said, "He has no sense of place, that man, and I wonder he lives in spite of it; but it is a good strong heart inside. Worthy, do you know."

"I think I do know." Longlight looked at her robe. "And I really ought to find my room—and I know Strange told me where it was, but I've forgotten."

"Upper floor, one more above us, the end room on the court-yard side. Climb the stairs where the hall turns, and enter the last door on the right hand. It is sure to be ready for you. Of the doors in the end of the hall, the locked ones are maids' cupboards; the one you can open, with the glass panel, is the stairway. Down a floor to the service kitchen, where you may help yourself if you're hungry, or ring down for anything, anytime. Dinner will be at nine, so there is time for you finally to rest."

"Thank you."

Dany inclined her head, and touched her right earlobe. It was deeply notched, a triangular piece a thumb's width at the base cut neatly out. Her left ear was intact. Something from a combat, Longlight thought, and let it pass.

She found what should be the correct door, hesitated for a moment with her hand on the handle, imagining the effect if she should burst in on someone else wearing just a robe (admittedly a perfectly modest one).

She opened the door, saw a parlor, a corridor past a brightly lit bathroom, another room beyond. Someone was emerging from the far room, and Longlight started to shut the door.

The woman bowed quickly. "Milady? I'm Pearsy, the day chambermaid. As you hau'nt'er been here, I ought show you the room. Where things are, and the hot water and all. It can be scaldin', if you've not used patent heaters. And short on I'll bring some dinner clothes that ought fit. Will that be well?"

"Yes, very well."

Pearsy pointed out the call buttons in each room, and the bedside cord—"They're all electrical, you know, needn't worry to pull hard, the cord's just easier to hand if you're sleepy, you see"—and demonstrated the bathroom water heater, a gas-fired copper cylinder tucked away in a ventilated closet that did indeed produce scalding-hot water to sink and shower. Longlight had never seen such a thing outside a public bath—even her costly City hotel had bathwater that might have been called energetically tepid—and questioned Pearsy about the device until the maid, with just a touch of fright, said, "Do please ask Butler Bliss on't, honored, or Strange himself."

"Thank you, Pearsy, I shall."

"Dinner's at nine, honored; shall I bring your clothes about a quarter after eight? The bedside clock has a bell, if you wish to sleep till then."

"Quarter after eight will be fine."

"I'll just be on, then. Comfort to you, honored."

The maid departed. Longlight showered again in the splendid hot water; she would have stayed under longer, but realized she was starting to doze off standing up. Inside the bathroom door hung a long robe of fine thick toweling, which was good, because she didn't have the energy to dry herself in the usual way. She remembered to set the clock bell, let the robe flump to the floor, slipped between the cool linens, and after what seemed one eyeblink was waking to the clang.

She got her eyes fully open and pulled the robe on in time to answer Pearsy's knock. The maid had one arm loaded with clothing, a shoe carrier in the other; she began laying articles out on the parlor daybed. "Will anything here suit, Honored? I tried to mind your sizes, earlier."

"Oh . . . I'm sure. . . . To whom do they belong?"

"Why, the House, honored. It's Strange's way to have what his guests might need. There is an ornament case on your dresser. Do you wish any help in dressing?"

"No, thank you."

"Then I'll leave you now, honored. But ring if there's anything you need. I'll be off by dinner's end, but Ginger will answer all the night."

Longlight nodded, still looking at the clothes, and made a gesture of dismissal. The maid went out, closing the door without a sound.

She sorted through the clothes. None of it was the strictly formal costume she would have expected; most of the fashions were not what she would have chosen for herself. She thought about the visit to Ivory's and decided that her Coronage ought to take some of the Cityish style journals by post, if only to lessen the shocks in future.

She chose a narrow, calf-length black skirt, plain but for a column of small silver buttons, and over it a short jacket of deep maroon satin, laced across the midriff, with a shallow neckline as wide as her collarbones. The lacings really did call for assistance, but she managed it herself. She meant to wear her boots, but they hadn't been polished. Of the shoes the maid had brought, a pair of silver sandals with slight heels seemed best, though they were awfully open; after some deliberation, she found a pair of long, opaque black stockings to wear with them.

The ornament case gave no trouble; the jewelry in it was all of classic pattern. She put large pearl drops in her ears, and slipped the armorial pouch Ivory's had made for her over a shoulder. She suspected that weapons, even ornamental ones, were not much worn in Strange House.

She opened the door, set her unshined boots in the hall next to it for whoever took care of such things, closed the door behind her.

"That outfit looks quite lovely on you," a voice said. "May I take you down to dinner?"

She turned. It was Birch, just closing the door to his room. He was wearing a long, black gown, plain to the waist, then falling in organ-pipe pleats to his ankles. There was white lace at his throat and wrists, and he wore high-sided house shoes of soft black velvet. The small silver astrolabe that had been in his waistcoat pocket earlier now hung around his neck.

"I'd be pleased, Reverence."

He nodded and extended the hand without the ring. "This is to take, if you choose," he said, "not to reflect to. Is that well, Longlight?"

"That is well, Birch," she said, and linked arms with him.

They took the northwestern stairs, at the elbow of the corridor; the ground-floor door opened onto the air, the colonnaded breezeway to the main house. It was full dark, the nearly full moon about halfway up, flickering in the woods to the north and on the lake to the south.

Longlight said, "Do we have time to look? Just a mim?"

"All the time you wish."

In the moonlight through the breezeway, Birch did seem to tower, his black clothes making his hands and face float in the dark; but to her he seemed entirely unthreatening, a kind of hovering calm.

"Can you tell me a bit about . . . some of the other guests here?"

"I will gladly tell you whatever I am free to tell."

"Who is Dany? Has she always been Strange's . . . companion?"

"Dany first came to visit, hm, hm, not quite nine years ago. She was in the company of the Prince Jule of Tisipha, in Nisimene."

"Where is that?"

"In the Southern Hemisphere. It's not on most Lescorial maps, it's half the world away, though it's as large as Ferangard, and richer. Back then, Jule was a regular guest, what we sometimes call a Player. They came every Cold Solstice for four years, until Jule became King in her own right. That was rather sudden: the two heirs before her were killed in a hunting accident, and the King's heart failed when he got the news. So Jule got the crown, and stopped visiting. Dany would have been first guardsman in the kingdom, but instead she asked for her discharge, to come here. Did you see the notch in her right earlobe?"

"Yes."

"The earring of Royal Service was removed, and cannot be replaced."

"I see. . . ."

"She brought Strange a letter from King Jule. It said, 'I give you my best and truest servant: and I would give much more to come with her, but I cannot so easily cut off a crown.'"

"So Dany is Strange's first guardsman."

"That is certainly literally true. But Dany is also a Houseguest, and guests are not in servitude. If you would better know what exactly is between them, you should ask them both yourself, and determine the meaning from the answers you receive."

"You sound like Varic," she said too quickly.

"I should. It is one of the things he taught me."

"But . . ." She was fighting the words she wanted to say, and it only made her think more strongly of Varic, the way he had struggled. "But he does not love Goddess. He's an Anticonist."

"No, Longlight. Varic is an Atheist."

She stared. For a moment, shimmering there in the dark, Birch looked whitely dangerous, as a Demon must look when waiting for a soul to call its name. But it passed at once.

Birch said, "That is a confidence, naturally. But I think it is safe with you."

"But what have you done about this?"

"Hm. Well, I have taught him to know if a horse is properly shod and to put a good edge on cutting steels. And I have tried to show him that there are priests who care about fair wages and adequate food for the Commons as much as the ascent of souls; and, I hope, a little of how to be patient with us when we seem not to care enough about the made world. In exchange, he has taught me to fish with a cast rod and understand the difference between what Ferangarders call 'war' and what they call 'peace.' Also, someone who has held a Coron's full power and authority since he was fifteen has spoken to a blacksmith's son as if the smith's-get were one day going to have great power and authority of his own, and ought to know how to bear it."

"I mind all he is a good soul—verra kind, tho' he'll not have't out so. But—in the light of all things—"

"In the bare glow of Goddess, yes, we're small. But a candle will burn at noon. Have you ever been part of a group Craft? Or a Communion?"

"Some Communions. My father took me to Windscapel a few times. Windscapel—because the roads to Capel Storrow, as I said—"

If he noticed her embarrassment, he gave no sign. "That would have been Whitedawn's tenure. A good example. Tell me then: When she invoked Goddess—before the actual requests, just when she was speaking before the crowd—did you see something unusual, among the people?"

"Yes. There was a—glow, in everyone there." She touched her chest, just at the point of the breastbone. "A kind of heart of light."

"The lucate varus," Birch said.

"Oh. Is that what it's called?" Her voice was slightly distant. "My Quercian isn't what it should be. . . ."

"It is a little like his name," Birch said with infinite gentleness and a clarity that dispelled any hint of condescension. "And indeed, what should your Quercian be, with no Quercians around to complain? As't may: The word means 'where the light comes to rest.' That's our name for it; in Alinsea it's 'the great well,' and in Dany's country Nisimene the name means 'the burning heart.'

"But I'm wandering inside my digression. The point is that any group Craft calls on the Spirit flow of all the participants. Everyone living has power, just as we have breath in our lungs; not everyone has the—wherewithal, call it—to work Craft, just as not everyone can use breath in beautiful singing. But everyone does have a song. Varic may insist that Goddess is only a story we tell one another. But I have *seen* his light shine toward the Absolute."

"In his way," Longlight said, feeling suddenly peaceful.

"Indeed. In his way. Are you ready to go in now?"

The breezeway door led to a room quite as big as the dining

hall of some grand houses, but there was no table set, and light spilled under double doors on its south wall. Silvern and Edaire were there, apparently waiting as well. Edaire came over to take Longlight's hands. "Oh, my, you're chilled! Are you all right?"

"We were just talking in the night air," Birch said.

Edaire was wearing a loose tailcoat and broad trousers of royal-blue velvet, with white frills at wrists and throat; there was a spray of blue-edged white bellflowers on her left breast. Silvern wore a gray silk jacket and trousers, a pleated white shirt with steel studs, a cravat of figured silver-blue satin. There were some miniature medals hung at his heart pocket, and below them the steel sunburst, sword, and anvil of the Archweaponer Sorcerers.

Longlight said, "Will there be place cards inside? Or do I sit with you?"

"Though I would be most glad of your company, you may sit where it pleases you," Birch said. "At this table there is no precedence. Strange will take the window end, for ease of maneuver and as host, but the rest of us sit as it suits whatever conversation is going on—and move about if it's convenient. Don't be surprised when someone shifts a seat; do it yourself if you like. However, as you're a new visitor, we'll leave you a seat next to Strange, and open one whenever you want it."

Bliss opened the doors to the grand hall, and Dany pushed Strange's chair into view. "Honoreds," he said, "there is a table prepared. We would have you partake of it."

Longlight waited. Silvern and Edaire waited, too, until Birch extended his arm to Longlight and smiled merrily. They went in.

The room was a large square, fifteen steps or more across. A long, narrow table, set for ten, was set down the center, north to south. The south wall was a deep, three-sided bay, all windows from knee height to the high ceiling; beyond it the gardens could be seen, framed by the residence wings, and farther on, the pillars of the boathouse and the lake, all gleaming in moon-light. The east and west walls had long fireplaces, paintings, and fragments of antique carving mounted above them, and swinging servants' doors. On the north wall, between the doors they had entered through and a matching set at the northwest, there was a huge tapestry, marked with great age, illustrating the tale of The People Who Hunted Goddess in high-allegorical Midreigns fashion.

The chandeliers had been discreetly electrified, glasswicks glowing through the crystal to generally brighten the room. The fine carved ornamentation of the ceiling showed up as one hardly ever saw by candlelight, or even gas. There were candles as well, four-armed silver sticks that made a warmer light on the china and crystal and a more conversational glow on the diners.

Dany's long, full gown was of dark brown cloth with complex geometric patterns in metallic gold thread. It was held about her waist by a broad belt, more than a span wide, with decorative grommets and lacing. A chain of gold links and pearls was wrapped several times about her throat, and her single earring was a leaf of hammered rainbow bronze. She wore high-backed sandals of leather and gold. Strange still wore a pocketed robe, this one of violet satin. Across the shoulders, extending around the back, were appliqué rain clouds. His cravat was of black and white check. A silver brooch was pinned to the glossy white lapel, a castelline with a silver chain that disappeared into a pocket.

Dany put Strange at the window end of the table, then sat on his left. She indicated the seat to his right for Longlight. Silvern sat next to Longlight, Edaire next to him. Birch took the chair at the north end.

Varic and Agate came through the door in the northwest corner. He opened the door for her and walked a step behind; they did not touch. Varic was wearing a short jacket of dark blue brocaded silk, with a black satin collar, black broadcloth trousers, a black cravat with a pearl pin. Agate wore a long gown of golden satin, with violet cording around the midsection and deep vertical pleats from waist to floor; it was a modern version of the Quercian robes of citizenship. Her shoes, incongruously, were high-buttoned white boots.

Varic said, "Milady Coron, I would have you meet the Archpoet Agate, an Accredited-Master-at-Large of the Lescorial Guild."

Agate bowed and pressed her hands together instead of offering one. Longlight did the same. Agate said, "I hope we shall find time to talk very soon."

"Yes. I hope we shall."

Agate took the seat next to Birch, Varic the one next to hers.

The northeastern door opened for Winterhill and Reccan. She held his left arm with her right; with their free hands, they were conversing in gestures.

Winterhill wore a plainly styled jacket of light brown velvet, an unadorned white shirt with a flap-over front and side buttons, tan broadcloth trousers. His boots had slightly elevated heels and the wear marks of spurs.

Reccan was in a hunter's-green suit of soft wool; the jacket was flared at the wrists and below the tight waist, the trousers were cut closely and tucked into high boots of the softest brown leather. Halfway to the table, she pointed at Birch, and whatever her hands were saying was clearly emphatic.

"She says congratulations, Archimage," Winterhill said. "Not that I was surprised."

Varic said, "You probably voted," and Birch burst out laughing.

"Me in a priest's robe?" Winterhill said. "Oh, I don't know. But . . . Birch, you wouldn't mind leaving me one of your old rigs, would you? Just in case." He stood behind Birch for a moment, as if comparing their sizes. "I could smuggle a *lot,* you know."

Strange said, "Winterhill, we're hungry."

Reccan took the seat between Silvern and Birch; Winterhill, finally, the last chair, between Varic and Dany. In a wounded voice, he said, "Not only am I blamed for national hunger, but I'm the only man at the table not seated between two beautiful women—oh, sorry, brother."

Varic lowered his eyebrows and laughed.

Strange said, "Birch?"

Birch stood up, and everyone was quiet. He said, "Through grace and fortune, will and love, here we all are, together again. We celebrate the turn of season, and we celebrate one another's company, old and new."

Silvern raised his wineglass. "I say you, Coron Longlight. Lasting returns, honored."

"Longlight."

"Lasting returns."

"Thank you . . . all." She waited, unsure if a longer speech were called for. Then Birch put his glass down and said, "Reccan, would you grace the Book?"

Bliss appeared at Reccan's left elbow, holding a polished wooden tray with a box covered in flowered green fabric. Reccan raised the hinged lid and took out the precisely stacked Book. The cards seemed to rise by themselves under her fingertips.

It was an old Book. The back design, of two jesters in motley coats, was faded, though the gilding around the edges had been renewed. In a movement almost too quick to follow, she shuffled, reversed half the pack, wove them together again. Then she sat back, and from the other side of the tray, Silvern slid a packet from the center, reversed it, dropped it on top.

Reccan turned up the top card, and the second. The Five of Stones, the Maze reversed. The Five showed a square, dark plinth in the middle of a green meadow; four spherical crystals were set at the points of an incised pattern. A woman in a white gown was placing a fifth crystal at the center of the design. The Maze card had a great stone archway, with hints of walls seen through a mist beyond; one of the card-back jesters leaned against the arch, playing a double pipe.

Bliss carried the tray around the table once, slowly, so that everyone could look silently at the pair.

Birch inclined his head, said quietly, "We ask, Goddess, for fair completions. We ask for straight paths. And we take joy to be dining again together, with such good and beloved friends." He raised his wineglass, and the others followed. "You are all aware that, as I am for the first time in my life what may be called fully employed"—everyone laughed—"my visits here will be much rarer, and my holidays will be rather, hm, taken up. But I do hope to see you all on every practical occasion . . . and between times, you are cordially invited to come and have a party at my house." He looked up. "Even if it is, strictly speaking, *Hers.*"

"Honoreds," Silvern shouted, standing up, "I say you all, the Archimage Capel Storrow; I say you all, Birch, our fellow guest!" He chimed his glass against Edaire's. All who could rise did so; all joined the toast.

"To our next meeting," Birch said, and they drank again more quietly, and then sat down.

Strange said, "Now here are the wineglasses all dry, and we haven't even touched the soup. Can't have that. Bliss, will you attend?"

Bliss did. Then the soup was brought out, served from a vast porcelain tureen: clear leek, with bay leaf and garlic. After the soup, as Birch had said, the conversations became multiple and continuous—new Ironways, the theater in Lystourel, sailing weather on the Southern Gulf—and the diners began to change positions, following thoughts—volcanic-repeater guns, the meaning of a Kólyan name, the gold standard—around the table. They carried their own plates and silver; another guest would pass the crystal, or a server appear to unerringly shift them. Longlight hesitated for a while, both at the novelty of the idea and the fear of crossing traffic. Finally Strange, who rolled about as well, more limited by the need to rearrange chairs, touched her arm and said, "She can't possibly hear you from here, my dear." After the first move, it turned out to be easy.

The main courses were a beef roast in a brown sauce, and venison in thin medallions, with a delicate apple-and-cinnamon glaze. There were potatoes with cheese and cream, buttered parsnips, asparagus steamed with just a little vinegar.

". . . that's exactly the problem," Varic was saying to Silvern, rather loudly. "The more strongly a Northerner is worked up, the more softly he talks, while an Easterner gets louder as his back rises. So if things are going well, each thinks the other's angry; and when they think they're about to agree is when the knives are ready to come out. Now: can we make the Kólyan understand this, while keeping our voices within the range of human hearing?"

Reccan conversed with Winterhill and Strange using hand gestures; Longlight began to recognize the simpler signs, yes and *no* and a twiddling burst of fingers in the air that must indicate laughter. With the others, she used her pad and flying pencil; if it was not as fast as speech, she did not waste pencil-coal on long replies.

Seated next to Strange once again, Longlight said, "It's all so . . . open. It's like I imagined Parliament must be, when I was little, and my father went away to the City for a session." She laughed. "But Parliament's more like a big, formal banquet, with bad food."

Strange said, "Oh, yes, we live as the Kings of Koss in the old tales, though our servants are not quite so insubstantial as theirs. Do you know of the Pandektine reasoner Pershex?"

"No. . . . But—wait." She smiled vaguely. "I was taught Pandekt, as well as Quercian. 'No Levels'?"

"Yes, very good! Pershex was dedicated to the abolition of all divisions between master and servant, owner and renter, and so on. His favorite method of getting his views across was to attach a declaration of principles to a brick and sling it through a window. And not just a wealthy man's window: true to his principles, he would pick any window that seemed useful. The message, he said, was not for just one group, but for all of them, because they all had to change."

"I suppose, if someone named him Pershex, he must have felt a sort of destiny."

"Oh, no, he was self-made. According to the best biography, he was born as Iknatus, 'fish breeder.' He's supposed to have learned the art of brick-throwing chasing away the cats who wanted to eat his stock. There's a painting of him in the East Wing, a marvelous, crumbly old frieze. Someone was going to knock the house down, but we saved the wall." Strange pointed through the bay window, at the East Wing. "Bottom floor, a little north of center. The political parts aren't such bad ideas, at that. Pity about the bricks, though."

From three seats away, Varic turned and said, "Sometimes people of whatever class need a little noise to make them pay attention."

Longlight said, "Am I more likely to read a political statement because it has just missed cracking my skull?"

Winterhill said, "Perish that! Imagine if Pinner got hold of the idea. '*The Lystourel Herald*, through your glass each morning.'"

Edaire added, "'Subscribe for two years and receive this lovely garden shed at no extra charge.'"

Strange was leaning back, his hands pressed together, his face luminous. "Oh, this is good," he said, not really to anyone else. "This is wonderful."

Longlight said to him, "Everyone here seems to have . . . been acquainted for some time."

"This holiday, yes. Reccan is the newest, but for yourself. Sadly, we don't have as many new guests as we once did. I had hoped that, with the coming of the Ironways, the House would always be full, but it hasn't happened that way."

"I'm sorry."

"I am, too, Longlight." He was smiling again at once. "Perhaps it's just a generational ripple. My friends here are all busy with the world, running trains and government; they are generous to me in spending their spare time here."

"My grandfather spoke of . . . That was so long ago. Did you truly know him?"

"It was truly long ago. And we were most excellent friends. Is the grand battleboard still in the north wing of your castle?"

"It is."

"We spent a good deal of time around that. Whole nights, sometimes. Your grandmother was a tactician of quite fiendish skill, did you know that? If your great-uncle Rangewell hadn't played alongside me, I doubt I'd have won a single match with them."

"You're flattering my family."

"I'm giving praise where it was earned. There can never be too much of that."

"And you knew Uncle Range, too. . . ."

"Yes. Another friend much missed. You understand, this was long ago, when I was more . . . agile. Since you have come to visit me, however, may I point out that we have a battleboard of our own?"

"I would be delighted to play."

"Proposed for tomorrow afternoon, then. Plenty of time to postpone if something more interesting happens."

She felt herself hiccup a laugh, blamed the wine, and let it pass. Strange hadn't blinked. "I begin to believe that it would be impossible for something interesting *not* to happen here. Nothing interesting . . . to . . . Will you teach me logic, Master Strange?"

"As I consider it the ethical duty of all mortals who can teach to do so, to anyone who wishes to learn, I should be delighted, Longlight. But I think you are already a rather logical person."

"Not by the standard here," she said, and this time forced herself sober.

Still Strange's expression had not changed. He said, "Is there any particular question about the House that you wish to ask?"

There were a hundred or so, but she said, "Just now, just one. Where do you get those patent cylinders, that make the bathwater so blessedly hot?"

Strange laughed out loud and clapped his hands. "Oh, my dear Longlight, welcome home, welcome home."

People kept their places during dessert, frozen cream and cake and tea. And then they began drifting again.

Varic and Agate vanished rather suddenly. Then the others departed, with hugs and kisses all around. Longlight tried to follow Strange and Dany, but they turned a corner ahead of her and were gone. She walked up a flight. Her room was all the way down the hall; Bliss had told her that Varic's was on the opposite side, three doors up.

Then, to her right, she saw the open doors of the Blue Parlor, and realized she was still a floor too low. She blew out a breath in annoyance, turned at what sounded like footsteps but saw nothing. She wandered into the parlor, which was lit by fire glow and one bright lamp. On a sideboard was a decanter of dark brandy and a row of glasses. She stood there, looking at it for a while, wondering where exactly to go next.

Winterhill came through the door. His coat, and the top button of his shirt, were open. It only made him look more conventionally dashing. "Ah. Milady Coron. The others have all scattered. What about you?"

"I suppose I should go to bed."

"Perhaps. Or there may be surprises yet."

"What do you mean by surprises?"

"If I knew, would they be surprises? It is the next-to-last night of summer, milady, and who knows what may happen." He sounded entirely sober, though with Winterhill it was difficult to be certain. A bit weary, possibly.

She said, "May I ask you about Reccan?"

"If you will bring that fine brandy over to these comfortable chairs, you may ask me anything, at a full remission of the usual price."

They sat down. Winterhill poured.

Longlight said, "Could she ever speak?"

"No." He put a hand to his throat, absently undoing another shirt button. "Nothing there. She is, if you will excuse the joke, deficient in the parts of speech. That's why it can't be mended; Agate tried—but there's no healthy pattern to heal toward. You'd have to build from nothing, and sorcery's not good at that. The Craft of resection produces monsters." His voice lowered. "It's good you asked me that, and not Strange; it makes him sad."

"She came here with you today. Did you first bring her?"

"I did. I didn't know where else to take her." He took a swallow of brandy and sat back in his chair, apparently not meaning to continue.

Longlight said, "You know the hand-spelling she uses."

"Soonest's Visible Speech. Old Dr. Soonest was a benefactor of humanity in oh so many ways. He loved his orphans; he spent his fortune and wrecked his health for them. And do you know, a strange thing in this bad world, most of them loved him back.

There are half a dozen members of Parliament who came from Soonest School. All in the Commons, of course. And the City Water Commissioner, and two good judges."

"And you as well?"

"Alone a boy sat,
On a wintry hill,
And if spring's not come again,
He's surely there still.

"Dr. Soonest usually found his pupils names in the homely classics."

"So . . . Reccan was in this orphan school as well? That's where you met?"

"Here, would you push the brandy this way? Thank you." Again he poured for two.

"Are you trying to get me drunk, Winterhill?"

"I get women drunk when I want to know what they know. I drink with women when I want them to listen to me. *Or* because I enjoy their drinking company." He picked up her glass, looked into it. "Anyway, I'm not pouring it into you. Just into this. Back to the tale: no, I did not meet Reccan at the Soonest School. When the doctor died, and the death taxes consumed what was left of his money, the school was purchased by a group of enterprise progressives, who understood that a knowledge of poetry and old plays is far less valuable than practical experience of being hired out as factory labor; and jaunts into the countryside, merely to see white clouds and trees that are actually green, only encourage an unwholesome wildness. That's how I came to meet Varic, as it happens; he did what he could for us, for the School, but when unbought judges face down fair-traded ones . . . well, enough. And it's just possible that even what Reccan had was better than the school after that."

"What did she have?"

"From her sixth year, a wet basement, or a sulfurated attic, or for some nights at a time a sewer arch or the shade of a lamppost. Six years old is her earliest recall; before that, no one knows how she lived. It's possible that she isn't an orphan in the precise sense, that her parents lost her. Imagine that you have this pretty baby, agile and bright-eyed, who never giggles or coos or cries. . . ." He poured them each a modest splash of brandy.

Longlight said, as if her mind were elsewhere, "You'd never know if she were hurt or hungry. You couldn't find her except by searching every corner."

"That is so," Winterhill said, and for once the touch of sarcasm was gone from his voice.

"Reccan. 'The Counter.'"

"'True Counter,' in Southern dialect. You'll hear 'Thay's a reccan factor,' for a trader who's exceptionally honest, or 'a reccan hand' for a sailor who's particular about wages. Either one could be a compliment or not, depending. And in Alinsea, *recaigne* is the word for a true report, as opposed to *marecaigne,* travelers' tales. Strange gave her the name on her fifteenth birthday—or anyway, what we decided was her birthday."

"What was she called before that?"

"I believe 'You there' was common. I heard 'the dummy' once or twice." He paused, then said, in the tone of a comic story, "I know you're not City. Maybe you just don't have the background to understand it; no blame if that's so. She was employed as a thief, in the same way a ferret is 'employed' in the catching of rats. You take it off its leash, it runs down the hole and comes back with the prey, and then you put the leash on again. The only real difference is that most ratcatchers like their ferrets, feed them, care for them, treat them well." He stopped again, looked directly into Longlight's eyes—something, she realized not pleasantly, he had never quite done before. "Yes, milady Coron.

You've the wit to understand now. So you can tell why she was ever so slightly a favored ferret."

"She could never tell tales on her master."

"Indeed. Provided she also never learned writing or the signs. Do you know what 'lucy-goosey' is?"

"No."

"The bailiffs have started to keep books of lucives of everyone they arrest. The gallery subjects call them 'Lucy Lockets'— you remember, 'Lucy Locket lost her pocket, Kitty Fisher found it'? Kitty-fishing's showing the book to a witness, hoping for an identification. Lucy-goosey is fingering the rascal. Even someone who can't talk, or write, can point and nod. Lucivitry's been the death of many a catspaw who once dwelt safe in her ignorance."

They sat quietly for a moment. From outside, toward the courtyard and lake, there was a splash. "Cool night for a swim," Winterhill said. "Makes me want another brandy. You?" He poured for both of them without waiting for an answer.

Longlight said, "How did you meet Reccan?"

"She dropped a plate of fried rabbit, in a rather bad restaurant."

"Ye-e-e-s?"

"I was in the restaurant, looking for the gentleman who employed her. He was about to shoot me from inside a booth. She dropped the plate on his head, causing him to miss, and eventually making honest labor for the City hangman. After that, since I had effectively ended her employment while she had allowed me to continue mine, I had a certain obligation to fill the gap." He sipped his drink. "I should mention that, given the restaurant, it probably wasn't *really* a rabbit."

"That was when you brought her here."

"A bachelor town house is no place for a girl of that age, even if I had a bachelor town house. She—no, Strange should tell it if anyone does. But it took a while to make the girl into the Reccan you see."

"Your Dr. Soonest . . . I imagine he was very proud of you."

Winterhill said, as lightly as usual, "Dr. Soonest, by the providence of Goddess, died before my career really began. You must know, milady Coron, that I am a spy, a thief, a killer from behind, a reader of others' mail, a breaker of true-plighted hearts. In my defense, I may say that I earn enough money by those means to be discriminating in my choice of employers."

"I can't say anything right to any of you, can I?" Longlight said roughly.

Winterhill stood up, put his hands behind himself, strolled behind Longlight's chair. More gently, he said, "I brought Reccan here because I simply had no other idea what to do. Strange saw her and immediately guided her hands to push his chair. She was too used to taking commands to rebel—the rebellion came soon enough, and as I said, it took some time before food and silver didn't vanish every time she left a room. But Strange is never wrong in his judgment of a human being. Those who learned from Strange—Varic, Edaire, Birch—are very rarely so, and Birch has Goddess on his side as well. Myself, I do my best not to think about it."

There was a sound of people down the hall. Strange came into view, Dany pushing his chair, and after him Edaire and Silvern, Reccan and Birch. They had changed into lounging clothes, nightgowns, and bed jackets. Reccan was a striking vision in a trailing robe of deep green satin, a six-string lute over her shoulder, like something glimpsed in a forest pool. Silvern wore a long gray gown, sashed with red, and embroidered red slippers with pointed toes; Longlight remembered pictures of Kólyan chiefs.

Winterhill said, suddenly merry, "Ah, the hallway dance arrives. Do you sing, milady Houseguest?"

"House—I mean—sing?"

"They have come bearing my old black lute, and I may talk with you no more. Come down to the great hall, and sing a verse with us."

"Yes, do come," Edaire said, and Reccan plucked Longlight by the sleeve.

They crowded around Strange in the lift, except for Reccan, who skipped weightlessly down the stairs around the cage as the others descended. In the hall, the dinner table had been moved to the wall before the tapestry, and soft chairs and large cushions set about. The glasswicks were turned out, and candles and oil lamps made warm, moving light. The fireplaces hissed softly. Moonlight through the large window, direct and bounced from the pond, over-sheened everything.

Winterhill sat down in a big chair near the window, settled the lute into position, and teased a few unearthly chords from it. "Steady now," he said to the instrument. "Girth a little loose, is she?" He tuned for a moment, as the others settled in, then swung full-tilt into "The Coron of the Grange," a song every child in Lescoray knew in half a dozen verses and at least two choruses.

Silvern sang first, his voice deep and window-rattling:

> "*The Coron of the Grange one day*
> *Went walking in the rain;*
> *He scolded at the falling drops*
> *To scare them back again.*"

Longlight, feeling herself looked at, joined in:

> "*The Coron went out riding once*
> *All splendidly in green;*
> *He sat his saddle backwards so*
> *He'd know where he had been.*"

And then everyone:

> "He had the moonlight in his eye,
> The people smiled when he went by,
> And all the folk who knew him say
> That he was passing strange;
> You never saw a fellow like
> The Coron of the Grange."

On the choruses, the singers practically yelled the words *passing strange;* it was obviously a Houseguests' joke, and Strange laughed every time.

They went on through the list of songs everyone knew: "Whisky, No Water" and "The Moon Rose Red" and "Six Roads Lead to Morning." Twice Winterhill gave the lute to Edaire. On a few of the songs, Reccan followed in sign language; for others, she produced a tin pipe from the air and played accompaniment. With pipe and lute and Silvern drumming martially on a pillow, they did a "Summer's Gone to Cavalry" that might have panicked an undefended village.

During "Deep in the Blossoming Somewhere," Reccan stopped playing and looked distantly out the bay window. It was, Longlight thought, a sad and thoughtful song; perhaps it reminded Reccan of something. Then, on the last verse, Reccan slipped a note into Longlight's hand. She tilted it against the moonlight to read:

AGATE IS OUTSIDE, BY THE LAKE.

IF YOU WISH TO TALK.

Longlight nodded. She moved quietly toward the door, waited there for a moment, not really wanting to leave, and then slipped out. She wandered for a bit, thought about leaving through one of the breezeways, until one of the staff led her to a courtyard door.

The path toward the columned boathouse was easy to follow in the moonlight. Agate was sitting on the grass, her white gown fanned out, leaning back on her hands and gazing up at the moon. The whole world was black and white out here, like a steel engraving; only when Longlight looked back toward the House and saw the great hall's bay window lit golden from within was there a touch of color.

"Welcome to Strange House," Agate said.

"Thank you." A slight breeze made the water splash on the shore, three steps away, and Longlight felt her skin tighten. "It's cold."

"Chilly. Come sit. Would you like some brantcider? Tacker brought me a flask."

Longlight took a few steps, sat down on the grass. The ground was dry and surprisingly warm. "Real brantcider?"

"Strange has very fine orchards." She held up a leather-covered pocket flask. "This is new stuff, be warned. There's older and mellower in the cellars. No glasses, I'm afraid."

"That's all right." She took the flask, carefully.

Agate said, "I can endure the brush of your finger. But I appreciate your caution."

Longlight drank. The unaged alcohol scraped at her throat, and the scent of apples filled her head. There was an intense flush of warmth. She felt herself sigh.

"It's an illusion, you know."

"What is?"

"The warmth. Doesn't really do anything but freeze you faster and keep you from minding. As I'm sure you know—Westrene mountains cold a' winters." She waited a moment. "Well, go on."

Longlight said, "Seil the wind, embrace the snow."

"Cleaven to the trail beneathan . . ."

"Minden an the fire glow."

"There," Agate said, "Now we have something, just you and

I." She took back the flask, tipped it. "I can manage a plain old verse. When I'm at rest, anyhow." She turned her head, facing Longlight eye to eye. "And I thank you for your part in that rest."

Longlight said nothing.

Agate said, "Has this still not been properly told you?"

"Edaire tried to explain it to me."

"Edaire is good at that. I hope she succeeded."

"I don't know."

Agate said, "I would be sorry if you were to be angry with Varic. I should be sad if you were so on my account."

"It fails to matter to you? What we did?"

"I knew that it must have been done, because I know what would have happened had it not been done. That matters quite a lot. There is nothing to *mind* in it and much to be grateful to you for. Do you not have another companion? Where you live, off to the winter-cold mountains?"

"Varic told you."

"He would not. I know such things because I cannot keep from knowing them. Well, then. Tell me to what standard you are holding Varic, and I will tell you how well I think he meets it."

"Concetta."

"Silvern tried to teach me swordgame," Agate said, "for the rhythm, and I think for the calm, too. Do you know that method? The sphere of calm?"

"I know of it. I'm no Palion, let alone an Armiger."

"Perhaps not. Dany helped teach, but it didn't really take. Not their fault. But I do know thrust and parry, point and concetta. And the invisible circle that one crosses only at peril. There is no such circle here, Longlight. Our play is furious at times, and we acknowledge touches, and sometimes surrender, but here there is no deadly intent."

"I'm only visiting here," Longlight said.

"And I cannot be touched," said Agate. She picked up a plate from the grass. "Would you like a bit of spice bread? Varic's butler's wife baked it. There's enough to share."

Longlight took the remaining piece of the loaf. Agate put the plate down, spread her hands to either side, and tilted her head back. The moonlight silvered her hair and gave her tanned face the cast of blued metal. Her fingers moved in the grass, tapping, and Longlight felt a pull below her breastbone: sorcery winding up. Agate said:

> "Feelings endure the profoundest removal,
> Water runs down despite mountains between,
> Some things can never be called to approval,
> All things exist in the way they are seen.
> Others shall pass us as others passed by before,
> From enough distance is anything small;
> There's not the time to stand still in the corridor,
> Waiting for life to make sense after all."

In the water, a few steps out, ripples spread as if a pebble had been tossed in. They were very black in the moonlight. Then the water hardened into the face of a sundial, a pointer of transparent ice rising from the disc.

"A cool night," Agate said, and her breath fogged with the words. "But it will be a fine, bright morning. It'll have melted by eleven. Good night, Longlight."

"Will you be—"

"I'll be up to my bed soon. I am somewhat nocturnal, as you may imagine." She pointed toward the West Wing tower. "The last light in the West, serenglow. I do not *like* to be lonely, you must know."

Longlight crossed the courtyard to the East Wing, went in at the southern end. She climbed two floors and walked out into the middle hall, knowing this time, she hoped, precisely where she was going.

She paused at the door. She could hear nothing from inside, but the doors and walls here were admirably soundproof. There seemed to be a light through the transom glass above the door.

She knocked. The House, she thought, was making her very bold.

Varic opened the door almost at once. The sitting room was in fact well lit, and he did not appear to have been sleeping; his hair was untied but still brushed smoothly back. He wore a dressing gown of night-blue flannel, loosely belted, gray silk pajama trousers that drooped around his bare ankles.

"Yes, Longlight?"

"I wondered if . . . you wanted to talk. I know that it's late—"

He opened the door wide, gestured to the parlor seat, shut the door softly behind her.

There was a large secretary desk in the parlor, open, with sketch maps and some sheets of notes under a lensatic lamp. Varic gathered them together quickly, slipped them into a drawer of the desk.

"That's military work," Longlight said.

"In a manner of speaking. You're playing battleboard with Strange tomorrow. Someone has to set up the forces. So, yes, it's a military secret, from you and Strange at least. And probably Reccan and Tacker as well; they all love the game. Or did you know what I was doing, and intend a bit of scoutcraft?"

"No. I didn't know."

Varic nodded and folded the leaf table up. He pointed to a cup and pot on a side table. "I was about to get something to eat and some fresh tea. What may I bring you?"

"Nothing, thank you. Dinner was lovely. And I've probably had enough to drink—though now that you suggest it, tea might do me good."

"Won't be long." Cinching his gown a bit tighter, he went into the hall. Barely five minima later, he was back, with a tray; it held some cold smoked salmon and thin toast, a large flask of tea, another cup and saucer, and a squat cut-glass tumbler of whitely fizzing clear liquid.

Varic held out the frothing glass. "Ginger the night man sends his compliments, and this to absolve your indulgence. Drink it quick, it tastes dreadful, but Ginger's a soul of much wisdom in these matters."

She gulped the digestive and almost at once felt calmer within.

Varic put the tea in easy reach and settled into the chair facing Longlight. "Now. What did you want to talk about?"

"Ironways," she said quickly. "There ought to be Ironways in my Coronage."

"I would agree that there ought. But I'm not an Ironway engineer."

"No, but you're in Parliament. More often than I am."

He looked thoughtful. "When Silvern does your military study, he can start the work. He's an excellent mapmaker, and lucives of the potentially difficult spots—bridges, tunnels—are a great help. Have you any experience of lucivitry?"

"I know people who do. And I could learn. What about Parliament?"

"Trains are, fortunately, not usually a hard case. Deerleap's the obvious contact, but there are others; Grandview, Plasher. I'll give you the names before you leave; write to them all. You needn't be too specific; 'We have languished on our muddy roads too long' will set them in their own motions. And by all means hold a conference with your Commons leaders. Then, of course, there is the population itself."

"What do I tell them?"

"You tell them that the Coronage is going to have Ironways—don't 'propose' it or 'suggest' it. After that there are no rules, but I would offer that you should listen to what they say in response, and be prepared for the complexities."

"Prepare me."

He offered her some of the salmon. "You may as well have something interesting to do. Very well. The land everyone understands, a strip ten steps wide, so that two hundred milae of line cut only a single square mila out of the world and the tax base. But, as any number of Corons have been surprised to learn, you can't just drop a steel rule on the map and consider it a survey. The motives will only pull up so much slope. Bridges are costly, cuts and fills costlier, tunnels absolutely dear. The surveyors are efficient, but on average they can chart only three or four milae a day.

"And then the motives want water and coal, and when they want them, not when and where it might be convenient. Cold cars for fresh food need ice. Livestock must be watered and fed and exercised. People have an infinite battery of particular wants, and invent new ones daily.

"And, of course, someone gives up the land, and someone the quiet, and someone has to live with the threat of fire and the occasional dead cow and the woefully frequent dead citizen. And have you ever seen a small town try to cope with a train wreck?"

"I don't suppose that I have."

"It doesn't matter a bit," Varic said, very seriously, leaning forward in his chair. "Even the simplest line—passengers between two towns, say, or a mine to a coal yard—has a hundred small complexities and two hundred hidden dismays. But so does an ordinary road: Where do we water the horses? How do we clear the dead leaves, the snow? Do we leave the track as dirt, and put up with mud and ruts, or pave and keep the paving healthy? Have you ever read Cornflower's *The Lost Way*?"

"No."

"He claims that the Quercians had to vacate Lescoray because road maintenance exhausted their resources. I'm not sure I fully agree, but it is a sensibly argued case."

She laughed. "In the end, though, there isn't really a choice, is there? Without trade, we're allun poor, and without roads, there's no trade. Ironways, ay mind, are the best roads, despite all your cautions."

"It isn't in doubt. Goods move ten, twenty times cheaper, and almost as much faster. The worse the terrain, the more benefit."

She nodded. "So my country needs them."

Varic said, "It would seem so to me. But I've never seen your country, and you know it well. The same with your people."

"You're Northesse. It's no easier there."

He moved a hand in acknowledgment. "And now that we have talked about Ironways, what did you come here to talk about?"

It took her a moment to catch up with him. He waited for her. "It wasn't easy for me to stay here, after you went away to another lover," she said. "It wasn't easy for me to knock on your door tonight—whatever I thought you would do when you opened it, that was not easy at all."

"Strange will have explained to you about Agate and I, or found someone to explain it—no, I neither asked him to or want to know about it; I just know it's Strange's nature that he did.

"In this House . . . remarkable things happen. I've seen them, felt them. People seem capable of more here than outside, and they are very good people outside.

"But I go back to the City, where the virtues and kindnesses of Strange House do not apply, fairly indeed do not exist. I remember that I am *not* a very good person outside."

Suddenly he covered his face with his hands. His knuckles went white as his fingers compressed his skull.

"Are you well?" she said, very carefully.

He seemed to be trying to speak, but did not for several long, hard breaths. Then his hands relaxed, and he said quite easily, "I shall probably live to be a hundred and see the world no better at all than when I entered it.

"I think I must say good night now, my honored lady. I have your war to finish, and then much sand to turn preparing it." He looked at the floor. "Always shape a battleboard in bare feet; it's gritty, and can be cold, but it's far better than sand lurking in your shoes."

"Hang the war."

"Never say that. You are in Parliament." He looked at the door, started to rise, but did not. He said, "Edaire loves Silvern so much that she leaves a door to her mind itself open for him, and so he in return. Winterhill loves romance and adventure, and the knowledge that he is far more free than those who consider themselves his masters. Birch loves the soul of the whole world, and soon it will embrace him. Strange's love of the mind's reach is more intense and passionate than most people can bring their physical bodies to." He looked at her exactly as he had done in the train compartment—the second night, not the first. "Everything I know of love is through the people in this House. They are rich in affection, and no one may go poor in their company."

"You do not seem to me to wear borrowed clothes."

He stood up then, walked uncertainly to her side, put a hand on her sleeve—lightly as nothing, but it made her gasp. "One of the marvels of the House is that borrowed clothes seem to belong to whoever wears them. Now, it is very late. Tomorrow night you may well knock on my door again, and I must be able to open it."

Once again she had to push her mind backward, to comprehend what he had just said so casually. She stood up and faced him, as close as she dared. "It oughtn't be so difficult, Varic."

"Surely it ought not. But then difficulty is in my own name, while you were named to look into the sunset." He opened the door and waited.

She walked toward the stairs. The corridor was lit low, silent, and all the doors were shut. She did not hear Varic's door close behind her and had to fight not to look back.

CHAPTER 4

THE MOON AND
THE BRIDGE

Longlight woke up in darkness. She blamed the last glass of brandy—one of them, at least—rolled over in the soft, warm bed and went back to sleep.

It happened at least twice more before her sense told her it could not still be the black middle of the night. It had, after all, been the middle of the night when she'd gone to bed.

She sat partway up. It hadn't been cold enough to close the bed curtains, and over the footboard she could see a brilliant streak of light on the floor, leaking under the heavy drapes. The sunlight was from rather a high angle. She found the bedside lamp and turned its switch. Electrical plumbing (was that what they called it?) was another thing she needed more of at home, along with hot water; no burnt fingers on dark mornings. The clock read a quarter to eleven. She sighed and forced herself awake and out of bed, grabbing at her robe; then the quiet of the room reminded her of the nature of Strange House, and she relaxed, went without hurry to shower and dress.

She dressed relaxed as well: a loose shirt of blue-gray linen, belted over black trousers that she tucked into her everyday boots. In the hallway outside her room, she paused to admire a beautiful scale model in a glass case, a two-horse coach. Her suspicion that it was the coach that had brought them from the station was confirmed when she saw Roan's name worked into the doorframe, in minute letters.

It was a bright day, and the halls were sun-warmed. The second-floor breakfast room was flooded with light; it was empty, though she could smell hot bacon. The two double doors to the terrace were open.

Birch appeared in a doorway, a great black silhouette in his plain black gown. "Goddess's morning to you, Longlight. And it *is* Her own day out there. Will you please to join us?"

The terrace was built on top of the bay window of the great hall. A waist-high stone railing ran around the outer edges, and wooden poles supported a canvas sunshade, though it was rolled back now and the sun was in glory. A table was set out, with a silver tea service and a partly covered basket of muffins. Strange, in a dark red gown, sat at the breakfast table; Dany, who wore a loose golden robe, was wiping what seemed to be a bit of honey from Strange's sleeve. A covered service cart was to one side; Birch lifted the lid. "We still have some kippers and bacon, and plenty of muffins. Would you like eggs?"

"Yes."

Birch leaned through the door. "Gaily, dear," he called, and a moment later a tall, thin woman in a white apron appeared. She seemed to be floating above the floor; she was almost frighteningly animated. "Morning, morning, Lady. So it's eggs, then? How shall they be?"

"Just shirred would be fine."

"No cheese? No mushrooms? And there's a lovely bit of salmon."

"The salmon, thank you."

"And then surely a little green onion." Gaily's smile and tone made green onion seem a treasure from afar.

"I leave it to you," Longlight said.

Gaily laughed aloud. "Leave it to me, now really. Well, I'll wrestle it out as I can, thank you, milady." She floated away.

Strange said, "The story is that, as a baby, she was named Grace, in hope. Then for her first half year she never smiled nor giggled. I think her parents were too worried to notice if she was developing any graces or not. The priest said, 'Call her Gaily. It can't harm, and if she doesn't laugh by her first birthday, we'll try Grace again.' You can see the result."

Birch pulled back a chair for Longlight. "Naming babies is a more daunting prospect than most people imagine. I've been asked only twice."

Longlight said, "How did it go?"

"Oh, one's eyes made him a Bluely for certain, and the other seemed to like Pineblossom. Fortunately I'm a country priest. If people want a Quercian name, or Pandekt, or something from literature, they usually manage on their own." He paused, thoughtful. "Strange, is there one of those *Ancient Names and Their Meanings* books around somewhere?"

"That should be in the downstairs annex. Or else upper west. Black or green tea, Longlight?"

"Black, please. No milk. Is there honey?"

"Certainly. And we still have muffins with bacon, apricot, and—no, the brown bread are gone."

"Oh. . . ."

"One of each, then. We probably won't have a formal lunch today. Hard to say when anyone else will be awake."

"I'm not the last one up, then."

Strange laughed. "Reccan's about somewhere; she hardly needs sleep at all. But certainly not Varic or Winterhill. Edaire and Silvern, well—I don't expect to see them before dinner, and possibly not until tomorrow." Strange's smile made the point without any hint of the improper.

Dany passed the butter and honey. A breeze rustled the canvas shade, and somewhere a bird sang. Across the courtyard, in the lake, as predicted, Agate's ice sculpture was entirely gone.

Gaily danced onto the terrace, bearing a covered platter. She whisked away the lid, and a cloud of scent, sharp and delicate, drifted up from the eggs with salmon. They glistened and shivered on the plate, rosy and golden.

Birch held his breath, said, "Thunder and boom. Dany, give me a muffin quick, before—"

"The hens won't miss them," Gaily said, "and the salmon's past caring."

"Oh—I suppose if you would, Gaily—"

Gaily said to Longlight, "You can give him a taste if he starts to pace and fret, but don't you wait him, or yours'll go cold, and he'll wait your seconds, and we'll be up to our eyes in cold fish and eggs." And she was gone again.

Longlight said to Birch, "*Would* you like some?"

"It would . . . be good for me to wait."

Strange was laughing silently, rocking in his chair, holding Dany's hand.

Longlight tasted her breakfast. It was, for just a moment, disappointing; nothing short of transcendence could have followed that presentation. But it was good beyond any question, the onion unobtrusive below the smoky-sharp fish. Bread crumbs, soft without being mushy, gave it texture, and there were at least two more ingredients she didn't wish to stop and identify.

Next to her, Birch ate a bacon muffin without any butter, sitting up straight in his chair. His eyes gave him away, though.

Longlight saw him, then, as he must have been when young: a big, happy boy, from a happy world where his size and gentleness did not mark him out as a fool or worse. Perhaps he had been scraped a little by the inevitable, meaningless cruelties of childhood, but not scarred by them.

As Gaily delivered Birch's plate, Strange said, "Longlight, do you still wish to play battleboard at four?"

"Of course."

"Then I will see you then if not before. Remember that the House and grounds are yours: if there's anything you desire, ask, and someone will find someone who'll try to remember where to find it." Dany pushed him back into the House.

Birch said, "I need to get some things from the Dark Room, for tomorrow. It would be nice to have someone else along. Would you care to come with me?"

"The Dark Room? Why—yes, I will."

"I will appreciate it. Do finish your breakfast. There's no hurry."

So they had more tea, and shared the last apricot muffin. Gaily did come back to check that more eggs weren't needed; told no, she rolled the serving cart away, singing something about an Ironway motive, with a great deal of "Huff, huff, *chuff*!" on the chorus.

Birch said, "Shall we go?"

They walked down the central stairs, the ones circling the lift—Birch said, "I prefer to leave the car wherever Strange did"—to the lowest level, and went through the door that did not lead to the arenetto. It opened onto a short corridor, lit adequately by glasswicks. Birch opened the first door on the right, held it for Longlight. As she passed, he produced a large bronze ring with three keys. Two were large but conventional finger bones; the third was about a span long, with a complex, slotted web.

Beyond the door was a rather small room, a little larger than one of the apartment parlors upstairs. It was lined with maple bookcases, from just above knee height to the low ceiling. Below the books was a bronze band, deeply cut with a knot pattern, and below that old, dark leather wainscoting. On the far wall, a glass case held a collection of coins displayed on plum-colored velvet. In the middle of the room were a large, soft chair and footrest covered in green plush, with a little bronze side table and a standing lamp.

It was a cozy little study, but it certainly was no Dark Room. Unless—Longlight looked closely at some of the books: masonry, gardening, history of arms and armor.

Birch said, "This is the annex library. Remind me to look for that names book when we come back out."

"Out?"

Birch grinned, a boy full of mischief, and knelt by the left-hand wall. He ran his fingers along the metal band, then took out the large key. Its web fit into a bit of the engraved pattern. Birch pushed it into the slot, turned it firmly. Within the wall, there was a series of muffled ratchetings, like a clock winding up to strike. Then came a sort of brazen groan. Birch withdrew the key, hooked his fingertips beneath the bookcase, and swung a section of the wall outward.

Longlight said, "I think I'm impressed."

Birch grinned broader yet. "It's something of a joke. There are a number of secret places and trick panels in the House, but none of them are very sinister. No peepholes in the bedrooms and baths, I assure you. Strange calls it the House's sense of humor. This way."

A shelf just inside the hidden door held some small lanterns and a box of phosphors. Birch struck a fire and lit two lamps, giving one to Longlight.

They were at the end of a hallway not much more than a step wide and barely higher than Birch's head. The walls were rough mortared stone; every few steps there was a wooden arch with an iron lamp hook. The floor was smooth concrete. The air was quite cool and fresh, with a faint draft in their faces.

Longlight said, "Are there set traps?"

Birch laughed. "No. But mind how you go; the walls scrape hard, as I've reason to know."

Longlight counted thirty of her own paces, just over twenty-five steps of measure, and four of the wooden arches. Then the hall turned right and ended in an alcove housing a large iron door that looked stout enough for the National Treasury.

Birch put a hand against the iron door, turned the heavy key ring over in his big hand. "Has Strange told you about this place? Not the Room, I mean, but the place it occupies?"

"No."

"When the House was being built, the crew digging the foundation broke into an underground chamber. The entrance had caved in, and there were two skeletons inside. It had been a sacred place, and a Seer's Seat. Eventually the local records were located—this was two hundred years ago, of course, and Corons weren't answerable to Parliament for this sort of thing—and it was worked out that the occupants were a priest and acolyte who'd disappeared about four hundred fifty years before the picks opened things up. The papers are in the House, if that sort of thing interests you."

"Is it still a Seat?"

"No. The lines of power are long broken. And the temple," he said, his voice even and calm and serious, "was one of those old faiths that any conscientious priest counsels against and the law sometimes has to forbid. However: I know of no danger within, physical or sorcerous."

"I see," she said, feeling a very small chill.

"I've been thinking on this ever since you asked about traps. Spiritual danger is harder to define than a crossbow and trip wire, but I don't think you're either weak of spirit or lightly suggestible. I tell you this because you ought to know it, not because there's anything you should fear."

"My own house has a Dark Room," she said. She did not say that it was at the center of a dank stone maze, purpose-built by her ancestors, and that a duty of every Coron of her line was to design a new scheme of death traps around the Room.

Birch nodded. "Usually Strange keeps the keys, of course. In Dany's country they have something like our Rooms, a house in every town, called *the end house.* But only a priest may go there, and afterward, the priest has to walk around town for half a day, so that any Demons following will lose interest. Our ways are hard for her, sometimes; it's her duty, as she sees it, to be with Strange, but when he goes to the Dark Room, well, that's the End House and she can't enter.

"But things fit together, in their own ways. In Nisimene, a very wise person may have the status of a priest, though the sage— they're called *Sky's-Bridges*—never claim such status, if you fol- low that. Agate pointed out to Dany that Strange was without question a Sky's-Bridge, and that put everything in place."

He put one of the smaller keys into a hole central on the iron door. There was a click, loud, but rather anticlimactic. He pushed the door open, with a visible effort. "Go in; the door is sprung to close."

She did so. Her lantern lit up a dancing skeleton, and she caught her breath. It was a painting on the wall, in colors that must once have been very bright. One bony hand held a jester's taddelix, shaking the clappers; the other pointed the way ahead. The bones were followed by flesh, a long line of people dancing after. Their clothes were of the earliest Midreigns and repre- sented the whole world: nobles and beggars, bailiffs and thieves, priests and dung-rakers, a sorcerer wreathed in thunderheads and a child clutching a toy horse. Longlight moved her light, following the mural procession halfway around the room. They were all the living, of course, on their way to the end. When the march was staged for festivals, the people in costume were called *Mori dancers.*

The dancing-master Death was wrapped in a white ribbon with an inscription: the letters were antique and faded past legibility, but Longlight knew what it said:

Who or why or when or whether,
You and I shall dance together.

The door closed with a boom and a click. Birch held up the two small keys on the ring. "One to enter, the other to leave. So you know." She nodded. In her memory, the traps in her own house had never caught anyone, but they were lethal enough. A Dark Room was the spiritual drain of its house, the place where rage and terror, all the nightside emotions, collected. If one believed there to be any reality to that, the Room had to be guarded by real force.

Birch set his lantern into a polished metal bowl, filling the room with hazy light. The chamber was an imprecise circle six or seven steps across. About half the circumference was plastered, with the Mori mural painted on; the rest was raw stone, with alcoves and ledges holding idols of stone and metal and ancient wood. At the center of the room was a stone chair with a low back, carved and pierced over its whole surface. Soft metal had been hammered into the grooves. It was a kind of work old before the Quercians had developed any thought of building an empire; before they had learned to build boats.

Birch bent before a heavy wooden cabinet, opened the doors. Inside were shelves, holding at least ten objects wrapped in velvet. He carefully drew out two of them, placed them on the top of the box. One was flat, the other narrow. The cloth wrapping them was old, though not seriously worn; it had faded to a dusty rose color, from either crimson or purple.

Birch closed the cabinet doors. "Take a look," he said. "I won't unwrap them again until tomorrow in the Bright Room."

He folded back the velvet from the flat object. It was a disk of metal, with inlays of wood and stone veneer around the edge. At the center, a circle of the underlying metal had been polished to what must once have been mirror brightness, though now it was gray and hazy. The long wrapper contained a tray displaying a short sword, no longer than Birch's forearm. It had a broad, double-edged blade with a triangular point, in dull gray metal that was glass-smooth, a crude design executed with great smithing skill. The hilt was in the same fashion: a heavy metal T that would have been hopelessly clumsy to hold in a fight, but was crisply and carefully worked, with unfaceted gems, like fat drops of colored water, set precisely into the metal.

"When I was twelve," Birch said, "some people from another town brought my father one like this; it had been damaged, I don't know how. They may never have said."

"He must have been a very fine smith."

"No, he wasn't. He was a good worker, you understand, but he was just an ordinary ironsmith, never did jewelry work, nor even weapons, beyond sharpening a soldier's bayonet or little knives like mine. But they insisted, and left it with him. He stood in the smithy, looking at it, and said—I was there with him, but he wasn't talking to me—'I don't even know how to pray for the mending.' And I said—*something* said—'It is a work for Coris, because the sword is no longer a thing of mortals, but of Nature.'

"He called Coris to guide him at the forge, and he mended the sword. He said later, 'They won't break it again, I'm sure of that.' We didn't talk about it for almost three years." He wrapped the cloth around the sword again, folding and tucking it with care. "Twelve to fifteen is a long time not to talk about a thing like that."

Longlight said, "Did it happen again? The—"

He looked down at the scroll box. "Yes. She spoke to me again. And when I was fifteen, we went to talk to our priest—her name was Enolesia, which if your Pandekt won't stretch, I won't explain—and, well, now I am bound for Capel Storrow."

"What does the Imagery's name mean?" she said, hearing her voice echo off the stone walls.

"Oh, it was 'Sorrow' originally. A few hundred years ago, someone tried to soften it with a hard sound."

His voice was hollow and ringing as well. Longlight looked up from his hands, lightly resting on the sword tray, to his eyes. For a moment they seemed to flash. She thought of Varic's eyes, in the whip of lights past the train window. The skin of her palms felt tight, and she thought of dark rooms, of mazes and set traps. She could hear the bowstring snap. She could feel the trip weight fall, its cord running in the sheave—

Suddenly Birch had his arm around her, holding her up. The sword and mirror were wrapped and tucked under his left arm. "It's all right," he said. "It happens. We'll go now."

When the lamp was removed from the reflector, the Dark Room was suddenly very black indeed. The iron door closed behind them, and they went back up the tunnel, followed by shadow.

They emerged into the book-lined room. Reccan was curled up snug in the green chair; the lamp threw a bright circle on the book in her lap. Another half dozen books were stacked in easy reach. She turned pages carefully, but with remarkable speed, gobbling down words by the plateful.

As Birch shut the concealed door, Reccan turned to smile at them. She held up a finger, pointed at a spot along the shelves, moved her hand in Dr. Soonest's sign, and then went back to her furious reading.

Birch went to the indicated spot, counted books. "Twelve,

thirteen—ah. Thank you, Reccan." She waved without looking up, as Birch pulled *Names: Their Voices* from the shelf. Without further sound, they left the annex.

As they climbed the stairs, Longlight said, "I suppose she's only recently learned to read."

"That is so. Did Varic tell you?"

"Winterhill did. . . . Seeing her like that, going through the books . . . she made me want to—to catch up. To not waste time."

"I think time is hard to truly waste," Birch said. "What Reccan learned from the book of streets and darkness saved Winterhill's life, as he will explain to you if you ask, and through that she was rescued. Play keeps us happy and agile, in mind and muscle; sleep and good meals keep us alive. We can misspend time— hurting people, ourselves included, making the world worse— but to 'waste' time—to get no motion at all, good or bad—to do that one would have to be not alive at all. Which, if you like, makes any untimely death the worst of wastes."

"Yes, I see," she said. "And Winterhill did tell me, about the tavern."

"Not a pretty story. But the spoon was what she had to hand, and a man will guard his eyes over almost any other threat." He stopped climbing then, looked her straight in the face; she realized that her mouth was open wide, and shut it. "I may have gotten the story wrong," Birch said with a distinct mildness, "and of course Winterhill was there, and I was not."

They paused at the first-floor landing. Birch said, "I shall take these upstairs. I'll see you at dinner, if not before."

"In your way," she said without thinking, but Birch just smiled and said, "And in yours."

She waited in the entrance hall until Birch's steps had died away above. She thought about hunting through one of the libraries, then decided that she still wanted someone's company. She went upstairs to the breakfast room. Winterhill was there, spreading strawberry jam thickly on a muffin. A pile of bacon was to one side, a pitcher of apple juice to the other. He was wearing a purple dressing gown over a collarless white shirt and loose black trousers, stockings, and backless leather slippers. "Another survivor," he said. "Will you join me?"

"I've—"

Before she could finish, Gaily had appeared. "Yes, honored? What else would please you?"

"Just some black tea and honey, thank you. And another glass, if Winterhill will offer some of his juice?"

"By all means," Winterhill said. He watched Gaily leave, and said, "I begin to think my lady Coron would have me say something improper."

"Would it be so . . . difficult?"

"It would be the easiest thing in the world." He took a large bite of his jam muffin, chewed meaningfully, swallowed as punctuation. "And having the swindler's expert distrust of easy things, I shall allow it to get . . . more difficult."

"I have something more difficult to ask you, then."

"I am *also* extremely lazy. But please ask."

"I'm playing battleboard later today. Reccan's playing as well. Could you teach me some of the manual speech?"

"School opens as soon as I finish my bacon. Kindly press the bell for Gaily, and I shall obtain something to keep my throat damp while I harangue you."

She did, and another pitcher of cider arrived. Winterhill cleaned his lips and fingers, sat forward in his chair, and pushed his shirt cuffs back with a fine flourish.

"First, inflection. You usually flash an inflection sign before a statement, though it can come anywhere. Experienced speakers can get a lot from where they put the stress flash. Now, hold your hand flat, fingers together. Yes. That means a plain flat statement. You can get away without it. Fan your fingers for imperative or emphasis—you can just gesture emphatically, but if you just use the hand, no one else will know you're shouting. Hand like this for a question. And *this*"—he tapped his first two fingers against his thumb, twice quickly— "is sarcasm: I mean the reverse of what I'm saying. Now that you know this one, watch for it: sometimes signers who can speak use the gestures as well. I imagine you can think of one or two uses for that."

"I can."

Winterhill nodded. "Then on to some basic vocabulary. . . ."

❧

The battleboard room was on the ground floor, near the arenetto. It was windowless, but lit brilliantly by glasswicks in a hanging fixture of polished brass and green glass.

The board itself was a wooden box a span deep, two steps across, and six long; it was on heavy wooden supports bolted with iron, to support the considerable weight of the sand that filled it. There was plenty of space all around the board, with side tables, paper and pencils, rolling carts to hold the miniature armies, and storage cabinets all along one wall. At either end was a door to a small side chamber, so the players could confer out of the enemy's hearing.

Except for the electrical light, the room was very much like the one at her own home. She remembered what Strange had said, about playing with her uncle and aunt, and wondered if the similarity was just a coincidence.

Tacker was standing behind Strange's chair, wearing a white

shirt, black canvas trousers, and a black vest with pockets for her cheroots and phosphors. Her hair was pulled back and tied casually with a leather braid. She seemed completely at ease.

Reccan was crouching beside the playing table, to see it from a trooper's eye level. She wore a loose tunic of green and gold flannel patches, with a sleeve pocket to hold her writing pad, narrow trousers, and deerskin boots laced up her calves.

Varic was in shirtsleeves, with a canvas shoulder satchel for his measuring tapes, cards, and other game equipment. He said, "It is a lovely spring day in our constantly embattled little nation." He pointed to a village of model buildings set up about a third of the way from one end of the table. Roads led from the town center to all four edges of the board; a river of blue glass, the sand carefully brushed into its banks, curved around the village in an L. "The stalwart footmen of the Blue Army are valiantly defending this small but important crossroads against the dashing cavaliers of the Gold Army, which I'm sure has a perfectly legitimate claim to its annexation. That concludes the political portion of the game. Since this is Blue's country, they will be allowed to see . . . well, at least the principal elements of Gold, and then prepare their defenses at least partially concealed."

Varic went to one of the wheeled carts, rolled it away from the wall. Miniature infantry and cavalry, painted in shades of gold and bronze and tan, stood ranked upon it. "Strange, Tacker, these are your initial forces. Your maps show the limits on placement. Reinforcements as yet unscouted by the defenders—if any"—he arched his eyebrows and smiled—"will be stored in the top drawer of the cart. Reccan, Longlight, your army is waiting in that conference room, same arrangement. After examining the table, you may wish to look it over and make some preliminary dispositions, and then come back to watch the enemy approach. I am, of course, at your service for any questions." He went to the side of the room, poured himself a glass of tea.

Looking from the defenders' end of the board "north" to where Gold would come from: there were hills to the east, built up from sand supported by slabs of wood a finger thick. A long, narrow, razorbacked ridge ran along the east side main road north, the road that would have to be the enemy's main avenue of approach. At the river just before it entered the cluster of buildings, the road crossed a substantial bridge, of wood carved and painted as stone. Across the river to the northwest of the village was a wooded area, perhaps a hundred tiny wooden trees leafed with green sponge. On the village's west side, the river was crossed only by a small wooden bridge that looked too small to bear cavalry. The stream banks around it, however, were shallow, and Longlight supposed that the river was fordable there.

Looking at the hills and the sculpted crossing, Longlight had a sudden, deep, pleasant thought of Varic working at the board, sometime in the dark hours of last night, his shoes discarded in a corner, his sleeves rolled up, shaping the sand with careful, patient strokings of his fingers.

Longlight made the sign for *Go?* and without a blink Reccan gestured *Certainly.* They went into the side room, where maps and blank pads for orders were laid out neatly on a table.

Their army, painted in shades of blue, with white facings and silver metal, stood neatly ranked on one of the rolling carts. They looked very trim in their upright pewter ranks, and their regal-blue banners had tassels of fine silk thread, but there were disappointingly few of them: perhaps half as much infantry as had been visible on the Gold cart; two squadrons of horse, one with muskets, one without; a single horse-drawn artillery piece, with its powder wagon; and an "organ gun," essentially a row of muskets bolted to a wagon and rigged to fire simultaneously, after which it was useless for the fifteen or twenty minima necessary to reload and prime all the barrels. They were sometimes called *bridge guns,* because the one place they could be useful was at points where the enemy had to crowd together—as at bridges. Longlight picked up the model—carefully, by its wooden base—and said, "I suppose we know where this goes."

Reccan grinned and nodded. She was running her hands over the maps, tracing out possible lines of enemy approach. She tapped her knuckles on the long ridge that paralleled the main road into town, then made the sign for an exclamation.

Longlight was confused for a moment, trying to interpret the sign; she felt inarticulate, rather painfully stupid. Then she said, "Surprise?"

Yes.

"There aren't any gaps at all in that ridge, are there? Our maps should show them even if theirs don't."

None. Then Reccan pointed to a notch in the far side of the ridge, something like a fishhook, open toward the town.

It was clear enough: troops hiding in the hook would be invisible to an advancing force at least until they were alongside— possibly, with care and luck, the ambush could go undetected until the Gold Army was entirely past, ready to be taken from behind.

"That would be a fine spot for the mounted muskets. There's no way back, of course—if we send them and Gold *doesn't* come that way, they'll miss the whole battle. And we'll surely miss them."

Reccan picked up one stand of the sword-armed cavalry, just two figures on a slab, and put it down on the ambush notch.

"Good. Write the order." Such a tiny force couldn't do much damage, but they could almost certainly stay unseen until the best moment; a charge then would produce enough confusion and noise to alert the defenders in town to enemy beyond the ridge.

Longlight looked at the other approach to town, the small bridge and ford over the western bend of the river. To the north was a fairly large woods. Outnumbered forces had been using forests to cover ambushes ever since there had been warfare; but, much as with the ridge, any troops they sent there would be far away on the wrong side of the river when the attacking forces reached the town.

The town was what counted; Varic had made that clear. But unless the estimate of enemy strength was wildly off—or there were some hidden factor, as if the Gold Army were green recruits who would panic and run at the first shots—there didn't seem to be any way of stopping them outside the town.

Longlight looked at the map again, at the spot where the bridge and ford were marked. It was an exceptionally small bridge, and would certainly be a bottleneck for infantry, but the horse would simply ride through the shallows—

Longlight banged her fingertip on the bridge. Reccan looked at it. Carefully, Longlight gestured her idea. When she was finished, Reccan took hold of her hand and adjusted its position. Then she took a pad and wrote, in her rapid and precise hand:

I DO NOT THINK IT WOULD BE A GOOD IDEA TO GIVE THE EN-EMY HORSES A BATH JUST NOW. BUT MEETING THEIR CAVALRY AT THE FORD IS AN EXCELLENT THOUGHT. VARIC DID SAY IT WAS SPRING.

They sat down to write their orders.

About a quarter of an hour later, Varic knocked at the door-way. "Gold have deployed, if you would care to see."

Gold cavalry were on the north road, beginning about half a span south of the edge of the table. They were in column of fours, six ranks deep. Behind the metal figures, stretching past the end of the long ridge, were wooden blocks the size of figure bases. Some were painted with symbols, the inverted V for horse and the slashed circle that was an infantryman's weapon and shield; others were blank. They represented troops too far away to precisely identify—or rumors of troops who were not there at all.

Varic said, "Do you wish to make any changes to your orders?"

"I believe not." Longlight looked at Reccan, who nodded in agreement. They had known the enemy must come down the road; there was nothing surprising in the way they came. At least, not yet.

Tacker pushed Strange into their planning room. Reccan retrieved the Blue Army on its cart. Longlight handed the Blue deployment plans to Varic, and he began checking the table to see what troops might be visible to the Gold vanguard. He took sightings with a long white stick, marked with the distances of movement and ranges of shot.

Reccan pointed to the ambush notch on the east side of the ridge. Varic turned slightly away, as if to hide his smile, and said, "They see no one yet. It's a comfortable spot to wait, though. I'll ask you both to step out for a moment, now."

In the side room, Reccan wrote, DO YOU THINK THEIR HORSE ARE ALL ON THE ROAD AFTER ALL?

"Not at all. They'd be mad to cram them all onto that bridge, even with our weakness in guns."

When Varic called them back, he had placed a few of their advance infantry at the tiny west-side bridge, and indeed the first ranks of Gold cavalry were visible, circling around the woods toward the ford. Some Blue blocks were placed about the town—less than half of them, Longlight noticed, representing real troops. The position of the organ gun was marked only by an artillery symbol.

Varic said, "Does anyone wish to give an immediate fire order?"

Tacker conferred with Strange. She crouched at the end of the table, looking toward the stone bridge and the possible gun beyond it, squinting one eye and rolling up the cheroot in the corner of her mouth. Finally she said, "No."

"No," Longlight said.

"Very well," Varic said, and began moving troops.

For three moves, very little happened. The advance column of Gold cavalry drew closer to the town, but it was a long road, and they were still too far away to charge.

Varic paused, scribbled a note, handed it to Longlight.

TWO RANKS OF HORSE, TWO ABREAST, HAVE JUST PASSED YOUR SCOUTS BEYOND THE RIDGE.

She showed the note to Reccan, who held up two fingers. Varic nodded.

"Why not?" Longlight said.

Varic took four cavalry from the Gold cart and placed them on the table, just beyond the notch. Then he placed two Blue horses behind the Gold. "Move to impact," he said, and handed Longlight a leather case.

She uncased the battle gauge, then paused to look at it. Like any gauge, it had movable slides, marked in red and black and gold for troop types and strength; the player adjusted it for the numbers engaged in combat, moved the bottom slide according to a die roll or card play, and read off the result. But usually they were made of printed cardboard, the fanciest just paper glued to wood. This one was of fine hardwood, with brass ferrules, with the slides running in milled tracks, not just butted together. The markings were engraved and filled with colored ink.

She turned the gauge over. Neatly inked letters signed it PLUMB. She said, "This is a remarkable piece of work."

"So is Plumb," Tacker said. "Though he doesn't see the guests much. Shy, a bit, and always busy. This is a big house. But he'll be happy to hear you liked his gauge, if I may tell him so."

"By all means do."

Varic produced a walnut dice box, a tray lined with padded green felt, with a rack of ivory dice to the side. He held it out to Reccan, who selected a die.

Longlight set the gauge—working a bit slowly, just to feel the fine motion of it—and Reccan tossed the die. It showed a 6. Longlight adjusted the gauge and handed it to Varic.

"Definitely a rout," Varic said, to no one's great surprise.

A 1 meant the troops had been little short of cowardly, a 6 called for medals all around. Each side also had five cards, numbered 1 to 6, held apart. At any time, instead of a random roll, a player could instead choose one of those numbers—but those, once used, were gone. When to play the 6 could be a crucial matter of strategy. The 1 and 2 were not often used, but there were ploys that called for an attack to falter, and draw a counterattack into a trap.

The Gold troopers fled off the east edge of the board. They might rally and return later, though in this case it could not make much difference. Longlight said, "Who else is there?"

"No one that your people can see," Varic said. "Apparently just a scouting expedition."

One of the staff brought tea, and they paused for a cup. Everyone sat but Reccan, who kept circling the table, taking sightings.

Strange said, "There's an old story that the Royal Marshal, being told that his officers were playing a game, stamped into the room proposing to, quote, hang the one most culpable and sack the remainder. But he saw the board and the pieces, and immediately ordered that every fortress in Lescoray should have a set."

Longlight said, "Which Marshal?"

"Oh," Strange said innocently, "knowing that would quite spoil the story."

A few moves after play resumed, more Gold cavalry appeared to the west of the woods, north and west of the bridge and ford. Longlight moved some of their musket-armed infantry across the bridge and waited. It could have been another feint, a few horse to distract them.

It wasn't. Varic placed a column of fours eight ranks deep on the packed sand, wheeling round the edge of the forest.

"Well, then," Longlight said, and Reccan made a sign that probably meant much the same thing. "Form line, three ranks deep," and Varic brought out more miniatures to follow the command.

"Fire by introduction," Longlight said, loud enough to bring Tacker's head up sharply. But she was grinning around her cheroot, and said right back, "It's to them or tail-for-home now, braves—Flag Centurion, sound the charge!"

Varic put down a line of cotton, stained gray to represent gun smoke, as the front rank of Blue musketeers fired. Tacker set her gauge, and Reccan rolled a 4. Two horsemen vanished from the charging column.

The rear rank of musketeers advanced through the just-fired line, prepared to shoot while the others reloaded. Fire by introduction was a continuous process of load, advance, fire in alternate lines, so that the battle line was continuously firing and continuously rolling forward.

Each wave of fire picked another one or two riders from the front of the column. Varic said, "Test for losses."

Strange said, "Use the six," and Tacker drew the high card from their packet.

"Their nerve holds," Varic said, and moved the charging horse the last distance to contact with the musketeers. "Test for impact."

Longlight looked at their own packet of cards, then pointed at the main deck, making a question sign to Reccan. She nodded and tossed the die. It came up 3.

Varic checked his tables. "The infantry hold. This is going to be rather vicious." Battle gauges were set, dice were rolled. To no great surprise, almost the whole first line of musketeers went down under the impact of charging horse. Musket fire was not allowed at close quarters—it was in fact almost impossible to reload muskets when so engaged—and given roughly equal numbers now, the advantages of height and mass would tell. The remainder of the second and third ranks of infantry broke and ran. Varic pointed with his measuring stick toward the far end of the table. "They won't make a sharp left turn to enter the town. Straight back; you'll have a chance to rally them before they leave the board."

Longlight said, "Contingency order."

Reccan handed an order slip to Varic, who read it with interest, then put it on his tray of equipment without further response. He said to Tacker, "Follow-through move," and measured out the advance of the victorious cavalry.

"Left wheel and form line," Tacker said, "and then across the river."

Varic adjusted the formation of the Gold horsemen. Then he put the powder wagon model on the table, at the end of the narrow footbridge. "With a suicidal effort, the caisson team sets a fuse to their powder." Varic dropped a thunderball of black-and-orange cotton on the bridge.

The room was still for a moment. Then Tacker burst out, "The *river*. I should have *seen* it."

Strange looked at Varic. Varic pressed his fingertips together and said nothing. Strange said, "Have the horse regroup and advance to the crossing anyway. It can do no harm to see for certain, and they are a long way from the point of decision if the water *is* too high to cross."

"It is now half an hour past five, in the larger world," Varic said. "Does anyone wish to concede?"

Tacker frowned. Longlight looked at Reccan, who folded her arms in an almost quarrelsome fashion.

Longlight motioned for Varic to step aside, asked quietly, "Would we then have some unexpected reinforcements on the way?"

"I fear not today."

She laughed. That was an old quote, from Lescoray's Quercian age: Three Imperial legions had moved north, to bring that part of the country under control. In the forests of Black Pines, they had been ambushed and cut to pieces. The commander, confronted with the local general, said, "This cannot have happened. The Bright Empire is invincible." To which the native, quietly as a Northerner, replied, "I fear not today."

Tacker said, "Let's go out glorious. Charge the bridge."

"Oh, Tacker, really," Strange said, "but I think you have a point. Pewter and paint can afford to be gallant. Besides, I shall feel much better if there *are* some Blue foot lurking in those woods.

There were not, of course. The organ gun gave a surprisingly good account of itself, bringing down the front ranks of horse and forcing the rest to pause and regroup; but behind them were companies of fresh infantry.

As the Gold foot reached the bridge, Varic said, "It would be interesting to play out. Street ambushes against formed infantry."

"But very slow," Strange said.

"True. I was somewhat too ambitious, as usual." He turned to Longlight. "You couldn't win it on numbers; you barely might if you could wear down Gold's morale. What do you say?"

She looked at Reccan, who gave a shrug that needed no special knowledge to interpret. "Very well, then. Concetta."

Strange rolled his chair to Longlight, held out his hand for her to shake. "Thank you for an excellent game. I shall see you at dinner shortly. We won't be dressing up tonight." Tacker pushed him out of the room.

Varic was stacking up the maps and papers. Longlight said, "It was a very good game."

"Too complex. I shouldn't have had both all that field maneuvering and the street battle. But thank you. And thank you, Reccan." He handed her a stand of figures, which she placed carefully in a felt-lined wooden case.

Longlight said, "I shouldn't have introduced fire. If we'd stood the bridge and braced, we might have held it. And survived."

Varic said, "Or if you'd had modern weapons. Mirit Opranas, or Challenge repeaters."

Longlight inclined her head, said, "That demonstration at the Embassy must have impressed you."

"Large volumes of gunfire generally do, in one way or another."

"I'm sorry. I spoke quickly."

"Nothing to be sorry for. But as the losers—however narrowly—you and Reccan owe a penalty."

"What might that be?"

Varic handed a trayful of figures to Reccan and said, "You are required to help me put the troops back in their cases. House rules, I'm afraid. If we're quick, we shall be comfortably in time for dinner."

❧

Dinner was informal. People wore coats, and Edaire was wearing a fine jacket of wine-colored satin with puffed sleeves, but

Bliss, the butler, had the only cravat in the room. The sideboard was set with warm meats and vegetables, and everyone served themselves, with Bliss keeping glasses filled and supervising the clearing of used dishes.

Afterward, the table was cleared and rolled on casters toward the sideboard, clearing most of the hall for conversation. Bliss moved around the room with glasses of a fine clarine, full-flavored and slightly sweet.

In one corner, Strange, Winterhill, and Edaire were playing arcquet. Dany and Agate were doing something with colored stones on a patterned scarf, either a divination or a game. Reccan and Varic had disappeared separately. Silvern was settled before the fireplace with his clarine and a clay pipe of something spicily aromatic. He waved Longlight to the chair by his.

He said, "I propose to leave for your Coronage in four days. The Ironways will be far less crowded. Have you sent a magnostyle home?"

"I told my castellan I'd be a few days late, and that he could reach me here. He'll make sure there are horses for us at the last Ironway station—that's in Caligo Pass, two days' ride out. The waycastle's comfortable."

"I've never been opposed to traveling in comfort." He smiled and adjusted his pipe. "Contrary to what you may have heard, not too many Palions wash their faces in snow and birch each other just for the practice."

She laughed. "Of course I had a copy of *In the Days of Lord Falchion*. With the color plates."

"Didn't we all?"

Longlight said, "I went to Lystourel looking for help against the bandits. When I come back with a Palion, there may be some winking and nodding when we say it's for a hunting lodge." She sipped her wine. "But your presence may make the raiders walk more carefully for a while."

"You overestimate me and undervalue yourself. I imagine they walk carefully in the lady Coron's presence."

"But I am not a Palion."

"It's a word. It is perfectly possible to live as a Palion, keep all the covenants and uphold the honor, without having the name. Varic would say that, since Goddess and all Her consorts are only stories, there must have been a time before the stories were told. And so, if there truly are any Palions, there must have been some such then as well."

Longlight wrapped her right hand around her left wrist.

"You see," Silvern said with great gravity and kindness, "you make the sign of the Willed Draw, even though you are not called a Palion."

"What would the name mean, then, if wanting it were enough?"

"I did not say that wanting it was enough. I said that, possibly, living it was." He held up his glass, clicked it to hers. "As was true in the days of Lord Falchion, as now."

Edaire came over, and rested her hands on Silvern's shoulders as they finished the clarine. The sight of them in such easy contact was suddenly difficult for Longlight to endure, and she said good night and walked away, down the hall.

Varic answered his door on her first knock. He was in his stockings and had taken off his coat, but was otherwise still dressed. "Please you to come in?"

He shut the door behind her. "Would you like to sit? I haven't anything but some whisky, but . . ."

"I don't need anything, thank you. And I don't really want to sit out here."

"Well, then." He walked down the hall toward the bedroom. The lights were on; he plucked an open book from the slightly rumpled, still-made bed and tucked it into the nightstand. He leaned against the edge of the bed, crossed his arms. "I am glad you decided to stay," he said. "And I apologize for the events that made the choice difficult."

"It was a misunderstanding. No one's fault."

"Still, there was an injury done, and whether or not it can be made right, at least someone needs to be responsible for it. As you are probably aware by now, I do not believe that the Dark Room solves these things."

"I'm not minded to argue it."

"Good," he said, loud enough to startle her. Then she remembered that in his country, what was spoken loud was meant gently. "For I would never have this done over argument."

He stood up then, and in an astonishingly quick movement, his fingers closed on the top button at her collar. "There is a spare robe in the bathroom."

She touched the back of his hand. The muscles were not at all tense. She reminded herself that he was in fact a fencer, and a dangerous one. "Aren't you going to go ahead with that?"

"Wilt do me a courtesy, and open the first yourself?"

"I'll trade you."

He nodded.

He did not move at all as she removed his shirt; relaxed to let the fabric slip away, but was wholly still. She wondered if that meant something; if it were supposed to answer a curiosity, about Agate.

When she returned from the bath, Varic had turned out the glasswicks and laid a small wood fire in the hearth; amber light shimmered over the room, leaving angles of deep darkness. He was sitting up in the bed, the linens drawn up to his chest, his hands clasped around his knees.

She hung her robe on a peg on the bedpost and climbed up, shivering slightly at the touch of cool sheets. He turned to look at her, and gave a small flat smile, but did not move.

She waited a moment, then sat up beside him and said, "Are you actually paying for Silvern to scout my country?"

"Someone needs to. And you've seen how Parliament does these things."

"We're not that poor a Coronage."

"And when you have Ironways to take out your ores and timber, you may be a very wealthy Coronage."

"How much do you know about . . ."

"Less than you, certainly. But my spies are probably better."

"But *why* do you—"

"My dear fellow Coron, at the risk of being rude at the worst imaginable time, put it aside for now. Silvern will offer a preferential rate for his services. Don't ask it of Winterhill, though—discounts and favoritism are looked on harshly in his profession."

"I meant, why do all of you—oh. What am I saying? I want to be awake for the service tomorrow, and I didn't come here for a discussion."

"Oh, I'm quite happy to have a discussion, and it's a long time until morning. Do you read gluebacks?"

She looked sidelong at him. "Oh, sometimes."

"That wasn't an accusation. More of them are good than you might think. And after all, what else is there in Ironway stations? Gluebacks, newspapers, *Lives of the Great Ironway Financiers,* and *Misty the Merry Motive.*"

"What?"

"Children's books. Misty lives in Steamdale with a whole yard full of humanized Ironway equipment—Swifty the Steamcar, Cranky Crane—oh, I'm sure it's all right to laugh—delivering the goods and the happy passengers. Hazel loves them. I mean, of course, he loved them when he was *much* younger." Varic smiled.

"Of course."

"When the rails run into your country, you can expect the adventures of Misty and company very soon afterward. It is impossible to do just one thing . . . but that wasn't my point. Or perhaps it was." He shook his head. "Aside all that: I know someone who writes gluebacks, the really red-litten sort. *The Wheatcombe Nightcryers, Fear in Amber, To Sleep with Shut Windows.* And what he tells me"—Varic's voice was serious now—"is that what those stories are always about is people forced to exceed their limits. Someone has to find a strength, of body or spirit, that wasn't there before, or lose everything. Fortunately, they almost always do find it—at least, in gluebacks."

"And if not, the story is a tragedy?"

"Tragedy itself."

"That word . . . it rings so drowe," Longlight said, her home accent coming up strong. "It means . . . 'hooves'?"

"*Tragadae* is the stamping of hooves. In the old Pandektine theater, a story where the hero failed—generally because he was fighting the gods—would finish with the chorus stamping their feet. The audience usually joined in."

Longlight nodded slowly, then said, "But why are we talking about the Pandektine theater? Nyne t'mind gruesome gluebacks and Cranky Crane?"

"We were speaking of the heroic reach. Have you never been in a company, late and a little drunk, who were daring each other? Snuff a candle with your bare palm, down a whole jack of ale without taking a breath, balance a knife on your nose. A deer may leap a long gap to escape the hunter, but I doubt very much that deer spend any time wondering if, should the hunter come, they can stretch enough to make the distance."

"Deer fight each other time on's, over territory, and mates."

"Yes. But do they *know* they are doing it? Or is there just some deep pressure to push the other away, take what's there? And do they fear losing?" He tapped his fingers on her wrist. "You told me a story about deer hunting. This is really nothing to do with that—unless, of course, it is."

"To talk of jumping gaps—"

"Yes, I know. There are an infinite number of ideas in the world, and I cannot make love to any of them for very long at a time. This is not true," he said with that sudden volume that was Northesse for tenderness, "not, somehow, true of people . . . the fascinations are not so universal, and not so easily given up."

Longlight said, "Last night, I was in a company, late and rather drunk. Dwillknow Winterhill was tapping me for echoes, but there weren't any dares that I could seil."

"No, not in the House. Not even at swords' length in the aren-etto." Varic rolled toward her, put his fingers very delicately around her bare throat. "Aye and this is different, here, is it not? What was sweet and desperate nights back, now is but sweet and calm."

Longlight woke in daylight, lying on her side facing the wall, conscious of Varic's weight behind her. The corner of a pillow blocked her view of the bedside clock. Carefully, so as not to wake Varic, she pushed the pillow down. Twenty to nine. She slipped her legs over the edge of the bed, turned her head back.

Varic was sitting propped up on a pillow, silently watching her. "Good morning," he said.

"Good morning. I was—"

"I know. I was about to wake you. I wouldn't have let you miss the service."

"But you're not going."

"No. I . . ." He reached out, pushed a curl of her hair away from her face with a fingertip. "No."

She watched him, then suddenly said, "Do you have to look so resigned?"

"I don't suppose I have to look like anything." His look softened, just enough to make it bearable. "Better?"

She turned toward him, put her arms around him. "Yes, better." He held her close. His skin was cool, and she wondered how long he had been awake, just watching her sleep.

"I suppose," she said after not nearly long enough, "I should hurry back to my room."

"This is Strange House. There are clothes for you in the hall closet and extra towels in the bathroom. You did notice that I had a spare robe?"

"No . . . I suppose I didn't."

She showered and dressed. The staff had brought several things; she chose a silver tunic and a blue pleated skirt.

"Very fine." Varic stood in the hallway, wrapped in his dressing gown. She swallowed a chuckle at the sight of his spectacularly disordered hair.

He caught her hand suddenly and kissed it.

"Oh . . ."

"Don't say anything," he said. "Don't inspire me to something I couldn't possibly mean." He turned away.

"I don't know where the Bright Room is. Do you—"

"Oh, I know where it is. Top floor of the main House, north side. You'll see it."

He bowed and went into the bathroom. She heard the shower run and had a sudden, terrible feeling that the water was supposed to cover some other sound. She went out into the hall. In the main house, she met Silvern and Edaire, on their way to service as well, and it was fortunately easy to smile for them.

The Bright Room was polygonal, twelve-sided, with a ceiling that came to a high point: quite literally a faceted jewel of a room. The southern half of the ceiling, behind the rows of seats, was clear glass, letting in the sky; the arc behind the dais had four stained-glass images of the Grand Aspects, and two panels of figured bronze mounted with crystal lamps.

The ancient mirror Birch had brought from the Dark Room hung on the wall behind him. The ceremonial sword was on a small table between him and the audience.

Birch was wearing a rather plain gray gown. It had organ-pipe pleats from the waist to the floor, and seemed to be made of a very fine, heavy silk, but there was no ornamentation on it at all, and the shirt that poked out at collar and wrists looked like, well, a white cotton shirt. He wore no headdress.

And it was, Longlight realized with something of a shock, quite right. It was not easy to imagine Birch in thick brocades worked with masses of gold wire, a hat as tall again as his head.

She would go to Capel Storrow, Longlight thought, attend his first Communion as Archimage, wearing something fine, but simple. She would tell her court to do likewise. Her father would have liked that. He had always been for Coris, taking his Goddess simple and thundering and elemental.

"This is Equinox Morning," Birch said. "In Her name, I welcome you to Her chamber, and to Her autumn.

"In this most fortunate house, first of autumn has always been one of our happiest holidays. It is still warm enough to play outside, the harvest is coming in, we're relaxing into the slower step of winter.

"It wasn't always like that. When we were new in the world—not that long past—the fall was when tensions rose. The winter would come after it, and winter was an ordeal every year that not everyone passed through. Would the food last; would our tempers explode, crowded into the few warm places; would there actually, this time, be a spring?"

She would announce a procession to the Communion: everyone who wished to go would go, the whole Mori dance from beggars to Coronate. The money saved by dressing the court plainly but well would dress the poor plainly, but well.

"They did not, yet, trust their Goddess. Partly this was because they laid too much upon Her; they supposed that She sent them deer, or fish, or apples, by whim, not yet aware that the deer, and the fish, and the apple trees, had reasons of their own, which they could understand and use. They were afraid that She would make a winter and stop, and they would die in the cold, and never know what they had failed to do for Her.

"We, of course, mistrust Her in a different fashion entirely."

Longlight looked around the room. She could see the lucate varii, the glowing centers of everyone there—everyone but Birch, but the lights were visibly refracting through him. He was the heart of their light.

"We know about the deer's scent and how to prune an apple tree. We know that faith will not hold a ladder if we tip it over, and the man who only prays over his sick family when the cause is a fouled well is worse than a fool.

"We are even close to really knowing the great thing: that Goddess can be different things to many people and still be Goddess. A soul may, for this reason or that, prefer Evani to Wyss, or Hand to Evani; but if he does not see that Hand *is* Evani, Evani Wyss, he rejects them all."

She would invite the bandit chiefs to join her, and make it clear that she did not fear what they did when she was gone to Communion.

She caught her mind wandering, and without really thinking made the sign of Coris-Calming-Beasts. A blob of roseate light tumbled from her fingertips, bounced softly on the floor, scattering silent flickers. She looked up quickly. No one else seemed to have seen it. Or was Birch smiling particularly at her?

"The first thing the Book teaches is that meanings must be found and interpreted." Birch held up his hand, and twisting light intersected on his fingers, forming a rectangle of translucent whiteness. He did not look at it; perhaps he had made only the gesture, and the rest of them created the card.

"When I put on the priest's gown, my favorite teacher told me, 'Sooner or later, but probably sooner, someone will ask you if there are any limits on what must be tolerated in Her name, and you had better have an answer ready.' I knew her well enough to know that this was a question.

"The question only seems to be about Goddess's nature. What it really says is, 'My mind, my heart, stick at accepting this. Tell me either that it is not truly of Her, so that I may reject it freely, or tell me that it *is* Her, so I can say I faced immortal will and not another soul as common as mine.' When it is not the rightness or the wrongness of the rejection, but the rejection itself, that troubles the person, that blinds the soul to Her. Sometimes the blindness leads a pilgrim down crooked ways, and we ought to bring our fellows back; but how can we bring them back if we will not look at where they have gone? We cannot change a thing if we deny it. We must accept its reality and its meaning.

"Still I say we are close to the full understanding, the true and total acceptance. Some souls, I do believe, are there already. But I think, here on balance day, that most of us are still on the edge between what we were and what we will become. I called this thing great, but when we master it, a greater one will follow. That is *wonderful*. That is what I ask you, now, to think about with me. The next wonder, and the next, and the wonder after that."

He tossed the card—or perhaps just waved—at the antique

mirror from the Dark Room, and it broke into butterflies of light that fluttered and vanished.

"We have learned enough to know," Birch said, his voice seeming to come from everywhere in the room, "that we cannot stop learning. When we say, 'Find Her, in your way,' we are not commanding or dismissing; it is not for us, priest or pilgrim, to command or dismiss one another. We are asking to be remembered on the journey.

"And now I say unto you, fellow pilgrims, find Goddess in your way; and as you find Her, remember me to Her."

After Birch's morning service, Longlight went back to her room, in something of a daze, intent on writing down some ideas before they faded from her mind. When she finished, back to normal, the House was very still; she wandered down the hall to the Blue Parlor, supposing there must be an interesting book there. She heard voices, and looked in tentatively.

Edaire and Hazel were sitting on the floor, playing with colored wooden blocks. It only took a moment to see that they were playing Ironway: a train of blocks was lined up neatly, and other rows and stacks were clearly enough signals and towers, bridges and stations.

Edaire said, "Steam up, brakes pumped, orders in hand, Captain! Ready to depart."

"Wait for me," Hazel said, and two fingers of his hand ran across the carpet and jumped on the trail wagon. "Don't tell the 'Specker Gen'ral I was late, will you?"

"She won't hear a word," the Inspector General said. Then the two of them took hold of the train blocks and slowly accelerated them away from the platform.

Longlight laughed. Edaire and Hazel looked up, grinning.

Hazel jumped to his feet at once and bowed. Edaire said, "Care to join us? Having only two people on a crew is strictly against the work rules."

"*Strictly*," Hazel said with extreme clarity.

"Thank you both, but I've just thought of something. I'll see you later."

"Goodbye, my lady," Hazel said, and bowed. Longlight returned it, then said, "Tell me, Hazel, what's the quickest way to the carpenter's shop?"

"Go to the very end of this hall, my lady, then out the door and across the road—you will be careful when you cross the road?"

"I certainly will."

"You'll see the stables clear then. The smith's is on the left, with the big chim-a-ney, and the woodshop's on the right. Our house is just past—it's the green one. I could take you, if you wish."

"I'm sure I'll find it. Thank you, Hazel." They traded bows again, and Longlight set off down the hall.

There was some cloud, and the air had become slightly chilly. The trees along the road were starting to turn color, and there were spatterings of red and yellow leaves on the green grass. She saw the blacksmith's and smelled its coal smoke at almost the same moment, then scanned past the long stable—big enough for at least twenty horses, she guessed—to the carpentry.

There was a whining sound within. Roan, in an open-collared wool shirt and a denim apron, was turning something on a lathe. The tool was driven by a belt to an overhead pulley and shaft; the shaft ran through the wall to the rear. The drive engine would be in a shed of its own, so any sparks were well away from raw wood and sawdust. Roan took the tool away from the work and said, "Good day to you, honored. What may I do for you?"

"That lathe is very quiet."

"Aye so. Ferangarder roller bearings; a third less power and half the noise."

"I saw your model coach upstairs. It was a proud thing to sign."

"I do thank you, honored."

"I would like to borrow some tools for small woodwork. And if there are some pieces of softwood—" She indicated a size with her hands, then described what she had in mind.

"Oh, that's lovely, honored. Will you just wait a moment? Plumb!"

A figure in wool and worn leather came through the back door of the shop. His black-haired head came up only to the middle of Longlight's chest, and he seemed almost as broad as he was high. Still, he moved smoothly around the machines and racked wood, stepping lightly in heavy metal-capped boots. He came around the last turn, and Longlight nearly flinched: his face was seamed with scars and seemed to have been pushed in, but his black eyes were bright and full of wit. She had yet to see anyone in the House, Longlight thought, who did not have that gleam of happiness. It was slightly disorienting.

Plumb said, "She's smooth as butter, Roan, I've only just oiled both th' lathe and th' engine—oh, me. Pardon me, honored, guest."

"Plumb, the lady Coron wants to do a little work at the carver's bench. Is it clear?"

"Well, of course it's clear, and every tool sharp. What sort of stock does my lady need?"

Longlight said, "Some softwood, clear pine would be fine, about a quarter-span square—"

Roan put in, "And a handful of harness snaps—we'd better have snaps in stock."

"We've buckets and barrels."

"And some flathead round nails, and a bit of that thumb-wide dowel. I take it you want to finish quick, my lady?"

"I should like to. But I hadn't even thought about the snaps. . . ."

"We won't paint, then. Just some emery cloth to kill the burrs."

Plumb said, "Better 'ad varnish 'em."

"Milady, if we varnish they will still be ready before you leave. Is that well?"

"Certainly."

Plumb ticked off materials on his fingers as Roan named them. Longlight saw that his hands were incongruously slender and long-fingered, almost delicate, though they were clearly a workman's hands. She had another idea, said, "Would you have a small burning iron? Something that could make a rectangle." She indicated the purpose with her hands again.

Roan said, "Two bits of angle around a block, that'll do 'en. Plumb, you get the lady settled and started."

"This way, honored, guest," Plumb said.

❧

Varic walked through the garden, bending over by a neatly trimmed bush to watch a hedgehog doze in the sun. He took another few steps, turned to look at the House; the crystalline peak of the Bright Room was just visible above the south cornice.

"What are they doing now?" he said.

Agate was sitting on a bench nearby, looking across the pond. Without turning, she said, "Midday service is almost over. Birch could have been quite a sorcerer, if he hadn't heard it as the Voice."

"If . . . My lady wizard is trying to provoke me."

"Never," she said, very seriously, and then more playfully, "never, for my life."

Agate was wearing a Pandektine chiton, a simpler version of the gown she had worn for the first night's dinner: black dyed linen, draped at the neck, sleeveless, with a skirt slit above the knee and a belt of knotted white rope. She had an elaborately knotted black silk cord holding her hair back, and plain black sandals.

Varic bowed to her, for no real reason, and followed her to the boathouse, where a small rowboat was moored. She paused on the landing, seemed indistinct for an instanta in the light off the lake, then got into the boat. Varic followed, tugged the mooring line free, and began pulling at the oars.

"I could rhyme us over," Agate said.

"It's only . . . a few . . . strokes."

The boat bumped against the small stone jetty. They fixed ropes fore and aft to pegs, making the boat fast, and then Agate stepped easily up.

Varic said, "The country life . . . agrees with some people." She laughed as he climbed onto the dock. They walked into the grove.

The entire island was only about twenty steps across. At its center, among the closely planted trees, was a little pavilion of white stone: a ring of slender columns, half again a person's height. Half a dome covered one side; the other was open to the sky. Inside the columns, three obsidian benches surrounded a sculpture of Goddess in Her four Great Aspects, each paired with Her Consort: Coris and Windrose, Shyira and Palion, Evani and Hand, Wyss and Mother Wolf.

Agate stood between two of the columns, touched them with her fingertips. She frowned. "The structure's not entirely sound. There's been subsidence, some gravel shift."

"Is it dangerous?"

"Not yet. But it should be attended to before winter and frost heave. Plumb and I will see to it. Come, sit."

He sat down on one of the black glass benches, cold and

smooth as ice. Agate perched on the sculpture, between Wyss and Coris, Knowledge and Nature. She kicked off her sandals and curled her brown legs around Wolfa's forepaws.

Varic said, "Disrespect is more my task."

"You know you can't disrespect Her. And I'm not flouting, I'm adoring." She laughed and leaned back, into the figures' arms. "Now, tell me how the City is."

Varic tilted his head back. "Dr. Whisper is Crafting a new lens for the Grand Oculus, over four spans across. It's quite a thing to watch, a glob of molten yellow glass suspended on his magic, in an airless envelope, spinning itself into a double meniscus. Whisper estimates it will take another week and a half to purge all the impurities and perfect the shape; he has two apprentices for spell sustenance, so he can get a little sleep."

"Sleep, yes," Agate said, quite without any immediate meaning.

"And Falconer's people have broken into a new chamber at the Castle. A library: scrolls, not books, so it's probably from before Falconer's era, meaning there will be a small war in the University over who's in charge."

"One would think that there were no more walls to knock through in the Castle, after all this time. No more rooms to find."

"Indeed," Varic said. "Indeed, in—" He caught the rhythm in his voice before it could set, held his breath and a ragged pause. A little brown thrush fluttered down from a tree limb and settled on his shoulder. Agate watched it with a small, rare smile.

❧

Longlight emerged from the shop, stretched in the afternoon light, exhaled varnish fumes, and took a breath of sharp clear air. It seemed quite silent, after the sounds of forge and tools, and red leaves under her shoe crunched like breaking glass.

Tacker was standing just across the road, leaning against a tree. She was tumbling two unlighted cheroots over in her hands, something hesitantly like Reccan's pencil trick. She turned at Longlight's next footstep, caught the cheroots in her fist, and tucked them away.

"A pleasant afternoon, my lady."

"And to you, honored Tacker."

"Thank you, if you will't so."

"So I do. It was a good move, with the cavalry."

"Better had it won outright," Tacker said with no special feeling. "We had some tricks in the woods, if you had come out. You and Reccan make a good team; she's awful bold, on her own. As I guess am I; Strange reins me. A fine game."

"Perhaps we'll play another before I go."

"Well by me. Wouldn't ask milord Varic again, though—he makes it too much work. My lord Strange might prepare, and Silvern play."

Longlight turned her head at a flare of light, from across the pond south of the House. She could see a lens of golden light, like a hovering eye, above a building that could not possibly have been there before, and could hardly be there now: a castle with towers and buttresses, bridges and narrow-windowed walls. As she watched, it shifted so that she seemed to see it from many angles at once. A vaulted hall stood open to view, shafts of glass-dyed light through its pictorial windows; then that space moved—revolved, folded, whatever—into a wall that crumbled away, revealing a room lined with scroll cases, its air sparkling with yellow-white dust.

"That looks . . . like the Castle, at Lystourel."

Without turning to look, Tacker said, "I wouldn't know, milady. I've never been near the City."

"But . . . it must be magic."

"The island, milady Longlight. Varic and Agate are out there, talking, I'd think." A little more softly, Tacker said, "It's like a dream, I think, milady: once you know it *is* a dream, it's over."

And then the structure was gone, except for a faint shimmer that could easily have been heat haze, had the day been warm enough for it.

Longlight nodded to Tacker and went back to the corner of the House. Strange was in the east breezeway, looking out over the gardens. "Good day to you, Longlight."

"And you, Strange."

"Agate says we shall have good weather all night—clear, perhaps a bit cool after midnight. We'll be able to have Masks out of doors."

"Oh! That's something I can never do at home. It isn't the same in the snow. What do you do here, that I should know?"

"Nothing so very unusual," Strange said. "A light early dinner, and we'll draw; then back to your room to see what you've drawn, and dress for it. The more creative you are, asking the staff for costumes, the better they'll like it. Then we'll gather in the garden and the Teller will tell the tale that's told. I ask you to pardon my absence—a mask could hardly hide me—but I will be watching, and with you."

They gathered at five in the great hall, sitting about in soft chairs at small tables, for meat pie and green salads, and a dish new to Longlight, of cold spiced noodles with groundnut sauce.

Bliss wheeled in a cart with a heap of black velvet bags. "Who shall draw first?" Strange said, and after some murmuring, Winterhill stepped to the cart, shut his eyes, and pulled a bag from the middle of the pile. He tucked it under his arm, said, "I shall see you all again, when none of us are to be seen," and left the room. One by one, they drew and departed.

Back in her apartment, Longlight pulled open the velvet bag. Inside, padded with paper so that it could not be identified by touching the bag, was a wooden mask, lacquered bright red; it had cheek and jaw pieces that articulated on leather cords. It looked rather Demonic in her hands, empty-eyed, the jaw hanging wide. She put it to her face and looked in the mirror; with flesh filling the gaps, the expression was much more placid, though still extremely formal.

She rang for the parlor maid, who listened to Longlight's instructions and quickly brought her a short jacket of red satin, ornamented with black embroidery. She paired it with a black kidskin skirt, just loose enough to walk in, and her boots. The maid checked fit and coverage, and showed her the short way to the garden, down the south staircase and outside.

Candles sparkled all about the garden, with high gaslights marking the paths and sitting areas. On the east side was a boxy building, one end open to show a shallow wooden stage with a dark curtain behind it. She had been told it was a theater; the stage could open on this side in good weather, for an audience out of doors, or to the covered auditorium inside. Now the stage was empty except for a small lectern and a high chair.

Reccan was standing near a gate, wearing a sleeveless dress of crazy-color patchwork, silver-buttoned black boots with high, slender heels. Her mask was woven of silk ribbons, as colorful as the dress, with many trailing ends twined into her hair and dangling over her shoulders. Some of them had been wrapped and tied tightly between her lips. She posed against the upright, clutching it, one foot drawn up, as still as a marble nymph. Then, as Longlight passed, her head revolved, slowly, slowly, her eyes straight and clear on Longlight's for a moment, then turning past to stare at—Longlight began to follow the look, then walked on by.

"My Red Lady," Dany's voice said.

Dany was wearing the Teller's golden mask. This one was a deep golden-bronze color, cut just below her cheekbones so that she had complete freedom of speech, with wide eyes of milk and blue glass. She was wrapped in a great length of metallic golden silk, wound from ankle to shoulder, trailing down behind.

Longlight looked at the mask and thought suddenly about the staring blue eyes, so different from Dany's beautiful, liquid black ones. The gilt complemented her dark skin, but where she came from, on the other side of the world, did they have such pale blue eyes? And if not, then what was it like to wear them?

Longlight put a hand to her own mask, feeling a brief shock of unminded fear, a childish fright that the mask worn too long—or too well—would not come off.

Dany said, "You are the Moon, the Bride of the Sun, and your love is true but troubled, your pride is the Moon's own. It is the lost time, when your faces are few and known, and you smile full every Shineday."

"I understand," Longlight said, and Dany nodded once gravely and moved on, a golden comet.

Longlight walked on as well. There were some small iron tables and chairs ahead, lit with candles in colored glasses. Two people sat at one of them, talking over plates of biscuits and meat rolls; after another step, Longlight saw that they were Winterhill and Edaire.

Winterhill turned, with something of a twitch, to face Longlight. He was wearing a mask of woven leather studded with bronze, and a Quercian Centurion's costume: leather, bronze, red cloak, thick-soled boots. It was well worn—in fact, it seemed about to fall to pieces.

"My good cousin," he said, his voice dripping honey, "how

good to see you here—you and your husband both. May I introduce my own wife? She is not of the family, of course, but comely, do you not think? For a mortal, of course, I mean. And I *do* love her so."

Edaire stood to bow. Her mask was sea green, with golden flecks that caught the candlelight like sorcery. It had a crease indicating lips, but no definite mouth. Her long dress was of translucent green stuff, off one shoulder and slit high on both sides. Quercian frescoes of the muses of art sometimes showed them so; indeed, when Edaire took a step, she showed flat sandals corded up her calves, precisely Quercian.

"I am pleased to meet you . . . half cousin?"

Edaire bowed her head, but did not speak. Winterhill said hastily, "My cousin of course meets so many of her large family. I am the Lord of Those Who Guard with the Warrior's Spear."

Longlight felt a laugh rising, started to stifle it, then thought of her role and let it bubble out. "Your gracious acquaintance, God of Spear-Carriers," she said, still laughing, and passed on, as Winterhill bowed and gestured his overwhelming gratitude.

Some distance on, Reccan skipped past, weightless and shadow-silent. Longlight did turn to follow her this time, and saw, beyond a hedge, Winterhill apparently adjusting Edaire's gown: he seemed to be trying to draw it even tighter across her hips and breasts.

Longlight did not know the play yet, but it was already full enough of unease.

Sometimes the funniest story slid uncontrollably into horror and death, and sometimes something that began like an old Pandektine tragedy, full of indifferent deities and brutish mortals, ended up in dancing and laughter.

A hand tugged her sleeve. She turned and saw no one; then from behind her Varic's voice said, "Here on your dark face, cousin Nightshine."

He wore an elaborate jacket of white leather, with wide shoulders, a peplum, and a short cape; tight leggings, one white, one black, and boots black and white counterchanged. His mask was of snow-white china that had been broken into pieces and reassembled, awkwardly and with bits missing. Iron bolts stuck out from it.

"Do I know you, then, cousin?"

"I know you. That's what matters. Your mate wants you: Shall we go?" He held out his arm, and she took it.

A few steps along, a dark shape came suddenly into view: Birch, in a plain black suit with a long silver scarf wound loosely around his neck. His mask was glossy black with faint silvery highlights, just suggesting a face.

"Enough, cousin Sky, enough!" Varic said. "Speak not; I am returning the lady to her lord."

Birch gave a slight bow of acknowledgment and stepped back into the shadows.

They approached a long table set with food and drinks. At the center sat Silvern, wearing a loosely draped cloak of intense yellow, a heavy golden chain around his shoulders. His mask was a hammered copper disk.

"This way," Varic said quietly, "I'm sure he'll be pleased to see you."

Silvern swayed in his seat, groped toward Longlight. "Come here, wife; I want you closer. Closing the gap is . . . difficult."

"My lord the Sun has been drinking."

"Ach! I am drunk on moonlight and I would taste more. Sit where I can reach you."

"I would not be reached now," Longlight said. "It is fast dark, and time I shone on others." She held up her head and turned away from him. Varic had disappeared.

Reccan whirled close to her, the ribbons from her mask flying. She produced a crystal goblet, filled it from a jug that seemed to float on nothing, handed it to Longlight with a deep bow.

She drank; it was sparkling cider. When she looked up from the glass, Birch, as the Sky, stood before her, offering a silver-gloved hand. She took it, and he led her in a dance step to mandolin music that came from nowhere visible.

The wind was sweet through the garden flowers, just warm enough to give no notice of itself, like water to fishes. Longlight did not see Agate, and wondered if she were responsible. The stars were soft and happy as Birch's eyes.

Reccan was juggling phosphors now, ten or more long wooden fire-lighters tumbling over between her hands, wreathing her in golden light.

Winterhill appeared, holding a wineglass none too steadily. He lit a cheroot from Reccan's cascade, blew a smoke ring. "Well met again, cousin Moon, cousin Nightmantle. So glad to see you dancing." He bowed, making his armor flap and clink.

"Where is your wife?" Longlight said.

"Oh," Winterhill said, nervousness apparent, "I'm sure she, um—shall we go over there and talk about, um . . ."

Varic stepped from behind an arbor. Part of a smile showed next to a bolt in his mask. He gestured back toward the main table, where Silvern had been sitting.

Longlight said, "Perhaps I have neglected my mate."

"Oh, surely not!" Winterhill said. "After all, he was all the wrong—I mean, you wouldn't—"

"I shall." She let go of Birch's hand and started toward the table. Birch looked silently after, Winterhill took a crooked step, then faltered.

The Sun was still seated in his brazen glory; but in the seat next to him was Edaire.

"Do you see," Winterhill's voice said from somewhere far behind, "how my lady, however mortal, is preferred of the Sun?"

"Indeed," Varic said, very dryly, "she does look a natural shade."

Reccan whirled by, her hands making the laughter sign. Then Varic was laughing as well, and Birch.

Longlight had to pause and sort her reactions. Silvern and Edaire were mated and more, and Varic's laughter was deeply bitter; but the masks set the meanings tonight, and the response.

"That is my place the woman sits in," Longlight said, "and you laugh that I am not in it? What is your meaning in laughing, and what is her right of occupation?"

Silvern said thickly, "I did not think . . . you wanted to be with me."

"Perhaps not; but if I am not, who shall be?"

"I have *decided* to offer *honor* to this woman!"

Varic said, rather loudly, "Who's off and who's on?"

Longlight said, "There is no honor when there is so much dishonor! I demand justice!"

Agate's voice said, "Demand it once again, and you shall have it." Agate was seated on the stage, on the stool behind the lectern. A book was closed before her, and a glittering aurora was above her head. Longlight thought at first it must be sorcery, then saw it was strips of metal foil, drifting in the breeze.

Birch, the Sky, said gently, "This is a folly of the Sun's, and within your power to forgive."

Longlight hesitated. She knew where the story must be going. Varic, the Trickster spirit, had allowed Sun and Moon to meet at just the wrong instant, and then persuaded the little follower-god to seek advancement by having the great Sun seduce his wife. The Moon had summoned the powers of Justice, and had one chance to change her mind. Which she could; this was Masks, and she was not compelled by any rule to speak any line.

But the story, the character, did compel. "I call again for Justice!"

Reccan played one long stinging chord on the mandolin.

"So be it," Agate said, "and it shall not be otherwise. Sun and Moon: until this night you walked to one rhythm, and the days themselves named your faces. Now that order is broken, and you are out of step, hour by hour and day by day, to your own distress and the confounding of mortals. They shall labor to know when you are full, and when fallow."

Longlight said, "I did not . . . desire this."

"Then let your desire cool slow," Agate said. She turned to Edaire. "You, mortal woman in the wrong chair, wife of the little god. You have failed your vow and your kind."

"I am not like you gods, who make things as they want them," Edaire cried, "nor even a King, who wants a thing and has it. I have only my own little power."

"It is not difficult as kingship is difficult, to save the people from starvation and war. It is hard in the way of ordinary things: to not be vain, to not break what should be whole. You did not fail to be a god. You failed to be what you should have been."

Agate threw out her arm, and something flew from it; Edaire huddled as it struck her. It was a wadded strip of soft red cloth, that uncoiled and dangled from her shoulder and arm, bloody on sea green.

"This is . . . my blood," Edaire said. "My inward blood."

"You are of earth, not spirit. Your suffering must be first of earth. But it will follow the Moon's wandering, so that you do not forget why you bleed."

"Justice does not consider me!"

"That is so," Agate said with a truly inhuman calm. "Justice considers nothing except itself. And for you, small god who loved this mortal, and should have loved her better, you will see your children scattered on the mortal earth, and see them fight and kill one another for a place in the Sun's favor, and never know why they do."

Winterhill fell to his knees, head bowed.

Agate turned to face Varic, who stood carelessly against a lamppost. "Now you, Trickster: you who were given more freedom than any god, and with it made this discord."

"A fine discord, was it not?" Varic said pleasantly. "It was splendid to see the gods' table disturbed. Where there is no seat for me, let all sit uneasy."

"Well you say: for unease shall be—"

"Oh, *stop it*," Varic said. "Don't pronounce: *do*!" He spread his hands. "Of course you will punish me! It is in our natures to do as we do, and we cannot alter it: Are we not gods? But if I had a choice, I would do it again." He raised his fists at the sky. "*Because it was a good joke!*"

Agate threw out her hand again. A kind of glittering black snowball flew at Varic, struck him, and burst into shining flecks.

Varic's raised arms stiffened. His spine bent back. He swayed, dropped to one knee. His mouth was stretched wide beneath the fractured mask, but he made no sound. His back hunched, and he pawed the ground with one clawed hand.

"A new shape for new tricks," he said, in a wavering screech. "Well, I have things to do, if you will pardon my going. When you see me next—I wonder if you will know me?"

He loped to the stage, vaulted up on it, gave Agate a crooked, courtly bow. Then he disappeared through the stage curtain behind her.

No one moved then. Dany came in from the boathouse, her gold much like a dawn; she removed her mask and placed it on the table. Then Silvern unmasked, and Edaire, and then the rest of them. Reccan untied her ribbon mask, tossed it in the air, where it spun like a firework wheel. She brought out a little black mandolin and began to play. Bliss served glasses of apple brandy, fiery in the cooling night. They drank, and embraced, and drifted back toward the House.

⚭

There was a slip of folded paper on the handle of Varic's door. Longlight unfolded it: it read UNLOCKED. ENTER. She did so.

The apartment was silent and seemed empty; a fire was going in the bedroom. When she came around the foot of the bed, she saw Varic sitting before the fireplace, looking into it. He was naked, and the light on his skin was like gilding on marble.

She crouched behind him, touched his side. There was a small, round scar on his lower back, an exit scar—the sword had gone in between his ribs. Every time she saw it, she wondered how he had survived the wound.

He said, "Are you thinking how helpless I am, how easy I would be to kill?"

"No. Why do you say such a thing?"

"I was thinking of your deer hunt, in the clearing."

"That was—do you think that was *anything* like this?"

"No. But a Coron must never show weakness toward anyone, didn't your father teach you that? Certainly not to another Coron."

"My father did teach me that," she said. "He also taught me that one can be tender without being weak."

"Then he was an exceptional man, and you rightly honor his memory." He turned, stroked her cheek, her temple. He took delicate hold of the cords that fastened her tunic. "May I?"

She put her hands behind her back. "I refuse to interfere."

"I may make you regret you said that," he said lightly, and touched one finger to her lips when she started to speak. A full half hour later, as he was folding her last stocking with an absurdly methodical slowness, she understood his meaning very well.

She fought for enough breath to speak, said, "Did you know tonight's story?"

"No. It's from Dany's country. I like it, though, better than ours; a quarrel among jealous but passionate and understandable gods is—oh, somehow more artful than a bunch of greedy sorcerers trying to grab more power. And the Nisimenish story comes back to touch life at the fundaments; ours just sees the Moon bumped loose from its old tracks and the bad old sorcerers all drowned in hot lava."

"I read a book once that told the story differently," she said. "The sorcerers all had their own characters. Kin more to real people, and some of them meant to do good. And it wasn't a mistake that stopped them, but one of their own, who saw they couldn't be trusted with the new power."

"Did that one still die in the volcano?"

"Yes."

"Well, there's art for you," Varic said. "From time to time the *Weekly Reasoner* prints a satire on one Parliamentary commission or another, casting them as the moonwreckers. They *always* end up in the volcano." He put a hand to his face.

"Is your head hurting again?"

"No. Truly, no."

She laughed. "And once again you make me wait while you tell a story, about stories. Now I want to play a game with you."

His eyes narrowed just slightly, striking sparks of reflected firelight, and then he nodded.

Longlight said, "I ask you a question, and you must answer. Then you ask one of me."

"I take it that I must answer truthfully?"

"I had not supposed you would lie."

"Point," he said. "And concetta. Ask."

She hesitated for a few instanti, then said abruptly, "Why Agate?"

"Because someone must, and I can. I am not vain or stupid enough to think that no one else on earth could take my place, but none of the others have made themselves available. I discount Strange, of course—I would never imagine Strange incapable of anything. At any event, it is . . . a rewarding thing to be needed."

She said, "Now your question."

"How many aces to a mark?"

"What?"

"A mark breaks down to how many coppers? In Lescorial currency, I mean."

"Ten plates to the mark, ten aces to the plate," she said slowly, "after Redlance's reform, of course. So: a hundred."

"Thank you. Is the game over, or do you have another question?"

She turned, gripped his upper arms hard, and pressed him to the carpet. The fire whispered and shifted. He offered no resistance. She said, "Here we lie and *are* a question, shoulda seiled it from the first. Be hard as you please, I'll be hard straight back."

"That is a good game, too."

❧

It was nearly eleven when Longlight got to the breakfast room. Only Edaire and Silvern were there; Silvern had a platter of sausages next to his eggs and muffins, and with only a little prompting from Gaily, Longlight had some as well. ("Three to start, Lady, while the two more you'll want are browning.")

As they ate, Silvern said, "Are my manners still asleep this morning?" and Longlight realized she was staring at his knife and fork. "It does happen—the Kólyan haven't read *Little Clarity*."

"No, no, I am sorry . . . I was just watching your knife work. I was thinking about . . . precision."

Edaire began to laugh, and was unable to stop. Silvern said, "Will you excuse me a moment?" set down his knife and fork, put his elbows on the table in bald defiance of *Princess Clarity's Little Book of Social Rules,* rested his chin on his hands, and gazed at his conseil with a broad and delicious smile.

Edaire held quiet with a visible effort. Silvern's eyebrows rose. Edaire said, "Oh," in a small, clear voice, and then began to laugh again.

"The honored will get hiccups," Gaily said, holding a teapot in each hand.

Silvern said, "Perhaps a pitcher of apricot juice, then, Gaily, just in case?"

Edaire finally controlled herself.

Longlight said, "I don't think I've ever been in a place where there was so much real laughter. It will be difficult for me to ever thank you adequately."

Silvern said, "Just keep coming back."

"I wonder if you know," Edaire said quietly, "just how good your company has been for Varic. That is more than thanks enough."

"Oh—well," Longlight said. "Now you'll get me to naughty laughter. I wonder that the Parliamentarian isn't here—Varic's friend Lord Brook. He seemed to need a rest and a laugh as well."

Gaily stopped in the doorway, turned, and went out again, without leaving the pitcher of juice.

"Brook no longer comes here," Edaire said.

Longlight said, "I'm sorry—I seem to have wandered off the path."

There was a long moment of silence between Silvern and Edaire. Silvern said, "Yes, I suppose it is my turn," and then to Longlight, "You should know this. The last time Brook visited was a few years ago. He brought along a companion who, to be honest, was something of an opportunist. There was certainly attraction, and I would like to think some real affection, but Rissi was interested in Brook mainly because Brook was a powerful Coron in Parliament. Rissi, who was a not-very-adept Archifactor, was attracted to other people's power. Strange saw through him instantly, of course, and I imagine Varic did as well. Before long it was apparent to all of us—except milord Brook.

"Varic had decided not to come to the House while Brook and Rissi were here. He didn't know that Agate was visiting."

"And the opportunist was a sorcerer."

"That's right. He wouldn't let Agate alone. He asked for lessons, trade secrets, everything novices think masters have to give away. May I be forgiven for a guess with cause, I think he believed she wanted seducing.

"Finally, Agate went out into the woods, just to get away. Rissi followed her, probably thinking he was going to discover some great mystery of Craft. What he found was the big mystery." Silvern made the sign of the Willed Draw, finishing it with a snap of his fingers so that it was just a gesture, without magic. "From time to time . . . energy builds within Agate—and then—"

"It's been explained to me."

Silvern looked suddenly at Edaire. "*Oh.* Well. At that point,

I'm not sure even Varic could have done anything, and Rissi certainly wasn't Varic. Ever hunted Nightcryers?"

Longlight signed against evil. "She—surely can't—"

"No. Even Agate doesn't have that power. But what happened to Rissi wasn't too far different. He lived long enough to print a memory on all of us who were there, and not long enough to raise the hard choice of keeping him alive."

"What did Brook do?"

"Brook woke up from his infatuation so quickly that he may have been under Craft all along. He went back to the City and hasn't visited here since. There must have been something said between him and Varic, but I don't know what it was, and I'm not likely to learn. Though he told Strange last night at dinner that Brook may visit for Solstice. That would be good."

"Would it?"

"If it needs mending, it can't happen at a distance. If it doesn't, then we will be happily together."

⸎

Varic entered Strange's outer office. Its walls were mostly bookcases, with a few glass sideboards displaying this and that. There was a large, tidy desk, and a world globe more than a step in diameter. Dany was sitting in a comfortable chair near the inner door, reading. "Thank you for a fine Mask Night," he said. "Is Strange busy?"

"I am sure he is not so busy as that," Dany said, "but I will call, if you please."

"Thank you."

She went to the desk, pressed a button, and uncoiled a speaking tube covered in green cloth. Varic could hear the tube whisper. Dany said, "Varic would like to see you. Yes." She put the tube down. "Do go in."

He opened the door. The inner office was the outer, but more so: more books, more gadgets and souvenirs, more paper in much less order. Strange had been writing, with the pen Varic had bought at the City Terminus. He capped it, stretched out the chain that held it to his robe, put it in a pocket. "Good morning," he said. "Why ever are you being so formal?"

"It's a formal business. Serious and legal."

"Very well. You won't mind if I remit my fee?"

Varic took a step one way, then another. He looked at a large wall map of Lescoray. "Reccan found something, in one of the provincial papers. A boy in a town called Sunsawe, down in Planes—have you noted it?"

"No."

Varic went to the wall and stared hard at the bookshelves. Calmly and firmly, Strange said, "Varic, sit down."

He did, dropping his hands into his lap. "The boy is . . . simple. Never did any harm, and people generally watched out for him. So far, so fine. Then when he reached his growth, he turned out to have the sorcerer's touch."

"How does he control?"

"Music. He's apparently a natural singer, knows all the favorites." Varic looked into the distance, past Strange. "One day he sang 'Summer's Gone to Cavalry' and let the power get into it. Well, you can probably imagine: a journeyman would have done damage with that, and any novice should have known better. A stone wall came down, and a horse barn. The barn had five horses and two people inside; one of the people may yet live."

"Does this involve Parliament?"

"It's going to involve Cable," Varic said, very quietly. "We passed the resolution establishing legal responsibility for the effects of magic. It's a good bill, but it's amazing what a good, sharp law can do in the hands of our Chief Justiciar. The law's like magic that way, I suppose—sometimes you get much more than you asked for."

"What do you think Cable will do?"

"I'd bet a mark to an ace he tries to hang the boy."

"Literally?"

"Cable has no use for symbolic acts. Certainly not executions. It'll be a fine, solemn, corrective spectacle, and everyone will see that the law for sorcerers is applied without fear or favor. Also without compassion, understanding, or regard to circumstances, but—" He stopped, shut his eyes tight.

Strange said, "I am going to summon Jingle about your headache."

"With all respect to your physician, it is the holiday, and my headache will pass." He took a long breath, and finally opened his eyes, spreading his hands wide so Strange could see that he was relaxed. "The Coron of Planes sends a proxy to Parliament. Decent fellow. Do you have an opinion on the Coron?"

"I recall her as a just soul."

"That's the best hope for everyone." He smiled crookedly. "One Chief Justiciar is like one King—it just won't do." He smiled faintly. "That was once a dangerous idea, too."

"I thought you and Brook had provided for that in the new Constitution."

"Article Twenty calls for a Chief Court of five equals. But I don't know if it will survive. It's on the second-rank list of provisions we're willing to bargain out, and I have very little hope we won't reach the third list." He pressed his hands together.

Strange said, "Will you at least take some feverfew? You can't help this young man if your head's off its pinions."

"I imagine . . . I've already 'helped' enough. Far away in Parliament."

"Where you cannot possibly see into every tiny village and surely cannot predict every consequence," Strange said calmly.

"If there's really no other way through the law, then I imagine that the boy will have to be responsible for himself and answer in full for his action."

The room was very quiet for a moment. Varic turned his head, and his eyes were unfocused, as if he were looking for something at a great distance. Then he said, "I believe I see your point. It's a great deal to ask. Especially of people barely old enough for their oaths to count in court.... No. I wouldn't know how to ask that."

"It's not difficult," Strange said. "You say, 'Your friend must be cared for, from now on, and protected from this ever happening again. It will be a special trust among all of you who accept it."

"Very well, those are the words. What gives me the right to ask them?"

"What gives you the right not to? It's better they be offered it now than realize, after their friend is dead, that someone *could* have made the offer. The hard choice isn't for you, Varic. It's for them."

Varic held his head in both hands as if to keep it from literally splitting open. Strange started to reach for the bell cord.

Varic said, "And twenty years later?"

"Twenty years from now the boy may have died in bed and the problem be solved by default. Or he and his friends may have found a way to solve it, a living modality.... It has been known to happen."

Varic let out an explosive breath. His shoulders relaxed just slightly.

Strange continued, "And there will surely be a different Justiciar in the country. Perhaps even five of them.

"You're right that it isn't your task. You have more to do than correct every injustice in the Republic. But it must be someone's. I'll send a message to the Coron of Planes: she'll either do it or know who can. And stop worrying about your law; you know that no good tool can't be misused."

"Well, I oughten," Varic said, his home accent strong enough to make the point.

Strange waited for half a minima, then said, "May I ask you to stay on here, a few days after the holiday?"

"Is something planned?"

"No. Everyone but Agate is leaving, so far as I know."

"And do you think . . . it might be useful if I remained?"

"I thought it might be pleasant."

"I'm sorry," Varic said, his voice rasping slightly. "I imagine it would be pleasant. The City will be turning damp and gray, and it doesn't need me for that. . . . I'll send a magnostyle to Brook tomorrow. If I'm not needed there, I'll stay—let's say another week."

"Very good. And now will you—"

"I will go to my room like a good lad," Varic said, dry-throated. "And I shall take a large whisky with feverfew and stanbark, and further ask that you make certain Agate has something else to think about for the next few hours."

"Point," Strange said. "Not concetta, but I suppose a draw. Are you certain you want your simples in whisky and not black tea?"

"Perfectly."

"Will you let Dany see you to your room?"

Varic started to nod, then winced and gave the hand-speech sign for *yes*.

Strange pushed himself to the door, opened it. Dany stood up.

"Walk me home, friend?" Varic said, and stepped uneasily through the door. Strange closed it, sat alone in the room. He rolled his chair to his desk, slid a blank magnostyle form from a rack of stationery. He plucked the castelline pen, Varic's gift, from his pocket.

Then he pushed back from the desk, ran the pen's chain between his fingers, turned the capped pen over and over in his hands.

❧

Slowly, Longlight climbed the stairs of Strange House's West Wing. The lack of any sound here was unsettling, without knowing entirely why; it was otherwise well-lighted, safe.

She knocked lightly on Agate's door, which opened. Agate was wearing a long, plain dress of raw silk in autumn colors; her fair hair was netted back. "Good afternoon, my lady Coron. Will you please come in?"

"Strange suggested that I talk to you," Longlight said. "I'm not sure what he had in mind, but . . . if you would like to talk, I would be pleased of the company."

"Strange has great faith in the power of conversation. Come in and sit down. I was just about to call for more tea."

Agate gathered up some papers from the parlor desk; they were covered with writing in what seemed to be several different hands: some spidery, some precise as engraving, some blocky and thick. Lines, and sometimes most of a page, had been struck out, sometimes with a single neat line, sometimes with savage hackings of the pen.

Not much was said until the tea came. Now and then Agate turned her head toward the hallway door, or perhaps the east in general, as if she heard something that way.

"Now," Agate said, nesting in her chair, "what shall we find to talk about? Or will our mutual friend do?"

"I would like to know . . . more about you and Varic. . . . It's prying, I'm sure—"

"Yes, it is," Agate said plainly, "but that doesn't necessarily make it wrong. With whom have you spoken already?"

"Edaire told me some things. And Varic—a very little."

Agate nodded. "I will tell you what Varic is thinking about, just at this moment, if you will promise not to repeat it to anyone. Not even Strange."

"Do I want to know?"

"A wise question. I think perhaps you do."

"Then I promise."

She turned east again. "He is in his room, drinking whisky and herbs, trying to sleep; because if he can sleep, he will not fret over a trial for death by sorcery. The case worries him enough, as well it might, but deeper down he is afraid of seeing me on the gallows. Or possibly some worse device, if he is correct about Justiciar Cable."

"He loves you very much."

"Be calm: I do not hear him when he is thinking of you. Nor at all, outside the House. Silvern and Edaire have more contact.

"But yes, he loves me, in his fashion. As how else can we? People can change, but they can't be something *before* they change to it. Have you begun to love him, in your fashion?"

"Yes," Longlight said. "Last night . . . I found I wanted his talk more than his touch—and I *wanted* his touch."

Agate's teacup shattered, not just into pieces but a cloud of white dust. Longlight gasped. Agate said, "You must pardon me. At the University they have a pavilion just for people like me, so that we may teach in safe isolation. Do continue."

"Edaire told me about you, and him . . . and I thought, as long as 'twas all flesh 'an 'tween'en, then 'twas—different. But it's never *sole'n* flesh, an't so?"

"So I hear."

"*Observate Coron.* That means—"

"I know that it means. I would respect your territory as well, Longlight. Have you read Mistral?"

Longlight started to speak, then shut her mouth. Agate said, "Do quote it; he's a good poet, won't hurt me at all."

Longlight said:

> *"Forest is forest, and sand is sand,*
> *But hearts shall be always debatable land."*

Agate shut her eyes for a moment. "There, do you see? No hurt at all. Tell me: most lovers take their companions candy, and flowers, and pretty little remembrances. Varic brings me quiet, and calm, and myself fit to smile at others. What has he brought you?"

"A Palion to protect my Coronage," Longlight said. "Ironways to feed it. And Strange House."

"You see: you do appreciate his peculiar fashion."

❧

Dinner that evening was a relaxed affair. The formal events of Equinoctials, Service, and Masks were past. It was now properly autumn, Shyira, Her aspect of body and senses, supplanted by Evani, Lady of Trade.

In honor of Evani, Birch brought out a set of Agora cards, and Strange, Winterhill, and Reccan were soon engaged in a spirited (and entirely wordless) game, indicating their trades with finger signals.

"Do you play?" Varic said to Longlight.

"I played Bourse when I was little. Someone at home was showing off a game called Kingscourt, all about politics and intrigue. It looked terribly complicated."

"It is. Even worse if you add the war rules. And the markers, and the toy money, and the special record paper. . . ."

"I take it you play."

"Yes. It allows things that real politics doesn't, or at least frowns on. Assassination is much more fun, for instance."

"Would you show me?"

He tilted his head, then said, "Bliss: Would you have someone send a Kingscourt setup to—your room or mine?"

"Mine."

"To Lady Longlight's room. And a large pitcher of cider, with spice and a fireplace kettle."

"Of course, my lord Varic."

They said good night and went up the stairs. As Longlight reached for the doorhandle, one of the chambermaids appeared from the south stairwell, looking agitated.

"Milord Varic, Jadey's called up from b'lowst'rs. A maggun-style's coming in for you: Will you go down for it?"

"Of course," Varic said. "Thank you, Liri." He turned to Longlight. His expression was abruptly that of the City politician, as it had not been since leaving Lystourel: polite and empty. It was horrible. "Perhaps you should go to your room. These things can be unpredictable."

"I'll come along, if I may."

"Quickly, then."

They went down the central stairs to the lower floor, into a small room smelling of chemicals and hot metal, the sharp scent of electricated air.

A young man with amazing green eyes, undoubtedly Jadey, was seated at a large desk, surrounded by machinery and paper, working a pair of hinged levers with his right hand. "I'm just telling the relay to send, my lord sir. Be coming in a moment."

"Leith Relay?"

"Tindale, my lord."

Strange came in, Dany pushing his chair. "Good evening, Varic."

"Possibly," Varic said without turning. "It's coming via Tindale."

Longlight said, "What does that mean?"

Strange gestured, and they moved back a little from Varic and the desk. Quietly, he said, "Most messages from the City go through two Ironway relay stations, then to the large office at Leith Meadows, before they reach us. The Tindale Relay is a small office only one link from the City. It actually takes longer, because of clearing the lines and finding someone to retransmit, but it is more secure, because there are fewer copy points."

"I understand."

Jadey gave the sending levers a last flick and snatched up a pencil and pad. In a glass-fronted box before him, metal jumped.

The magnostyle receiving case held two long needles on central bearings. Magnets driven by the electrical fluid could pull each needle to the left or right; a particular series of combinations indicated a letter. A trained operator could read over a hundred letters a minima, though the standard speed was only about half that, to keep errors down.

As the pointers oscillated, Longlight looked around the 'style room; it was, like her own, and every other she had seen, lined with reference charts for coil windings and electric pressures and all the other knowledge to keep the system clicking. She looked especially for one piece of paper, and soon spotted it, framed behind glass: it was a verse by Shoredrake. It was always somewhere in the room, came packed with children's toy 'styles; Longlight had learned it as a child, from her father's chief operator:

> *Listen to the needles,*
> *Listen to them click,*
> *Auntie's coming visiting,*
> *Uncle's taken sick.*

Messages upon the wires,
Sparking up and down—
Spelling out the wider world
To every little town.

Something better secret,
Something better known,
Someone's left a legacy,
Someone's left alone.
Anyone may get a message,
Any time of day—
Anything the needles bring
They, too, can bear away.

Telling of a baby,
Telling of a crime,
Song of matrimonials,
Song of fallow time.
Never blame the messenger,
That's the truth of it—
Life's the common fabric
The electric needles knit.

Varic was watching the needles as if there were nothing else in the room, in the world. Longlight wondered if he could read the code.

The needles stopped. Jadey worked the levers, acknowledging the message. He passed the message form to Varic. "Shall I relay it, milord?"

"No, thank you, Jadey. I'll see to it."

"Certainly, milord."

Varic turned and walked out of the room as if he saw nothing and no one else but the message form. Longlight followed, and Dany pushed Strange's chair behind.

In the hallway, Strange said, "Yes?"

Varic handed over the paper.

BROOK TAKEN ILL. ASKS YOU INFORM CORON RED MOUNTAIN
   TO CANCEL APPOINTMENT. NOT SERIOUS, FULL RECOVERY
   EXPECTED.

FRESHET

END

Longlight said, "Who is Freshet?"

"Brook's physician. Excellent soul, rarely wrong."

"Was the key word *red*?"

"You have some experience of this," Varic said distantly. "Of course—there are bandits in your country. And friends of bandits. Will you all excuse me now?" He walked up the stairs, and they let him go.

Longlight turned. Strange looked thoughtful, Dany questioning. Both of them were very still.

Strange said, "Perhaps, Longlight, you would explain to Dany."

Longlight said, "If you think the wrong person might read your messages, there are ways to hide the meaning. For example, the word *red* could mean that the message is to be understood as far graver than its surface meaning, or even its complete opposite."

"Then Brook's physician," Dany said, "believes he will not recover."

Longlight nodded.

"But did you then read this code so easily?"

Strange said, "I believe the code is sound enough. My lady read Varic."

"You flatter me, Strange."

"Not much. What do you think he will do now?"

"Go to the City. Tonight. However he can get there."

"You see, I don't flatter."

❦

Varic raised his hand to knock on Agate's door, then stopped. His head seemed afire, and he could feel his pulse in his fingertips. This was no state to visit her in, but he needed her.

Delicate fingers slipped within his skull, cooling the flames, and he heard Agate's voice say, *Sorcerers are always wanted for some thing or another, but so rarely needed. And to be needed by you is a rare thing indeed.*

"Brook is . . . please, Agate . . ." He put a hand to his head.

I will take my hands away, if you will not weep.

He nodded, and the touch went away. "I need—I need you to work the Long Mirror."

Then come in and help me find my robe.

He went inside. Agate was pushing a chair before a tall dressing mirror. She was wearing a short cotton bed jacket that barely reached to her tan hips. "Look around, will you? I tossed it somewhere."

He found it behind the parlor chair. "Do you want your slippers?"

"I'll work better without them. Earth and Air. Sit down."

He sat facing the mirror. Agate stood behind him. "Who is the message for?"

"Freshet. Brook's physician. I would suppose she'll be at the Gate Park Hospital, but I can't be certain. She'll be in the City, though."

"Of course. She won't have gone far from Brook at such a time."

Varic nodded. "It's grave, yes."

"Freshet. *Fresh*-et, *Lys*-tou-rel. *Heal*-er, *hos*-pi-tal. Couldn't be better."

"I don't think I'd ever considered the disadvantages of an un-metrical name," Varic said. "It must be a great convenience in Ferangard: *Teph*-ar Di-*an*-te, *Or*-ic A-*dor*-ni."

"Varic."

"I'm sorry."

"Face the mirror. And don't turn."

"I know."

"You also have a great deal on your mind. I can't grow you new eyes in less than three days."

"Very well."

She sat on the floor behind him, began to speak softly and rhythmically. The air felt tense, charged. The room lights dimmed. The image in the mirror wobbled, then cleared, and the lights flared bright again.

"She's not at the hospital," Agate said. "Where shall I try next?"

"Let me think. . . . Oh, of course. Try Brook's house. Walnut Row."

"*Wal*-nut-Row. Same as *hos*-pi-tal. Good. Look forward."

The chant started again. This time, the room lights faded entirely, and the mirror image cleared to show a woman sitting at a table, beside a lamp, playing a solitaire card game. The view was bulged, as in a spherical mirror.

"Eh, now? Oh, Varic. You look very curious, peering from a silver teapot."

"My apologies, Freshet."

"None needed. This is over Brook, after all."

"Tell me what has happened."

"His butler found him on the bedroom floor. It appears to be an apoplectic seizure." She sighed. "His eyes look without blinking, until the lids are shut for him; they do not respond.

He breathes quietly, his heart beats slowly. He is alive, and no more than that."

"And recovery?"

"It has happened in similar cases, and it has mostly not happened. We both know Brook; I would like to say that, if there is a will left inside the body, it will find a way back. The Archipath I usually work with is away, and I am being cautious. . . ."

"Send a message to Master Whetstone. He will arrange something."

Freshet nodded. "You are, if you don't mind me using the word, his executor. What do you want me to do?"

After a long pause, Varic said, "What is to be done?"

"His brain is wounded, Varic. Even if we can locate his mind and then bring it back—it may be in pieces. What do you want me to do?"

Varic started to turn. Agate shouted, "Face the mirror!" and there was a sudden sheet of blue-white light. Varic winced and turned back. Agate said, in a ragged and angry voice, "It's not a matter of minutes, and probably not hours. If he's gone by the time you'll reach him, he's gone now."

"Varic?" Freshet said, pressing her face close to her end of the Mirror. "Are you still there?"

"Have Whetstone find a sorcerer, but don't act until I arrive. How much of the news is out?"

"None, so far as I know. The butler called me directly, and we haven't yet moved him from the house. Being the holiday, there have been no appointments. There was a card from"—she picked it from the table, read the name—"Linnet, asking about dinner."

"Linnet can be trusted. But . . . tell him gently."

"Why, Varic, you surprise me," Freshet said lightly.

"One other thing," Varic said. "Is this definitely a natural illness?"

Freshet's look darkened. "Oh, you vile little man," she said, more sadly than angrily. "I have no reason to believe otherwise."

"Thank you, Freshet. For everything. Is there anything I can do for you?"

"Spell me watching him," she said wearily.

"I will be there as soon as I can."

"Very well."

"That's all, Agate," Varic said, and the Mirror image faded. Agate groaned, and Varic turned quickly.

"I'm fine," she said, breathing deeply. "And I am sorry, Varic. You will send word if there is anything I can do?"

"I will."

He helped her back to bed, hung her robe on the bedpost hook, and tucked her slippers beneath the step. "Now I have to disturb Edaire's sleep."

"A word before you go."

He stood still.

"You thought it would be you, not Brook," she said quietly. "That the bullet or the knife would take you, and Brook would go on, probably forever. It was never likely to happen that way, Varic; and with no lack of sympathy for Brook meant, I would ask you not to feel guilty that it has not."

"Just a little ordinary grief, then."

"Your grief is not ordinary, Varic. Not to me above all people."

He kissed the tips of his fingers and pointed them at her. She nodded. He went out.

❧

Breakfast the following morning was very quiet. Everyone but Agate, and of course Varic, sat around the table indoors, mostly still in nightclothes; there had been very little sleep since Varic's departure. Even Gaily was subdued as she came and went with the meals, though she still had smiles for everyone and told the joke about the chicken and the pig who agreed to race to the breakfast table. "'You win,' said the hen, looking at the bacon and eggs. 'I'm glad there wasn't money on it.'"

Strange managed to laugh, and then they all did, Reccan merry with her hands. Brook excused himself to the Bright Room and prayers.

Hazel came into the breakfast room then, carrying a box covered with a painter's cloth. "Excuse me, my lord Strange, honoreds, but Master Plumb told me to bring this to my lady Coron Longlight."

"Thank you, Hazel," Longlight said, and took the box.

"Shall I go now, honoreds?"

Strange said, "Stay just a moment, Hazel. You look worried. Is something wrong?"

"If I may ask you, honored."

"Of course."

"Milord Varic left the House very late last night. Mama Roan drove the carriage, and Mama Tacker was sad when she called me this morning. Milord Varic is always sad when he leaves the House, and he never goes away in the night like that."

Strange said, "Come here, Hazel." The boy went to stand by Strange's chair. "One of milord Varic's good friends in the City is very sick, and Varic had to go away quickly to visit him. You know how far away the City is."

"Yes. Will milord Varic bring his friend here, to get well?"

Strange took Hazel's hand. "I don't know, Hazel. But that's a very good idea. It may be that he will." He looked across the table. "And now, I think milady Longlight has something for you."

She took the cloth cover from the box, held it out to Hazel. The boy's eyes went wide. Longlight said, "Go ahead. They are for you, an Evennight gift."

Hazel carefully lifted one of the wooden Ironway coaches,

turning a dowel-slice wheel with a fingertip, tracing the wood-burned window frames, making the snaps at the vestibule ends jingle. "Do you see, honored Edaire? They can train up!"

"I see, Hazel. Isn't there something you should say?"

"Oh. Thank you, my lady Longlight. Thank you so much."

"You are most welcome, Hazel. And your mother Roan helped me make them, and Master Plumb. You must thank them as well."

"I will, Lady. Honored Edaire—could we go to the parlor?"

"I think we might, Hazel. Perhaps milady Coron would like to join us?"

"I would be delighted," Longlight said. "It is ripe time that I should learn more about Ironways."

II

THE PALE TESTAMENT

I found you sleeping, quite as still as death:
The moonlight on your nakedness shone blue
And cold. I could not sense your heart, your breath;
Yet knew you only slept—I hoped I knew,
And feared not knowing. I drew near, and read
Your pale testament, my legacy:
Long silences, dark nights, a colder bed,
Disordered sheets, disordered memory.
Of late we'd said that our estates were too
Intangible, uncertain ground—but then,
The land I longed to live upon was you.
You snored, and I was propertied again.
And as I moved to enter on your rest,
I paused—and felt the cancer in my breast.

CHAPTER 5

JUSTICE AND DIVISION

Varic sat by the compartment window, watching the dark world pass by. From time to time a light showed, yellow-white and unreal in the fog; there was no real sign of dawn yet.

He had been sitting so for at least two hours, when the train stopped at Leatherwood Halt to take on a carload of fresh milk for the City. Milk and mail was the main purpose of this run; there was a coach with a tea and pie counter, and the short sleeper for souls with early City business. Varic's bed was still tightly made; there had been no point in trying to sleep.

After Leatherwood came a series of momentary halts, to deliver the milk and transfer the post. Station names slid out of the darkness for a minima in bright yellow gaslight, then vanished again into the wings. The signboards spoke of distance and isolation: Greygates, Alders March, Solus Post, Fartheron—outposts turned to postal districts. Corons a hundred milae from the zero stone worried that they would be absorbed, become mere City councilors, and sometimes they were not joking.

It could not happen, of course. The steadily increasing complexity of supplying Lystourel with fresh food, clean water, gas, and passable streets—and now electricity as well—pointed directly to the limits of city sprawl.

As Varic thought on this, walls appeared by his window as if by sorcery, swallowing the train in a swirl of confined smoke and flickers of lights passing nearby. The wheels clacked loudly over crossings and points. The whistle blew, and they began to slow.

Shortly they were in the Terminus approach. Lights glittered on the great fan of tracks, polished rails in the darkness like a spiderweb bright with dew. Switch and service crew waved lanterns, signals shifted color.

Varic stood up. His knees were uncomfortably stiff. He picked up his bag and left the compartment, sidling down the dim corridor to the vestibule.

The captain was there, by the open window, examining a huge bronze-cased watch. "Good morning, honored," she said, just above the wind and steam. "Right on time today."

"Indeed," Varic said, and took a deep lungful of the oil-smoked air.

"Did you have a pleasant holiday?"

"Exceptionally pleasant. But now back to work."

"Find Her waiting," the captain said, and went down the corridor. Varic nodded and leaned against the wall as they rolled to a stop beneath the glass Terminus canopy.

He got off almost alone. A family that had been traveling in the coach was sorting itself together beneath one of the dim platform lights; the sleeper passengers were allowed to stay abed for another two hours yet. Those, that is, who could sleep.

The great curve of the Terminus was supernaturally empty, the upper arches lost in darkness, all the shops shut but for the news vendors and a tea cart. Varic pushed through a side door, into air abruptly cold and very damp; it shook him fully awake. Ahead, through icy-blue mist, the rank of waiting cabs were black silhouettes, like holes cut in paper. He boarded the first coach in line, and they rolled away with a startling clatter.

The life of Lystourel's streets never quite stopped. On the ride, Varic could see milk and meat wagons starting their rounds, the friendly light of an all-hours corner shop with the early newspapers still bundled on the curb outside. A watchman stood under a lamppost, hands in pockets, rolling his weight from one foot to the other.

That brought Varic's thoughts back to the New Constitution: the judiciary Articles were to reserve cities and chartered towns the unquestioned right to maintain their own patrolmen. Justiciar Cable had been making noises for some time that any such force should be under the control of his Bailiffs' Corps. He had not gotten far with the idea; the town watch was an ancient institution, and the Corons were jealous of their privileges of law.

For his part, Cable would not give up the notion—and in fact, he had a point about establishing the authority of the national police above Coronal or local forces, which all too often enforced a Coronal whim or a local prejudice rather than anything that could be called justice.

It needed consideration, and work, and certainly it needed Brook well and working on it.

The cab stopped on a quiet, well-lighted block of detached town houses, set back from the street behind small, iron-fenced yards. Large walnut trees lined the curbs. Varic paid the driver and passed through one of the well-oiled gates. He saw that it was the only house on the block showing a light upstairs.

This was Walnut Row. Its first wealthy inhabitant had made her money in lumber, and put the trees in. There was as yet no central electricity here; the few houses that had electrical light generated their own fluid. Brook still lit with gas. Setting up one's own light service required time and effort and additional house staff, though what he said, smiling, was that electricity was obviously a temporary fancy—after all, could one cook with it?

Varic climbed the steps and turned the bell-knob. Clarity, Brook's butler, opened the door. She was tall and looked almost absurdly delicate. Her raven-black hair was smoothly brushed and cropped close, like a helmet. Her long, black coat, though it was the same as she wore every day in service, today had a look of mourning.

"Please come in, my lord Varic. It's terrible sharp out—will you take tea? Or some broth? But you've been traveling all night, you must want breakfast."

"No, thank you, Clarity. Perhaps a cup of the broth, a little later on."

"Of course, my lord. Let me take your coat. The doctor's in the upstairs parlor. Shall I announce you?"

"No need."

Clarity gave a birdlike bob of a bow and disappeared with Varic's coat.

Varic glanced around the entrance parlor. There were three neat piles of mail on a side table, each wrapped with a ribbon and a note showing the date received. He went up the stairs, past a dozen glass-fronted frames on the blue watered-silk wall-covering, holding honorary University degrees and diplomatic awards from any number of nations.

At the top of the stairs was a large framed engraving of Thorn-grove House, Brook's Coronal Seat. Varic had visited it twice. The picture emphasized the central hall, a massive frontage of Midreigns stonework. It was attractive in its way, but exception-ally uncomfortable. Three of Brook's ancestors had each added a wing in a different direction and architectural style. Brook re-ferred to them as the Grotesque, Runagate, and Derangée Halls (the last in an Alinsever coastal style, eighty milae from open water). "Other souls dread retirement because they fear being idle and forgotten," Brook would say. "I fear having to live at home."

Brook's bedroom was quite warm, with a good fire going to one side of the large canopied bed. A table lamp made one corner bright, and there sat Freshet. Her coattails were draped neatly over her lap, her watch chain and rimless eyeglasses caught the firelight. She put the book she had been reading next to the tea service and stood up, holding out one hand to take Varic's and massaging the back of her neck with the other.

"I'm glad you've come," she said, "and I wish I had some news. But there is no change." She gestured at the bed.

Brook reclined on pillows. He had been dressed in a quilted bed jacket over satin pajamas; the bedcovers were drawn up to his breast, his hands pale and still upon them. His face was perfectly calm, his mustaches combed neatly (that would be Clarity's work, Varic knew), though his cheeks were dusted with new beard. His eyes were shut; above them, a nightcap held back his hair, overemphasizing the height of his forehead, making it skull-like.

Freshet brought the lamp over. In the better light, the grayness went away, and Brook seemed not so marble pale. Freshet said quietly, "There would be no harm in touching him."

"No. Tell me what arrangements you've made."

She put the lamp down, looked at her watch. "It's just five. The principal nurse will be in at six; he'll be living in, napping on the daybed there, with another nurse to spell him for a shift every third day."

"He'll sleep?"

"This is the usual arrangement. It is safe. And it keeps the number of nurses to a minimum—which I'm sure you will agree is a security measure."

"Point," Varic said.

"Fortunately, Brook can swallow liquids."

"If that changes?"

"Sustenance by Craft. It isn't difficult, but it requires much more tending—two sorcerers by shifts."

"Very well."

"Clarity's quite a nurse herself, do you know—she's insisted on dressing and bathing him, and done it right well."

"That does not surprise me," Varic said.

"Nothing ever does, I suppose," Freshet said.

Varic said, "How did this all begin? In as much detail as possible."

"May I sit down?"

They did, across the room. Freshet said, "Three days ago—what was that, Shineday? Third night of Evenlight. He stayed in all day; I think Clarity said he was answering letters. Linnet brought dinner, and they had that. He makes a remarkable lamb broth."

"Just the two of them?"

"I thought you'd ask that. No, Clarity dined with them; Brook told her it was an Equinox party. He asked her to bring her friend Trammels, the hammerjack at the house up the street, but they were having their own party and Trammels had to work. Some, as they say, are more equal than others. At any event, Linnet was asked to stay the night. A quarter after two, he woke Clarity; Brook had made a noise in his sleep, waking Linnet, and Linnet couldn't rouse him. Clarity called me, and I was here by half four. No sign of anything but an apoplexy. And if Linnet *had* had some intent, he couldn't have found a less subtle way to carry it out." She said, almost kindly, "Does that clear your mind a little? About Linnet, at least?"

"It begins to."

Freshet sighed. "I may not have sorcery—as people never tire of reminding me—but I *do* have an apothecary's certificate, and if there was poison, it is too subtle for me. And I also know that it's difficult to kill subtly by Craft; I've seen it done a few times, and there's always been a grand old mess. Varic, listen.

Brook isn't young, and he worked too hard. Something inside him wore down and gave way. There's no good or evil in it, just the terrible, awful fact. And the hope of restoration."

"Yes, of course. The hope." He took a careful step toward the bedside, stood watching Brook. After a full minima, he slowly stretched out a hand, placed it across Brook's knuckles.

"Yet he does not stir," Varic said. "And both of us nobles of the blood. Where are the strong tales of yesterday?"

"Varic, I—"

"Yes?" He took his hand away, turned to face her. "*Were* you expecting something miraculous?"

"I have never been able to like you, Varic. I respect you, I admire your work in the Parliament. But—" She interlaced her fingers. "Doctors are taught—even the ones without Craft—that people are flesh and spirit interlinked, inseparable and complete. The end of a finger contains humanity, and with it Goddess. But you're like—a machine operated by something at its center, separated from the world by levers and wires. Separated from—"

"From Goddess. Yes. I am."

Slowly, she unwound her hands. "I can see that you'd want vengeance on whoever might have done this to Brook. For my part, I think if I really believed someone had deliberately caused it to happen, to Brook of all people—I think I'd regret that I'd ever saved a life—given any comfort at all to such things as we would have to be."

"Well. We have a thing in common, then. Not that comfort is what I've given."

"Brook has told me otherwise."

Varic turned back to Brook. "How long can a person survive, like this?"

"At the Teaching College in Ascorel, there's been a patient sustained in coma for six years."

"Of course," Varic said, the memory ticking into place. "That would be Coron Fairlane's son. He was thrown from a horse. Fairlane's sent a proxy since then."

"Care is rarely so prolonged, Varic."

Without turning away from Brook, Varic said, "I take it you are about to tell me why it is not."

"Entry to the mind is delicate work, but not exceptionally difficult. Done under observation, by a Guildmember, the patient's statement is legally binding. And—in the majority of cases—"

"Yes, of course. I believe that is why Fairlane refuses to allow it."

"It will be your decision, as executor."

Varic was silent.

There was a knock at the door. "Milord Varic. Dr. Freshet."

"Yes, Clarity?"

"The nurse has arrived, honoreds. He awaits you downstairs."

They went down to the parlor. A man was standing to attention by the fireplace, a battered Linkman bag by his feet. He was as large as Brook, powerfully muscled. His hair, which was bushy on top but cut well above his neck, was red brown with gold threads. He wore the usual nurse's uniform: short-sleeved white shirt and trousers, a linen vest with large pockets. His skin was deeply tanned, looking even darker against all the white. A topcoat was folded neatly over his left arm; the hand upon the coat had a tattoo of fouled anchors. He wore thick-lensed glasses, and a gold-and-red pearl drop hung from his right ear.

"Trevan," Freshet said. "I'm glad to see you. My lord Varic, may I present Trevan Dain, nurse and physician-auxiliary. Trevan, please to know Varic, Coron Corvaric. My lord Varic has authority for the patient during his incapacitation."

"Of course, my lord," Dain said, and gave a small, military bow.

Varic said, "You would have been in Alinsea's marines?"

Dain tilted his tattooed hand. "My lord is observant. I was in the Home Island Division. Corporal, invalided out as serjeant."

"If I may?" Varic said, and stepped closer. He could see shiny, unnaturally smooth skin around Dain's right eye. Dain looked at Varic directly, and Varic noted the slightly oval pupil: an eye regrown by a sorcerer of less-than-perfect skill.

Dain said, "My lord may be aware that as the fleet changes from sail to steam, many of the plank-and-halyard marines are no longer in demand. So after the injury, I took my severance in training, and my auxiliary's certificate from Ascorel Physicians'. I am, of course, a Lescorial citizen now. In case my lord was wondering."

Freshet said without inflection, "The agency was necessarily told some of the circumstances of my lord Brook's condition."

Varic said, "I know of nothing to question in the record of the Home Island marines, honored. But I appreciate your frankness. Perhaps, when I am intruding on your work with my visits, you will tell me something of your service?" He turned, saw Clarity standing in the hall doorway. "Clarity, will you take the honored's coat?"

Dain relaxed to parade rest as he handed over the coat and picked up his bag.

Freshet took the nurse upstairs. Varic followed Clarity down the hall to the coat closet and then into the kitchen. It was a small room, all white porcelain and dark blue tile. A teacup and an unwashed plate were on the central table, along with household papers.

Varic smelled lamb broth, and at once it seemed the most desirable of things.

"Are you certain you would not like some breakfast, milord?" Clarity said. "There are biscuits with cheese and greens, and a fresh berry linka." She looked apologetic. "Linnet keeps bringing baskets. It is something to do."

"A biscuit, then, and some broth. Have you time to join me? While the doctor is busy." He took off his suit coat, hung it on a peg. Then he turned and raised a finger to Clarity, who was hurrying to assist. He took down an apron from the rack and tied it over her tidy black coat. Then he sat down.

She nodded, poured him hot broth from a pan on the stove, and went to heat the biscuits.

He could not, he knew, really have a casual meal with her, as if he were the mail carrier after rounds or a handcrafter from the house up the block. But just now, while there was something of Strange House still around him, they could at least be two people who cared for Brook. It was something to do.

Clarity handled the food expertly, and Varic could see the tension in her face and hands lessen as she worked. As with Varic's City house, Brook had no full-time cook. Most of the full meals they took were at work, whether a conference over lunch or a diplomatic banquet. On the rare occasions when they entertained, the food was brought in, by someone like Linnet. For the rest, there were their own resources, or Midden's wife, or Clarity.

Her name in the fullness of the law was Clarity After the Kings. No one remembered now whether it had been a historical enthusiasm of her parents' or an overly literal transcription by a dozy clerk. Varic had wondered more than once what it had been like to literally be Little Clarity—people who had never read the book and had no use for etiquette anyway knew the name—but he had never asked, even asked Brook. And this was not the time.

She served Varic his biscuits, then seemed about to stand aside or leave the room; he gestured for her to sit across from him, and she did, but without removing apron or coat.

They talked a little about Varic's holiday. Clarity had grown up in Grand Bluffs, on the Estuary. At the time it had been fairly open country, but now there was a cluster of warehouses, waterside industries, and an Ironway yard. She admitted that she missed open fields, but where else was she to go on holiday? Home was home.

Varic made a meaningless noise of agreement.

"Milord Varic—this is a difficult thing to ask—"

He put down his fork, wiped his mouth carefully. "It is a difficult time, Clarity. Do go ahead."

"I simply . . . do not know what I shall do, if we lose Milord Brook."

"I am entirely certain that Brook has made provision for you."

"I did not mean to question his generosity, my lord. I meant that . . . I am not certain how to think about service with someone other than Brook."

"Yes," Varic said, controlling his voice carefully, "I believe I understand you. Well. We must maintain hope, and if we pass that, I will do what I can. There are many great houses in the country."

"Thank you, my lord."

"Perhaps it shall not come to that."

A half-formed thought finally crystallized. Should they move Brook to Strange House, for the duration? It would probably mean a new physician; Freshet had other patients. That would not be good. But the surroundings would be healthier and infinitely more secure.

Clarity would go along, of course. She would be torn between Brook and the house, but posts were easily forwarded. She would not have to carry the whole load of staff work. It would certainly be better for her.

And if the worst happened, Brook's testament assured her of enough money to settle in the country, whether Strange's Coronage or another. She doubtless knew that, but it was not to be thought on now.

On the other hand, there were people who could not easily

shift two full days from the City for the uncertain duration of Brook's illness. Linnet could not.

And Varic could not.

When he left Brook's house, the sun was up but short of the housetops, the streets still shadowed beneath a clear, pale-blue sky. He had declined Clarity's offer to summon a cab. It was over two milae, and the Grand to cross, but a long walk and river air would not harm him, and there were always cabs for well-dressed folk in the better City quarters. He accepted the loan of a walking stick, knowing from its balance and the thumb catch on the grip that it was a swordstick. Clarity would not have chosen it by chance.

He must, he thought deliberately, set aside the idea that Brook's condition was anything but natural. If evidence to the contrary should appear, there would be things to do; if Justiciar Cable was really so interested in prosecuting destructive sorcery, that would be a fine and proper thing for him to pursue. But Varic was going to be pursuing too much else, whether Brook recovered or not.

That was another thought that must be dealt with, of course.

Brook's testament was in a concealed safe box in the town house. Varic knew only those parts of it Brook had spoken of; he could not now remember how Clarity's endowment had come up in conversation. It was possible that it dealt with his wishes in circumstances such as this. Varic would have to examine it, soon. Certainly before any decision was made about entering Brook's mind.

His thoughts were interrupted by footsteps and metallic squeaking behind him. He turned. A young woman in a neat blue dress was pushing a baby carriage. Varic raised his hat.

"Good morning, honored," the—nanny? Mother?—said, in a quite musical voice. She passed on by.

Something about her face had reminded him of Longlight.

He supposed he had not said a proper farewell to her, or indeed to anyone at the House. Letters were called for. Strange would want to know Brook's condition, and Varic could be more detailed and much more direct in a sealed post than a magnostyle. And to Longlight . . .

He wondered how long it took the mail to reach her home, past the limits of the Ironway. A 'style to the last station, and then a copy by post, ought to be waiting when she and Silvern arrived. It could be quite discreet—*Thank you for a pleasant holiday, hoping you are,* and so forth—and a proper letter could follow.

He wondered what was really going to happen to her nice young Palion. Was it withering, as she had said? Or—

No. *Not now.*

He turned onto Cashgoods Street and headed west, toward the Grand River. More people were appearing on the streets, once more the early change of shift. House staff were sweeping the first few fallen leaves from neat lawns, walking briskly to the corner shop for a newspaper and a pint of milk for the breakfast tea, oiling fence gates so the owner's morning departure should not be interrupted by grinding metal.

A few of the owners were stepping forth, in morning coats and silk hats, some with satchels, others lightly hoisting their canes.

This, the northeast riverside, was a prosperous, businesslike part of the City, settled during the rise of the merchant classes— people like the lumber dealer on Brook's street. They had gone upriver, so that their drains emptied above the older neighborhoods of the Estuary. A few of the houses still had more-or-less unimpeded water views. The primacy of drains could not be maintained; too many people thought riverside and upstream both good ideas. A three-block-wide strip of parkland had been established to the north side of the district, keeping the even newer money at a certain remove.

Varic thought about walking north to the parkside promenade, but kept his course. He was determined to walk the mila
and a half farther home, but there was no reason to be extravagant about it.

The street ended at the river. There was a narrow iron bridge,
mainly for pedestrians but wide (and strong) enough for a
mounted constable or medical van. It had semicircular platforms
to either side, to step aside from any such emergency traffic or
just enjoy the City view.

Varic stopped at the top of the arch, looked downriver. The
water was placid, shimmering. The masts of docked ships made
a spider forest. To Varic's right, even the sprawling architectural
mess of the Castle gave the illusion of order and rectitude.

The bridge iron hummed in the breeze, a baritone guitar
chord. The tuneless music made him think of Agate, the bridge
builders she had met in Blackice Gorge.

He wondered if, should it come to that, he could ask her to
enter Brook's consciousness. Freshet had offered it as a simple
and logical decision, but in Varic's understanding, the Crafting
was particularly delicate. And not without risk to both patient
and sorcerer.

Varic's head began to ache. He shut his eyes, pressed fingers
hard to his forehead, and the pain receded.

He would not ask Agate, because Agate would consider it necessary to agree. He would go to the Guildmaster; Whetstone
would know who was right for the work.

The wind picked up slightly, and the bridge sang. Varic resumed his walk.

❧

The parlor was very dark, all the curtains drawn tight. Varic
turned up a glasswick. Everything was just as it had been, though

the secretary desk seemed to have a particular sheen; Midden must have waxed it. On the desk, Varic's post was racked by date of receipt. There seemed to be an unusual number of letters for a holiday.

A handwritten card caught his attention. Linnet requested the pleasure of the Lord Varic's company for a meal. Varic felt himself smile. It was not the technical form for inviting a member of the Coronate to dine. He did, hang protocol, certainly want to see Linnet. Tonight, he thought, or tomorrow's lunch.

There was a large, heavy envelope with the crossed sword and tipstaff of the Justiciar. It was addressed to Varic, marked *By Hand,* and was filed in the slot for two days ago, the day after Brook's attack.

He slit it open.

Salutations to my lord Coron.

I have been much remiss in not complimenting you anent your work upon the Revised Lescorial Constitution. Constitutional matters are, as you may imagine, a close interest of mine, and I should like to discuss the proposed Revisions in a setting more private and less formal than Parliament House.

I would have my lord meet the Grand Captain of Bailiffs Heartsease, who brings this message. Would my lord consent to a dinner with the Grand Bailiff and myself, at the first convenience? Heartsease will gladly await your reply, or I may be reached at my home or official addresses.

[The sign of Justice]

Cable

Chief Justiciar of Lescoray

Well, that was rather closer to the technical form. And Varic was interested in discussing the Constitution with Cable, especially so given the timing of the message. It did not mention Brook's illness. Surely it did not have to.

He was also curious as to what a Grand Captain of the Bailiffs' Corps was.

There was another piece of formal-looking mail, a large envelope with a steel-engraved cachet of machinery above indecipherable interlocked initials.

The letter inside was from the Exposition Organizational Partnership, whoever they were, asking for a meeting to discuss the Lescorial Grand Exposition, whatever that might be. It was written in someone's idea of technical form, taking four times as long as necessary to deliver its point, with enough personal praise and honorifics to embarrass actual royalty. It was dated before the holiday.

The rest was periodicals, bills—electricity, water, Ivory & Co.—and a handful of stationery he recognized, friends of Brook's. He would deal with them later.

He went into the kitchen. The icebox contained neatly wrapped patcakes, beef and seasoned chicken, and several bottles of brown ale. He took a bottle and one of the beefs upstairs, got into pajamas, and sat eating in bed, reading the *Weekly Commodities and Trade*.

An article on Ironway construction in mountains caused him to think again of Longlight. He turned in the sheets, feeling a sudden real pain for her.

He had turned lights in at Strange House before this particular holiday. It had been six years ago, at the Warm Solstice. Her name was Coquil de Nive. She had come to the House with her cousin, who was a trade negotiator; she was herself from a sea-freighting family.

She had been unusually pale for an Alinsever; even those who dwelt off the water were near it. But Coquil was fair, with gold hair of an extraordinary fineness, and eyes the color of dark blue pottery, like the tile on Brook's kitchen walls. She wore a touch of perfume that had a dark, smoky scent, imported from somewhere exotic.

She brought with her a game called Caravels, about sea-trading and piracy. Varic and Strange introduced her to King-scourt. She played both ferociously, sinking paperboard ships or beheading wooden nobles with a triumphant laugh.

Varic had been surprised, therefore, to find her patient and still in the dark, light of touch. They spoke in low murmurs. He could still remember the words. And the rest of it.

He remembered the first time he had seen Agate after that holiday, uncertain if he had upset a delicate and irrecoverable balance. He could still perfectly see her complex expression: amusement, a dry grin, and the pleasure of truce with the jangling world that was particularly Agate's.

He had not seen Coquil after that. She had ships of her own now, he had been told.

Where *was* memory? In the brain, the naturalists said, and indeed when the brain was wounded the memory was as well. But how did it live, inside the knotted tissue? Varic's legs remembered how to walk without his telling them, his hand recalled the grip of a sword or a pen, but where was a summer night at the House, cool air rustling the curtains, the scent of smoky rare oils and warm skin?

It could not be found with the naturalist's knife, nor with fingers. There was an old tale that during the Great Famine, when people had finally begun to see one another's dwindling flesh as meat, that some of those had deliberately fed on the brains of the best and wisest dead, trying to preserve their knowledge, assimilate their wisdom, and solve the problem.

But not a thought was saved.

Varic's hands were crumpling the magazine. He had been staring at the curtained windows, dreaming awake, seeing Brook lying coldly in the firelight. The thought made him tense, the tension made his head ache, the pain behind his eyes made him think again of Brook, and that made him angry.

He wondered if, if one could justify opening up what most people believed was their one inviolable place—as the closest companions could not, as even the conseil could not—was there not, then, a justification for any act at all?

And if they *did* Craft-cut into Brook's mind and found no certain answer? Did that mean he was gone, just a breathing shell? Could you then starve that shell, could you bury it, knowing in the best of conscience that you could no longer feed of its wisdom?

He shut his eyes, tried deliberately to relax his muscles. The bed pressed at him in ways that seemed unfamiliar. His arm rested on the curve of a pillow, and again he thought of Longlight, with the same pain.

If he dressed, went out again, it was half an hour's walk or ten minima by cab to Cold Street, where (as Brook had said) they liked him. They would treat him very well and listen to whatever he had to say with the same kind of calm equanimity he tried to display on the floor of Parliament. He could certainly go there angry—a good number of people went there precisely because they were angry, and the houses had elaborate methods for handling that.

But if he were to be alone in a room with Longlight, and angry, he had strong reasons to believe that she would understand, be able to confront his anger, not just distract him from it. Thus, the pain.

He moved his fingers on the cool pillow, allowing himself to think very particularly of Longlight. Somehow it calmed the storm in his skull. He felt his breath come easier, which struck him as paradoxical.

Then suddenly the air was chilly and the sheets were warm,

the bed damp with sweat as from a broken fever, and the mantelpiece clock said it was early evening.

Dinner at Linnet's tearoom ended early, at nineteen or so. If Varic moved briskly, he could be there just before closing, and they could sit in private. It would be better, he thought, to meet there, Linnet's home territory, avoid any idea of being summoned into the mighty presence of the lord Coron.

He tossed aside the moist linens. The lord Coron would need a shower as well. Best to hurry.

It was a gray, clammy twilight when the cab arrived at the Blue Rose, and the restaurant's lamps in their petal shades looked quite friendly.

The driver asked for eight plates, presumably expecting a full mark. The ride should have cost no more than five, with perhaps one more as tip, but it was still the tail of the holiday, and shortage was sorcery, as the Commoditor liked to say. Varic handed up a kingsir. The cabman had mastered the trick of hiding his license number with a flourish of his high hat; Varic noticed this with a welcome amusement.

He went inside. Most of the table lamps were out, and only one table was occupied; Linnet sat there, with a man whose back was to the door.

Varic thought for a moment about stepping immediately out again, but the door chime had already rung, and Linnet looked up. "Milord," he said, and rose. The other man just turned in his seat.

"Why, my lord of Corvaric," the seated man said. "How pleasant to see you, though not at the most pleasantest time." Then he stood as well, and extended his hand. Varic took it gladly, pumped it vigorously in the Ferangarder fashion.

The man was Merus Arayder, an art dealer who had reset-
tled in Lystourel years ago, and married a Lescorial. Lapis was a
painter of considerable reputation; she had designed cards for
several well-respected Books.

"We would have seen you, the party of the Ambassador's, but
we came late and you had early gone. But—do tell me—Brook:
Is there anything to be done?"

Varic held his reply for a moment. In Gerade, the Ferangarder
language, *anything to be done* was a specific offer of any assistance in the speaker's power to grant. "I know of nothing," he
said, "but your care is precious."

Merus Arayder waved a hand. "For Brook, what is too precious? But you, Varic, you must come to visit. Lapis said it mo-
mental we heard of Brook. Time, have you?"

"I shall make time."

"Ah. Tell me then: Dinner two nights from now?"

"Gladly."

"She will be as pleased as I." He turned. "*An du, kus'ne—
vieder, all's I kann.*"

"*Sen hoffen seit obernvell, kus'ne,*" Linnet said with a small
bow. He held out his hand, and Merus Arayder shook it in both
of his.

Merus Arayder took Varic's hand again. "And good night to
you, cousin." Since Ferangarders never shortened names, and
private names were only for the most intimate, relational words
were the usual short form, *cousin* if you were not related, or
uncle to an elder.

He got his hat and topcoat, accepted a white paper parcel from
Linnet. The scent of warm herbs reminded Varic that he was actually very hungry.

After the door closed behind his first guest, Linnet latched
it, turned out the outside lamp, and drew the window shades.

"Please do sit down, my lord," he said. "May I make you some dinner? And then we can talk of the unspeakable."

Linnet lit the lamp on a clear table and snuffed the one where he and Merus Arayder had been sitting. He took Varic's coat and hat and held the chair. "Would you care for the ham? Or the fish—it is a fine fish, but the best parts are gone. I'm sorry there isn't more; I've spent most of my time catering holiday dinners. I should have saved some for you."

"I shall have the ham." He could not suggest that Linnet might not have known he was coming; it was inevitable, even without an invitation.

Linnet nodded. "I think beer will be better with that. Though I have a couple of wines tough enough to meet it on even terms. Or would you prefer a fortifée?"

"Let's look at the beer." They went down to the cool cellar, and spent a while examining bottles. Varic put his fingertips on a large flask of Brookbank Fire Bock, strong, smoke-flavored stuff from Brook's Coronage. Linnet took it, and a bottle of Coasters Cream Ale. They climbed the stairs, and Linnet set the table for both of them. A Book was uncased nearby, where it had undoubtedly graced Linnet's earlier dinner, but he did not touch it. Varic thought that was most considerate.

"The ham" proved to be a steak as thick as Varic's thumb, with a luminous maple syrup glaze that was somehow not at all heavy or too sweet—cider vinegar? Some sort of acid fruit? The marrowbone was garnished with brightly colored herbal florets, looking like needlepoint. Piled against the inner curve of the meat were fluffy white peaks, turnip furiously beaten and blended with goat's milk and strong white radish.

Varic lifted a forkful. "You do know what the Kólyan call this?" Silvern had often spoken of it, with something very like reverence.

Linnet said, "'The First Snow Is Sharpest.' The Kólyan usually serve it over 'firs and shale'—hard sausage and brittle bacon. The cook who taught me how to make it disapproved of my changes." He had set himself a small plate of the turnips, with a sliver of the ham, cut from the edge so that the caramelized rind ran its whole length. He lifted a bite, ate it along with Varic, and then they touched glasses and drank.

Not much was said as they ate. Linnet asked some purely friendly questions about the holiday at Strange House. He had served dinner to Edaire and Silvern, and knew of some of the other guests at second hand. Now, of course, most of Lescoray knew of Birch, and Linnet asked after the health of the newest Archimage.

"I believe he shall do honor to his office and his calling," Varic said, perfectly honestly.

Linnet offered dessert and tea. Varic said, "There is not enough will in the world to decline one of your pastries—but I am very full, and we have things to talk about. I promise I shall take something home. Will that serve? And the tea will be welcome in any case."

The tea came out, along with a bottle of harborside rum, dark as old oak and rough as brambles—"less liquor than lacquer," the saying went. They each drank off a short, blazing gulp, and then Varic said, "Tell me what happened that night."

"He was tired. He had been tired a great deal lately—but I suppose you'd seen that."

"Yes. Just tired? Or did he seem ill?"

"Not ill. I think he would have told me. Usually he did, when he had a cold or his joints were hurting. And anyway, Clarity would have known whether he'd said so or not."

"True enough."

"I hadn't planned to stay the night—cooking to do—but he asked me to. He didn't sleep well."

"How not?"

"He trembled. And his breathing was rough. It didn't seem to be waking him, at least not fully."

"Did he say anything?" After a moment's silence, Varic said, "Anything that might be meaningful."

"I'd repeat anything that might make a difference," Linnet said, "but he said nothing that I heard. I know I must have dropped off from time to time—I wasn't quite tired enough the next day to have spent the whole night awake, but it seemed like I did. Just holding him, listening to his breathing. Usually—usually that assured me a restful night. Both of us." He made a vague gesture in the air with both hands, as if trying to feel out the shape of something invisible. "Then finally I heard him making a choking sound—"

"Choking?"

"No," Linnet said. "I know well enough what choking sounds like. I mean death rattle. I just couldn't say it."

"I understand. Go on."

"I must have been asleep, and it woke me. I don't know how long it had gone on. Maybe half a mim after I was aware of it. Then he was just silent, and still. His heart was beating, but he wouldn't answer me. I got Clarity, and we both tried to rouse him, but nothing happened. Clarity sent for the doctor, and I cried all over her until Freshet came. I stayed until almost dawn. There was a banquet to cook for, and it was . . ."

"Something to do."

"The host said he'd never had such a luncheon. He insisted I come into the dining room and take a bow. I just managed to get back to the kitchen before I broke down again." He took another swallow of rum. "You know how to honor a cook, honored; you enjoyed the meal."

Varic said, "How long have you known Merus Arayder?" and suddenly hoped it did not sound like an investigation.

"Some years. He came in search of a linka as good as an aunt—well, an aunt in the 'Garder sense, at least—had made. Do you know the children's story they have, of the baker who's conscripted into the artillery?"

"Tell me."

"He loads the guns with linkas, and the enemy are so pleased by the taste they stop fighting. Merus Arayder—who was War party, I suppose you know—told me that in one version, the short rounds take the friendly skirmishers out of action in the same way.

> *"Und so der Maxl Linkakuch'*
> *Lasst sich bei sein Soldatbuch*
> *Und hiebt kein mehr der Kesseltrom*
> *Sondern der Linkabatter um.*
> "If you follow that."

"'Beating the batter instead of the drum,'" Varic said. "Though your Gerade is certainly better than mine."

"Down in the far southeast, you either learn Alinsever or Gerade. It's too philosophical to explain. Like the way native *Geradesprecker* never can get used to Lescant word order."

"Merus Arayder's is good," Varic said. "While the new Ambassador, Rocha Serestor, either cannot construct a sentence to our plan or wants it believed he cannot. Interesting that the merchants do so much better at it than the diplomats. Of course, the servants seem best of all."

"My lord is generous."

"It was not meant in that way," Varic said, his voice lower than he would have liked. He tried to reach for the fading gift of Strange House to make him decent, and said, "You are Brook's friend, as am I, as is Clarity. It is a world of distinctions, but in that we are all one. If I should forget this—because I have many distractions ahead—I should be grateful to be reminded."

Linnet nodded slowly. "If anyone ought to be friends in this, we should." He turned then, looking at the curtained windows, and said, "Do you really think someone hurt him?"

Varic resisted the impulse to follow Linnet's look. "Not really. Not now."

"Good," Linnet said. "I've never wanted to do anyone any real hurt, and I shouldn't be happy to want it now."

"Freshet said much the same thing."

"More rum?" Linnet said, and they rested from the hard topics awhile in discussing drink and desserts, finally returning to the cellar for more of the Brookbank beer, which was a way of continuing.

Settled again, Varic said, "You said you were from far southeast. East of the Estuary? Beyond Gildenstrand?"

"Much farther. Past Erlenspine, the out islands. I was born on Coreyn Tay, just in from Coreyn Windward. Do you know them?"

"Not more than location."

"If the Quercians had come to us first, in their leaky rowboats, we'd have sent the strong swimmers home."

"Seil thou, sailor, Northish we did send the strongen home, in bronzen caskets."

Linnet laughed then, and Varic nearly did; boasting how your people had given the Bright Empire the bloodiest nose was a national sport.

Then Linnet said, "I think you're coastal."

"Yes. But not seagoing."

"Still, you'll have seen. Our mother had a blue glass bottle, with a bit of guidestone hung on a hair inside it. It went up on the kitchen windowsill when Dove went out. Whenever she came home again, something she'd brought back would go in the bottle—a pearl, a little shell, a coin from somewhere far away—and it would disappear into a cabinet for the rest of the visit. I think we really did believe that the bottle would bring Dove home safe. And it did, right up until it didn't.

"We kept faith with the bottle for, oh, two years after her ship went missing. You know how slow news can come from sea. Dove could have been stranded on some happy little island, or kept by Alinsever pirates—if there's not a story to fit, we cut a new one.

"After two years with no word, there was a service at Sailors' Hall. It's a very careful sort of service—no one ever says that the crew are anything but missing, hoped well. But it serves the same purpose as a funeral; it lets you make a mark in your life and go on.

"When we came home from the hall, I saw that the bottle was gone from the window. No one but Mother would have touched it, and I never could bring myself to ask what she had done with it—but I'm certain it's still in the house, somewhere it won't be come across unexpectedly. And if Dove ever does come home, as she may, when she goes out again—as she will—the bottle will be in the window. You have to have something."

Linnet looked at the windows again, and this time Varic did look as well, but there was nothing but a glimmer of light on glass above the still draperies. Then Linnet said, his voice thin and distant, "Do you know what they say to me, in the market? 'Linnet, a soul who treats fish as you do should have their respect in return.' I've never tested it, though."

"Despite what the Parliamentary secretaries may tell you," Varic said carefully and definitely, "I shall be available to you. If there is any trouble about this, find a woman named Leyva."

Linnet looked stricken. He gulped a sob, pressed a napkin

to his eyes, and then said in a firm voice, "Do you know how many times he said that? Even about Leyva. And of course you are right. He would insist that we all go on. Sometimes . . . when I've visited, after . . . I think he is insisting. I cannot tell how. The guidestone, turning . . ."

Varic said, "It has become late. I thank you for the meal and the company."

"The meal was leftovers. The company has been more than repaid."

There was another pause. Only mediocre conversations could be brought to an easy end. The intolerable and the important always found momentum to roll on.

Linnet stood then, and took a small, green-shaded lamp from below the counter. He lit it and placed it in a front window. "You'll have a cab soon. I'll be just a breath; call me when it comes."

Varic stood by the door for no more than three minimi before the cab horse clopped up. "Linnet," he said, opened the door, and waved to the driver, who tilted her hat and sat patiently.

Linnet came from the kitchen and put two warm paper bags into Varic's hand. Varic caught a whiff of warm bread and olives. "One for the driver," Linnet said, and then, "This has been Brook's way home more than once. And—so good night, friend Coron."

Varic knew what Linnet had begun to say: *And my way to Brook, in the empty hours.*

Outside, a light fog was illuminated weirdly by the small green lamp. Varic handed a bag to the driver and boarded the cab. As he shut the door, the lamp went out, turning the street suddenly to a clouded lucive, all black and gray. The cab rolled away, clattering not too loudly on the pavement.

When he got home, he changed into a dressing gown and

slippers and sat down at the secretary with tea and some of the olive bread. He was not hungry, but wanted to taste the bread warm from the oven.

It was after one when he finished writing. He set the letters—two by messenger, the rest for the post—in the rack for Midden to deal with come daylight. He rubbed two sharp granules from the corners of his eyes, stared at them blank-minded—two specks, the color of dried blood, tears dead of waiting. Finally he shook his head and went up to bed.

✺

Toward eleven the following day, Varic was still in his dressing gown, puttering with breakfast in the kitchen, when the front doorbell clanged. Varic glanced through the spyhole and pulled the door open to admit Winterhill from the bright, cool day.

Winterhill was wearing a dark green infantry officer's coat, wide-lapelled and ankle-length. The shoulder insignia had been removed, the regimental buttons replaced with plain nickeled steel, but there was still a Companion Major's gold braid winding up the sleeves. His broad-brimmed black hat was not regular army, though it might have passed muster on a cavalry scout of one of the more idiosyncratic squadrons. He was wearing a long knitted scarf, the red and blue chevronny of the Ascorel College of Surgeons. As he hung his coat, the conventional dark suit and boots beneath came as rather a disappointment.

"Wedding or funeral?" Varic said.

"Ah. Edaire told me her old confidant Lix was tripping the line between Coldmere and the City. I was hoping to run across him—and you can't travel with Lix in just any old rags."

"Someday I should like to meet Lix."

"Perhaps. Though the Lamerick Finny's never as wonderful eye to eye."

"The what?"

"There's an old Alinsever song about a ghost ship that no one ever quite sees. 'La Marecaigne Founef.' Our sailors turned it into 'The Lamerick Finny,' making the ship into a sea monster on the way. Now, brother, I have told you a merry thing, and I have earned my tea."

"And a cinnamon sticky as well."

"Bless you, honored, and Midden's honored lady. 'Soonest's honest men and maids earn their honey by their grades.'" He paused then, and fingered the doctor's scarf. "Do you know, old Soonest gave me this. I cannot now call to mind why."

Varic led the way into the kitchen, poured the tea, and set out the cinnamon buns. He was certain that Winterhill remembered in precise detail how he had come into possession of Soonest's scarf, but Winterhill's lies, however frequent, were never unworthy. Rather they were boneset leaves for a fractured world.

Varic leaned against the counter. Winterhill sat, arranged a napkin in his lap, then picked up a sticky bun and admired the fat raisins and the cinnamon glaze. He said, "How fares my lord Brook?" and ate as Varic told him.

Winterhill made precise use of his napkin, and said, "And have you come to agree with Freshet's medical opinion?"

"As a first conclusion."

"Only an exceptionally stupid person could see any possible gain in destroying Brook," Winterhill said, "and I know the inherent flaw in that argument. While one imagines that merely hurting Brook could be conducted with much greater efficiency." With a studied offhandedness, he said, "My lord Varic has received no further invitations to a disputation at sword point?"

"None."

"Just so. My lord here present is an old player, and needs no telling what shape 'proof' shows in these matters. If there is such a handful of smoke about, however, I shall bring it to my lord in the pocket nearest my heart." He reached into his jacket, then showed his hand empty, waving it like a fingersmith who had just brought off some remarkable vanish. "A question, though, brother. What with that pale testament will you to do?"

Varic said, "If there's vengeance in it, there is no shortage of avengers." He felt suddenly very wearied with the idea.

"Does that surprise you?" Winterhill said, softly and evenly.

"It shouldn't." Varic felt a whisper of pain above his eyes. "One must not forget the quantity of rage in the world."

"In the civilized world," Winterhill said.

"Yes?"

"I'm not civilized, as you very well know. So, from time to time, and after careful animal consideration, I can kill without rage or the release of rage. People like you, and Brook, aren't and can't."

"I've had a sword in."

"Into animals like me, turned loose to tear out your liver. The hunting pets of the civilized classes." He stopped, sat back in his chair. "But I give my game away. Listen, brother. I haven't much wisdom, but this is mine: if the bad thing needs to be done— and grace Her it doesn't—leave it to those of us who do not contradict ourselves in the act."

Varic stared for a while at the toes of his battered slippers. Then he asked briskly, "Tell me about Captain Heartsease of the Bailiffs."

"Heartsease! Have you met her?"

"Midden has. I've been invited to dine with her and Cable. Assuming that a Coronal reply carries weight with the Justiciar, we shall meet tonight."

"I should not be surprised if you were much in demand as a guest," Winterhill said thoughtfully, "now."

"What about Captain Heartsease?" Varic said with a touch of impatience.

"Well, it's Grand Captain, actually. There are only supposed to be three ranks in the Bailiffs—ordinaries, sergeants, and captains."

"That's in the old Constitution," Varic said, almost without conscious thought. "They aren't supposed to be too large or too hierarchical."

"A little over a year ago, Cable made Heartsease a 'Grand Captain,' with authority over all the City Captains. The rank extends to the whole country, but since Lystourel is the only city big enough to have more than one captain of Bailiffs, there's only one Grand Captain. And while the other captains are subordinate to their district Justices, the Grand Captain answers only to the Chief Justiciar of Lescoray."

Varic did not speak. Finally Winterhill said, "Serious question, Varic: *Did* Cable violate the Constitution?"

Carefully, Varic said, "I can see arguments both ways. The Bailiffs are a national force, and the Justiciar is the only national judge, so it makes sense that he should have control over them. But one could also hold that his control is supposed to be filtered through the district Justices, and an attempt to seize direct command is highly un-Constitutional."

Winterhill said, "Understanding that people must be polite to one another, what do you have to do these days to have it called treason?"

"The silly question gets the serious answer," Varic said. "A large number of the Commons and a possible majority of the Lords don't consider offenses against the Constitution to be treason; at worst it's lawbreaking, and some cases might be thought commendable. And that isn't necessarily—do you know that a clause in the Fourth Article establishes a permanent state of war between Lescoray and Ferangard? And a subclause requires that we sever diplomatic relations with anyone who *trades* with Ferangard."

"No wonder Tephar Diante looked so weary the other night. Though I assure you, I had no economic relations with Davesque Isle."

"Both points were overridden by an amendment passing the relevant powers to the Ministry of State."

"Varic, even peasants like me know we don't *have* a Ministry of State."

"The entire Cabinet of Ministers was dissolved with the Monarchy. Parliament was supposed to create a new, Constitutionally based Cabinet, but no one could agree on how to do that. Instead there's the Advisory Office, which has run on interim powers for eighty years. And now Brook—"

Winterhill said quickly and loudly, "So *are* we at war with Ferangard?"

"No."

"Then I shall have another cup of tea, if I may."

As Varic poured, Winterhill said, "Returning to your earlier question, Grand Captain Heartsease is well spoken of even among my class," Winterhill said. "She used to be one of us, you know."

"Before continuing, I trust you will explain what 'one of' that is?"

"I mean a stone-corner, lamp-shun, light-foot, light-fingered orphan, of course, who found a way off the pavement. I didn't know her then, but this is on true report. I got out through Soonest's, Reccan through Strange House, Heartsease through the Bailiffs' Corps."

"Go on."

"She had a master, like most of the stone-corners with any

skill—as I say, stop me if you've heard this tale. When she was twelve, he tried something too foul to be funny, and she broke his arm and his leg and hauled him to the Thunder Street Barracks. He was hanged in a chair. Something about her took the company's fancy, and they took her in. She is the law's child right truly."

Varic said, "That must have attracted Cable."

"In the abstract, I'm sure you're right," Winterhill said, "but if there's anything beyond the professional between them, it's utterly circumspect." He wiped cinnamon from his fingers and took a sip of tea. "The most interesting rumor about her is that she once killed an Armiger, one to one, in what is supposed to have been a fair fight—though what 'fair' could mean in a duel like that I couldn't say."

"Really," Varic said. "Does anyone know the Armiger's name?"

"That's too much to ask of a rumor. Anything else?"

"Yes." Varic fetched the Exposition Partnership's letter from the desk. "This is signed by a Collier and one Ryeflower."

"May I?" Winterhill read the letter. "Well! Should be quite a party. I wonder if they'll let us common folk in." He pointed to Ryeflower's signature. "I very much imagine this honored used to spell his name Rye-flour, like the bread stuff."

"Do you know him?"

"You always say that as if it's a formal indictment," Winterhill said, sounding almost wounded. "If he's the one I know, he's from Red Plains. The family made a heap in the grain business. This one came to the City, gentled his name, and has been trying ever since to become minor nobility. Which is more than a little silly, given the rate of exchange these days between minor nobility and major merchants. That as it is, I don't know anything against him."

Varic nodded. "Anything about Collier?"

"Collier's not a rare name anymore, but I'll find out. For which you will pay me, and the world will go on turning. When do you need to know?"

"I'm meeting them this afternoon, but nothing will happen today, as I should hope they'll be aware. I won't need to know until after the session starts—say, six or seven days."

"Oh, now, brother, that does hurt. *Anyone* would find out in six or seven days."

"Nevertheless, I will not reduce your fee. Does that ease the hurt?"

"I feel scarcely a twinge now. . . ." He seemed to have swallowed the rest of the sentence. Varic supposed Winterhill had been about to make a joke about healing wounds and thought better of it. In Varic's world, not knowing when to jest and when to smile within could be socially fatal. In Winterhill's, it could be fatal plain and simple.

Varic said, "If you can spare the time, we might have lunch at Castleview."

"Milord is generous."

"Milord wants to know what happened at the House after he left. I'll dress."

Castleview was a restaurant on the Grand, just at the river junction; it did have an excellent view of the Castle across the water. It had been founded as a water-drivers' tavern when the Castle was still a center of government, before bridges or Parliaments. Though time had brought wooden floors, drinking glasses, and tablecloths, the owners were determined that it never become so fashionable that a Coron in Parliament and a rogue in a doctoral scarf could not dine there together in comfort, and talk of whatever might mutually concern a rogue and a Coron.

Through the first glasses of beer and the soup, Winterhill said nothing, just looking out the windows at the river.

Finally, and impatiently, Varic said, "The end of the holiday at the House."

"Of course. Do you want what did happen, or what ought to have happened?"

Varic managed to stop himself from speaking too quickly. The glow of the House was still there in Winterhill. "I am buying the meal," he said.

"Then you shall certainly receive an accurate report. First, your new Player has charmed everyone. Reccan particularly says . . . no, words won't do it, and in Soonest's Visible I might shock half the waterfront. Well, good, you're smiling."

Varic made the sign for *yes*.

"Apart from that, the holiday was ending; you missed very little but farewells. Longlight and Silvern should be leaving tomorrow for her Coronage. Edaire has two more days before hopping the rails; I believe Reccan intends to travel with her a way. Birch left as I did, and—true report, my lord?"

"True report."

"Then his message for you is: 'Remember that, at some dark hour, you will have to take a step without Goddess. It does not mean She is not there.'" Winterhill looked straight at Varic, eyebrows lifted.

Varic said, "From Birch, that is no reproof."

"No, I think not. To resume, then. Agate is staying for a time. From the staff, the usual good wishes; Bliss says to tell you that there will be new smallclothes and some shirts for you next visit."

"Is he burning the old ones?"

"Papermaking was mentioned."

"And from Strange?"

"Strange proposes that, when Brook is able to travel, he take his convalescence at the House. He asks to be kept informed of my lord Brook's condition." Winterhill paused deliberately. "My lord's schedule is very full. I can make the reports if he wishes. My lord Strange's commission."

"By all means, then. Though I shall try to write to Strange." On the edge of his vision, Varic saw the waiter holding their main courses, waiting almost out of sight and more or less out of hearing. Varic motioned for her to serve.

As they began to eat, Varic said, "You may also report to Strange that I am well."

"On true report?" Winterhill said, eyes on his beer-battered fish and grilled potatoes, voice coming from somewhere a little distance off.

"*Le recaigne*," Varic said, and they ate. Winterhill added a few more anecdotes of Equinox-end at the House—one of Gaily's jokes, Agate lighting the pond with Craft verses, an acutely observed little picture of Silvern and Edaire making ready for separation. "Oh," he said, as if about to ask for the salt, "my lady Longlight will write you soon."

Varic nodded.

Winterhill gathered up his hat and coat, bowed, and departed. A minima later Varic saw him through the windows, standing on the riverbank, looking possibly at the Castle, looking away.

Varic paid the bill, checked the time, and caught a cab to Parliament House, for his appointment with the Exposition Partnership.

⁂

When Collier and Ryeflower arrived, Varic was seated behind his office desk, in coat and clean cravat, unimportant papers on the blotter to look properly at work.

Collier was of average height and muscular build, squinting behind gold-rimmed glasses. Ryeflower was slightly shorter and potbellied. Both men wore brown coats with velvet facings; the color was flattering on Collier, not on Ryeflower. Their waistcoats were ornately brocaded silk, and Ryeflower's watch chain could have anchored a small sloop. Collier's dispatch bag was from Velon of Alinsea.

Varic wondered which one would speak first. He bet on Ryeflower and won.

"May we say, honored, how much we appreciate your lordship's making time for us."

"Thank you, honoreds. The office has responsibilities of service. Though I would begin by asking why you have asked to see me in particular? Both of you are, I believe, from midlands Coronages."

"My lord is well informed," Ryeflower said with a nervous tremor.

Collier said, in a voice almost mechanically even, "We approach milord as a leading voice in the Parliament. Particularly as a leading Constitutionalist."

"May I assume, then, that you have been in contact with my lord Brook? Or intended to do so?"

"That was our intent," Collier said. "After his sudden illness—" A waved hand for period. "You seemed the natural choice."

"Do not mistake our meaning, my lord Coron," Ryeflower said. The words hung for a few instanti, as Varic—and apparently Collier as well—waited for the meaning to be clarified, but nothing happened. Finally Varic said, "Your letter was brief. Perhaps you could expand on what I might do for you."

Ryeflower looked deeply relieved. "We propose a Grand Exposition, honored. A kind of universal market fair, at which every city and Coronage would display its produce and achievements. Commerce, science, and education, all together celebrated— and the nation itself, naturally, on show to the whole world." He smiled with genuine pleasure.

"There was a fair of this sort some thirty years ago," Collier said. "The Railways and Industries Exhibition. Perhaps the Coron has read of it, or seen the famous engravings."

"Yes," Varic said. "The old Exhibition Grounds are now built up, as I would imagine you know. Where do you propose to hold this fair?"

Collier opened his bag and unfolded a map. "This area to the southeast of the City. It is partially marshland now, as you can see, and can be acquired inexpensively."

The area was labeled *Site of Grand Exposition* on the neatly drafted map. It was more commonly known as the Fresh Wets. Varic wondered how much of it the partnership had already inexpensively acquired, and who would pay for the drainage and roads, not to mention what would be done with the more-or-less transient population that lived in the unused space of any large city. But he just nodded and said, "This is to be a stock company, of limited loss?"

Ryeflower said, "Several types of securities will be issued, including limited stock. There are still openings, however, in the primary partnership." He smiled. "Those will be selectively offered, of course."

Collier put a hand into his bag and held it there. They all waited, looking at the map.

"Honoreds, you have my delighted approval in your project. I should be pleased to subscribe a quantity of your shares—let us say, ten thousand marks of the initial offering?"

"Ah," Ryeflower said, sounding puzzled. Then he said brightly, "That is most generous, my lord, and I think we can promise you a return—" A glance from Collier stopped him, and he cleared his throat. "Yes, a proper return. But our true hope of your support comes in the Parliamentary sphere. You can surely imagine how many issues of government will be involved with such a large undertaking—the uses of land, the collection of tax—"

"The construction and operation of Ironways to the Exposition, among many other things," Collier cut in. "Things which will require the approval of the Parliament."

"It sounds," Varic said, "as if we must craft up that dread creature, a Parliamentary Committee."

"And would my lord see his way clear to assist in this?"

"I can start the procedure. It is not a thing one member does alone, you understand. And, naturally, as I have a financial interest, it would be inappropriate for me to serve on such a committee, though I could offer advice."

The two men seemed confused by this. Varic could understand that. There was not, naturally, a formal rule against such interests for committee members, but Brook had taught him that certain principles were more useful than rules.

"I bank with Charterhouse & Chequers. I regret that it will take me a few days to arrange the documents—if you will apply to them, say, Paleday next, with the shares, I am sure we will all be satisfied. I might add that the honored Chequers takes a particular interest in this kind of investment; I commend you to her about your remaining partnerships."

"We shall be most happy to make her acquaintance, my lord," Collier said, sounding quite sincere.

Shortly after they left, Leyva appeared with a pot of tea and a slice of cherry linka. "I thought my lord might appreciate a little something."

He did. Leyva asked after Brook, and Varic told her what there was to tell. She had every right to know, and would make certain that no rumors spread down the Parliamentary back stairs.

Varic cleared his desk and began a letter to Chequers the banker. He had been honest with the Exposition Partners; Chequers had a serious interest in such investments. An unblinking and merciless eye for them, in fact. Collier and Ryeflower were certainly out to turn a profit by their fair; that did not make them swindlers. If they *were,* they would not be happy at all to make Chequers's acquaintance.

Later in the afternoon, he called for a records clerk, and had the second-floor porter open Brook's office. He opened an unlocked file cabinet and removed folders on Constitutional judicial reform and City land use. The clerk copied their titles and numbers to a form, which Varic signed. After a look around to make sure that all was in order, the office was closed and locked again. Varic thanked the clerk and went upstairs.

He set the land-use papers aside and began reading the judicial documents. After two pages he put it down and poured the last of the tea. It was cold; he didn't care.

He would read the files, but they were just an excuse to visit the office. Certainly the porter would have let him in for no reason at all, but this was not a time to do anything outside the rules.

About seventeen he left the office and went to Brook's house. "I apologize, milord," Clarity said at the door. "I did not expect you until tomorrow." Her hair was untidy; she gave it a tug.

"My apology," Varic said. "I'm only intruding for a few mims. Is the nurse upstairs?"

"Yes, milord. Shall I announce you?"

"No need."

As he approached the door, Varic heard a voice, muffled, from the other side. It did not sound like Brook, but—

He opened the door without pausing to knock. Trevan Dain

was in a chair by the fire, a book in his lap, his glasses far down his nose. He stood at once.

Varic held himself still. Brook was just as before. Varic said, "Please keep your seat, Serjeant Dain. I am only looking in. Anything to report?"

"A little roughness in his breathing from time to time, my lord. It may be dehydration. Honored Clarity is fixing up a steam kettle to moisten the air."

"You were . . . reading to him?"

"Sometimes—rarely, I should say—the sound of a voice brings a response. It seemed worth trying."

"Certainly. I shall try it, when I take the watch tomorrow afternoon. Do sit."

"Thank you, my lord."

"'Honored' will be sufficient. At least when there are no officers about. *Ou 'maitre,' a'vot'plaisance.*"

"Honored Varic, then."

Varic said, "There is a point of your employment here that may have been passed over."

"Not at all, honored. I have had the care of delicate cases before. Anyone wishing to reach my patient will have to pass me."

"Then no more need be said of it. Good day, Serjeant."

"Honored."

It was nearly dark when Varic arrived at Cable's house. The Justiciar's Residence was a converted stronghouse from the Midreigns. A gray stone wall, three steps high and topped with embedded chunks of glass and rusting iron points, surrounded it; the arched double door was iron-studded wood, dead black with age. To one side was a small box with a shiny brass bell-push. Varic pressed it.

He heard a heavy bolt thrown, and one of the doors opened, with a disappointing lack of metallic groaning.

A tall, broad-shouldered woman wearing a Bailiff's uniform appeared. She removed a cap and bowed slightly. Her face was not finely drawn, but smiling and quite pleasant. "My lord Coron," she said in a calm, unmusical voice. "I am Heartsease. Please you to come in?"

Within the walls there was a formal garden, stone paths in rigorous angles and geometrically arranged plantings, lit here and there by gas streetlamps. Some of the trees were gilding with autumn. As they crossed to the house, Heartsease looked here and there around the garden, but Varic could not tell what, if anything, she was seeing.

The house itself was a cube of stone, like the outer wall, with a few shuttered windows. Ivy had been allowed to grow over it, and the lower windows were lit a pleasant amber, but it was still an extraordinarily ugly structure. As it had lasted for four centuries, however, and seemed fit to stand for as long again, the Parliament saw no need to pay for a replacement. The Justiciar could live anywhere that suited, at the Justiciar's private expense.

Heartsease led the way through the front door and took Varic's overcoat. "I have a very rude question, milord. Do you carry a weapon?"

Varic opened his dress coat. "I have never carried a handgun. There is no sword in my stick, though it is weighted. I shan't be carrying it into the house, at any rate."

"Of course, milord. I am told, by the way, that you are a fine swordplayer. Perhaps you would honor me with a game at splintans someday."

"Certainly. But—if I may be rude in return—is the Justiciar at such a risk?"

"Persons in authority make enemies," Heartsease said, "as milord must know. I ask all who enter, so none can feel slighted."

Varic nodded.

"The Justiciar proposes that we dine at once, so you may converse without interruption later. Does that suit?"

"Excellently."

Cable was waiting in the dining room, in a formal coat of the gravest cut and blackness. The table was set for three, and the sideboard was covered with dishes. Cable said, "We have only a few day servants here. I hope my lord does not mind . . ."

"Not in the least."

The meal had been brought in—Bovery & Co.'s mark was on the dishes, and while very good it was also very elaborate, with expensive dishes: lobster bisque with wild mushrooms, quail's eggs, and so on. It was exactly the sort of thing people ordered when a Coron was coming to visit. As every Coron learned to, Varic ate in the spirit of the offering. The food quite superseded conversation.

After the last course, they moved to a parlor with comfortable chairs and a large, full bookcase against one wall. With a velvet drape over the arrow-slit window, and the lamps soft, one could forget the house's rougher aspect. Heartsease brought light and dark whiskies and a box of cheroots. Varic took a glass of the dark and said, "Do you smoke?"

Heartsease said no; Cable shook his head. "I rarely do," Varic said, and passed the box on.

"I understand," Heartsease said. "If the Coron does not smoke, no one is likely to."

"Captain," Cable said stiffly.

Varic said, "The Grand Captain is exactly right. Sometimes one lights up simply for general comfort. Your health."

"Yours." They drank.

Cable said, "I am delighted that you could visit so soon. I am sure you have a great deal to do, especially now." With a genuinely sincere tone, he added, "I would like to say how sorry I am at my lord Brook's illness. Is there any new word?"

"None, but thank you. And the invitation was very welcome, especially at a difficult time."

Heartsease said, "Your butler was most hospitable, to a bailiff on the doorstep."

Varic saw the small, dark look Cable gave the Grand Captain, but it was milder than the last had been.

"Midden is an essential part of my life," Varic said.

"Midden?" Heartsease said. "There must be a story to that."

Without waiting for Cable to interrupt, Varic said, "There is a long line of Middens, older than the Midreigns. They were the official custodians of the village refuse. Here in the City, with our rubbish removed by an agency, we tend to forget how important that was, then; the midden-keepers were as vital as the pindars—or now, the lamplighters and gutterers."

"That is indeed so," Cable said with a sudden, surprising animation. "And spiritually—have you ever seen wispels? The glowing mist that rises from wastes and marshes? When wispels were thought to be the spirits of the dead, the middeners were the defense against them; they had to be of the very highest character, better in most towns than the mayor."

The mood in the room had relaxed considerably. Aware that he might be about to wind it tight again, Varic said, "Your letter spoke of the Constitutional Revision. Did you have any specific ideas on the subject?"

Cable looked more serious, but his tone was still easy. "I understand that my lord was instrumental in passing the bill bringing sorcery within reach of the law."

"I studied it. It seemed a good law, and I voted for it. No single person's labor can outweigh a full voting quorum."

"Still, single persons must do a great deal of work before any vote."

"The Justiciar has seen the chambers at work." After a pause and a sip of whisky, Varic said, "I take it you do have some Constitutional thoughts."

"Yes." Cable leaned forward in his chair. "In Alinsea they have established what is called the Bureau of Resolution. If you will pardon me a moment?" He stood, went to the crammed bookcase.

"I have read Master Michet's book," Varic said, "and had the good fortune to speak with him briefly, two years ago. His ideas, applied with care and certain controls, seem to me most useful."

Cable paused with his hand half a span from the books. "Two years . . ."

Heartsease said, "*Maitre Coron connaitre-le d'Alinsetre?*" Her Alinsetre had no attempt at all at accent; Varic supposed that she was more a reader than a speaker, as he was.

"*Nessu bon, Grand-Capitain.*"

"Of course," Cable said, recovered instantly. "It must have been an interesting discussion. But what controls does my lord speak of?"

"Our conversation did not reach that far. To you, honored, I would first say that I find nothing to fault in the idea of the *Resoleurs*—'students of evidence,' as Michet calls them. The application of natural study to taking criminals is simply a logical development of naturalism itself. Would anyone have imagined, fifty years ago, that the pattern of lines on a fingertip is as absolutely unique as the lucate aura?"

"And stronger than sorcery, because employable without Craft," Cable said, interested. "Or is that your objection?"

"I have no grounds for objection," Varic said without raising his voice. "I would suggest that one of the things to be learned from Michet's excellent work is that there must be firm outlines of the Resolvers' proper employment. Alinsea, I think, is not specific enough on this point—particularly in the secret use of the officers, and their employment as what Michet calls *agents provocateurs*."

Cable said, "I would agree that Michet too freely hired thieves to catch thieves. We would certainly have more exact standards."

"Indeed," Varic said. His understanding of the Justiciar was becoming much clearer.

"As to provocative operations, though," Cable continued, "surely an official who accepts a bribe, or a broker who buys stolen property, is corrupt whether the offer comes from a criminal or a bailiff? Is it not much better that we make the test, and know who will fail it?"

"A definite point," Varic said. There was, he understood now, no use in mentioning the point's utter lack of utility among real human beings. It would be good if officials were not bribable, as it would be good if soldiers were bulletproof and sailors immune to drowning.

Cable's vision of the law, and the people under it, was a marvel of clarity; there were only those who applied the law and those it was made to punish.

Since this was still a friendly conversation, Varic thought he would experiment a little more. "Captain Heartsease," he said, "I was reading recently of a captain of Bailiffs in Blueport who was apparently involved in a smuggling ring. I have not been able to find the disposition of the case."

"Captain Stave was executed by hanging, along with one of his Bailiffs and two civilians," Heartsease said crisply, "one a secretary and the other a receiver of goods. Most of the smugglers were Alinsever or of no provable nation, and were fined by the Customs. Three Lescorials were branded to deny all ports by an Admiralty Court."

"Not that it will make any difference," Cable said, quite coldly. "A few marks of stolen money, and a new tattoo for a sailor! But we dealt with our own turncoats. That is why such behavior is rare—and because it is so rare, it is immediately obvious."

Varic just nodded. After a minima and a long draw at his glass, Cable was smiling again.

"Returning to the new Constitution," he said, "I have another thought, which might prove less complicated. I should like to see a provision requiring that the more fortunate feed the hungry. A Constitutional law that could not be evaded by lower rulings."

"I can see that such a rule would have broad support," Varic said, and added, he hoped without audible irony, "especially in the Commons."

"I am glad that my lord thinks so."

"But do you think a law—at whatever level—is necessary? Lescoray, it would seem, preserves the memory of the Great Famine very well."

"That is a tradition," Cable said, "not a fact. Like the Harms and Judgments."

Heartsease suddenly made the sign of the Willed Draw and recited:

"To harm one's neighbor harms Shyira, and shall be judged.
To harm the land harms Coris, and shall be judged.
To harm honest produce harms Evani, and shall be judged.
To harm the truth harms Wyss, and shall be judged."

"Indeed so," Cable said, in what seemed an extremely leading fashion.

Varic indicated that his glass was empty, to buy a few instanti for thought. He decided to pull the lead.

"That is a foundation for law," Varic said in a precise voice, observing Cable with each word. "A reasoner's source for law. But it is not itself law. No more than to draw the card of Justice from the Book is to execute justice."

"That is so," Cable said with a tremor of the shoulders astonishingly like sexual release. "That is the difference so many reasoners—and too many judges—cannot see. I cannot tell you how it pleases me to hear you state it so clearly."

Varic had a slowly turning, terrible feeling that he understood the Justiciar; Cable was sane enough, but there was the sign of madness in him. His vision of the law was absolute, unsparing, and not human. He genuinely believed that evil could not hide from the sight of the pure and that the righteous, in delivering punishment, were unchanged by it—if anything, more purified.

Very well then, he thought, such was the nature of the Justiciar. Cable was not eternal in either person or position. It was possible that the nation was well served by such a Justiciar, as a miser might be a proper master for a countinghouse.

The problem came when the miser decided the countinghouse's money was his own, or when the Justiciar decided that his own vision of the law was infallible. Then there was no safety anywhere.

With that understanding came the awareness that Varic would have to deal with Cable alone. Even should Brook revive, there would be a recovery period, likely a long one, and this would not wait.

Strange had told him: Never confront madness eye to eye, because it will not blink, and the longer you stare, the more of yourself you give up to it. Look past it. Look through it. There is a soul inside it; speak to that.

Varic wished it were a better memory. He had been unable to look past Brook's—*madness* seemed a good word for it, now— over Rissi. He had stood aside, telling himself it was out of respect for Brook's feelings.

It was possible that he was doing exactly the same thing now, for exactly the same doubtful reason.

He would deal with that tomorrow. Now there was Cable, across the room, to be looked—through.

What, then, were Varic's grounds for objection? Birch was now committed to walk with the invisible. Strange could go into the end houses, looking for a means of redemption. Varic was just a thimble-rig mechanic trying to get some utility out of an off-center engine.

Varic was aware of Heartsease watching him. She had extraordinary eyes, brown and doe-like. He remembered what Winterhill had said. Was that how she had killed an Armiger, craft-binding with those eyes so that no killing thought could form in the victim's mind, and so no weapon or defense?

She said, "My lord Varic seems tired."

"No, thank you, not at all."

"But I have run on," Cable said graciously. "I am sure milord has had a crowded day, and this will surely not be our last conversation."

They shook hands, and Heartsease led Varic out. In the middle of the garden, she paused. "Before my lord departs . . ."

"Yes?"

"Do you see the house in the wall, there? The old smith's shop. That is where I live. It is just large enough for one—though some would say I am at least one and a quarter." She smiled then, as she had when Varic had arrived and not since. "I tell you this because I want nothing misunderstood."

"Of course, Grand Captain. Thank you. And good night to you."

❧

Despite the time and the chill, he took an hour to walk home, wanting to think without the distractions he would have there. He was thinking especially of the Harms and Judgments, and

Cable's clear dismissal of them as anything beyond a worthy notion. That had the ring of Anticonism, if not actual Atheism. But could Cable possibly be an Atheist, given its illegality? Such a tension might turn a soul to insanity.

Insane or not, there was a point that could not be dismissed. It was an authentic wonder how the few words of the Harms and Judgments could create so much trouble. There had been arguments for centuries about what they all meant. Did it harm one's neighbor to build a fence on your land that shaded his land so his grass died? Or was that harming the land? What constituted "honest produce," sacred to Evani—oh, it was generally considered that the intention was the protection of property from damage, but . . .

Judged might be the most troublesome word of them all. Some people claimed that it demanded not just legal process but a particular sort of process. Others held that it really meant "punished," or at least "recompensed." It did not help that the source of the word itself was disputed: was it from *jusicato,* "to balance," or *diadero,* "to discover" or "expose," or—oldest word and most contentious—*jagah* (*diagah* if you were Southern), "to hunt down"?

Everyone agreed that there was such a thing as justice, whether or not they thought it was an absolute, and everyone agreed that it was a good and useful thing, at least for certain people. Beyond that it was in the arenetto, with points on all sides and no concetta in sight.

❧

When Varic reached home, the light on the secretary desk was lit, spotlighting an envelope. It was blank, but Varic knew Strange House's guest stationery at once. He turned it over: the seal was blue wax, with a setting sun on a blade. Longlight's sign.

Winterhill had left it, before they had gone to lunch. Varic remembered Winterhill's touching his pocket, in the kitchen. He ought to have noticed that; Winterhill was several parts finger-smith (to put the nicest polish on it) and did not make absent-minded gestures. The logic was easy to follow; the letter would not be for public reading, and Varic had made clear that he was in for a very public day. The message would not go stale in a few hours more, and Varic would not be distracted by unanswerable thoughts of it.

He slit it open in a single stroke, slid out three folded sheets of heavy, smooth paper, the color of double cream. It was note-paper, small in size, and Longlight had large and sweeping hand-writing.

There was no salutation. In considering the letter he had not yet written, Varic had still not decided how to begin it: "My lady" or "My lady Coron" were not the thing at all, "My dear Longlight" or "My most Flattering Adjective Here Longlight" not much better, a single naked Longlight—enough of that, she was correct, the letter would know its object.

> *Tomorrow Silvern and I leave for the west. I cannot write legibly on trains, to say nothing of horseback, so you will not hear from me until I am home again.*
>
> *Archimage Birch has been persuaded to travel part of the way with us. He asks me to remind you that his investiture comes soon, and he hopes you will think of him.*

She went on for a few lines about the house after Varic's departure, much the same news Winterhill had reported. Varic saw that there was not a single scratched-through or blotted word.

The second page ended:

At breakfast, Gaily told me a story that she said would make you laugh. That seems like a good idea to me. It is about a Quercian emperor who visits one of his victorious generals in the field, and demands a victory banquet on the moment. . . .

"Quintillius Varus, where are my chickens?" Varic said aloud, and then laughed. It was, indeed, a good idea.

There was one more page. It had only two more lines of writing and then a boldly slashed signature, a double-blooded Coronal mark. Varic read:

Sometimes I also need to laugh.
I have cause to think you know the word.

Not *words.* Word, singular.

There were several concealed spaces in the secretary desk. He opened one, a steel-lined pigeonhole, put the message inside, and locked the door.

There would have been a time when he would have read the letter over again, just enough times to memorize it, and then burned the paper. There had been such times, such messages.

But just now, he needed some things to exist outside his own mind: to be absolutely, independently real, where he could return and touch them at need.

❦

He thought the letter would ease his sleep, but it did not, nor did anything else. There was dewbell in the nightstand, but it quickly lost its effectiveness if used too often, and whisky did not last the night. Varic read for a while, lay in the dark awhile, lit the lamp again and read some more, then snuffed the lamp again and tried to deliberately relax, loosening one muscle at a time, trying to think of nothing but that limb. But clearing one thought from his mind only allowed another to come in, limits on judicial power followed by the issue of entering Brook's thoughts, the choice of an Acting (the word used by courtesy) Parliamentarian giving way absurdly to the layout of avenues and buildings for the Grand Exposition.

That last seemed to help, perhaps because it was not quite a real issue yet. Varic was free to imagine crystalline pavilions of glass and iron, prismatic at beginning and end of day, broad, straight ways (with excellent drainage) for the easy passage of thousands of visitors. Perhaps a small-gauge Ironway stopping at the principal sights—should it be an electrical tram, or an elevated way as was proposed for Lystourel's streets? That might be useful. Something could be learned from that.

He imagined the visitors: couples, families, groups from schools and guilds and labor societies wearing bright ribbons to show off their affiliation, hardly aware that an old malodorous bog was a few spans below the pavement. They would be smiling. There would be music, food, buskers, fingersmiths, street artists, market fair for the City and the nation, and true enough they needed it. . . .

Somewhere on the promenade he slipped into heavy, dreamless sleep.

❦

He did not wake until almost eleven. He dressed hastily, swallowed a muffin and cold tea, and caught a cab to Walnut Row. Clarity met him at the door with a pot of tea, and they went upstairs to relieve Trevan Dain.

"Thank you, honored," the nurse said. "I shall see you in four hours."

Brook's room was quite warm, the air moist from a kettle

boiling in the corner. Clarity pointed out a pitcher, to refill the kettle at need. "Is there anything I may bring you, milord?"

"The tea will be fine for now, thank you. Perhaps later."

Varic sat down. There was a large book just beside the chair. It had a worn green cover, faded gilding on the pages. A green ribbon in the binding marked the spot where Dain had stopped reading. The cover showed a child peering through an opening in dense woods, at a wonderful, impossible city beyond. The title, which had been gilded once, was *Tales of the Green World*. Varic knew it; some of the stories in it were older than not just books but written language.

Varic had owned a book like it, when he was young. He supposed everyone had, in the classes with money for books, once the steam press and the glueback binding had made books an actual commodity with an actual price.

Brook had told Varic a story about books, something from Brook's childhood.

Brook's family was as old as Varic's, but Brook's had been Mid-country, under the Quercian occupation, and the Quercians had brought literacy with them. In those days, before the press, manuscripts belonged either to the Church or the sorcerous, and the association had never entirely faded. Thus, Brook said, it was not so much that anyone was hostile to his reading as unable to understand the purpose of it; he was going to inherit the Coronage, so what was the point in pursuing a second career, since no one could hold two seats in the Lords?

Varic's house had not been bookish, either, but matters there had been more immediate.

"A story for the Coron, now," Varic said aloud, and opened the book to the green ribbon. "Once in a forest village—"

He stopped, feeling his fingers tighten hard on the binding. He took a breath, looked straight at Brook, and said, "I don't know what you would most like to hear, my friend, so perhaps you'll tell me?"

Brook did not stir.

"Very well—another time. Then I'll deal us a tale, and this one I *will* read." He slipped a finger between the pages, turned to the chosen place, and then went forward a few more pages to the start of the next tale. From the engraving, a pirate ship drawn to resemble a vulture with black sails for wings, he knew what story it was, but he had said he would read what the draw chose.

"Long ago and far," Varic read, "in the cold and cruel lands of the north . . ." He paused a moment, said, "That isn't the way I heard it," then continued, "there was a girl who had grown up so wild and forward that her parents feared the family line would end with her. 'She will never bear a child if she can choose not to,' said her father, and her mother, who may have been afraid or may just have been weak, agreed. So they decided that their child should never know the source of children, and never learn Wyss's Cares.

"And this was how the girl, whose name was Plaisance, was raised: either lies or nothing of that which she most should have known, and as they lived in the lonely North, this course was successful.

"In Plaisance's seventeenth winter, there came to the house a young man, the son of fur trappers who had been killed by . . . wolves. He had become lost trying to carry one with the trapping, and now sought shelter with Plaisance's family."

Varic put the book in his lap, closed on his finger to keep the place. He watched Brook for at least two full minima, until Brook's still image began to wobble. He then looked up at the framed prints on the wall before the bed.

Finally Varic let the book shut and said, "I know the story

now, Brook. It's somewhat long, and full of foreshadowings and repetitions—oral tradition, you know—and neither of us have any use for circumlocution, so I'll summarize. The trappers' boy assumes that Plaisance must know the Cares, but she knows nothing, and so in the course of things they have a child. The child grows up knowing that no one wanted it except to keep a particular bloodline going, and everyone it meets considers it to be the product of a peculiarly awful offense against Goddess. The requisite adventures follow—usually the Unwanted becomes a pirate king or bandit chief, this being long before government service and professional sport widened the opportunities for hateful bastards.

"So in time the gang of cutthroats captures someone who falls in love with the Unwanted, not knowing its origin, and so on. Suspense is maintained. There are at least two endings."

Varic set the book aside. "Because we are both very tired, I shall guess that this is the version where true love redeems the couple, and it is made clear that, whatever mortals may judge, in the eyes of Goddess no child is truly Unwanted."

He stood up, poured more water into the vapor kettle, went to stand by the bedside. Brook's breathing was even, just barely audible this near. There was nothing else: not the stirring of an eyelid or a finger, not the turn of a hair.

"Can you wait through the first days of the session?" Varic said, too softly to be heard beyond the door. "It won't take long—if this was done, they won't be able to hide it. They'll *want* me to know, and then I'll have them. And it will have meant something."

He opened the door, stood in it with his eyes still on Brook, and called, "Clarity?"

She was up the stairs in three steps. "Yes?"

"I—should be going. Is Serjeant Dain here?"

Dain stepped into view behind Clarity. "Waiting your pleasure, honored."

"Nothing to report, Serjeant. Your watch."

He allowed Clarity to serve him a cup of soup and a patcake, then rode to Parliament House to shuffle papers and write letters reporting Brook's condition.

There was time to spend before going to Merus Arayder's, and he wanted words; plain, organized words. Tales were good—tales were vital as breathing—but he had grown up where the air was bad, where tales were held to a superstitious standard of literality.

The story he had found when he opened the *Tales,* the one he had not read, was about a girl in a village of the deep forest—forest villages of the long-ago were not kindly portrayed in books for literate children—whose talent was for fine embroidery, and was a wonder at it. But her guardian (jealous stepparent, barren aunt, natural parent widowed and embittered, it was told all ways) punished her for such a frivolous activity when there was plain sewing to be done, not to mention the inevitable water drawn and wood split.

The girl keeps up her work in secret, in the time supposedly her own, spinning her own threads and dyeing them with forest plants, hiding the cloth between times against the guardian's threat to burn it before the girl's eyes.

Which threat, of course, is carried out. "She saw the threads glowing, brighter than ever, seeming to leap up, be reborn as light, more beautiful than an autumn sunset; but like the sunset it passed, leaving only black shadows of its passing."

Yet the girl continues to spin and color and stitch, and watch her labor burn, until a voice from nowhere tells her to reach into the fireplace and take what is hers.

As with the tale of the Unwanted, the story ends two ways. In one, the voice comes from Hand, consort of Goddess-as-Evani, sacred to handcrafters, and the girl suffers no harm. The wicked guardian flees, and the embroiderer is allowed to be what she divinely is, growing old and wise and beloved as a master of work.

In the other ending, the fire, "hungering for the vine as well as the blossom," catches the girl's clothing, envelops and consumes her. "But for a moment there was no pain, neither of the flesh nor the spirit, but only light, soft, brilliant, sweeter than the Sun; and she entered that paradise of those who have never turned away from what they truly are."

∽

Merus Arayder opened the door. "Forstel!" he called. "Here is Varic!"

"Coming, Rahme!" came a voice from a far room.

Forstel and *Rahme* were intimate names between husband and wife, in the Ferangarder fashion. They meant "Image" and "Frame."

People expected Lapis to have eyes of a deep blue, as her name, but they were a striking honey gold. Her skin was an even tea-with-milk, the blue veins not prominent. There was no obvious reason for the name, and Varic had never asked it; his whole life people had smiled and nodded to themselves to hear that his own name meant a shipwreck coast.

She usually dressed simply, as now, in an unbelted long robe of autumn-maple silk. It made Varic think of Dany. Lapis spread her arms, and Varic, awkwardly raising his own, allowed himself to be embraced.

Their house was, unsurprisingly, filled with artworks. The entrance hall was lined with Lapis's designs for the Book: a Gateway, naturally enough, a Sky, a Huntress, a wistful and unthreatening Death. Farther in were paintings, sculpture from any number of cultures and countries, a hanging device of sparkling prisms and tubular chimes.

There was only one piece in the dining room, however: a three-paneled screen of stained glass, carefully lit so that color washed the whole room. The imagery was complex; Varic understood that it was the cycle of Time, drawn from an epic poem by Bourne of West Riding. Here were the stars coalescing from water, here the planets from the fragments of dead stars, here the birth of life . . . standing back from the triptych, one could see that all the smaller images fused into a spread hand before the face of Goddess, Her eyes the sun and world.

"Is this yours, Lapis?"

"I'm flattered, Varic. But no. That was made by Cova di Genedi. Rahme bought it for me, at a hard time for both of us. Now, will it please you to sit?"

Dinner was pork roast in a sauce with pear cider, served with thinly sliced fried vegetables. It had certainly been a good deal of work for them, and Varic hoped his appreciation showed.

After they had eaten, Lapis said, "There's something I want to show you. Bring your wine."

They climbed stairs to a large loft room, Lapis's studio. "Bring me one of those, please, Rahme? Any one will do."

"Moment, Forstel." Merus Arayder put down his glass, wiped his hands carefully on a towel, and unfolded one of several flat cloth parcels on a table.

Lapis uncovered an easel. Mounted there was a subtly colored image of the Joker from the Book, a slender figure keeping three crystalline spheres airborne with one hand and holding a grinning white mask before his face with the other. She said, "This will go to a lucargent master. It's the same principle as lucivitry, but instead of darkening a glass plate, the light-chemicals etch a tin sheet. You end up with something very like a copper engraving—in fact, an engraver usually touches it up. Ah, here."

Merus Arayder was displaying a smaller metal sheet between his fingertips. He tilted it to catch the light, and Varic saw the negative image of a King of Steels, his sword point downward, his head bowed in token of peace. It seemed incomplete. Varic said, "How is the color printing done? Light filters, and multiple plates?"

"This one will be," Lapis said. "The one Rahme's holding is from the simpler process, where there are just two or three main colors filling in the black outlines. But now we're working with additive full color—three mixed colors and black. It takes four print passes, and getting them to align is something of a mechanical miracle—bad as banknotes. In fact, we're printing with Hatchen and White. If they're good enough for the national currency, they might be good enough for the Book."

"More wine?" Merus Arayder said, as they descended again. "Or other? Tea?"

"Tea, please."

They sat down with teacups in the front room, and Varic told them what there was to tell about Brook.

"You said nothing before, *kus'ne*," Merus Arayder said, "I ask it again: Is there anything to be done?"

Varic felt suddenly weary, and his head ached. He took a long swallow of tea and felt slightly better. Perhaps it had been solvents, up in the studio. Or he had acquired a cold on the long walk home last night.

Or he was just worn thin with saying, *I do not know what is to be done*. But he said it again. "Perhaps—if there finally is no solution—I would commission something from Lapis. As a memorial."

"And do you think I would take money for that?"

"I am sorry," Varic said, feeling his head ache again. "Such manners as I possess have deserted me. I don't—I—your gift would be welcomed."

"It is forgotten," Merus Arayder said. "There are losses that do such—when our child—" He linked his fingers together and made a tugging gesture.

Lapis said, "One does not recover, really. But one goes on. To go on is the only stand against Death."

"I know not at all if one can be strong at such an event," Merus Arayder said. "What would strength be? What, then, mean it? Silence, perhaps for a moment—it wants no music—but if one speaks not at all, then I think the words can be forever lost."

Lapis said, "I broke pens drawing, and then Rahme and I burned the pictures. It was a kind of screaming. And then, I think, a kind of offering. There are places where prayers are written on paper and burned, so they will rise to Her." Merus Arayder frowned, but Lapis put her hand on his and he nodded. "And again, I wanted to break and burn things. Beautiful things, because what is the point of there being beautiful things in a dead, ugly world? But Rahme brought the triptych . . . and I remembered what beauty was for.

"Rahme has already said it for both of us. What may we do, Varic? If not for Brook, then for you?"

He turned his head, and the hinge of his jaw cracked like a dry stick. The room tilted. "I—" he said, and swallowed the rest of whatever he had meant to say in a convulsive breath. Dark fog closed around the edges of his vision. He was already thinking of Brook—who worked too hard, who had too much to do—and had a small but absolutely clear thought that if the same thing were happening to him, *whatever the reason*—he preferred to die now.

He could not get out so easily, of course. Not now. Merus Arayder was out of his chair, reaching for Varic. Varic tried to get up, to get out, gasp some excuse and flee to a room with a closable door to collapse or vomit or whatever he was about to do in front of his friends, but the room tipped again, and his knees wouldn't agree on a direction. He tumbled forward and was caught, held, supported on two pairs of hands. His collar was opened, his hair untied. He knew they meant only comfort, and he felt only ashamed, dissolving when he needed to be strong.

The clear, small thought was there again, but now it offered a little hope; yesterday his first thought, choking and tumbling, would have been that his hosts had poisoned him.

He shuddered, and another wet noise escaped from his lungs, but he did not weep. He was perfect at that. He could freeze tears with his hands in a fire, clutching beloved pages as they crumbled to ash.

CHAPTER 6

THE MISTRESS OF STONES AND THE ROAD

The day following Varic's sudden departure from Strange House, Longlight did not rise until midday. She had awakened, or partly so, three or four times, aware it was day despite the curtain-sealed windows. But the bed was warm, and it held her. And . . . before she got to the next reason, she was asleep again.

The holiday is passing, she thought finally, and struggled up from the turbulent pool of linen. It occurred to her, in a fit of irrelevance, that her house needed better bedding along with new water heaters.

She swung her feet out of the bed. The fire had gone out; the room was chilly and genuinely dark. She found the switch of the electrical side lamp. A fine thing to have light at a touch, doubtless good for reading, but firelight was right for bedrooms. Fireplaces were . . .

She had thought she would dream of Varic, but hadn't, or at least could not remember it. She had been very still in the bed, in the firelit, empty room, for a long time, thinking. Perhaps she had used up the thoughts and left nothing to dream about.

She was quite awake now. She smoothed down her nightdress and walked to the bathroom.

The Lord Brook—who was, she understood well enough, more than just Varic's friend—was gravely ill, and Varic had gone to attend him. He had abandoned his holiday; not any of the people here, not her. She could not fault him. She tried to think if there was anyone, any event in her own life for whom she would have flown on the instant. Her parents were gone, her household, like any such, ran on staff and custom.

No one at home, to the best of her ability to discover, was in any sort of rebellious mood. It was anyhow considered bad sport to overthrow absent Corons; usurpers were expected to face the incumbent down properly.

And then, naturally, one of you had to die.

She was expected at home. Plans had been made with Palion Silvern—indeed, they were largely Varic's plans. She and Varic might circumspectly leave Lystourel on the same train, but to arrive together . . .

She turned the shower valve up hot, and fog enveloped her. There was no way Varic could have asked her to join his midnight's errand. She could not have accepted had he found a way to ask. And still—

She knew then what it was. She had had the thought herself, just a moment ago. In her country, when you took something from a Coron, you fought for it face-to-face.

⌘

Dressed, she crossed the open breezeway to the main house. The day was beautifully clear; the pond and woods beyond were like carvings of sapphire and jade. The crystal air was sharpening distinctly toward autumn, though, and she thought she saw a little copper in the green.

Inside, the doors to the dining balcony were shut, and lunch was laid out on the sideboard. Strange and Dany, Silvern and Edaire were moving about, filling plates with cold meats and several sorts of bread. Longlight smelled chicken soup. They all exchanged quiet greetings and began to eat. The conversation was, for this House, very thin.

Then Gaily appeared, with pitchers of elderflower water and warm cider, and told the antique joke about the Quercian emperor whose general had mislaid the Imperial feast. It finished with a play on Varic's name, and they all were struck silent for just an instant. Then Silvern laughed out loud, and the others followed, and then it was all right to talk about him, and Brook, and the message in the night.

With a look of profound satisfaction (and maybe just a little relief), Gaily brought the apple pie and thick cream.

Longlight, with what she knew for severe impertinence, wondered silently what Gaily's intimate life was like. It did not seem possible that she could be unpartnered, but she had seen into enough dark corners in her own household to keep silent. In most great houses—her own included—the master knew little enough about what the staff did among themselves, until there was screaming and weeping below stairs, some blood perhaps, and rumors of foxglove. Strange, she was certain, would know all the facts. Perhaps there would be a time to ask him alone.

Provided that she ever came back here again.

Silvern said at that moment, "We will be returning for Cold Solstice. Do you think you will want to go to the City then as well? Possibly for the end or beginning of the Parliamentary session?"

"I had not thought about it," Longlight said, honestly enough. "Just at this moment, I do not believe so."

Strange said, "I gather you have not spent much time in Lystourel. I think that Varic would be pleased to show you about. He knows the Castle extremely well. And all the historical collections. Art . . . somewhat less so."

She said, "If my lord Brook is improved . . ."

"If he is not," Strange said very seriously, "so much more need for diversion. Lystourel can be an abomination to the senses, but it is also filled with wonderful things. Which is, I suppose, only saying that it is a great city."

"I will certainly consider it."

"All it needs, just now," Strange said. He had, Longlight thought, the marvelous quality of urging you toward a thing, without disguising that he was doing so, yet never insisting; of making it seem desirable of itself. It was said that her great-uncle—the one who had apparently played battleboard with Strange decades ago—had possessed that. Until he was murdered.

If she asked, politely, as a Coronal favor, could Strange convince her that she was content to leave his House, and go home to her Coronal Seat, and not think about things and people she had no right thinking about?

It was getting too complicated. No, it had been that for days now. She excused herself before she should say something irrecoverably stupid.

In the hallway, she met the boy Hazel. He was holding the motive of his wooden train, clenched in both hands. He bowed and said carefully, "My lady Longlight?"

"Yes, Hazel?"

"Uncle—Honored Birch would like to talk to you, if he can. May. He is in the downstairs lib'ary . . . I can take you there, if you wa-wish it."

"I know where it is. Thank you, Hazel." The boy shuffled a shoe, turned slowly. "Wait, please. Are you allowed to take an ace for your service?"

He turned back, said rather more rapidly, "My mamas say yes—if I don't ask for it."

She held out the coin, trying to keep her smile from spreading too wide. Hazel had a little difficulty easing his grip on the toy to accept it, but gripped them both whitely tight and bowed again. Longlight returned the bow, and the boy hurried off.

She went down to the book-lined room, expecting to find Birch by the hidden opening to the Dark Room, but the panel was closed, and Birch, in a black robe trimmed with red, stood at the back wall, examining a case of medals. He turned, bowed slightly. "Good day, my lady."

"And to you, Archimage."

He looked slightly embarrassed. Silence followed. Longlight said, "Does Strange collect these medals?"

"They are all his, if that's what you mean." He turned, pointed to a particularly impressive one. "From the colors and design, I think this one is from your part of the world."

She recognized it from half the room away, then had to move close to be certain. "But . . . that's the Order of the Field of Clay. It was given by the Westrene War College—the highest award for an instructor."

"Oh. That would make perfect sense."

"Not to me. That award hasn't been given since Westrene was absorbed by the National Academy. That was over a hundred years ago."

Birch smiled. "I keep showing you the limits of my knowledge. First about Reccan, and now this."

She tried and failed to think of a proper reply to that, and found herself saying, "You wished to speak to me?"

"*With* you. Shall we sit?"

They did, facing each other in the comfortable chairs. Birch adjusted the lamp so that the light was in no one's eyes. He looked directly at her and said, "This is about Varic."

"Has there been some word?"

"Varic will not arrive in the City until tomorrow. Winterhill is departing this evening and will see him the day following."

"And . . ." Had the message come that she should follow, after and despite all? Traveling with Winterhill might not be circumspect, but from what she had heard at the Ferangarder ball, it was not a lapse likely to attract much notice. ". . . what of Winterhill?"

"If you would write a letter to Varic, Winterhill will deliver it. His discretion in such things is absolute." Birch grinned. "I would say renowned, but—well."

Back to secrecy, she thought, very well, then. "What would this letter concern—particularly?"

"It would concern Varic alone." His smile disappeared. "I see I have made another awkward joke. It would particularly concern Varic not alone—Varic and yourself, my lady Coron."

"I cannot travel to Lystourel for some time. Certainly not for a month or more. Possibly longer. My affairs in the Parliament—"

"I don't need you to tell *me* these things, Longlight. And I think Varic knows you are needed at home. He also told me a few things about your difficulties with the Parliament. Varic understands obligation. Though he did not say so, he wishes he could have done more for your cause."

"He tried," she said, feeling suddenly miserable. She pulled herself taut again, said flatly, "What, then, should this letter say?"

"Save your grace, Longlight, *I* don't know. Only you do."

"*Goodbye* is a difficult word to speak, and a brutal one to write. So perhaps we can both imagine it said already."

"Very well," he said, in a tone that did not at all end the conversation.

She pressed her eyelids shut for a moment. There was no hint of tears; that was no part of her. But looking burned, sometimes. "He said that this place . . . made him good, and decent, and that he was not those things away from here."

"And do you believe that?"

"No. It . . . lifted a weight from him, I think. I saw him in the City, and—I would not have followed a bad soul here."

"He would not have brought one." Birch paused. "A weighted one, as you say, yes."

She noted the sudden shift of the weight, let the thought go by. "The house *did* do something terrible, though, to both of us, something worse than—" She stopped.

"Tell me."

"We are both Corons. Lords of the blood ancient, or at least the generations since the last usurpation."

"Three, in Varic's case."

"Five in mine, seil 'an. Whoever we partner becomes partan allsey—part of that, will or no. Our lands are half the world apart; we couldn't graft them, even if our people would stand it. So who sets by? You say Varic seils handness—obligation—*it cannot be.*" The thump of her words made her pause, but Birch just sat, looking straight on, attending.

She said, "For a few nights, this place made me forget that . . . and I think that if I stay here much longer, I will begin to hate it for that. So I will go. It may be I can come back again, even when Varic is here. But I do not know."

Birch said in an ordinary tone, "Once, Strange held Agate in his arms. Touched her skin to skin."

"What?" she said, disoriented.

"This is a grave secret, and I expect your word that you will never speak of it to Agate. Because she doesn't know."

"What has this to do with Varic and me?"

"You know about the business with my Lord Brook's lover. After Rissi died, Agate fell into a fever, hot enough to singe wool. What could anyone do? Strange said, 'This is a darkness on my House, and it must be met.' He nursed her for five days." Birch's face was illuminated with awe, and terror as well. "He is what

Dany calls him: the soul that can meet the powers you and I cannot." He relaxed a little. "When Agate recovered, she remembered nothing after Rissi's death. I don't know what story Strange told her. But she does not know. Because *that* is a touch that cannot be. And to think that the only break in that isolation came through death and sickness—" He shook his head.

"Or worse, to know it," Longlight said, "and have it be gone again."

"Yes," said Birch, his voice much less tense. "Like losing the experience of Goddess."

"Are you suggesting," she said, the release bringing a weird, light-headed irony, "that I am an experience of Goddess?"

"Yes, of course."

Her short laugh made him smile. "That is what we all are, when we are just and true. That is what love is, Longlight. Why we need it. Varic perhaps more than you or I, because—just now, it may be the only one that can reach him."

That stopped her still. "You are . . . thinking of his spirit."

"Yes. Though never only of it."

"Have you ever had this discussion before? About Varic. With another . . ."

"There were opportunities. But I missed the one, and I rejected the other." His smile was very faint. "If I am wrong now, at least it is a different error." His eyes finally lowered, just slightly. It was not, she realized, really a shock to see the loss and regret there, and know that she now had one more secret to keep. She was more surprised that she had not seen it before.

He recovered in three quick heartbeats. "I shall be there for the sake of his spirit, for all the life She gives me. But that is not the whole of my calling, any more than the spirit is the whole soul. If Varic's heart withers, there is no hope for his spirit. Light without joy . . . burns, destroys."

"You ask a great deal," Longlight said.

"True."

"What would we . . . *be* to each other?"

"You have a great house of residence, do you not?"

"I have a large house."

"If you looked out on a stormy night and you saw a traveler whose candle was guttering in the rain, what would you do?"

Longlight's hand moved involuntarily: Shyira-Guarding-Seed. "You know that mine is a hard country. There is only one rule for that."

"One rule everywhere," Birch said gently, "but you remember it. When you had taken the traveler in, something would happen. She might sleep the night and barely speak a word. She might keep the household laughing all night with stories. She might be a thief or give birth to a perfect new soul. She might even be a wispel and show you the terror of death by morning. You don't know what the visitor will be to you, or you to her. You only remember the rule. The candle must not die, because then there is no story."

They were both quiet then. There were faint sounds of life from elsewhere in Strange House.

Longlight opened her mouth. It was absolutely dry. She drew up enough moisture to say, "When is Winterhill leaving?"

"Not for some hours."

"Still." She stood up. "Don't allow him to go without speaking to me."

Birch nodded, and she went out.

❧

Birch leaned forward in the deep, soft chair and shuddered. He felt that if Goddess should look wide just now, Her single eyelash would blot him out. He had done what he ought do, and therefore must do. What would happen was not the great issue;

that was up to Her, and to Longlight and Varic. But if Birch did not try to draw his friend's spirit from the void with whatever means were put before him, then it was time to stop playing priest, *now*, before he should play at Communion and their first conjoined breath burned him to ash.

The power was just too great, he thought one more time; the mechanism was too big, and all the gears and levers were inside cabinets he could not open. *Were* Varic and Longlight paired, truly? None of them was past the sudden flare of plain heat that went cold and bitter as quickly.

He stared at the wall of the library, apparently solid, that hid the entrance to Strange House's Dark Room.

He heaved himself up and went upstairs.

∞

Agate got up from her chair, put on shoes and a plain blue dress, and was standing three steps from the door when the knock came. "Please come in," she said.

Birch opened the door.

"Good afternoon, Birch," Agate said, not closing the distance between them. "I can tell from the shape of your shoulders why you have come to visit. Are you certain you should not wait?"

"Needs to be now," he said. She could hear him shifting tone from word to word. He broke the music of his speech for her sake. It was not necessary, at least not now. But she did appreciate it.

"What do you think, then?"

"Earth."

"I will meet you in the elm grove, then."

He nodded—he even did that arrhythmically—and departed. She shut the door, then exchanged her shoes for the loose black sandals. For Earth she would want the touch of earth.

She walked down the south-end stairs, all the way to the lower floor. Birch would be in a hurry, Agate knew, but she was not, and she had not eaten today; she stopped in the kitchen, and Lilia the cook brought her warm bread and a mug of chicken soup. She could just hear the murmur of onions and potatoes, the whisper of growing wheat, below the song of the chicken: she was moving toward the poetry of Earth.

For Agate, the most important thing about a language was its rhythm. That was where her Craft was. But the most interesting thing was meanings, and how they shifted like light on water.

In Lescant, when someone spoke of a "soul," they meant a person, of any sort, but a whole person, body and mind. In Gerade, *seil* meant only the mind, the invisible part of the person, what Lescorials called *spirit*. The confusion was compounded by the old Lescant *seil*, meaning deep understanding. In Alinsetre there was a spectrum of words for bodies and minds and various combinations thereof. Dany told her of a country near her own that had no specific word for *human body* at all, or indeed the body of any animal; the names of beings meant their spirits, all bodies being the same temporary shells of meaningless stuff.

The voice of Earth—and Fire, and Air . . . they were not things sorcerers spoke of much, because they were not to be understood in human speech. One did not get too close to the reasons underneath the languages of things. Agate doubted that it was understandable: like a field mouse, nibbling wheat, trying to comprehend crop rotation.

Any sorcerer could rattle his Talent Archain and move stones about. There were proofs of that stacked and aligned all over the human landscape. But to move stones in the other sense, one had to address them in their own language.

Agate thanked Lilia and went out the lower door, past the

cold and dry storage houses, the kitchen wood and coal piles. A right turn put her on the stone-flagged path to the elm grove, and twenty long steps along the House was hidden by masses of green leaves streaked with red and gold.

She began to think as Earth thought.

> *The moving touch gone,*
> *I shiver, sleeping;*
> *I break within.*
> *Return, or do not.*
> *Broken is just another sleep.*

The leaves stirred around her feet, and she felt a push as the soil hardened beneath her soles. She pulled off her sandals, placed them by the path, continued on toward the clearing where Birch waited for her.

They had first done this almost two years ago, when it became apparent that he was on the path to the Archimagery. He had wanted Fire, that first time. She understood. He wanted to be worthy or die at the very start: no slow torture of doubt. She had given him Air instead. Air flowed around, forgave, passed on, and forgot. It was still entirely able to kill.

By now they had passed through all the elements several times over, a little worse, a little more dangerous, each time. It was never quite enough for Birch, apparently, never the proof he needed. This time, she knew, would be the last; after this the Archimage would face his congregation and open himself to their Goddess.

The stone path ended in a circle of smoothed earth perhaps eight steps across, ringed by tall, old elms. Birch was kneeling on the far side, a step or two from the trees. She stood just opposite, spread her feet as far as her shoulders. "Are you ready?" she said. It came out as a rapid chirp. Birch just nodded, once.

She spoke to the ground, murmuring as earth to earth, kindly asking the great stones to pardon her company. It answered, formally. She did not intrude. It did not mind. She was just there.

Her spine was straight as a finger of quartz, her fingers spread like branching crystals. Slowly, like the rise of hills, her eyelids opened.

What she saw was stone within blur: carbon and calcium, silica, traces of metal, wrapped for the briefest of moments in water and air, temporary matter that would in another instant rot and deliver itself up again.

Birch (as part of her remembered it was) was a rick of white sticks, within a cloud of mist glowing with life as it pulsed and faded. Around the bones, pinpoints of iron and copper glittered, red and green.

The language of Earth barely had words for the delicate stuff that flickered over it, lighter than dew. Mostly it was beneath notice, a kind of superficial itch. Sometimes there was a palpable event, a deep burrow, a scar. Of late, a river might be moved, just a little. It did not matter; when the river was ready, it would move back.

This was, Agate's mortal mind knew, what Birch wanted, what he needed to cope with: the infinite unconcern of Earth. Not patience, because to be patient with something was to give it attention. People thought they were patient with the land, when their crops died and their houses collapsed and floods swallowed what was dear to them, and they did not move on. It was nothing of the kind. The people often died in such a patience. The land did not care.

Birch wanted to stand in the full blast of that riverine indifference. If he could endure it, no mere human passion would be unendurable. Or so the reasoning went.

It could kill him. In truth, it was very unlikely to just *hurt* him, if it did any damage at all. She might return to mortal time and vision to see a sort of puddle with a fan of bonemeal blasted out beyond it. Or a standing stone, ensorcelling the grove for the rest of human time; legend and place-name said that every rock of a familiar shape had once been something alive. More of them had been than most people believed. Or she might see nothing—just a gap in the air, closing up, and one last word.

And if that happened, what of her?

There were very old sayings that a sorcerer who had not killed three dear friends wasn't really trying; that all Masters walked alone, sooner or later. The newer sort of Crafters liked their society, and those sayings were not popular now.

She must not think of this. Soon she would have to, and it would be ugly, but now—

She felt energy move from her like a slow exhalation, a creeping wave of distortion visible in the air and palpable in the stuff of space itself, shouldering reality aside as it bore upon the bone stack in its momentary veil. It was in no hurry. What the Life did before it was unimportant.

The Life held still, and the wave passed through it. Little waves rippled to its sides; one of them was probably a sound, another air, another perhaps water.

Agate looked up. She could see the sun gaining speed, visibly moving, the shadows bending as she watched. She reached for another heartbeat, pulled it to her and past, pulled another on. The sun paused. The wheeling universe slammed noiselessly to a stop.

Her breath came in thick as water, and she nearly choked; but the next one was smooth and easy, and her heart found its pace.

Birch was as he had been, though his hair was disarrayed and his knees were sunk half a span into the ground. His eyes were shut tight in a wrenched face, and he breathed hard, but he breathed.

He got his eyes open, moved his hands unsteadily to their lids, and began to scrape out sandy gum. "Agate—?" he grunted.

She waited until she was certain the reply would come in Lescant, or at least in something human. "I am here. Are you well?"

He started to get up, then thumped forward on his hands and knees. She waited. It was all she could do. He got to his feet. "I am . . . yes, I am very well. It was—not so hard. . . ."

"Look behind you," she said.

He turned and stared at the elm that had been directly behind him. It was heaved up so that half the root system was exposed, and the trunk was mangled by pressure, like the blow of a great fist, splintered down to heartwood. Some of the boughs groped at the sky.

"Too much of Water," she said, then swallowed. "Stay clear of it, fall at a touch." He moved back. It was a shame to kill the tree. Perhaps Roan could make something beautiful of the remaining wood.

Birch—she kept thinking this was a joke, the tree left standing when the elm died, but she couldn't parse it, it needed Gaily— came toward her. "What may I do for you, Agate?"

"Serve Her in your way," she said, not meaning it unkindly. "Go now. I will be . . . along soon."

They had done this before. He went, quickly.

It was good to be stone, she thought, against herself. You never died. Broke, yes, but it was only another sleep.

After she had so soundly punished Brook's lover's last bold move, she had fallen into an affliction, for days it turned out. Strange made the others believe Agate knew nothing of what had happened in the gap, to spare them when she was present; but who else could it have been, sponging her cracked skin, speaking little comforts into her incoherent ears, covering her indifferent modesty? He was a Sky's-Bridge, as Dany called it, the soul who could enter the house of the desolated spirit, tell it to hush, sleep, find what peace it could.

Only one other might have done it, with the strength of the House behind him; but he was not there, or the thing might never have happened at all.

Let everyone believe she remembered nothing of it. These things were necessary, even if one did not make a Craft of it, like Winterhill.

Let Varic believe it most of all. If he should think—and he would—that anyone else, even Strange, was fitter for her side than himself, he would cease to intrude. In that were seas and continents of desolation.

And if, and if . . . Birch was, to be most absolutely certain, not Rissi. She knew, though, that she would never break in just that way again. Which meant, of course, a new and different way.

The delayed rage came then.

What if she had killed Birch? No—what if she killed him, *too*? Did that save his congregation, the glory of Goddess, the honor of the priesthood? All that, for a little more human grease on her fingers?

Who did he think she was?

She dug her toes into the hardening soil, trying to earth the fury like electric fluid. Birch did not ask this for himself. He asked it in Her name, trusting that She would guard them both.

Varic had no such safety, or at least he believed he did not, which probably came to the same thing.

She threw her long senses into the ground, down the road to the Ironway, along the rails, but moving lightly, so lightly—

Varic, please. For just one of your spirit's cool breaths, I need you.

—light as a very breath, because he must not know he was needed and absent.

She knew it was a mistake at once, to reach for Varic in a house full of people who cared for him, were thinking of him. The echoes and resonances fell on her like a collapsing building, rebounding, splintering, closing around her—

Birch, struggling between hopeless loss and unquenchable hope—

let go now

Strange, his incandescent spirit glowing through every crack in his defenses, burning with grief—

Dany, her care for Varic almost outfacing that for Strange—

you have to get out of this

Lilia, pounding her sorrow into brown wheat dough that a guest had departed the House unhappy—

Reccan, in an intolerable wordless radiance that was terribly close to the voice of Air—

not her, stop before

And then, as she feared, Longlight, clutching a pen, soul-and-spirit-deep in thoughts of Varic. Agate raised her hands to push doors shut on her mind, feeling fire and cold marble on her skin, the tightening of—

I reject caress and token

She knew he was gentle, knew he was patient—

nothing promised nothing spoken

The deer in the glade, bound and helpless, its throat white and naked under the knife—

and by this the charm is broken

Who did she think she was?

"Good afternoon, Agate," Winterhill said, simply and loudly, and saved any number of things. "I trust you are not unwell, on such a fine fall day." His fingers echoed the words in Soonest's Visible, giving her dumbstruck mind more language to seize on.

She signed, *Only tired, thank you,* back at him, knowing he would find it as absurd as she did.

"I think it might be good to sit," he said, and pointed to one side of her. "There is a conveniently sized boulder just a pace to your left."

What she had just done, just below Longlight's awareness . . . some sorcerers called it "honorary conseil." It was universally considered inexcusably rude, so no one ever attempted to excuse it.

Worse, it was so horribly, cruelly *lonely* . . .

Winterhill watched as Agate carefully took a seat on the stone. He felt himself poised, wound up to . . . well, run, most likely. He couldn't help her to sit, or catch her should she fall, nor was there anything he could imagine to do without help. He would go for Strange first. If not him, then Roan; her particular combination of mother and tool master let her cope with a vast range of problems. And after Roan, who? Edaire, perhaps . . .

Agate relaxed into her seat, crossing her tanned ankles with a very pleasant delicacy. She smiled at him. "Thank you, Winterhill. Is there anything now that I may do for you?"

"A man might faint at an offer like that," he said at once, and then stopped his runagate tongue. Agate just laughed, dispelling the last of the tension like bells driving off a thunderstorm. Winterhill had done that once, and it had actually worked. Fortunately for him, and the bell tower, and the six tons of powder and primers at its base.

Considering explosives—*did* Agate have any idea how summer's-day desirable she was? Varic must have told her; the man was a live Dark Room of secret things, but if Winterhill understood one thing about Agate, it was that loving her would require absolute, more than mortal honesty.

So Winterhill had meant what he said to her; fainting was all that might save him.

Agate said, "Never stop, Winterhill, lest the world stop with you—" And he said, "You're right, of course, much to do," turning to go just not quick enough to miss her "—never, ever die," at the end.

He supposed that might be nice, never dying. He ought to ask Strange about it sometime. Not that he would. Strange could see around the corners of the most obliquely phrased question, and give you just the answer you were terrified was coming. The reason, he supposed, that none of the Players ever asked Strange who his heir might be. It was a thing that would find its own bad time.

He imagined Varic must be thinking that way, just now. Varic was odds-on to be Strange's heir, in everyone's calculation but Varic's own. Winterhill doubted very much that Varic had thought of Brook ever dying. Certainly not before Varic himself—and at a duel every half-year with people he didn't really want to kill (but who did not return the courtesy), Varic seemed determined never to face the difficulty.

Not that you ever really had to worry. When the trouble was ready, it would let you know.

He saw Reccan on the plaza before the pond. She was wearing a loose coat and trousers, black slippers, and she had a sword extended. She pivoted, swinging the blade up and over, then down in a sudden brutal cut.

Winterhill paused a moment to watch. It was a medium-length blade, flat but not wide, a little too long and curved for a swordstick but concealable under a long coat, or even up the back of the one she was wearing. He could tell from the movement of her right foot that there was a throwing blade strapped to her calf, just out of sight.

If she had been anyone else but Reccan—that redoubtable Lady Longlight, for example—he might never have seen any of this. Or rather, he would have seen every bit of it, every motion, every flicker of light in her eyes, until one blade or other split his heart in the material sense.

Just beside him, some long-stemmed flowers with large,

spherical violet blooms were growing. He picked one, with about a forearm's-length of stem, held it loosely in his right hand, and took two long quick steps behind Reccan.

She pivoted with no sound but moving air. The tip of the sword cut the flower stem just below the blossom; it tumbled in air, and Winterhill caught it in his left palm. *Point and concetta,* he signed, and flicked the fingers of both hands in applause.

He signed, *I am returning to the City on the late train. Are you coming?*

No. Dany wants to practice. And I want a little time with Agate. I will be there again in a few days.

She had signed *there,* and not *home.* It wasn't a word he had much use for either. He bowed, as if in the arenetto—which was a joke, as they had both learned most of what they knew about fighting before they had ever been in such a place—and went on, into the House.

He had never brought a companion of his own to Strange House. Nothing to do with Strange, of course; he liked laughter in his chambers, even if it went mostly unheard. It just fell out that—well, the only woman he had ever brought to the House was Reccan, and Reccan was . . . very different. Once Strange had calmed the feral edge from her, she thought she owed Winterhill something. That was absurd; they were at least even on lives. Her former owner had taught her a few elementary forms of gratitude; it had been almost harder to get past those than the fear and rage. The worst bit was convincing her he was not repelled by her vocal deformity. *The Lady bless Dr. Soonest, and gild his fingers with Her kisses.*

Dashing souls like himself were supposed to always be saving lovely folk of compatible inclinations and then dancing off the page and into the snuffable lamplight. It was a lot harder than they made it look.

He went up to the Blue Parlor, where Edaire was sprawled on

the carpet with Hazel, playing Ironways. She looked up. "Yes, Winterhill?"

"Reccan's staying on awhile. Alone into the darkness ride I, alone."

Hazel looked up, with something like awe, at this. "Will there be danger?"

"Naught that a swift hand and a swifter wit cannot defeat, honored," he said, and swept a bow. Hazel laughed.

Edaire said to Hazel, "Motives stop for water and coal, Inspector's orders," and Hazel quickly moved the wooden motive beside a tin canister that was presumably a water tower.

"You still want the night express?" Edaire said.

"Yes."

She found a pad and pencil on the parlor secretary and wrote out what looked like a string of nonsense words—COPAX LYSTL NTHRU and so on for a line. They were magnostyle code, precise instructions and authentications to the Ironway staff compressed into five-letter groups for rapid transmission. "'Style this to the station, copied to Chantery Junction. You'll have a compartment, through to the City."

"Thank you. Any message for Varic?"

"Love and trust as ever, if he'll hear it. And another thing—if you see Lix on the cars, thank him for me. In fact—to thank him properly—"

"It would delight me to share my compartment with Lix," Winterhill said. He held up the message. "Best stitch this off."

A moment after Winterhill had gone, Hazel said, "I met Lord Lix once, when he came here."

"Lord Lix?"

"Well . . . only Lord Strange called him that, but Lord Strange would know, yes? Like with Lady Longlight."

"Of course that's right," she said firmly. "What did Lord Lix do here?"

"He talked a lot with Lord Strange. And he did fingersmith tricks—'conjuring,' he said it was called. He did those for Honored Reccan, and she smiled so much I thought—" His face tightened up.

"Yes?"

In a small voice, Hazel said, "I thought she would laugh, really."

"It's all right, Hazel. I think Lord Lix might have hoped she would, too."

"Bessa gave me some apples and patcakes for him, when he was going. He made them all disappear right out of his hands!" After a moment to let this sink in, he said, "All but one apple—he gave that to me, and said a proper lord always shares. So he was a proper lord then, wasn't he?"

"As you say, Hazel . . . milord Strange knows these things. What did your mamas say?"

"Mama Tacker just laughed all the time when he was around. Mama Roan told him he was a wicked man, but she wasn't mad when she said it, so I think she was joking. After he went away, she told me . . ." He paused. This was a lesson, and it had to be called back. ". . . that I always must work hard to really know people, because a great soul might come in wearing any sort of clothes." Another deep pause. "I don't know if Lord Lix is a great soul—I mean, like Lord Strange or Mistress Agate. But I think he was a good one. I worked hard to see, and I think so."

"Yes, Hazel. I believe you are right." She pointed at the train on the carpet. "I think that motive's well serviced by now. What did you say her name was?"

"*Queen Beryl*, from the Ashfork Shops."

"What have you been reading, then?"

"Strange said I could look at the big Ironways book in the upstairs library, as long as a grown person was there, too. And I didn't have anything to eat or drink in the room. And I was careful." He knelt by the toy motive, then looked up at Edaire with a deeply thoughtful expression. "How old do you have to be to work on the real Ironways?"

"Well, there are some jobs that you can start when you're fifteen. Message runners, lantern tenders. They aren't fancy work, but they're important. Do you understand why?"

"Course. You can't run a train without lanterns and orders."

"Right. And if you stay with them, the time you work counts for you when you're old enough for other jobs. That's called seniority."

"How much of it do I need to be a motive driver?"

Edaire suppressed a grin. She had never met a child who wanted to be anything *but* a motive driver; the only near exception had thought the captain with the fine brass-buttoned uniform must drive the train as well. Carefully, she said, "Usually you can apprentice to the Drivers' Guild at eighteen, but if the drivers get to know you, as they will if you've been handing them orders and clean, filled lanterns, they can vote to start you a year early. Whichever it is, you then have to apprentice for at least two years, sometimes more."

"What do 'prentices do?"

"They work with the motive crews, helping take care of the machines and learning all about how they work. You stay near one of the terminals, so you're around motives all the time. It's like horses, you see?"

Hazel nodded. Edaire could tell that this was going to lead somewhere unexpected, but she went on, trusting Hazel to drop the word at some appropriately startling moment. Edaire said, "Sometimes you go out on the road with a crew. Then you oil the rods, and rake ashes, and break up the coal. You get dirty *all* over." She saw Hazel's eyes brighten at the thought. "Finally you take a test to prove you know all about the job, and if you pass, you get a license. The drivers call it a 'card.'"

"A writing test?"

"Partly. Long ago, before I was born, there was a test for people who couldn't read or write, but that was when all the lines were short and there weren't any magnostyles. You have to be able to read orders, right?"

This was absorbed. "And when you have the card, you can drive motives?"

"Yes. But there are more drivers than work—there have to be, because people get sick or hurt, and take holidays. New drivers, without much seniority, mostly move equipment in the yards and shops. Some people like that job; it means they can always go home at the end of the day. The next step from that is stopping trains and then the expresses."

She could see him mentally adding all the delays and *eventuallys* into more than the years of his life so far. "But there are long trips? All over the country, like you take?"

"For some drivers, yes."

Hazel paused. This would be, Edaire knew, the windup to the Big Question. When it came, it was just a little more unexpected than she had supposed.

❧

In the battleboard room, Strange was examining a terrain of high plaster hills, heaped sand, and dense groves of fiber trees, while Silvern adjusted the positions of miniature soldiers. Some were painted in Quercian scarlet and bronze, others in dark brown leather and black iron.

Strange tapped his fingers on the arm of his chair. "That's very close to Summerleaf's description, however accurate it may be."

"It makes sense, though," Silvern said. "The Empire would have deployed according to the manual. Even their own historians give Florius no credit for imagination. So, if Wander is sensible, she has to put the spearmen here"—he indicated a narrow pass—"the archers and slingers up above, here and here, with the trees for cover."

"We can't be sure of the trees' location. But there must have been trees. The cavalry, then?"

"If I were commanding, I'd have told them to leave their horses at home and prepare for serious hand-to-hand. But Wander couldn't tell Westrene hill-riders that."

"So you believe she would have divided them?"

"That is an interesting thought." Silvern examined the two groups of cavalry, one in front of the pass, facing the Quercians, the other in to the rear, in the narrow valley. "Give me Summerleaf's line again."

Strange touched a book that lay in his lap, but did not open it. He said:

> *"Knowing their chances and chancing to naught*
> *Wander divided the bold riders there*
> *Half for the drawing and half for the stroke*
> *Half for each Lady—Commander and Goddess."*

"It's a strong translation," Silvern said.

"It ought to have rhymed, but I was very young and in a great hurry. Interesting, you said."

"My thought is . . . there's nothing Wander can do with those horse. They can't do serious damage to armored Quercian heavies in close ranks, and even if Florius has to retreat, he'll retreat in good order, by the manual; Quercians could do that if the village fool was commanding. And if the cavalry charge after that as if the Imperials were a bunch of panicked village levy, they will be very sorry they ever learned to ride." He looked up at Strange, who nodded.

Silvern continued, "So Wander says, 'I want half of you to wait out here, dare the Empire to attack you. The other half will wait behind the pass, as a reserve if it's forced. Decide among yourselves who is in which party, and do it quickly.' So the rowdy ones—"

"Who won't be commanded anyhow," Strange said.

"Yes. They're out where they'll probably wound a few Quercians and almost certainly die trying. Goddess's portion. And the sensible half—because rash or not, none of them are cowards—stay back, Wander's half, to use in whatever fashion suggests itself."

Silvern turned his head away from Strange then. His lips moved, without a sound. Strange watched him, but said nothing.

After perhaps two minimi, Silvern faced Strange again and said, "Hazel has just asked Edaire when his time will come to be a Guest of Strange House."

"A question he was certain to ask eventually," Strange said. "I should have given more thought to the answer."

"Perhaps he means . . ." Silvern shook his head. "Something other. I don't know. Children sometimes see the world very oddly."

"Distinguishing them from adults."

"Point."

"I should think he means the obvious: when will no one give him orders, when will he rise when he pleases and eat what he likes, when will there be no need to ask permission. When, in short, will the world out there be like the one in here."

"It seems to me that many good people are working toward that."

"Yes, since before Pershex, and he was long before even my time. Society's not just a pyramid, it's a range of mountains; it takes time to level them. More time than one soul gets." Strange shook his head. "He's grown up with Corons and professors and engineers and the occasional monarch running about the halls as if they were so many other children—and soon we'll have to turn him out into a world where a servant's child can still be whipped for standing on the same carpet as a Coron."

"You haven't spoiled him," Silvern said, gently but firmly.

"No, but we may have ruined him. For life anywhere but here, I mean." Strange looked up, suddenly smiling. "But you're right, we haven't spoiled him. If they throw him out of an Ascorel college for believing the teachers are no better souls than he is, he'll have learned something precious. And we'll be one spirit closer to the mountain coming down."

"I might speak to Hazel."

"Because you do not count yourself among the guests here—in that particular, Players' sense?"

"I will not be the one who inherits your burden."

"If the choice were a thing that could be refused, you know as well as I do who would be first to set it by. And Varic is the only other one who would dare to call it a 'burden.' Or am I missing some secret within you, Silvern?"

Silvern gave an elaborate shrug. "You? Never. I was only thinking—it is not for one of the Order. If I were old, no longer fit for combat, but . . ." His smile evaporated. "Pardon me, Strange."

"Nothing to pardon. You are correct; it will not wait for you to grow old. . . . Go on, ask the next question."

"*Do* you know when?"

"No. That would be unbearable, I think. It's hazy—months, a year, possibly two, and I may be foolish even to count. It's curious . . . a year, the full turn of seasons, hundreds of rich days, so much that can be done with them—yet when there's only that one year and no more, one fears to blink and lose an instanta." His face seemed to smooth, his eyes to grow luminous. "I think that's why the Palions refuse such prophecy."

"To live always ready for the moment, take it in its time, the instanta edaire," Silvern recited. "A surprise, and a wonder. She laughed so, when first I told her that saying."

"When you did, did you already know?"

"We knew. We set the date for the ceremony later that day." He paused, his lips open. "Very well. The following day."

Strange was relaxed now. "Silvern, if there is any distinction among this House's visitors, it is not of my making. I am not a Palion, but I have known many, and there comes a time when the Order is best served by retiring to pass on one's wisdom. How long before the Kólyan winters touch your joints?" He paused. Silvern said nothing. Softly, Strange said, "Do not think on the instanta Edaire, but on the years of her."

"Point," Silvern whispered.

"You should go to her, now."

"Point and concetta. May I take you somewhere?"

"No, I thank you. If you will hand me that shawl, I shall go inspecting my domain. . . . I believe there is to be mutton pie for supper, and I had best examine that very closely."

Silvern opened the door, and Strange rolled his chair into the hall. As they waited for the lift, Strange said, "Perhaps it is time for a new translation of Summerleaf."

"This one could rhyme."

"Too young then, too old now. Besides, one never knows when one will need to make the sunset orange and the moonlight silver."

Silvern laughed and exited on the next floor down. Strange continued down to the ground level. He watched the pulleys and cables working as the car descended. Of all the things he had built into the House, he thought, was any quite as crucial as this one? The indoor plumbing, perhaps. The old ramps had been a nuisance, the manual lift a group nuisance, but one did not have to go out in the cold, incompletely dressed, to use them.

Yes, the plumbing was good. Longlight's pleasure at the hot water had pleased Strange greatly. He was thinking of her as he rolled into the courtyard and saw her, something clutched in her hand.

"Good afternoon, Strange."

"And to you, Longlight."

"I was looking for Winterhill. But everyone around here seems to have disappeared."

"Large houses do that. One moment it's like an Ironway terminus, the next everyone's down a different hole. May I know why you want him?"

"I have a letter for him to carry. To the City." She showed the envelope, though not the address. There was no real need to be curious. Strange said, "Do you know the secretary desk in the first-floor lobby?"

"I'll find it."

"Place the letter in the red box."

"Oh, yes. I saw him there just after we arrived. Thank you, honored."

"Most welcome."

She walked purposefully into the house. He watched her; she did not seem troubled, but certainly in the grip of a thought. Well, troubled perhaps, but not in a destructive way.

He gripped the wheels of his chair tightly, so that if Longlight turned back she would not see the sudden tremor in his hands.

After the door closed, he turned the chair and moved to the fountain. It splashed off-center in the light breeze. In ten days or so they would shut it down and drain it, ahead of the frost. He would talk to Agate about Crafting the garden; it would save a great deal of work, and a few winter flowers would be good for everyone's spirits.

As Longlight had said, the area seemed entirely empty of life. Strange put his hands inside his shawl and let them shake. They ached a bit, that was all. Younger souls than he—very much younger—felt chills.

He did not imagine feeling regret for the House. He had friends who believed, earnestly and with hope, that their spirits would return in new bodies, live new lives, grow toward wiser, better selves. Strange did not believe in that. If age made a better spirit, he . . . well. Perhaps there was some next world, better or worse or neither; he would go into it with all he had brought to this—that is, himself and nothing else. There might be another House—but that was too much to think: infinity was not so large.

Varic had agreed to stay on, before Brook had been stricken. Strange had wanted that time with Varic, wanted to talk with him while the House was uncrowded. Goddess was the fount of sorcerous power, and Craft was imprecise by nature. Was that why Her timing could be so perfectly bad?

Maybe not perfectly. There was Longlight.

He would speak to Agate about the garden, but he would take the long way there, around the House, and by the time he arrived, thoughts of Varic would have subsided to a level tolerable for her. Just a little patience, and it would be well.

Impatience, and therefore patience, were human concepts, he thought. Goddess made whatever time She needed.

❧

The next day was chilly, with hazy golden curtains of sunlight breaking heavy clouds. The courtyard fountain splashed the flagstones in the breeze, and dust danced along the ground. It smelled of coming rain.

Longlight stood upwind of the fountain spray, watching Tacker load the coach for the trip to the Ironway station. It wasn't a major task; Silvern traveled as light as she did, and Birch just had a waxed-canvas knapsack. She supposed his Archimage's wardrobe would be waiting for him at Capel Storrow. . . . And somehow, despite their time at Strange House, it was hard to imagine one of Lescoray's four chiefest priests in a shirt and old trousers.

But that was what Birch was wearing when he came out of the House, with infantry-style boots, a long, brown trail coat, and a black hat with a broad floppy brim. He looked like a rogue from a ballad, the sort who was always a prince in disguise.

"My lady Coron," he said, and bowed, waving the hat.

"Archimage." She inclined her head.

"That's over, good," Birch said, grinning hugely. "We can go back to names for the rest of the journey. Have you made your farewells?"

"To Strange. He said he would pass my respects to Agate. And I watched Dany and Reccan in the arenetto, just a little while ago."

"That's good. We try not to make too much of leaving here. It's hard enough to do, without elevating it to a ceremony." More quietly, he said, "You do intend to return?"

"I do, if life allows it."

"Exactly the proper mood."

"I . . . did not see Edaire."

"Nor I, but I imagine we will." He pulled an oversized watch from a trouser pocket, opened its case. "Just about now."

He turned just as Silvern and Edaire appeared on the stairs, descending with hands firmly clasped. They paused at the turn, and Silvern said something into Edaire's ear, inaudible from where the others stood. Then they came on, hands still held.

Silvern said, "Into the Western sunset. I have not been west in a very long time."

Edaire said firmly, "You will find the sleeping cars tidy and the tracks smooth as far as they take you. Or there will be more riding west, and thunder with it."

Silvern turned to Birch and Longlight. "She means it. Longlight, if you find a smudge on your mirror or a hair on the carpet, avoid anything that might draw the lightning." He faced his conseil. "Now, give me a kiss, before the honest Coron and the good priest; there's all oaths in one breath."

Longlight turned just her eyes away, enough to see Birch's hands move in the sign of Coris's Union. She vaguely remembered that as part of the conseil ceremony, though people tended to better remember the wineglasses of blood.

She had never, she thought suddenly, been among so many intimacies in as short a time. She could not decide what to think of it—except that it did not seem a bad thing. Indeed, she would not believe that it was.

"In your way," Birch said, and hugged Edaire. Longlight, not sure of what to do but wanting to do something, held out her hands, and had them gripped tight.

Birch had taken a box from within his coat. He slid it open, removed the Book, began shuffling and turning the cards. "Edaire, will you grace for the travelers?"

Silvern held the Book. Birch held his palms level, Edaire turned two cards onto them. The first showed a pentagonal window framed by five thick stone slabs, opening onto a twilit sky. The second had a slender human figure, feet together and arms upraised, wrapped in sheets of flowing water. Streams from the extended fingers made a hazy rainbow over the person's shoulder.

"Five of Stones, Master of Springs," Birch said. "The way opens into the West; good to know the cards can be plainspoken sometimes. And the Craft in water. . . . Change surrounds us." There was, Longlight thought, just the faintest hesitation in his tone. "Change comes to us all." He grinned again. "And that is a plain thing, too, even if I will be dressing up proper for it. Thank you, Edaire."

Behind them, Tacker said, "Time to go, honoreds, if you will."

Birch put away his Book. Edaire and Silvern embraced. Longlight looked slowly over the face of Strange House, trying to burn it into her mind like a lucive on glass. Varic had said something— she had barely marked it at the time and tried hard to remember clearly now—about carrying the House with oneself. She had told herself, ever since Varic had gone in the night, that she would return here if chance and the world allowed it. That seemed not good enough at all, now.

The three travelers boarded the coach; Tacker shut the door, climbed on the box, and they were off, circling the House in a whisper of fallen leaves.

As they passed the edge of the pond, and the House disappeared from sight, Longlight said, "I had thought Edaire might accompany us to the station."

"That would be work," Silvern said. "Once she was on the platform, she would begin looking for things out of order. For her sake, I try not to notice anything short of imminent disaster. Now, would you hand down the decanter and glasses for all that's willing?"

Longlight looked at Birch, who nodded pleasantly. She passed the bottle across the coach and took down three glasses.

As Silvern lifted the cut-glass stopper, the spirit of apples floated up. "New brant'cy," he said. "Not too deep a pour, then." He poured out three neat splashes of the brantcider.

Longlight breathed the sharp aroma. An old toast came into her mind and was out before she could think: "To your stomach, in its way—" As she felt her face heat, Birch laughed aloud.

"I'll have to remember that one," he said, trying hard not to spill his drink. "Here's another: Coris calm your waters." He turned to Silvern. "Your turn."

Silvern sat very still for a moment—was he conversing with his conseil?—and then said with only slightly overdone drama, "Down runs one spirit, and this soul is due one; up floats another, and there's a Communion."

"And so farewell to these things," Birch said, and at once raised his glass; the others followed, and they sipped together.

The coach passed a stand of maples, their branches incandescent gold and red. Birch said, a little dreamily, "New brown sugar for Solstice. . . ."

"If you may not visit," Longlight said, "I shall bring you some." She hiccupped.

Silvern said, "So you do propose to return, my lady?" and before she could answer, "Good and well."

Birch's melancholy, if that was what it had been, seemed to pass then. "I would be happy of that, Longlight. And I would invite you—both of you—to the first Communion of my tenure."

Longlight said, "I shall certainly be there."

Silvern said, "As I am in my lady's service until Solstice, I shall of course attend, attending her."

Another hiccup. She understood his meaning; it was a Palion's phrase, a duty Silvern had accepted, not any sort of specific fealty to her as Coron or—otherwise. It was what he would say. But . . . Varic had spoken of taking Strange House with one, but he had also said that people were worse away from it.

She felt a sudden pull within, as if something just below her heart were draining out, leaving her hollow. She wanted to go back to the House, undress, crawl into the steaming shower and wait . . . wait for . . .

She blinked the thought away, looked at her companions. They were watching her, casually, not staring. They knew, she thought. They knew it, too. Perhaps they were only waiting for it to happen to her.

Birch said, "I understand that Capel Storrow, while not luxurious, has comfortable quarters for a few guests at a time. Riverglass—my predecessor—said it was the rule of hospitality. You must both know that you are welcome at any time convenient to you."

"Birch," Silvern said, very kindly, "I would visit you if I had to sleep on the ground, and you would do the same for either of us. The gravity of your office will wait until you arrive at it."

"Mm," Birch said. "I'd also been telling Longlight how we don't ceremonialize farewells and then pulled the Book out."

"And Edaire was happy you did," Silvern said. "You may trust me on that."

Birch said, "You're right about the office, waiting. On the train, perhaps you should avoid the title. No, even my right name."

"Calling you 'heysoul' will turn heads."

"Smith will do. It's true enough."

Longlight said, "The same with me, I think. No 'Coron.'" She wondered why that thought had never occurred to her before, but the answer was plain enough; she had always gone to and from Lystourel alone. "My name shouldn't be a problem. I don't think most of my own people know any name for me but 'milady Coron.'"

Silvern looked thoughtful. "I think I shall remain Palion Silvern. It will draw attention away from both of you, and I am less likely to forget it when you call."

At the station, Tacker took down their bags, politely declined a kingsir from Longlight, and disappeared around a corner with Birch.

"Come," Silvern said, "that's clearly duty. Birch will join us on the platform."

Which he did, looking distracted but not displeased, a few

minimi before the train pulled in. They boarded the sleeping car. Silvern said, "Birch isn't overnighting, so he'll store his bags with me. Shall we meet at dinner?"

Longlight agreed, watched them go down the corridor to Silvern's door, then opened her own.

It was a single compartment, large enough to take a few steps to and fro in, with a narrow door in the corner hiding the toilet—from whom?—and an oversized, comfortable chair against one end that folded out into an undersized but still fairly comfortable bed. A lap desk hung on the wall.

There was a wool throw on the chair, green with gold stripes and a satin edge. She sat down and spread it over her lap. Outside the window, cottages were passing, some with thatching and some with wooden shingles, all with stone-fenced yards, here and there a spot of bright color from a flower bed. Laundry fluttered. In the distance, not seeming to move at all, were hills, pastel green with dark stands of forest. Light struck a river—that would be the Leith, she thought—an instanta of silver.

Soon there would be hills whose names she knew, and rivers she had drunk from, and mountains. Home. Things might come to make sense then, if ever they would. Or did.

She jerked out of sleep at a tap on the door. "Longlight?" Silvern's voice said.

"Yes."

"We're two hours from Birch's stop. Would you like to have dinner?"

"Oh. Surely. Just let me—"

"Take your time. We will be in the restaurant car."

She shuffled into the tiny bathroom, pried her eyes wide before the mirror. Was that all her, or was the bad light doing its part? Washing her face and brushing her hair improved matters considerably. She shouldered the bag Ivory's had made for her, on the night of the Ferangarder ball, and was halfway down the corridor before recalling that it displayed her Coronal sigil. Well, she thought, nothing for that now. Anyone who recognized it, would.

Birch and Silvern were talking across a table when she reached the car. Neither of them had dressed up; in fact, the general level of attire in the restaurant was, while by no means shabby, not elegant. Post-holiday exhaustion, of course. There would have been quite enough fine turnouts during the Equinoctials.

She sat down. Birch indicated the open bottle of wine on the table, poured for her. It was a pleasant, fruity red, strong enough to hold its own with Ironway cooking.

They did not talk much during the meal. Three or four times Longlight thought of something to discuss, and at once discarded it as not for public airing. The train passed a fire, a barn completely wrapped in yellow flame. The diners stared through the windows at it, then recoiled as something struck the side of the train in a burst of sparks. And then it was gone.

Birch kept looking out the window, at the fading glow. He waved to the steward. "Where are we?"

"Thrassos Coronage, honored. The last town was Smokestone. Your stop is . . . ?"

"Not until Capel Storrow. I was just wondering. Thank you."

Birch looked at his companions. "You must remember to visit as you can," he said. "Do not think I will be too busy."

"We shall," Silvern said. Longlight wondered who the "we" included—her? Edaire? The company of Strange House?

Birch nodded and the conversation slept again.

They did not linger after the meal. In the corridor, Longlight said to Birch, "How much longer before your station?"

"Half an hour at least."

"Then might I—"

"Certainly. Silvern—"

"I will see you before you leave."

Only back in the compartment did she remember that a single did not have enough room for two to sit. Birch gestured her to the chair and leaned comfortably against the wall. He said, "Now, whom did you wish to speak with? The smith's-get, the village priest, or the Archimage?"

She held her breath a moment, then said, "Who's here?"

He laughed. "Point."

"When you asked about the town . . . where the fire was . . . you weren't just curious."

"Of course not. Those are about to be my people. In trust from Her, naturally."

"I have people," she said. "In trust."

He was still smiling. As she looked up at him from the chair, he looked huge—he was a big man, but there were moments, as in the breezeway at Strange House, when he could seem immense. The voice from that presence was clear but small—words in a vast space. "I am only Her priest, Longlight. I am as driven by my own wants and needs as anyone is. I may be wrong for good reasons, or right for bad ones. And I am only where I am. *She* is different.

"She will not abandon you. But sometimes She will not answer your question—at least, not in a way that will clear all mysteries at once. Not all mysteries are to be cleared, not for us. If there were nothing to discover for ourselves, what would the point be? Too much revelation withers the spirit."

He took a step forward. He knelt. She nearly gasped. He took her hand. "In your way, Longlight. I will always listen to you, and I will help however I can. But you must find Her in your way."

"Yes," she said, hearing it as from a long way off.

Birch nodded and stood up. "We are getting near my station."

"Yes. . . ."

He opened the door. Silvern was in the corridor, leaning against the window, looking out. He picked up Birch's bag, then looked right at Longlight, who was still in the chair. "All well?"

She stood up, nodded, and followed them to the end of the car. The captain was in the vestibule, braced comfortably, examining her watch and a passenger manifest. "Who's for Capel Storrow?" she said pleasantly.

"Just me. Birch."

"Very well, then. Baggage?"

Silvern hefted the bag.

"An easy one. Thank you, honored. Just about five minimi, now. Wait for the platform attendant to open the door, will you?" She tucked the watch away and went on to the next car.

The whistle blew, and the brakes echoed it. The train came to a halt at a platform lit greenly by gasmantles. A few people were waiting, waving to the train; Birch looked them up and down but did not return any of the waves.

"We could make this long, but it wouldn't be any easier," Birch said. "So: In your way, Silvern. In your way, my dear Longlight."

"In yours, Birch," Longlight said, "happy meet again." Silvern said, "Find Her waiting," and grasped Birch in a tight two-armed hug. Longlight felt her mouth open, dry; it was like seeing giants wrestle, in the friendliest of ways.

Then the door was opened. Birch took his bag and was down the steps. He stopped on the platform, turned to face the train. And there he stood, watching them as they looked back, until the platform guard closed the door, the whistle blasted twice, and the train creaked into motion. Birch held up his hand, standing there alone, and they did the same, until he was gone from view.

Longlight said, "Someone is surely coming to meet him. The Archimage . . ."

"I'm sure," Silvern said with an uncharacteristic faintness. Then, more strongly, "If we wish him home, he will get there."

"Yes."

"Would you like some tea before retiring, my lady?"

"No, thank you. We have to be up early tomorrow. And I would like to write a letter."

"Good night, then, Longlight."

"Good night, Silvern."

She went back to her compartment, closed and latched the door. Just near her hand, the lap desk hung, awaiting her pleasure.

She had said she wanted to write a letter. Had she really meant that? The Ironway ride was smooth enough for most purposes, but not legible handwriting. She wondered if Varic had a method for it, drafting Coronal and Parliamentary papers as the milae flew by. He knew how to shave in a moving train; she remembered that.

Then she wondered if Silvern had for a moment believed she had letters to write.

Strange House at the Cold Solstice . . . three months. A season until she could see Varic again, have any sound idea. And not spring, no buds opening, no promise of birdsong and golden delight, no summer incense by night. The snow would fall and the air would harden, and anything that did not have true heat within would wither and die.

Which would be just what they needed to know.

She drew the window blind and undressed, wriggled into a plain white nightdress. She turned the lamp down—yes, electrical light was a fine thing for bedrooms—and looked out the window at the dark world passing. No moon now, and only a few sparks of villages.

There was still the night to be got through, alone, in a single compartment, just as she had left home however long ago it had been. She slipped into the cool sheets as into water.

Your bed, Coron's-get, she thought, you lie in it.

⁑

Silvern woke to north light through the car window. He went to the bathroom mirror, gathered Craft, and a razor shimmered into being between his fingers. His Craftmaster had taught him the trick—and it was a trick, trying to keep control of the acute little blade, so close to the skin. "But if you can do this," the man had said, "a sword will seem easy."

The Master had said that at least three times before Silvern understood it properly: the important word was *seem*.

There was a knock; it was Longlight, dressed for the road, with two paper cups of tea, hot and blackly strong. "There's no breakfast aboard," she said. "Too early, never enough passengers. Sometimes I've gotten off this car alone." She paused a moment, but Silvern said nothing.

The train halted at a sturdy, plain little station; they were, in fact, the only sleeper passengers, though at least three dozen people got off the coaches.

Once the train had moved off, Silvern could see that the end of track was a substantial village built from the trainyard. They had an excellent breakfast at a place just by the station, full of Ironway workers, redolent of coal smoke. Two excellent horses were waiting for them just down the street; on the way, Silvern paused to buy fresh bread, sausage, and three sorts of cheese.

Beyond the town, the air was crisp and the road was fair. There were a few hills here, with more and higher ones clearly visible in the western distance; to the north, there were mountains beyond blue haze. Longlight did not speak much and seemed to be looking at everything in the countryside, reacquainting herself. Silvern was pleased to do the same.

After an hour or so of this, Longlight began to look fixedly forward, and Silvern decided it was time for conversation again. "Have you decided to visit the House for Solstice?"

"To speak now of it, I have. That isn't a promise."

"Not taken for one."

"I am a Coron-Resident. I have no proxy in Parliament. Nor," she added, looking away from him, "do I know of anyone I can spare who could act as one." She took a long breath. "I am sorry, Silvern. That was badly said."

"To say it once more while we are alone, we three"—she looked at him then and was smiling a little, which was what he wanted—"you are still the friend my friend loves. Of that there is no doubt in our minds, none at all. What will come of it—that we don't know."

She turned aside again. "Did you speak with Birch?"

"Of this? My lady, even at the House, even to Strange, nothing would draw that from Birch. Not the Seven Fires of the Soul and a bottle of Ferangarder red."

She laughed, and he did, too. She said, "I must try a bottle of Ferangarder red wine someday, to see if anything can be as bad as the tales. The Seven Fires, now—do Palions learn things like that?"

"We have a rounded education." They laughed again. The Seven Fires was a method of interrogation so spectacularly gruesome as to have become, at least to some people, the same kind of joke as the red wine of Ferangard: a thing so horrible one laughed.

She said, "We have not spoken of how long *you* will stay."

"As long as seems useful. I should certainly like to attend Birch's Communion, and I will go to Strange House for the

Solstice. I would think the survey should be done by then—and there's only so much that can be done in midwinter. So let us suppose three months, with no obligation implied. Unless—"

"You will be welcome. I only wondered about your other obligations."

"My work with the Kólyan is also only advisory. And one does not usually go to Bryna Kóly between the Cold Solstice and spring."

"Are you suggesting," Longlight said, grinning, "that our winters are not the coldest and fiercest on earth? Don't you know that, in the depths, one has to snap off bits of air and suck them to breathe, and an untended fire will shatter like glass?"

"There must be a fable of Corons in love," Silvern said on the moment, and stopped at the change in Longlight's expression. "But . . . I don't know it."

"Yes, there must be," Longlight said. "Ahead is the border to my country."

There was a small guard post at the foot of a rather insignificant hill. Silvern guessed that the hill was part of the border demarcation; there was nothing much else to indicate where the line might be. The road was open, no barricade across it.

Two soldiers in long blue coats came out to meet them. Longlight raised her hand, said, "Good day, honoreds," and they bowed and saluted as the riders passed without further ceremony.

Two milae later, the path curved past a small hill. Silvern could just see a figure on the hilltop; there was a wave, and Longlight raised her hand in response.

They cleared the hill. Beyond it was a valley, perhaps a third of a mila across. There was a settlement: a few large houses, a blacksmith's with the forge going, two watermills—no, one was a foundry; he could see, and then hear, the trip-hammers. A rack of pole weapons, and one of bows, stood a little distance from one of the houses. And it wasn't just a military post: children were playing ball in a marked court, a man and woman were exchanging back-fence conversation while laundry hung in the cool, still air.

Past the village, the road went on, paved and straight. There were low walls along it, and more stretches of parallel stone wall to either side that did not seem to enclose anything. Silvern knew what they were for. The walls would break up the front of an advancing army, compress them into narrow columns, perfect targets for arrow and bullet and cannonball.

At the end of the road, the hills rose up steeply, looking from Silvern's position like a vertical wall, gray and tan, with coppery streaks in the rock. The sun was behind it, creating an unnatural darkness, except for a red-gold blaze where the afternoon light washed through a cleft, just to the right of the road. Clumps of trees stuck out here and there, evergreens looking nearly black, more trees than one would have thought could find space to grow up there.

"Wander's Gate," Silvern said. "I've never actually seen it."

"Then I am pleased to present it to you," Longlight said, and he could hear the warmth of pride in her voice. "I would like to show it to you properly . . ." She looked toward the village. "It would mean spending the night here, instead of at the wayhouse. Certainly more comfortable. If we left early tomorrow, we would be home a little after dark."

"If my lady pleases, let us go on."

"Another time, then," she said, and they went on toward the notch in the hills. A few people waved or saluted as they passed; Longlight returned all the signs.

Beyond the linear walls, in the last open dying-ground before the pass—where Goddess's portion of Wander's horse would have gone first to the Quercians and then to Her—were two stone blockhouses, one small, with magnostyle wires running to it, one large enough to be barracks and mess for twenty or so. Silvern caught a smell of messroom cooking—some sort of stew. A man walked from the small house to stand in the center of the road and waited for them. He wore a dark green uniform jacket with brown leather trim, tan riding trousers, black boots. He had ridden awhile in the boots since their last polishing.

Longlight reined in. "Anscient Argentan."

"My lady Coron." He bowed smoothly. "Welcome home." He looked at Silvern, politely but very directly.

"Palion Silvern," Longlight said, "please you know Argentan, Anscient Coronal and Commander of Wander's Gate. Argentan, the Palion Silvern, also Armiger."

The officer relaxed just perceptibly as he bowed. "Happy of the acquaintance, Palion. And thanks for my lady's safety."

"I am glad to meet you, Anscient."

Argentan nodded and turned back to Longlight. "My lady, there is a 'style at the station that should have your attention—with your pardon, Palion—"

Silvern waved idly. Longlight, who had seemed about to speak, dismounted and followed Argentan to the small blockhouse. Silvern sat placidly, examining the Gate, trying to imagine which of the clusters of pines had been there in Wander's day. Difficult to say; the trees were old, but not a thousand years old.

But the stones could not have changed much, except where people had changed them, and the places trees could and could not grow would be much the same. It was worth study. When he came back—and he certainly would, if at all possible—he would make some sketches, take some notes, perhaps some lucives as well. That would make a fine Solstice present for Strange. And Varic could plan the battleboard game.

His mind back in the present, he supposed that there were two rifles on him. One from the guardhouse, another from a good cross fire point—probably above the pass. And unless the bows in the village had all been for sport shooting, which he doubted, there would be a sharpshooter with six broadpoints and six bodkins at the ready somewhere.

He looked up at the hilltops again, and across. There was a snowcapped peak in the distance to the north. That would be past Longlight's Great Rogue Hills, in ... what, Greyfort? It made him think of Bryna Kóly, that and the bows. The Kólyan did not use the long wooden bow of the Lescorial Middle and West. They made short, recurved bows of horn and sinew that were brutally powerful, often using iron broadpoints that could cave in a chest, or smash a skull apart. All the Kólyan words for bow shot were the same as their words for snowfall, of which they had a rich collection—"whisper," "smotherer," "white eternity." For their kind of warfare, which was, no altering it, several parts hill banditry, the quiet, close, definite kill was central. And the explosion of a gun in the snowy heights had an excellent chance of bringing a real white eternity down on you.

And it was hill banditry that brought him, in mind and in fact, here.

Longlight and Argentan returned. She carried a small leather bag; she tucked it carefully into her saddlebag, then remounted.

The Anscient said, "I am sorry to have detained you, my lady, and you, Palion. Necessities of state. Will you require an escort to the wayhouse?"

Longlight said, "No need. Thank you, Anscient. And sleep snug."

He bowed. "My lady." He turned to Silvern, said, a little stiffly, "Palion?"

"Commander?"

"I am sorry to have so little time for you today. If you would visit again, we shall be pleased to show you better hospitality. And I imagine you would like to be shown around the Gate."

"I would be more than pleased, Commander."

"May I suggest within the month, while the weather is still fair?"

"If it is at all possible."

Argentan saluted, and Longlight and Silvern rode on to the pass.

Beyond the cliff face, the path kinked to the left for a dozen steps, then to the right, and there was another valley, shallower than the one before, opening out toward the west. The golden sunlight hit them straight on; Silvern automatically shaded his eyes. He saw another stone barracks, with ready weapons outside, and another small mill. A stream crackled along to the left of the road. Two soldiers stepped to the roadside and saluted as they passed.

"Was there really a magnostyle?" Silvern said when the soldiers were far enough behind them.

"Yes, but it wasn't of consequence here. Coal for the frontier posts; it would have been passed on with the next post. He did not like treating you so." She nodded at her saddlebag. "That's eggs and butter for tomorrow's breakfast. An offering for the road."

"And glad of them. But he was entirely polite and correct. I said I was a Palion; I might have been anything. He could well have been saving your life."

"I know. I thought of that just before I said something unkind. So all is, I suppose, well."

Silvern waited. He was certain that Coron Longlight could not be baited into saying good morning against her choice. But he knew other people like that, and they would speak easily enough if they felt sure of their listeners. He let the horse carry him, watching the scenery; the canyon was opening out, and there were dense stands of deep green pine to either side, the creek glittering white and gold. There was no wind at all, and the still air seemed warm, though his horse's breath was misting a little. He was, he thought, going to like this place.

Half a mila on, the stream ducked under the road and wound up a defile to the right. "Come this way," Longlight said, and they turned their horses to follow the water.

The way was easier than it had looked, though slow. A great many people and horses had passed this way, over a very long time.

They came to a flat, open area, strewn with big rocks, speckled with lichens; the stream leveled out. Up ahead were two upright stones, one to either side of the creek, half again Silvern's height, black and shiny. His mind immediately saw them as human figures, robed perhaps, slightly bent toward one another.

"Yon's your fable," she said, and pointed to the stones. "The Corons who loved 'gain love. Facing one another across the border, always just apart, with a spring clear as tears to speak for them."

Silvern sat unmoving in the saddle, looking at the stones and the water. "Is this really the border?" he said finally.

"Not for a while. You don't know the tale, then?"

"No."

"No faulten that. It's bitter and bad. But my coin says Varic knows it. Sort of thing we get with our porridge." She picked up the reins.

"Wait," Silvern said, still looking at the rocks, like a lucivitor framing an image. "What's the other end of the tale?"

"Oh, that. The same, except that there's a war before the Corons freeze." She turned her horse. "Come. This is a cold place."

They reached the wayhouse about two hours before dark. It was of mortared stone, with slate shingles and a squat slate chimney. The windows were covered with wooden shutters reinforced with iron; the door was made the same way. It looked more like a prison than a hostelry, but Silvern understood the design well enough; it was meant to survive by itself, between travelers.

Longlight started to dismount, but Silvern stopped her with a raised finger. He swung down, pulled open the heavy door with one motion, and shouted, "Goddess's evening to all within!" There was only silence. He went inside; even in the dimness there was nowhere to hide. He unbarred a window and opened it, graying the black. "My lady?"

He found a lamp, got it alight as Longlight entered. "There's wood in the box," he said. "If you'll lay a fire, I'll cut a refill."

He found a saw and a small sledge near the woodbox and went out. He walked farther than he had to before choosing a tree; after the first good snowfall, guests of the house wouldn't have as much choice.

When he returned, smoke was curling slowly up from the house's chimney, the horses had been moved to a shelter at the back, and Longlight was carrying a kettle of water inside.

Half an hour later, their bedrolls were made up, the kettle was heating, and the place seemed close to comfortable.

Silvern set the small table—there weren't any chairs—with the sausage and cheese, and took a Book from his saddlebag. He uncased it, shuffled. "Grace, my lady?"

"Call me Longlight just a little longer," she said, cut, and dealt two cards: Two of Springs reversed, Maker of Steels. They both looked at the cards for five minimi, perhaps longer, without speaking. Finally Silvern restored the Book and put it away.

Silvern went to the shuttered window, looked through the small vision slit in the wood. It was quite dark outside. He bolted the door, then sat down next to the table, sliced off meat and cheese for Longlight.

She said, "I should tell you something, before we reach my house."

Silvern waited.

"For about two years . . . I've kept informal company with a Palion of the household. That is about to change."

"The name?"

"Graven."

"Not one I know."

"I don't know that you should. He was made Palion three years ago, by my Marshal at Arms, Praxitae."

"That name I do know. But go on. Does Graven have any warning of . . . ?"

"No. I would say it was because I didn't have any, but that wouldn't be true. I said a little of this to Edaire . . ." She waited, but Silvern just nodded slightly. "None of this is your problem, seil 'an. But you have a right to know, before we arrive, together, and he decides—something incorrect."

"Is he a right Palion?" Silvern said, very seriously. "No. Does Praxitae have any doubts of him?"

"Twice or three times she's said, 'Well, he's young,' and there's the kind of sharp talk one hears from any Marshal"—Silvern smiled at that, and Longlight felt considerable relief—"but nothing to mark." She considered another thought, then spoke it. "I don't think she approved of our relation."

"To speak only honestly, my lady Coron, I doubt I would have either."

"That's"—she swallowed hard—"only fair."

Silvern said, "Both of us are given to the truth, my lady. I will tell this Palion the truth about you and me, and Edaire if it seems useful; if he does not believe me, the fault is his. My suggestion, politely tendered, is that you decide well in advance which truths you will tell him."

That ended the conversation for quite a while. Finally Longlight said, "Would you answer a question? About yourself and Edaire?"

"I will listen to your question," Silvern said amicably.

She nodded. "Well enough. How do you . . . converse? Is it words, or pictures, or . . . something different?"

Silvern laughed out loud, startling her. She started to speak, but he raised a hand. "Oh, my dear lady. Of all the things I have been asked about conseil—and there have been some whistlers—I do not recall anyone ever wanting to know how we *communicate.*"

He went to the fireplace, lifted the boiling kettle with a bare hand that suddenly was heavily gauntleted, filled the teapot. The kettle went back on the hook, and the glove evaporated.

When they were settled with hot cinnamoned tea, Silvern said, "It is words, mostly. There are expressions that come across in a moment, as with any of the signs that two people develop over time—it takes no time at all to say, 'I love you.' Otherwise, it is much like speaking, and as you may have seen, we do speak aloud at times.

"Images are more difficult, which surprised us."

"Do you know why?"

"Possibly because words are how we're taught to communicate. If we were both painters—or better, sketch artists—it might be different. We've wondered what it would be like for Reccan—though she's a power with words now, just given her hands."

Longlight said, "Sometimes one of you seems to feel what the other feels."

"Oh, yes. Especially if it's sudden. And . . . do you know what Longsight is?"

"I know about the Long Mirror, of course."

"If we agree to try, sometimes one of us can see through the other's eyes. The sender has to think as nearly of nothing as possible—getting the spirit out of the way. You can't talk while it's happening, and the receiver can't move much. It's not much more than a trick, really." He smiled then. "But it has shown me some wonderful things."

"I don't know if I could do that," she said, and at once regretted it.

Silvern took a long sip of his tea, and then said, very carefully, "So said Varic, once. Or did my lady know that?"

"Who should take the first watch?" she said.

"The door is strong," Silvern said. "Any attempt to breach it will wake us both. Your country, milady; but I think sleep is the best thing."

"Yes."

He turned out the lamp, and they finished their tea by the firelight. Silvern tucked into his bedroll, and she did the same. After a moment, she heard him singing, too faintly to make out the words; then, somehow, she thought there were two voices. She turned to hear better, but was swallowed by a sleep that was mercifully without dreams.

⚭

Silvern woke to the hiss of butter in a pan. Longlight had a skillet and the teakettle over the fire. She said, "We have three eggs each, travelers' gift from Argentan. Would you like something with yours?"

"Some of that soft cheese would be good, I think. With the rind, if you please."

"Argentan sent some grated onion as well, and sea salt."

"The onion by all means. I'll salt it myself."

She cut off a lump of the cheese, chopping at the firm white casing, stirred it into the eggs with the edge of the knife, turning and moving the food as she sprinkled the threads of onion into it. The scent rose up wonderfully. Silvern dug his plate and fork out of his bag, and Longlight slid the high road omelet from the skillet, adding a slice of lightly fried bread.

"My compliments," Silvern said. "And to the Anscient."

"If you're lucky, he'll cook for you when you visit."

"Argentan *is* an Alinsever name."

"Point."

"He's a long way from there."

"He was wrecked on our coast when he was young—ten, I think. A few others made it, but no one of his. My father took him in. He thought Praxitae might have him for a Palion, but he said no." She shrugged and cracked her share of the eggs into the pan.

And did you say no? Silvern thought with his lips tight. He waited for a comment from Edaire, but there was none. He poured tea from the kettle and dug into his breakfast.

Longlight joined him a minima later. "What do you suppose is going on at Strange House just now?" she said.

He thought to reach for Edaire, but she was likely busy or asleep. "Most of the Equinox guests will be gone. My guess is that Strange and Agate, and perhaps Edaire, are having a quiet breakfast. I hope it's warm on the balcony." He added, "It is purely a matter of crowds, not company."

"It must be quite a different place with no guests."

"There are almost always guests, even if it's just one or two— but you're right, it's different. Strange doesn't feel the need to play host in all directions, and more serious things are said and done. I hope you understand that I mean 'serious' in a sense rather special to the House."

She smiled. "It's not a pleasant thing to imagine."

"Hazel would be delighted. I wonder if you know just how much he adores his model train."

"I'm glad of it. Hazel is a wonder. He's going to grow into a fine and noble soul."

"Do you think so?"

"I don't see how not, raised in such company."

"Strange would be pleased to hear you say that. I hope you will tell him. When Hazel is not in hearing, of course."

They laughed. Longlight said, quietly, "Did you have a happy childhood?"

"Better than most, from what I've seen. My mother was a physician; my father taught history at Ascorel."

"So that's how you met Strange—"

"Not at all. I'd heard of him, one couldn't not hear around the University, but Edaire first took me to the House, a year after we joined."

"Oh." In a softer tone, she said, "How usual is a past like that for a Palion?"

"Not very. But there have been many changes. In the Midreigns, it was the stuff of stories when someone not noble-born was inducted. Then, as soldiers became less the lord's personal warbands and more like armies, it became much more a matter of individual merit. The Monarch still had the sole power to nominate candidates, but almost anyone might qualify—remembering that not all who try the course endure." He glanced at her. "Some of the greatest came from that—Redlance, Moonhawk, Sunderhand. Also some of the worst. Their names let none recall.

"Now, with the Monarchs gone and the selection among the Order itself, there's a tendency to choose what one knows. We're gradually becoming more like one another. Not all of us think too well of that." He stopped, smiled, said, "Not that we can't still change."

"So who chose you?" Longlight said.

"The Craft did. I would not have been a Palion if I had not first been an Armiger. And I did not choose that."

"What do you mean?"

"The power behind sorcery is a will. But it is sometimes difficult to say just whose will it is. For myself, I have nothing to compare it to, but I'll try anyhow. You know that Birch is not a sorcerer."

"Yes."

"Yet you have seen power flow through him."

"But that's not—"

"Indeed. Yet despite that you know who gives that power, you weren't fully at ease with Birch at first, were you?"

"It showed, I suppose."

"Do not worry. He has dealt with much more. Think of it, though. We're speaking of a soul that Goddess reaches right into, projecting Her light through his hands. It would scare anyone. And one has to live with it, daily, or . . . not live."

"I hadn't thought of it that way," she said, from a distance. "I suppose I thought you began with the Talent and chose the Craft?"

"It is easier to let people believe that." He looked at the ground. "And I ought to be ashamed of that. It is deep in our mortality to prefer easy ways. What else is the attraction of sorcery?"

Longlight said, quite gravely, "Would you be ashamed of the color of your hair?"

Silvern chuckled. "My father would have liked that. He would have found it beautifully Pandektine. And then said something like, 'But of course, they kept the Quercians out.'

"But I was speaking of the Archana. There are usually signs of what's coming. Sometimes it turns out to be a thing you've fought for a long time, not really knowing why."

"Fought?"

"Oh . . ." Again he held back from reaching for Edaire. "Suppose a child refuses to sing, even when everyone else is singing together, well or badly, no one judging. Once in a while a soul like that turns out to be an Archvocal—and may eventually be a strong and sure one; but the first sign of it was something un-settling and terrible every time she tried a verse, so that verses were like nightmares and one could not sleep for singing."

"Are you speaking of Agate, then?"

"No," he said firmly. "Agate was good with words from her fourth summer. I'm told she was always expected to show power. That anyone foresaw what she truly would be, though, I would not believe." He scraped up the last of his eggs, went to scour out his plate. "There are still places where a child like Agate wouldn't live to know her power."

"I know there are," Longlight said, and her tone made clear enough how she knew it. "Will you tell me how you fought?" Silvern could hear a rough line in her voice, though she was trying to hide it.

"I will. Once we're on the road. It wants the fresh air."

The morning was clear, the sun warm on the skin in the still, dry air. Silvern closed up the wayhouse to await the next traveler. He and Longlight set their horses at a steady, unhurried walk up the road.

"Now for the Armiger's Tale," Silvern said. "My father died of heart failure when I was eleven," Silvern said. "My mother wasn't there—she was with a patient at the time, just where she ought to have been. Made it no easier.

"His specialty was Pandektine history—he'd taken me on a long trip to Pandreas two years before. I loved those ruins. Their temples are like no one else's—not even our copies. I can see now that much of the love was his, radiating; he adored their culture and very literally mourned its ruin. He didn't hate the Quercians—he was too deep in history to believe in bad con-querors and innocent reasoners—but I don't think he fully for-gave them, either.

"What my father hated was war. And for that he was too deep

in history to make excuses. He wouldn't even enter an arenetto for exercise." He paused. "He spoke a few times of Strange,
and I would hear that they'd met when Strange visited Ascorel.
But my father could never quite see how Strange reconciled the
wish for peace with the study of war. Strange told me, much,
much later, that they had been quite friendly, meeting in the
University common rooms; but my father never brought that
home to me."

Longlight glanced at him, but said nothing.

"About half a year after he died, I was playing ball with some
friends, in Stringer Quad Green. The ball took a ricochet at a
crazy angle, and one of my friends—Clay, who was bigger than
I, imagine—dove blind for it and slammed into me like a horse
trying to vault a pikeman.

"I didn't go down. Lights went off in my head, and I hurt, but I
was still standing. When I could see again, I saw Clay sitting on
the ground, just staring—he wasn't hurt, Wyss's mercy. I was
wearing full Midreigns iron, helm to spur—do you know the
Green World storybook? The Defender of the Bridge?"

"I know it."

"I ran all the way home, the armor melting off as I went. No
one was there—my mother expected me to be out playing all
afternoon—and when she got home I was still staring at myself
in a mirror, terrified the armor would come back."

"Did you understand what had happened?"

"I'd felt the hum of the power since before my father died. It
fascinated him. He wanted to see my Craft come and sharpen.
He was a teacher. But here I was, something I—well, it isn't hard
to imagine what I thought."

"And he wasn't there to tell you that you were wrong."

"So I fought. For a year and more."

Longlight said, "Could you have won?"

He said slowly, "It is possible to deny the Craft. To choose another Archanum, at which one will always be clumsy and misfit, or to choose nothing at all—wild light. That works only if one's very thinly Talented—the best of us can only partly control the work; to have it come in its own time and direction is just no way to live.

"So: one can be unhappy, or one can go mad, or one can die fighting."

"I see."

"I think you do," Silvern said. "And I am sure that I would have fought to the end. Talk about not knowing one's enemy. But how it did end was this: my mother said, 'I know too well what I cannot do. I haven't the power to stop you. But know two things: You disserve your father by judging his will for him. And know that if you go on with this, you are going to have to do it looking at me, with me looking back, until you're cold and I'm alone. . . .'

"Oh, dear, dear, dear, I'm sorry to have awakened you to such a fit. It's well now. It's well." He looked up, faintly smiling. "This happens. Your pardon."

"None needed," Longlight said. "I saw it from her side as well."

Silvern said, "We say, 'In your way,' so often, sometimes it slides right by us that people must find the way, and in the dark. I decided that if my father could not understand warriors, it was not because he lacked understanding but that he hadn't found one who showed him an understandable face. If I was going to be a warrior, then I would try to be the one he was looking for. And—*wait*."

They halted their horses. Ahead, the path curved to the right; the road was cut narrowly against the side of a steep hill rising to the right twenty spans or so to a line of pine trees, dropping clean away to the left, at least a hundred spans down.

Silvern said, quietly and casually, "Do you notice?"

"Someone's up there," Longlight said, not needing to indicate where she meant.

"What's behind the trees?"

"A rough patch for maybe an eighth of a mila. Then more hills. People live in the hills, isolated houses."

"Bandit houses?"

"A few of them."

"Ride ahead. Say ten steps. Don't look for me unless I call. It could be someone hunting small game or gathering wood."

"We can hope," she said, patted her horse, and rode forward, at the same quick walk as before. To anyone on the ridge, it would seem that she had simply passed him. He couldn't let her get too far ahead, but if nothing happened in the next quarter mila, it wasn't going to happen here.

Ought not, anyway. One could never be certain of these things.

As it went, he saw a cloaked figure appear from the trees, looking down the slope even with Longlight, just as he heard the thump of a crossbow from his own right. He threw up his hand, and a shield spun itself into place around his forearm just before the bolt slammed into it. He felt the shock down his arm and spine, but it wasn't a heavy bow—no more than a bird bolt. His horse checked a bit, but didn't shy or rear—a good beast. Silvern flipped his arm as he let the spell shield dissolve, and the bolt tumbled away.

Ahead, the other ambusher was stumbling down the steep, bare slope toward Longlight. That made no sense at all. He turned to look up; maybe someone sensible was still up there, waiting for them to get entangled with the decoy.

As his eyes left the running figure, he registered that the person was either quite short or quite young. What he saw above himself was a straggle-haired boy in a rough shirt and baggy trousers, scrambling down the hill no more surefootedly than the other ambusher.

Silvern took a deep breath from the diaphragm, pulled Craft to himself, and vaulted out of the saddle. When his boots hit the road, he was crown to heel in blue-gray armor.

Ahead of him, the panting boy looked up, directly at Silvern. His eyes went big as the moon. The knife wobbled in his hand.

Silvern slapped at the knife with a gauntleted hand. It went flying. He picked the boy up bodily, slung him over a shoulder, locked his left arm around the body. He turned toward Longlight.

She had a sword out, was bringing her horse around to face her own attacker, who was fumbling within the cloak.

The bandit brought out a pistol.

Silvern raised his right hand, and a long drover's whip spun from it. He recoiled and flung it out.

Craft is uncertain. Silvern had meant to crack the whip near the bandit's head, to startle and distract. But he had at least two steps more length than he needed; the tip coiled around the target's neck. The figure fell.

Silvern let go of the whip handle, and the weapon vanished instantly. The bandit, staggering, hit the ground.

The pistol fired. The body twitched, the cloak fluttering over it.

Silvern went forward at a trot, still carrying the boy. Longlight dismounted, crouched, sword ready, by the cloaked figure.

Longlight turned the body over. It was a girl, perhaps fifteen, her chest a red and dirty mess.

Silvern put the boy down, as gently as he could. Longlight moved at once out of his way. He crouched by the girl, letting the gauntlets evaporate, moving the power into his hands and chest. He put one hand on the wound, spread the other on the girl's forehead.

There was no heartbeat. On his probe, the heart seemed intact; the bullet had split the liver, perhaps the spleen. Hardly any better. He started to pull the rip together; wet tissues hissed like bacon frying.

He felt with the other fingers. Life was drying in the nerves, and he couldn't touch spirit in the brain. He thumbed an eyelid open, snapped his fingers, making a bright spark. The pupil didn't move.

He thought hard. His mother had taught him wound aid, and a soldier got practice. The Craft could help in some ways—he could make a surgeon's knife sharper than steel and cleaner than obsidian, and seal bleeders with heat. But for death he had nothing. This was death.

He let go, drawing the girl's hood to cover her eyes.

He stood, turned to the others. Longlight was watching the boy, who was just staring at his fallen partner. Silvern let all the armor but a backplate fade, and moved, without fuss, to put the boy safely between himself and Longlight.

Longlight said, "What's her name?"

"I don't know," the boy said in a tiny voice.

"Do you know yours?"

"Huh—Hilt."

"That's a start." She made a gesture, a tight fist with the thumb pointed to herself. It was meaningless in itself, but any field officer would know its intent: she was to be the Bad Interrogator, Silvern the Good. "So, did you agree to attack travelers together and trade names over the loot later, or was this all a supreme coincidence?"

"What?"

Silvern let the helmet and most of the armor melt from him. It was a bit of a risk; there might be another gun up in the trees. But he doubted it. In an even voice, he said, "You cannot have met just now."

"I . . . She didn't say her name." Hilt swallowed hard. "She said she'd help me. With the fight."

"Such thoughtful strangers one finds on the roads," Longlight said, and though Silvern knew she was acting a part, he could hear the real anger in her voice. "Listen very well. We haven't time to waste here. I'll take the body on my horse, you'll travel with my companion. If you try to run away, he will kill you. If we are attacked again on the way to town—by friends of yours, by no one you know—he will kill you first of all. So if you *have* any friends ahead, and know any signals to warn them off, don't forget them. Now, help me with your short-time friend."

They got the dead girl on the rear of Longlight's horse. The boy was no real help; Silvern knew that this was something one needed experience in. Longlight obviously had it. She folded the cloak to shroud the body, fastened it with some rope from her pack. When she was done, it was neat as a blanket roll.

"Come along," Silvern said, and led Hilt back to his own horse. He helped the boy into the saddle, climbed up behind him. There was no protest, no sound at all. He let Longlight take her ten steps' lead, then followed at a quick walk.

Silvern reached into his saddlebag and took out the last of the cheese and sausage. He broke the pieces in half, chewed a bit, handed some of each to Hilt. "Take this."

The boy took it cautiously, then devoured it in a few bites. Silvern supposed he might have refused it if given a choice.

After about a quarter of an hour, Hilt said, "What she said . . . Would you do that, if . . ."

"Would I kill you? If you do what she warned you against, I *will* kill you. You should know that neither of us tells lies. If we say a thing, we will do it. But also know that neither of us has any wish to harm you. What she was really saying is that what happens to you on the way to town is mostly your choice. She said it as she did so that you would have to listen. Do you understand that?"

"I won't run away."

"I hope you will not. And if you have any more companions out there, I hope they will let all three of us pass in peace."

After a moment, Hilt said, "Does she pay you well?"

Silvern laughed. Ahead, he saw Longlight turn her head slightly, but she did not look back. "She isn't my employer. She is a friend I am going to visit for a time."

"But you . . . take orders."

"I followed a friend's wisdom. If you choose to take it as a command, then I will say that I chose to be commanded. I trust her. Perhaps you should as well."

"To do what?"

"To deal justly with you. Do you know what justice is?"

"The gallows," the boy said, and went instantly silent.

"That may yet be," Silvern said as simply as he could. "You attacked complete strangers without cause or warning, and people are indeed hanged for that. We could also have cut your throat on the pavement, thrown your and your companion's bodies down the ravine, and no one would have questioned our right even had they ever discovered you. But we didn't. And having not done it then, why should we want to do it now?" He nodded toward the lead horse. "I'm sorry for your—fellow traveler. What happened was an accident I couldn't mend. Maybe if I knew more about her, I'd know better just how badly I went wrong."

Hilt didn't answer.

There were no more incidents. After about two hours, the road entered a dense green grove, the trees trimmed comfortably back from the roadway. It might have been good ambush country, if it were not so obviously tended and patrolled. A quarter mila on there was a square-sided gatehouse, with guards at attention. Hilt looked around, as if it were all quite strange to him. Beyond the gate, a last bit of straight road through green led into a cluster of buildings. Above and beyond them, Silvern saw an obviously defensible mansion. That would be Longlight's Coronal Seat. Her home.

They rode into the town.

It was substantial, given that it was almost as far from the City Lystourel as it was possible to be and still in Lescoray. Silvern guessed its population at ten thousand; Longlight would surely know precisely, but it was impolitic for strangers to ask such questions, even casually. Perhaps especially if "casually." If he were to do a military survey of the Great Rogue hills, he would need some kind of approval beyond a piece of paper. Being a Palion would help, but the right companions would be necessary. Silvern wondered if Graven, Longlight's . . . former companion, would be a good choice. He was another Palion and would understand the mission; he would know the country. And—not to avoid the issue—it might be good to take him away from the Coronal household. Even if Graven knew that was exactly what was being done.

Praxitae would be able to advise him and would give an answer absolutely clean of ambiguity.

The town was laid out in the typical plan of the early Midreigns: a broad avenue from the gateway to the market square, and from that, smaller, turning streets leading off in several directions. It caused as little interference with the flow of commerce as possible, but an attacking force would find itself in a killing-ground, surrounded by thick-walled, impenetrable buildings, every window hiding an archer. They could either stand and be shot down, or scatter into the side lanes, to meet knife and catchpole at every unfamiliar turn.

Silvern had ridden more than once into a square like this, to find it deserted, with the certain knowledge that there were watchers behind the shutters, around the corners. It was not a comfortable feeling. But after an instanta, people came flowing into the market, a dozen on horseback and twice that on foot, dressed for show, not combat. A small crowd of children, herded by two women and a man, came around a corner, giggling and whispering.

One of the riders came forward from the pack. He wore a blue leather jacket with bright red facings; black hair spilled from under a blue cap with the Coronal moon and sword in silver. His face was handsome, a little sharp, a little northern-pale, and his eyes were bright, a blue Silvern could see from this distance. This, he thought, would be Longlight's Palion. The one who obviously had no idea he was riding straight into an ambush.

The young man swept his cap off, bowed from the saddle, started to vault out. Silvern could remember being that young, and they had all read the same tales.

"Keep your seat, Graven," Longlight said, pleasantly enough. "We won't be pausing long."

The Palion aborted his dismount with fair grace, got his cap back into place. "As my Coron commands."

Silvern felt Hilt go absolutely rigid. He thought about putting a hand out to steady the boy, but supposed it would only make him jump or scream.

He saw Graven's look move to the bundle tied behind Longlight. "But, my lady . . . these are . . ."

"The man accompanying me is Silvern, Palion and Armiger. You were told of his coming."

Hilt squirmed. Silvern said, just to the boy, "Be still. You are in no danger from us."

Longlight said, "Is Praxitae with you?"

Someone near the back of the crowd dismounted; the others moved aside for her. "I am, my lady. My greetings to you. And to you, Pentepalion."

"And to you, Teacher," Silvern said.

Praxitae nodded. She was a short, very broad-bodied woman, who walked with a kind of sailor's roll. She was wearing riding leathers set with a few pieces of metal, military but not really armor, and a short sword on the Pandekt pattern, definitely a weapon.

She said, "I am pleased to greet you after so long, Silvern. But this one can't be yours, can it?"

Longlight said, "The boy's name is Hilt. Beyond that we don't know much of him. For now, we entrust him to your care."

"Go to her," Silvern said quietly, "be mannerly. And believe me, do *not* try to run away from her, or you will be very sorry you tried."

He helped Hilt dismount. The boy was dazed and kept glancing at Longlight, looking away before her eyes could meet his. He walked unsteadily to Praxitae, who took his hand with a gentle dignity—it was odd, Silvern thought, that her students remembered that of her so little and late, when she gave them so much of it.

"As for the young woman," Longlight said, "there was a disaster on the road. If she is not ours, she is not from far away. It would be good to at least have a name to rest her under. Put the word about."

Praxitae raised her voice. "Young honored Pelter." Pelter identified herself by sitting spear-straight in the saddle. "This will be a good exercise for you. It involves a sword and is not done on horseback. You will find the Dead Services in volume three of your manuals, on the uncreased pages."

Give Pelter credit, Silvern thought; She saluted the Master, dismounted smartly, and led her horse to Longlight's side. She bowed to the Coron and stood to attention.

"Proceed," Longlight said. Silvern watched as Pelter transferred the body between horses, cinching it down with care, if not Longlight's efficiency.

Silvern looked at Hilt, who stood next to Praxitae with his face rigid. It wasn't kind to do this to the boy, but no one here was making him keep silent, either. Silvern wondered what was.

"I thank you all for your greeting," Longlight said with an elaborate wave to the group of children. "I trust you will allow us a little time to rest from our journey; audience will be held the day after tomorrow. Any more urgent matters should be addressed to my secretaries."

The crowd sorted itself about. Most moved to the sides, leaving a mounted party to accompany the Coron. The way was obvious enough: a broad paved way that curved up a hillside, toward the great building Silvern had seen from the approach road.

There were, in fact, four rectangular buildings, arranged on an arc down the hill like stairs for a giant. The structures were similar: walls three stories high, round towers at the corners; a notched parapet around the top for a protected view all around. It was apparent on a closer look, though, that they had been built a long time apart, as the Coronal Court had grown.

Silvern had been fortunate enough to see the expansion process in action a few times. One day the Coron would ask why dinner was late, again, and be told, again, that the temporary pantry was just too far from the temporary kitchen, which was just too far from the dining hall. Or it would take three extra days to assemble the Coronal Council, because there was no room in the house suitable for a visiting Councilor to stay—or, even more dramatically, the suitable apartments had to be vacated by the usual occupants and their belongings for the duration of Council, after which the process would have to be reversed. A number of Coronal Seats had excellent inns, subsidized by the Coron as a way of putting off the expansions just a bit longer.

And if the line were held everywhere else, eventually the Coron would visit another Coron's house, or at least one of those subsidized guesthouses, and notice that lighting and heating and plumbing had all moved irrepressibly onward, and the builders would at last be summoned.

What happened then was more variable. Sometimes the architect was given great freedom, and sometimes that proved to be a fine thing. More often, when the builders asked the Coron's pleasure, the Coron would wave at the existing structure in a general fashion and say the equivalent of "Continue and improve."

So it had happened here: there were four houses, all in some ways the same house repeating itself down the hill. But one could see the passage of time: the windows becoming larger, the arrow slits being replaced by gun embrasures and then vanishing (except for a few decorative imitations, to keep things harmonious), the stonework subtly changing as the chisel was replaced by the saw and then the power saw.

The elders descending in slow dignity, their children hurrying ahead, Edaire said, making a pleasant warmth in Silvern's mind.

They passed by the lower two buildings and came to a halt at the next—the second oldest, it would be, still with narrow windows that had been refitted for better glazing. It had a fine, smooth-paved oval courtyard with evergreen shrubs and an artificial waterfall—doubtless more durable through the winters here than a mechanical fountain would be. Praxitae, Hilt on her lap, nodded to Longlight and led her Palions away down a side path; the rest dismounted, and attendants arrived to take the horses.

The doors were opened and the Coron entered her house. Silvern followed, five steps behind. One did not walk behind a Coron at less than twice a sword's reach, unless one was a bodyguard on duty.

Beyond the door was a long entrance hall, meant to provide a long gauntlet for invaders to run, and more ordinarily to keep the cold air away from the inner door. It was lined with worn tapestries, pieces of antique armor, the mounted heads of game brought down generations ago.

After a crossing hall, more doors were opened—these metal-reinforced and highly defensible—onto an audience chamber, big enough for eighty or so, perhaps a hundred with a little squeezing. Chairs were pushed to the walls, and the decoration was tastefully underdone. A raised platform with blue carpeting and a large, heavily carved chair hung with an armorial drape was at the back. An exceptionally tall and slender man in a blue butler's coat with silver buttons stood—well, upright—on the platform.

He stepped down as Longlight stepped up. She sat down, rather heavily, in the audience chair. "We are home, Pike, and we are well. Palion Silvern, I would you know Pike, my secretary for household matters. Whatever you should need or wish within my house, he shall provide."

Silvern said, "My pleasure, Pike."

"Mine, honored. You shall be staying in the Third House, one below this. A few more steps, I regret, but I believe you will find it comfortable."

"I live here in the Second House," Longlight said. "Take the offer." She turned, looked past Silvern. "And this is the Palion Graven. Graven, come to know Silvern, Palion and Armiger."

Graven came forward and saluted—elaborately, but not too much so. "I have most eagerly awaited your arrival," he said. He had an odd, toothy grin that made him look skull-faced, impossible to tell what, if anything, it might mean. He went through the standard greetings of the Order—duty, service, fear not for your back while I am with you—in a voice that went from tight to galloping. "And further, Pentepalion—"

"I should be pleased if you would use my name," Silvern said, extending his hand. "And may I call you by yours?"

The hand was vigorously shaken. "Most certainly, honored Silvern."

"Excellent, Graven. I hope we shall find much time to talk. I do remind you, though, that I am here only as a guest of your Coron. I have duties here for an absent friend, but I do not come representing the Order."

Graven seemed to relax slightly, but now looked puzzled. "May I ask—"

"We will discuss it later," Longlight said. "Pike, what immediate business?"

"Little of great consequence, my lady. A small grease fire in the west kitchen, no one hurt and little real damage. Two new foals, both doing fine."

"One was Cracknel's?"

"An excellent mare, my lady."

"Very good. Proceed."

"The curtains for the south-light rooms in the First House have arrived and wait my lady's approval to hang. And Boneburden gave the best estimate for repairing the south steps, so I gave approval; she will start in three days."

"Very well," she said. "Especially the steps; I'd entirely forgotten about them. Anything further?"

"I believe we should discuss the powder store. Some of the loose musket grain is getting old enough to worry me. It would seem that if we are actually reduced to firing our muzzleloaders—well."

"Is it actually dangerous? Or can we get something for it?"

"Not dangerous yet. But it would be difficult to get a price for it. The kegs are probably worth more than their contents."

"What if we gave it away for hunting, with the caution that it was for this season only? Would that offend the merchants too much?"

"Not if we purchased cartridges to replace it."

"Which puts us down on the balance. But see if it can be made to happen."

"My lady."

"Thank you for your attention, Pike."

Pike bowed—it was like watching a pocketknife fold—gave a smaller bow to Silvern, and departed through a side door.

Longlight said, "I am withdrawing until dinner. I shall see you all there. Palion Silvern, one more moment of your time."

Graven said, "My lady—"

"Thank you for your attendance, Graven."

Graven stood still for two long breaths, then bowed and left the room, leaving only Longlight and Silvern in the large space.

Longlight stood up. "That was badly begun," she said, looking after Graven. Then she turned to Silvern. "I have something to do before I rest. Perhaps you would like to accompany me to the First House?"

Silvern bowed and followed. She led him out the back of the audience room, then reached behind a wall hanging. A door concealed by paneling opened up, exposing a stairway up. It was dimly lit by narrow skylights; lanterns were hung along one wall.

"Not the Dark Room," Longlight said quickly. "That's better hidden."

At the top, another hidden door opened onto a spacious room, with a large chandelier refitted for gas. There were half a dozen large, comfortable-looking chairs and tables in a variety of sizes; bookshelves stood at intervals around the perimeter. One wall had a large, beautifully carpentered map rack, a table with study lamps, and a stand magnifier just before it.

Compared to Strange House, the library was light on books—five or six hundred. The shelves, Silvern saw, were much newer than the structural woodwork.

Longlight crouched by a corner alcove, took a key from her clothing, and opened a waist-high cabinet. Inside were four shelves of miscellaneous books.

"When I was six, this was all the library there was. The maps were here—we still call this the Map Room—but no other books, except in the cooks' and the healers' rooms, and a few references in the Coronal offices." She spread a hand, touching spines with her fingertips. "There are one hundred twenty-three books here. Exactly that: one-two-three. I know them all, and if one were to be missing, or their order altered, I would know it on sight. I am the Coron now, and everything here is mine, but these were mine at six. I found them, and they became mine by abandonment."

She looked up at him, with an expression of both defiance and pain. "Your father was a teacher. . . . There must have been books."

"Yes. Though we had the use of the University libraries."

"At Ascorel . . . I couldn't have dreamed of that, then." She turned back to the shelves. "After a year, when I was sure no one touched them but me, I had one of the hammerjacks make a new lock for the cabinet, and only this key. It was our secret. Not that my father didn't know.

"One-two-three. I thought that had to mean something, back then. Something sorcerous. The only sorcerer I spoke to was our healer, and I didn't dare ask her. There must be a word for a Crafter with numbers, but I've forgotten. . . ."

"Archimate," Silvern said, "sometimes Archreckoner. It's one of the rarest Archana. I've only known one—and a second who might have, but music found him instead."

"Are numbers so terribly hard?"

"Not hard, but terrible. Archimates tend to slip out of the world, to another one made of numbers and truly straight lines. It looks like madness, from our side. I wouldn't guess at what it looks like from theirs."

"I might," she said. "Each time I counted them, I sorted them. First by color, then by size, then by title—I didn't really understand about authors then—so that, every time I came here, I could check and account that nothing had been altered or taken, that the number was still perfect."

"And was it?"

"Oh, always. After a while, I didn't need the count, I had the image whole. I was only eight, of course. . . ."

"Which is a cubical number," Silvern said, "two times two times two. If you had been nine, that's three by itself, a square of primes. Do you know Shoredrake?"

Longlight's hand fell at once on the blue spine of *Shoredrake's Backglances*. "'In bottom drawers and backs of books, one only finds these things who looks.'" She pulled out another volume; Silvern was sure she could have done it with her eyes shut. "Do you know this one?"

He nodded. "That's Catchpenny."

She gave a sharp, bright laugh. The sound startled him; it was clearly her, and felt, but it was quite unlike the Longlight he had been with the last few days. It was like—

Like she is eight again. And it is better than that old, hurt look, Silvern and Edaire thought, both as one, like hands slipping together across distance.

Longlight handed him the book. The cover showed a Quercian decenion in field dress, standing by a table covered with scrolls and surveying instruments; in the background, legionaries were bridging a river. The title was *Bones of the Empire*. The letters were set in a curve—a kind of pun, given the scene and the Quercian association with the arch.

The cover gilding seemed new; Silvern looked inside. "This is a first printing."

"Are you going to tell me that it's worth a lot?" she said, her voice still childlike. "Even with the jam stain on page two hundred thirty-four? And the grooves on plate fifteen, where I traced the diagrams of the model siege engines? Now, I wish I had those still, but I broke them all conquering the west garden."

Her head turned sharply. Silvern followed her look. Pike was across the room; he had entered quite silently. "My lady's pardon . . ."

"It is all right, Pike. Do come here." Her voice was still happy, but entirely adult again.

Silvern handed the book back to her. "I should see about my room and unpack my kit."

"If you would wait a moment. . . . Asking you to see the library was not completely a whim. I knew Pike would come to collect me. Pike, the Palion is here to survey the country, with the intent of advising on our difficulties in high road maintenance."

Pike nodded once. Silvern told himself the click he heard could only be imaginary.

"Publicly, he is looking for a property site, for the Coron Corvaric to—"

"I have been thinking," Silvern said, politely but firmly, "that we should abandon any pretense about what I am doing. It will be obvious enough to many people, and if anyone chooses to suspect that I have a secret purpose here, I would rather they be wrong."

Longlight looked thoughtful. "Yes, that's right. We made the plan on the spot, and things have changed since then."

Another click from Pike. The sound was real, from somewhere far down in his throat. Silvern did not think Pike could have any idea, yet, just what had changed between his lady and Varic, but that was not Silvern's charge.

Longlight said, "Much of the survey will be properly Alecti's business—my secretary for Coronage business, Silvern, you'll meet her at dinner—but is there anything Pike may assist with?"

"Lucivitry equipment. And someone to use it, if possible."

"What about Ventry, my lady? This would seem to suit him very well."

"I believe that it would. Have—no, we'll go to see him, that'll be a surprise. Tomorrow we rest, next day audience, next day rest from audience—four days."

Another click. "It will be arranged. And now, Palion, would you care to see your quarters? Your luggage has already been delivered there."

"Thank you, Pike."

Pike pulled a bell cord. Less than a minima later, a young woman in household livery was at the door.

"Briary," Pike said, "this is our lady's guest, the Palion Silvern. You will show him to the Falconer's suite, and see that he has everything necessary."

As the two of them went out of the room. Longlight heard Silvern saying, ". . . but my name is Silvern, and when things are not too formal—"

Pike was standing at attention.

"Yes, Pike," she said, "there is another matter. It involves Graven. At dinner tonight—and from now on—he is to be seated among the military staff, not with me. If he chooses a new companion, that is obviously his business."

"Very well, my lady. Who else may I inform of this change?"

"I will tell Alecti. Use your discretion otherwise."

"And who will tell Palion Graven?"

"I shall. Thank you for reminding me, Pike."

"Will my lady be retiring now?"

"I think that I had better."

Pike withdrew. Longlight put the copy of Catchpenny in its place and locked the bookshelf doors. She crossed the Map Room and took the other hidden staircase—the one that, after a few more defenses, also led to the Dark Room—to her office.

As Longlight had expected, Alecti was there, poking at the office fireplace. "My lady is welcome home," the secretary said, put down the fire tools, stood, and bowed.

Alecti was wearing a black riding jacket and a long, dark green skirt. Her hair was a vivid red, which looked terrible with the Coronal blue livery; it had taken a special instruction from Longlight to force her into more suitable colors.

She was slender, shapely, but very slight—"Stack me on Pike and we'd be two people high and half one wide" was her own comment. She had been born almost two months before her due time, to a household brewer dying of summer fever. The healer had denied any part in saving her, giving the child herself all the credit, and Longlight thought that was probably true.

They had been as close as circumstances allowed, growing up: two girls close in age (Longlight was two years older), in the same household, who had never known their mothers. Longlight wondered, just now, what their lives would have been like in Strange House; something like sisters, she supposed. But not here. Nor anywhere else she could think of. Ascorel, perhaps. Alecti had a degree in estates management from Ascorel Applied Sciences.

She was the only member of the household in her generation with such an education.

Longlight could remember hearing her father say, "She can already cipher better than any two of my clerks. You say it costs money to send people to the University, and I say it costs more money to hire stupid clerks. Find the money and don't ask me again."

The belowstairs tale had been about for years already that the two girls *were* sisters—half, anyway. Longlight understood that such stories hung on every Coron, man or woman, partnered or not, a Coron's loose lambs would multiply. Longlight had avoided the tales so far, but her time would come. There were sound ways to prove or deny bloodline. There had to be; too much was involved. But proof was for lawyers.

"Is my lady well?" Alecti said, and woke Longlight up.

"Tired. I have Pike's report. May I hope yours is as quiet?"

"There was a killing near Wolf Trace. A woodcutter, solitary, in his house, with his axe. It seems to have been revenge for a breach of promise, but it's being looked into."

"Do we know who was responsible?"

"We will. There is unlikely to be further revenge, and the guilty family will probably be amenable to fine and service. By the Coron's justice, of course."

"Of course."

"And the hop harvest is nearly complete. It looks to be a very good one. The oasts are full, and given the storm damage to the south last summer, the sale should be excellent."

"Ill winds. Speaking of which, I propose to visit Ventry in a few days. We have some work for him. Would you care to come along?"

"If possible, my lady."

"We'll make it possible. Besides, the work will involve him

leaving the weather station to make some lucives around the countryside. He'll be persuaded more easily by you than me."

"My lady flatters me. But if I cannot accompany you, tell him that he may plate clouds for his studies, along with . . . I assume this is military, as the Palion is visiting?"

"It is."

"And what does my lady have to tell me? There was some talk about a corpse."

"That rose the hill fast."

"Such things do."

Longlight described the ambush and its aftermath.

Alecti said, "Giving the boy to Praxitae should be justice enough. Do you think the girl was his sister?"

"I'm sure of it, given their looks. I'd guess they were orphaned up in the wild parts, and when the food ran out they decided to be bandits—"

"Lost princes so frequently do."

"Yes. . . . They certainly wouldn't have been much as hunters. It's possible the boy, Hilt, is the only one living who really knows."

"Not many people are that isolated, but it's possible. I'll put ears out. It may take time."

"Naught for it save patience."

"Or the suren-draw."

"All the hurt was on their side. Let's leave his spirit alone, howan gently done, an't some crime to catch out."

"Your accent is coming back. That means you're relaxing. Good, an I may bolden say."

"An ye leiter seil me, when I go soft?"

"Anyone is easier read at ease, my lady. But I think you mean something particular."

Longlight took in a breath, let it out. "I met someone. In the City. We—this is private."

"I see."

"Do you?"

"Only one thing could be so private that my lady would need to tell me so."

"Yes."

"Praxitae has said much of the Palion Silvern and his conseil. I do not think he is the person you met in the City. Do you choose to tell me? Understanding that any visit would be Pike's responsibility."

"There are no plans for a visit. He is the Coron Corvaric, and his name—"

"Varic?" Alecti said with an explosion of breath. From her, that was as startling as a scream.

"Do you know him?" Most of Alecti's life at Ascorel was blank to Longlight; she had decided it was no business of hers to know. Now she felt a thin, sharp chill.

"I know of him. He overlapped me by a year, I think, but we never met. Even in the openness of the University, there are . . . many rules."

Longlight sensed something unsaid in the last words, but let it pass. *We never met* was a plain statement. She was sure Alecti was not lying. She suspected she could not have. The last touch of cold in her breast said that if Alecti *had* met Varic then, she might never have come home at all.

That red hair was so very beautiful, when it was not bound up with cloth or cord or a wire cage. But—it was inevitable, given the uncounted hours of a secretary's service, that Longlight should see her with her hair down, barefoot, her clear green eyes full of sleep. . . .

Are you mad, woman? Have you not made enough trouble for yourself?

"So what, then, my lady, of Graven?"

"Graven and I are done, I believe."

"In that my lady does not have the option of faith. If you do not yet know, very well. But you must know; no one else can. And then he must."

"You're pleased by this."

"I owe my Coron my honesty. I am grateful of hers."

Alecti had a look in her eyes that Longlight had not seen often, and never forgot when she did see it: neither defiant nor abashed, a cool acceptance that was not defeat.

A Coron's heir, nine years old and thoughtless, could torment any same-aged girl she might choose, but that look deprived the game of any reward and taught her more than a hundred scoldings could have.

She had lost herself the last night with Varic, and he had taken on the same look—just for one short breath, but it had registered just as sharp. And he had *been* Coron's heir: Where and how had he learned it?

Longlight said, "I will tell Graven. You will excuse me if I take my own time in finding the words."

"Graven's world does not work like that, my lady. If you try to explain why you no longer want him, he will take it as a challenge to meet your tasks. Give him a rival and it will be even worse. You were best to give him nothing he can fight. Be an imperious Great Lady, casting off a servant's affection as if it were a soiled glove. He will understand that, and it will hurt him less."

"Would you do the same for the weatherman?"

"I would tell Ventry that the wind had turned, the clouds broken, the rain fallen into the sea. Which is how he would tell me."

"Point."

"A word I do not think you will ever obtain from Palion Graven," Alecti said.

"Point and concetta," Longlight said, her mouth quite dry.

Much more softly, Alecti said, "I see a difference here, my lady. I heard it when you first spoke of this man.

"Graven never loved you, nor you him. For a time you answered something necessary and useful to each other, and however sharp I have been about him, that was a good thing. But it was always going to pass, and now it has, in favor of—I'm sorry, I have no idea what."

"Of another Coron."

"Lescoray is a vast country, my lady, with hundreds of Corons, who change with the wind. And there are single paintings in the First House that would bring enough money to sustain two lives."

"What are you talking about?"

"A story. No more true than any other."

The long silence after that was broken by a tap at the door. Longlight was still trying to find her voice when Alecti said clearly, "Yes?"

"Briary, honored."

Alecti looked at Longlight, who nodded. "Enter."

The maid came in. She held out a folded paper, said unsteadily, "Message from Pike, milady."

Longlight took the note. "Were you told to wait for a reply?"

"No, milady."

"Thank you, then."

Briary curtsied and hurried out.

The paper had Pike's trademark fold and tuck, that made it all but impossible to open without tearing. There were rumors that a few of the oldest staff could get a look at Pike's messages undetected, but Longlight knew of no one who had dared to try.

She didn't either, ripping a thumb's-breadth gash in the paper as she folded it out.

The Palion has asked for clothes that reflect our house-hold, and not the City fashion. I shall do my best to accommodate his considerable grace.

    P

Pike's initial was a little sketch of a pikestaff and pennon; it was his signature as much as the secure fold.

She handed it over to Alecti. "If this is important, I suppose I'll find out. Now I must nap, or I shall fall into my food, and Silvern will think badly of the Westrene. I *am* joking."

"Of course, my lady. I will have Merian wake you in adequate time."

⌘

Dinner was in the large hall of the Second House; it was darker and chillier than the newer halls below, but it had more of home about it, old things in their places.

Merian had brought out one of Longlight's better gowns, a brocade of pale blue and silvery gray. She wouldn't have picked it for herself, but seen in the mirror, she had to admit it looked well.

The hall was bustling when Longlight arrived, the tables set and about half-occupied, the fire going, the first drinks being served. The household seemed happy, and that was well, too. There was no sign of Silvern, but Pike would make sure he was found or awakened in good time.

And then she saw Graven, purposefully crossing the room toward her. She saw that Praxitae was absent; how fortunate for Graven that the Teacher of Palions did not see him approaching a Coron in such a fashion.

She ignored him and took her seat at the main table. Silvern's place would be next to hers. She imagined Graven knew that very well by now.

He stopped in mid-stride as she passed, then waited for her to sit, and came politely toward the table.

"Graven?"

"I . . . find myself . . ."

"You do?" She stopped herself; even if Alecti were right, there was no need to humiliate Graven in front of everyone at dinner.

She hoped there was not.

". . . less than well informed."

She looked around. The hall was still disorderly, and no one was seated near her. They could have a quiet conversation to themselves, if it stayed quiet. She gestured him closer.

"You imagine there is someone else, and that is true, which is all that you are entitled to know."

"More than that, I think," he said, but he did not say it loudly. It was not a demand, just the first thing that had entered his mind and mouth.

"Then you need to think harder," she said, "and you will say no more of it unless and until I raise the subject."

"My lady . . ."

She turned away from him. It was frighteningly easy.

Graven went back to his seat.

The first course, a light fish soup, came out. There was as yet no sign of Silvern. Longlight watched the upright clock by the wall count off two full minimi, then said, "Shall we begin, and hope for absent friends?"

As the soup plates were removed, Silvern entered the room, and there was an instant and absolute silence. A plate chattered on a tray and was clutched still.

The Palion was dressed in a long black gown with silver embroidery on the breast and massed pleats from waist to floor. It was fastened with a heavy belt of red leather, ornately figured in steel.

On the wall, above and behind him, hung a life-sized portrait of a gray-haired man leaning against a map table. He wore the exact same robe, with only the addition of a long dagger hung from the belt. His expression was not pleasant.

"I am sorry to be so late . . ."

Alecti laughed. It died away alone.

Longlight dragged her thoughts together. "That is no fault of a guest's here. Your seat is waiting and your meal is hot, and we are delighted of your company. But if you will look—" She gestured at the picture.

Silvern turned. "Ah," he said, "no wonder then. I *am* the ghost at the banquet." He laughed, and then others did, and the tension was broken. The Palion took his seat and dinner resumed.

The main course was sausages, made with apples and the household's own black stout. They seemed more delicate than usual; she wondered vaguely if the kitchen had been experimenting, if that had led to the notorious grease fire. That was fine, she thought, however it had happened. They needed more experiments, out here at the end of the world.

She turned to Silvern, saw him looking curiously at the portrait.

"You're too polite to ask," she said. "That is my twice-great-grandfather, the first Coron of the line. The dagger on his belt was the means of his ascent; I'm surprised Pike didn't provide you with that as well."

"He did," Silvern said, just to her. "Armigers do not borrow weapons except under the most extraordinary necessity."

"I'm told it flatters him greatly, which must say something about what he was like. But let's spare that for another time. Here's to good company and your most welcome stay."

"I'll drink to that always." He raised his glass. "This is your local beer?"

"Ours. It's been a good year so far. Maybe we'll finally run the magnostyle wire to the house. If we can keep it safe . . . but not now."

"We'll try." He looked at his gown. "I'm not an easy fit. Does it bother you?"

"No. It's Pike's style of joke. He even warned me, but I wasn't paying enough attention." She drank; the beer *was* good this year. She had already drunk enough of it, which was probably why she didn't mind having some more. "I have two jesters in the old sense, though neither bears the taddelix," her tongue ran on, "souls who remind one that nothing needs laughter more than uncomfortable truths. Pike is the deep-laugh sort. The other—isn't."

"That would be the honored Alecti?"

"You've met?"

"I heard her spoken of, wandering about this splendid house." He lowered his voice. "You know that, usually, either the leader must be feared and the lieutenant loved, or the other way around. But here . . . well. I would hope you are pleased, because you should be."

What made you such a good man, she thought, so patient, so calm? Varic was patient—oh, Shyira, yes—but she had also felt the tension in him, knew there was rage in his bones. She gulped at her beer, sloshing it, just like a bad, old Midreigns Coron of the stories.

Varic had called his own father one of those.

Dessert was warm berry pie with thick cream, with a light wheat beer for those who had not had enough and tea for those who had. Longlight had a short glass for the honor of the Coronage and moved to tea.

The staff came in to shift the tables and open up space in the hall. Seats were moved into a circle, and cushions set about on the floor. Guitars appeared.

Longlight noticed a ripple of talk in one corner. Someone moved, and she saw who was at the center of it.

"Alecti," she said, "are you leaving us so early?"

"No one seems to wish it," she said.

"Come on," someone else said. "One song and we'll let you sleep."

Silvern said, "I should like to hear you sing, Alecti."

She said, "You have a fine voice, Palion. And first place as guest. I wonder, would you sing? Or tell a story? I would wait for that." She looked around at the people circling her. "Yes, yes, and sing one, too."

"I'm not a storyteller," Silvern said, "but my father was. And I will tell one for him."

"A Pandekt story?" Alecti said, quietly, but cutting straight through the noise of the room.

"A Pandektine version of the story," Silvern said.

There was a ripple of approving noises from the audience. Naturally, he thought. Here they had thrown back the Quercians; there would be a great sympathy for the Pandekts, who had failed to do the same, and lost so much more.

That was a sympathy he knew very, very well.

So he told the story as his father had, sitting on the perfect green grass of a University quadrangle, while Silvern, six years old, leaned against his shoulder and watched the arc of rapt students seated and sprawled around them. Silvern himself had been lost in wonder that they should be so still, so unaware of the playgrounds all around them.

"Once in the day when people were far apart and the sky much closer," he said, "Goddess's aspect of crop and seed Shyira decided to go among mortals as one of them, as She did and as She does. This time, for reasons She never told me"—he got his chuckle—"She took with Her not Palion, Her usual companion, but Hand, the consort of Evani; Hand, the craftsman and artificer. And also, though it seems that even Goddess may forget such things, Hand, the trickster, whose word must always be true but is hardly ever straight."

The audience nodded and muttered approval. That was good, Silvern thought. It had been a long time since he had told this story, and sometimes the Pandektine view of Goddess and Her consorts—able to be arbitrary, to forget, even to lie to each other, so remarkably human—startled people who thought of the Pandekts as marble-white reasoners from an age of long ago.

"Shyira took on the shape of a poor woman, in linen that had once been fine, hair woven with cracked beads, barefoot on the hard road. Hand was bent and one-eyed, with a clubfooted boot, and though his fingers were still long and delicate they were wrapped in rags of gloves and mostly hidden in his sleeves.

"When they passed a house that seemed prosperous, they would stop and ask the traveler's aid—a little food, a cup of water, an ace against the shadows down the road. Twice they were given a little water, once some bread with olive oil. But they were never offered admittance, or even shade to drink and eat beneath, and most of the houses, even the finest, told them to move on.

"Once a vicious dog was set after them. Hand produced a fine-looking marrowbone from his shirt and tossed it to the dog; but when the beast gnawed it, the bone roared like lions, and the dog ran yelping away. Hand laughed, but Shyira's look was cold.

"Then they came to a small house—no more than a clay hut, with a tiny garden inside a stick fence.

"'We ought stop here,' Hand said, 'and see what gifts they have for us.'

"'Why do you say that?' Goddess replied. 'So you can laugh at them as well?'

"'Perhaps. Sport is taken where it is found, and being sportive I am always curious. But my lady calls the game.'

"'Very well. But I am already weary with mocking today.'

"There was no door to the house, only an old piece of sacking hung in the opening, so Shyira tapped at the clay wall, which shed itself at the attention. An old man appeared, and behind him an old woman. Both were dressed more poorly than the travelers, if such can be thought, but their thin-worn gowns were clean. Shyira asked the same as She had asked all day.

"'We were just about to dine ourselves,' the old man said. 'It is not fine, but it is yours to share.'

"In the voice of the spirit, which the mortals would not hear, Hand said to Shyira, 'They were not about to eat, nor have they for some time. What a terrible thing it is, to lie to strangers.'

"The old man's name was Beller, and the woman's was Clare. They moved around the tiny house, covering a bench with a worn but soft cloth for sitting, pouring oil into lamps that were obviously lit only in need. Clare fanned up the cooking fire as Beller got out a kettle; filled with water, it took the both of them to set it in place. Clare rubbed herbs between her hands and sprinkled them into the pot, while Beller went out to the garden.

"'This is a good day for guesting,' Beller said when he came back. He had a fine cabbage under his arm, and the skirt of his robe was full of ripe olives.

"'What a fine garden you have,' Shyira said.

"'Ah, You lie worse than the mortals,' Hand told Her. 'There were a few half-dry olives and a scrawny little cabbage out there before You put Your fingers in.'

"'I do not understand you,' Goddess said in return. 'And I do not enjoy your company.'

"'No one does,' Hand said. 'But parting from me brings such joy. . . .'"

More laughter. It was going well so far. Of course, Hand had far to go yet.

"And so," Silvern continued, "when the meal was over, the couple and their guests sat with a little tea Shyira had drawn from Her pocket, pretending it had been given them somewhere up the road. Goddess and Her sometime consort asked the old people about their lives, and though Beller and Clare insisted there was nothing to tell, in truth there were many tales, of travel in their youth, of the change of seasons, of the happiness they had found together, poor as they might be.

"Then, for no reason—though Shyira would later blame Hand for it—a gust of wind blew the doorway drape wide, and a clay lamp was knocked from its hook.

"Goddess moved Her finger, and the lamp gently floated toward the floor, landing intact and still burning.

"The old people knew just what they had seen. They at once dropped to their knees and begged Goddess to forgive their miserable hospitality.

"In response, Shyira blinked Her eyes, and the world around Her and Hand stopped still, its colors fading to gray. 'They must have a reward,' Goddess said.

"'That is fair enough,' said Hand. 'Have You any ideas?'

"'Their garden shall always be bountiful, come plague or bad weather.'

"'Your sister Coris will have something to say about the weather. And anyway, all that food will only make them fat and slow. They don't want that.'

"'Then this house shall become a temple, and they shall be its priests; and all those who were turned aside as we were will find hospitality here.'

"'Seems like a lot of work, though they are happy workers and would serve You gladly. But it isn't what they want.'

"'Then they shall be—'

"'Oh, don't say it! They've lived and lived and lived already, and they know what it means to grow old! Don't prolong it, and don't make them endure it twice! *They don't want that!*'

"'Then, you hateful little thing, what do they want?'

"'Why not find out? In Your way, I mean.'

Giggles became chuckles became a full, rich laugh. It was going to be fine.

"So Goddess cast light through the gray, stopped air and looked through the bodies of Beller and Clare, to their spirits. Hand turned away from the sight and groaned as if his eyes hurt. 'So,' he said, still wincing, 'You know now.'

"'No,' Shyira said.

"'Oh, yes, You know. But You will not do it.'

"'To kill one in the arms of the other?' Shyira said. 'Will they wish that? Not now, when it is a dream of gods and somedays, but when the one is truly dying and looks up into the other's eyes, will the wish then be *live no more*?'

"'I see Your point,' Hand said. 'They will worship You the less, for worshipping one another more.'

"'You ask me to tamper with Death,' She said, 'and you know very well why we forbid that Ourself. I wish Palion were here: he knows Death.'

"Hand said, 'I wish he were, too. Palion is brave and handsome, and I am an ugly fool, unfit for Your company. Evani loves me for my uselessness, for I rest Her soul of the tumble of commerce; but You, ah, You see things differently.'

"Shyira's voice was many voices now, a chorus of Herself: 'What if others should wish this? They are the creatures of fashion and whim, as Evani should, or ought, have told you. And they come together in our Communion; someday they may learn to come together of themselves. What if the whole of mortality decided to abandon life as one, and in love, not in fear? Would we have to remake all things—and if we did, should we not shape them new, to a different end?'

"Suddenly grave, Hand whispered, 'We are all Death, all of us—Wolfa devours, Palion slays in his legions, Windrose breaks stone and furies water, I make the tools for all destruction. And we are but Yourselves' shadows.'

"'*Stop*,'" Goddess said, and Hand stopped, as still as the stayed mortal world.

"'I came here to know things,' Shyira said, 'and I am come to know them.' She moved then, and the world around them moved as well. The old couple blinked and looked at one another, as if they had woken from a sleep.

"'Would you grace for us?' Shyira said, and produced the Book from within Her clothing. 'The two of you. One each.'

"The old people seemed surprised at the request, but then the woman chuckled and said, 'That is a pretty custom. We must remember it.'

"'Assist me, friend,' Goddess said, and Hand stirred and spun the Book, holding it out to the couple.

"Clare drew Division reversed, Beller the Two of Staves. Then the woman gave a small cry, showing her finger bleeding on the edge of the card. The man took hold of her injured hand, setting the cards aside; then his companion reached to his other hand, showing it cut and bleeding as well. In an instant each was kissing the cut on the other's finger.

"'And it is done,' Shyira said to Hand, 'and so it shall be.'

"And so it was for the old people, a few more precious years, in which their garden always fed them and their house somehow failed to fall down. Until one day, in the absolute clarity of the sun, as Clare filled the kettle with water, her heart that had borne all things with joy gave way. She cried out, and Beller ran to her, and embraced her. There were no words, because there are no words. I do not know what they felt, or if they saw the end, but as the man held his wife, wood enclosed them, oak leaves on one side, elm shoots on the other, and where there had been two mortals there were now two trees, an oak and elm with their trunks and branches intertwined.

"It is a wonder, and you can see it if you go there—but I shall not tell you where; for as with the Goddess and Her companion, some things are not sought out but only found."

Silvern shut his eyes. Someone pressed a mug of beer into his hand, and he drank gratefully as the room cheered.

He looked up. Alecti was standing next to him. "A wonderful story," she said, below the other sounds. "A shame the Quercians learned nothing from it."

Silvern was surprised. There were not many people who knew that slant on the tale—that the oak was the Bright Empire and the elm was Pandekt, and if the two would join their strengths they would be eternal. His father had known it, of course, but even he never told the tale that way.

Before he could say anything, Alecti had settled herself on a chair and nodded to a young woman with a guitar. Slow, sharp chords chimed soft from the strings. Alecti counted off the beats, and began:

> "Though the journey's incomplete, the wind is turning colder
> Gather all your burdens in, the night will be here soon
> Shake the dust from off my feet, the shadow from my shoulder
> Shut the door against the wind that's falling from the moon.
>
> "The inconstant moon, they say
> From the sea was torn away
> Bringing into night some day

Just enough for shadows' play
Once abandoned, not recovered
Pale the look and cold the lover
Is it not the faith of men
That which rises falls again."

Her voice was obviously not trained, but it had that unpretty strength that could put words between the ribs just like steel.

How like you, my beloved, Edaire said. *Agate would call it raw and beautiful, the music of the first juice from the cider press.*

He did not answer, so that she could hear the rest of the song, but he pressed his left thumb against the first two fingers, and felt her sigh.

"If a soul can catch itself, what quarry can escape her
Tears and kissing ne'er come right, and folly 'tis to swoon
Set the heart upon the shelf, and wrap the bones in paper
Shut my eyes against the light that's falling from the moon.

"The inconstant moon has seen
Heaven, earth, and all between
Bright to dark its face has been
But whatever can they mean
Seasons changing, sea-tides bringing
Set the wolf and owl to singing
Ask the echo of the sun
If it answers, tell no one.

"Weep not at the end of day, the morning's where it's leading
I can't make the verses knit, the loom is out of tune
Put the words and notes away, my eyes are red with reading
Shut the heart against the spirit falling from the moon."

The audience was quiet a moment, holding its breath, and then they applauded, furiously. Alecti got quickly to her feet, bowed in all directions, and hurried from the room.

There were more songs, some unsteady dancing. The group thinned, imperceptibly at first, by ones and twos, and then suddenly Longlight was thanking everyone for their attendance and the party was over.

She said to Silvern, "You are a fine old warrior, to last the campaign. Is there anything else we can provide you?"

"I would like to look at the library for a few minimi before bed," he said. "The general shelves, not—"

"There is only the one key to that," she said, "and I am too tired to turn it. But all the rest is at your disposal. Roper."

One of the servants was instantly at her elbow.

"The Palion wishes to visit the Map Room. You will see to light and direction."

"My lady. At your pleasure, Palion?"

"Oh, now, so we're back before dawn."

Roper brought a lamp, and led the way up to the library. Silvern dissuaded him from lighting the whole room. He found a book on Wander's Gate he had not seen before, and one on beer making that simply looked interesting.

As they passed through the Second House, Alecti met them in the corridor. She had a pink satin pillow securely tucked under one arm. Silvern caught the resinous scent of hops.

Alecti paused. "Good evening, Palion. I am sorry we have not properly met before now. I have an errand, but if you have a moment . . ."

"I can find my way from here, Roper," Silvern said, and the man bowed and disappeared.

Alecti could mean "chosen one," or "one given power." It was a rare name, because even sorcerers were afraid to summon the Talent to their children. Silvern's mind reached out to politely touch her aura, but there was only the trace power of any living soul.

"My lady has told me about the Coron Corvaric," she said. "She said they met in the City, but I believe that you have just come from Strange House."

"Both are true."

"I know of the Coron Corvaric, though we have not met," Alecti said, then added in a very precise tone, "You are his close friend?"

"I do hope so. We have known one another for many years."

"He is not forgotten by the New Reasoners of Ascorel. His close friends know this, I do believe."

"Some of us do," Silvern said. The group she spoke of was unofficially known as the Atheist's League, but even the University dared not call it that openly. Illegal beliefs must be addressed with misdirections and silences. "I am certain you would have much to discuss."

"That can hardly be. Unless the Lord Varic were to visit here—and that, too, can hardly be."

"The Lady Longlight and I will be visiting Strange House again at Cold Solstice. Varic will be there as well. I do not speak for Strange, of course, but I do know him. And though I am a guest there only by grace of my conseil—*What untruth is this?* Edaire said in the corner of his mind—"I am sure that you would be most welcome."

"The Lord Strange told me the same, at Ascorel," she said. "But that was a life I did not live, and it is too late to return there now. To the choice, I mean, though I suppose I mean Strange House as well. But for what it is worth, Palion Silvern, I am glad that my lady Coron found her way there. And I am very glad for what else has happened to her. Happier, I think than she will be these long-drawing nights until Solstice." She bowed politely.

"May I ask—"

"As you are my lady's guest, I am at your disposal in all things, Palion. But I am no more than my lady's servant." Her voice had not wavered a fraction of a note, but her arm was crushing the pillow it held.

"You have an errand, and I keep you from it. Good night to you, Alecti, and sleep well."

"Good night to you, honored. And thank you."

Silvern turned away. He could hear Alecti turn the corner, and then Edaire was with him.

Oh, my dear, don't you know what hop pillows are for?

"Not, I take it, easy breathing."

Her laughter tingled within him. *Surely not. If one sleeps on a hop pillow, one will dream of the true beloved.*

"And you think—"

If it had been Alecti's own, you would never have seen it. Now, you have your books, and I am sure someone will bring you some tea. Come to bed.

⤜∞⤏

In her room, lit by the fireplace, under the heavy canopy of her bed, Longlight tossed awake. The hop-stuffed pillow, Alecti's cruel gift, was shoved to one side.

It was not difficult, and not unpleasant, to recall Graven sleeping there, flat on his back, smiling with a justifiable satisfaction. He was a Palion, after all, and to be daring and bold was not the same thing as to be presumptuous, no matter how it might look to Alecti.

And then the firelight shifted, and the image became Varic's, a reclining sculpture, looking at her with . . . was that presumption? He was a Coron, after all.

The first morning on the train from Lystourel, when it had

been simple enough to believe that all was passing and past, the first thing he had said to her was, "Hello." And looked her straight in the unfocused eyes. Then kissed her, on the forehead, as if he were afraid to be too passionate.

That was funny.

Graven's idea of morning was a gulped breakfast and a brisk ride through Rogues Wood near the house, or an hour down to the seacoast. If she did not wish to join him, that was his lady Coron's pleasure, and he would ride alone.

Which was no judgment against him. Those early rides could be, had been, very beautiful.

Suppose the Coron were just to have two lovers, one at home and one away? It was done, all the time and everywhere, and not just by Corons. But—

But she had told Edaire, within minimi of their first meeting, that whatever had been between her and Graven was dying. Had that been a boast, or a dismissal, or a lie?

What it had been, she was suddenly certain, was a breath of relief. The affair with Graven was done, and when she arrived at Strange House it was safe to admit it, because something had appeared to take its place.

It was apparent to her that Varic would never literally be in this bed, and she would never see his Coronage, perhaps never even his house in Lystourel. That separation, too, was done in many times and places.

For a Palion to romance a Coron was the stuff of stories, and to fail at it would still be glorious. Of course Graven had taken his chance.

For two Corons to fall in love was a story as well, of cold stone and long-drawn pain and the taste of blood and ashes. She and Varic had known this and not stopped, and that was all the difference.

She grasped the hop pillow and stuffed it beneath her head,

pulled the covers to her chin, and shut her eyes. She would see what dreams came, but it didn't matter. She was dreaming of Varic this moment, awake, and her spirit knew that he was dreaming likewise of her.

CHAPTER 7

The River and the Road

Varic woke in gray light. He had grown very tired of gray light. He turned his head, and the light moved. That was better. He felt about with his feet; they were moving. He slid his legs out of the bed, to the floor, and eased himself up. After a few moments of experimentation, he was standing independently. He pulled on his dressing gown, which Midden had placed where he could find it by touch alone, and shuffled out of the bedroom, to the bathroom. Everything seemed remarkably easy.

The stairs stretched away and down. It would not do to fall; his bones were all intact, whatever was awry within his skull. But the muscles were responding well enough that he was almost tempted to hurry.

In the kitchen, Midden's wife had fried bacon and cut four perfect slices of bread for him, all still warm beneath a cloth cozy. The butter and jam were neatly set by, a spreading knife, dull as a Coron in Parliament, at the ready.

He ate his breakfast with honeyed black tea, and then waited. His stomach seemed to accept the offering. Then he found the bread knife—nearly the length of a Quercian short sword, with a toothed edge—and cut another piece of bread, as thin as he could, buttered and ate it.

He rinsed the knife and dishes and put them up to dry, just as any normal, healthy soul might have done.

Very well, then, his body was his own again.

He opened the door to the basement stairs, brought up the electrical lights below, and descended.

The Dark Room in Varic's town house was in fact just a cabinet, underneath the stairs, with a waist-high, brass-fitted door. If the shelves inside were torn out, a grown soul might barely be able to crouch inside. This was not a great house, with many residents and house staff; it did not need a large space for the underthoughts of those within. Still, there was a blade trap attached to the complicated lock; Varic was a Coron, and the forms had to be observed.

He put a hand on the door. It was cold, in the warm atmosphere. Or perhaps his hand was only warm by comparison. There were any number of stories about the real and measurable effects of a Dark Room, everything from nightmares to murder induced by exposure to the accumulated malice within. There were always stories, and stories never grew less in the telling. And compared to any given gin house cellar in Cutsail Street or Fiveways End, the toll was modest indeed.

Still, like everyone, Varic had a Dark Room, and like everyone, he kept certain objects locked inside it, things that required special handling but which could not simply be thrown away.

One of the items was an old thumbscrew. He had no idea how old; it could have been Midreigns, though it was very probably newer. The design had not changed much. Varic had found it when he was quite young, in a box of old iron in Corvaric Castle. He hadn't known what it was—some sort of mechanic's clamp, he supposed—and had used it a few times to crack nuts, but it was slow and clumsy for that. He kept it as children keep the few things that are genuinely theirs. And then, when he was ten, he saw such a device in use, and the knowledge changed him.

On the top shelf inside was a pistol, an old powder-and-ball weapon with ornate inlay on the stock and gilding on the lockworks. His father had carried it while traveling. Varic had been brought up to know weapons and in his youth had never understood the choice; anyone who expected to need a pistol carried a cartridge repeater. The only exceptions were those who were bound by some kind of ritual, such as a duel—and even there, only the proctor was still required to carry such a weapon. The duelists themselves could use light artillery if they wanted, and it had been known to happen.

Varic had known better than to ask his father for a reason. Much later, after asking was no longer possible, he understood that it had in fact been a kind of ceremony, a Coron saying that he went armed because that was what a strong man did, but he did so merely as a sign, not because he feared for his life.

When the coach was found with Varic's parents dead inside, the gun was there, still loaded and unfired. That was still a puzzle. There should have been at least one dead bandit. Possibly two; his mother could also load and fire with acute skill.

It was a puzzle, unless the Coron and his wife had been approached by people they had no cause to suspect. But they had been killed by bandits. Everyone in Corvaric agreed upon that.

The weapon was not loaded now. Powder would have gone bad and eventually corroded the lock. And there was such a thing as granting a symbol too much power.

His parents had died more than half his life ago, and he had not been at home when it happened; he had, in truth, found every possible excuse to stay elsewhere. He had gone to Ascorel, and then discovered Lystourel. At fourteen, he had even tried to be appointed his father's proxy in Parliament. There was an elaborate letter from the Coron's secretary saying that the Coron had found this an interesting, and a very worthy idea; that he was pleased his son had such serious thoughts.

If that were true, and not the secretary's flourish, it was the greatest praise Varic had ever received from his father. But it had not happened, for reasons he never knew. Proxies could be refused by a committee, to prevent infants, farm animals, or inanimate objects from being appointed by humorous Corons, but there was no specific age rule, and heirs as young as fifteen had held the job, with various degrees of success.

But it had not happened. A year later, he had been Coron in his own right, and shortly after moved his permanent residence to the City.

His family memories were becoming like a book of old lucives; some were stiffly posed, some candid and awkward, some blurred with motion. Most were at least a little faded. Varic could call back memories of his father; of his humor, which was not all coarse and unpleasant, though his merry moments were rare indeed. He had his own headaches as well, and Varic understood now just how terrible they must have been, though the Coron was incapable of admitting pain. He was just angry, he said, and always had a reason for the anger. And his rage was as visible as lightning, freezing the moment like the luciver's flash.

Varic wondered, by no means for the first time, if they would understand each other now. He supposed they would, though to what degree he could not know, and he had no clue whether it would have brought them closer.

He also wondered if, had he been in Corvaric when his parents were killed, if something equally sudden might have happened to him. On the rare occasions when he visited now, he was a stranger politely met, and much praised as a good Coron. (The Corons who lived in Lystourel would occasionally call themselves the League of Good Corons.) And he would hold court, and listen to requests. But no one ever suggested that he could do more good if he stayed in his country.

He ought to ask Longlight about that. She would have the humor not to be offended, and her answer would be instructive.

He closed the cabinet on his past once more. He was hungry again. He had a sudden thought of how soldiers on the march, deprived of salt, sprinkled gunpowder on their stolen eggs. There was nothing human that was not connected to food, or death, or both at once.

He went back upstairs and made a pot of tea. Freshet was due shortly. As he carried the service into the parlor, her knock came.

"I hope that you will excuse my dress," Varic said, plucking at the silk lapel of his dressing gown. "I'm very pleased to see you, but it is still a bit early for me."

"In my work," Freshet said, "we are used to seeing any sort of dress and none. The dressing gown is quite usual for consultations."

Varic saw her to a chair, poured the tea, and sat down. "I suppose that first we should talk about the other night."

Freshet sat very straight, holding her teacup like a child visiting a strict aunt. "Is milord doing well?"

"His lordship is much improved, thank you," Varic said. "And he does believe you have been in the forbidding ancestral manors of Corons before now."

She laughed then, rattling the cup. "Yes, I suppose I have."

"Mind you, both Brook and I have home manors that are quite out of a glueback thriller. But in the City the crypt and the ruined tower have gone out of fashion."

"Milord does not frequent the Central Hospital. Are you in fact improved?"

"I will allow you to examine me. But how is Brook?"

"No great change. His breathing is shallower than it was ten days ago, but that in itself is not significant. His pupils are still fixed. Will it please you sit on this chair?"

"I will do it to please you," he said, and she did smile slightly. She moved his limbs, tapped his knees, and watched the twitch. She tilted a small mirror to shine a spot of light into each of his eyes.

"Your eyes respond normally, as do your muscles. Have you had any other signs? Any bruising or bleeding? Any pain?"

"A few headaches. Nothing severe."

"Not severe by what standard?"

"I assume that my own measure is what matters."

"Blinding head pain is not normal for anyone, my lord. It is always a sign that something is wrong."

"But you are not in a position to say exactly what."

"You were unconscious for nine hours and could not rise from bed for a day and a half. Doctors see denial all the time, but an event like that gives most souls a little perspective on their conditions." She paused, drew a long breath. "I will readily admit that our knowledge of the brain is poor. We also know very little of how the liver works or even all its functions, but I can do many tests that will tell me if it is performing well or poorly. And an episode such as you have had is a clear warning. It is certainly true that I do not know exactly what is wrong with you and may well have no means to find out. But I believe you have enough respect for my skill to accept that, if I do not know, neither do you."

"Point," Varic said.

"I asked that man Winterhill if he knew anything about your health. He said that he only reported things like that when he was paid to, and he was not at the time for hire."

Varic laughed. "I do thank you for the care you took in the matter of my indisposition."

"Your friends managed it all. I had no idea who I was being called to see, or for what reason, until I entered their guest room. It was a surprise. But when one attends Corons and other persons of status, it becomes a familiar sort of surprise. Anyone is entitled to be ill in privacy.

"But I wonder, milord Varic, if there are actually no permanent effects."

"You did say 'a temporary collapse, from overstress and exhaustion.'"

"It is apparent that the collapse was temporary, and those were the immediate causes. But there were signs of it being a transient apoplexy. Not definite, but the way your eyes responded to light. The slight instability on your right side—"

"Which has passed." He held up his cup, balanced on its saucer, without a rattle.

"Which has passed *for the present*. Milord, a physician who is indirect does no good, and may do considerable harm. I strongly suspect that you have had such symptoms before. Perhaps you have not fallen, but you have stumbled. Am I right that you do not see any physician regularly?"

"You could no doubt learn that from your colleagues."

"We all observe our patients' privacy. If you had died, the law would have obligated me to ask. You are still here, so I am asking you."

"My apologies. You suppose correctly in both cases."

Freshet said, "Is there anything else it would please you to tell me?"

"No."

"Very well, then. I take it that I am not welcome here again."

"You are Brook's physician and are welcome at any time whatsoever. You are not my physician, however, and while I most sincerely appreciate your assistance and your discretion, that association between us is now over."

"You seem more concerned that no one hear of this than the possibility that it could cause you to die."

"That is true. It is a matter of personal priorities."

"My lord, there are people who care for you. It shows quite clearly in those around you. The couple you were dining with. Winterhill, who one would not take for a soul of sentiment. And milord Brook, who spoke of you nearly every time we met. You will probably not forgive my saying this, but if Brook does not recover, you will need to carry on for him."

"You're wrong," Varic said. "I forgive you that."

She paused a moment. "There is something else I would like to discuss with you. As regards Brook."

"Please proceed."

"A number of years ago I met an Archreader named Shandrey. She's from Westfaren, though she doesn't live there now. She has been working for some time on using her Archanum to reach people with limited ability to communicate and, after some success with the deaf and mute, focused on comatose patients. She will be visiting Lystourel shortly, and there is a possibility that she would see Brook."

"Where does she work now? Ascorel?"

"The Institut Preuszen."

"I am glad to know that there is at least a traffic in natural knowledge between Lescoray and Ferangard."

"I do not know all the details. I am given to understand that she has had some successes, though as with any sorcerous method, perfect work is impossible."

"I ask this very politely: What do you mean by 'successes'?"

"She has been able to discover whether a spirit endures in an unresponsive body. In at least one case I know of, the person was aware and, after intensive medical sorcery, returned to consciousness."

"If it can be arranged, I should be very pleased to meet her."

"I will make the request."

Varic said, "Brook is much respected in both nations, even among those who disagree with some of his beliefs."

"It would be a good thing on both sides, then."

"It would be significant. In such matters, 'good' is a judgment that depends on one's individual interests."

"I have known milord Brook well enough not to quarrel with you, milord Varic. But I shall still hope."

"So, I trust, shall we all. Thank you very much, Freshet. You have brought light into my day. Now, Winterhill will be arriving very shortly, with a cab. May I take you somewhere?"

"I have other appointments in the area. But thank you."

After she had gone, Varic dressed in heavy canvas trousers and a short wool sailor's jacket. He was not going anywhere formal today; the Parliament had been without him for five days, and its respite could last a little longer.

Half an hour later, Winterhill came to the door, with a cab waiting at the curb. "Where are we lunching?" he said.

"In a swamp," Varic said. "But don't worry, I guarantee the food will be good."

The cab took them to the Blue Rose, where Linnet had a warm and aromatic basket waiting for them. "May I ask after Brook?" he said.

Varic said, "You are always free to ask. I regret that there is no news."

Linnet looked very worn. "Then I will wait for some," he said. "Tomorrow I am taking dinner to Clarity and Trevan Dain. Would it please the both of you to come?"

Varic said, "I shall do my best."

Winterhill said, "I am not a man to turn down the gift of a meal. What do you like to drink with your dinner, Linnet?"

"Oh . . . I have a wine to go with it."

"Then a little whisky for afterward?"

"I would appreciate that. If you could find something Alinsever, I believe Trevan is feeling a bit homesick."

Varic and Winterhill reboarded the waiting cab. Linnet watched them go from the corner door, waving a napkin.

The driver took them down a narrow waterfront road to the undeveloped area on the west bank of the Grand River, not far south of the docks. It was not actually a swamp, though it was certainly moist. Varic gave the driver instructions to return in three hours, and they walked inland to a flat, stony, fairly dry spot. Winterhill spread out a clean horse blanket, and they sat on it to dine on Linnet's patcakes and apple cake.

"And this," Winterhill said, "is where the honored Ryeflower and Collier propose to hold their fair?"

"They've purchased this plot and have options on two more nearby."

"Doesn't appear to be marked."

"There are a few small signs. Enough to make it legal. And a patrolman wanders by now and then to make sure no one has put up a solid dwelling. There are enough dry places to flop at waterside that it isn't a problem."

"Still, following the least requirement of the law is fairly common when running a one-way investment program."

"Even lawmakers know that."

"Then what is this about? I will grant you that there hasn't been a real public fair in the City for so long that people would probably go to one held in high street traffic, but do you really think this 'Exposition Committee' has any actual plans of an expository nature?"

"Let's look at the map," Varic said, and unfolded a large sheet of paper, spread it on the blanket. He picked up some small stones, dried them with a handkerchief, and weighted the drawing. "We are at present seated at the north of the Avenue of Nations, which will stretch for half a mila to the south, parallel to the Grand. And we have chosen a most excellent location for lunch, as we are in the middle of the Alinsever pavilion, at the precise site suggested for the *parc de plaisance*. Have you ever seen one of those?"

"Several. They go back to just after the Midreigns, when the nobility were trading the castles for comfortable new houses with real windows and heat. Some of them put in little parks. Depending on how rich and playful the owner was, they'd have fountains, bandstands, courts for games. There's a huge one at Alin-le-Grand, can easily hold three thousand people without crowding. What goes here?"

"Across the way, there, will be the Ferangarder area. Just across the Avenue of Industry to our north, Lescoray will have the position of honor, and on the fourth corner, either a fourth major country to be decided later, or a market and dining plaza."

"I'm impressed," Winterhill said. "Usually these things have every last detail in place."

"Other countries will take space along the Avenue of Nations, which is to be electrically lit. There's a note somewhere about 'persons in the unusual costumes of their distant lands will be on display.'"

"Will the visitors be allowed to feed them?"

"If they're well behaved, I don't see why not. About halfway down is the Avenue of Knowledge. Ascorel and other centers of learning are expected to install museum collections there, along with various countries' Sorcerers' Guilds. Here's a Telescopium, although how that's supposed to work with all the lights it doesn't say. And there's supposed to be an 'Exhibit of Artifacts from the Castle, Lystourel.' Will that please or worry Falconer?"

"Is there a Dark Room? You're going to need a big one."

Varic picked up the map and stood. Winterhill followed suit, and they began walking. "There are all the things one expects from a fair. Museums of the fine and applied arts, plenty of food. The spectacle showgrounds would be that way."

Winterhill said, in a spec-talker's chanting voice, "One million and one great beasts under one tent, ladies and gentlemen! Rosie the Educated Horse performing alongside one million mosquitoes!" He looked at the map. "What's the long, winding line?"

"'The Light Railway, to carry Visitors about the Site.' There's a note suggesting it should be electrical as well."

"Less coal smoke."

"True, though the fluid generators will burn coal. Though we'll need a generating plant somewhere."

"I take it that isn't on the map."

"It is unaccountably missing, along with water supply, sewage, and service roads."

"This is a dryish patch," Winterhill said. "Practically a commanding height, in fact. What's to go here?"

"The Hall of Commerce, which will rent stall space to tradesmen. There's to be a similar Hall of Earth's Bounty, with food vendors. The idea, I think, is that everyone who builds their own structure will be free to choose a design. And down there at the end of the Avenue of Nations is the 'World Center,' for the countries that want a presence but not an entire building. That should probably be larger. It wouldn't do to turn a country away because we were short a few steps squared."

Winterhill looked down the empty space. "So there is Ferangard, and there is Alinsea . . . and there Nemera and down that way Bodolingo and Coromaestra."

"There are not many people in Lescoray who have heard of those places," Varic said.

"There are some in Lystourel. One can see their citizens any day and every night, working in our docklands and basements, hungry and thinking it paradise because they aren't starving. They come off the ships and never get back on. They do a little better in Alinsea, where if you can do anything around ships, you can at least make a living. One doesn't hear much about what happens elsewhere. At any rate, from the stories their people tell, their rulers aren't likely to put up any booths, unless we make it legal to sell the poor."

Winterhill blew out a long, faintly foggy breath. "I am sorry for that. It's a good thought, and I can imagine many good things coming from it. But I wouldn't count on the whole world visiting."

"No. The world is a very large place."

"I think you know," Winterhill said, "that even if Ryeflower and Collier are absolutely sincere about this fair, spectacle show, and parliament of the world all in one, they intend to make a profit out of it, even if it is strictly speaking a lawful profit."

"I am aware of that. And if they can be forced into making a lawful profit, why should they not have it?"

"I can only give you the answer of a thief and a liar and a scoundrel. It's because thieves and liars and scoundrels only partly do those things for profit. They do them because they are allowed to. It's great sport to find a way to ride a cab without paying, and there are more ways to do it than a bailiff has brass buttons. But the ladies and gentlemen who drive cabs carry whips and are good with them."

"Petty crime is endlessly interesting," Varic said. "Murder, however complex the plan or exalted the victim, is always a base thing. Grand thefts and swindles are never as clever as they appear in the gluebacks or onstage."

"They'd never succeed if they were," Winterhill said. "I once saw *A Million Marks at Hazard* at the Rose Court with half a dozen souls who made their living doing banks; they treated it as the best comedy ever."

"Would these have been the people who stole the office receipts toward the end of the run?"

"That is not a thing I would say, milord. Not to a man who is on dining terms with the Chief Justiciar of the country and his first officer. And if I may ask, how did the dinner proceed?"

"Slowly but surely." He gave a brief recounting of the dinner. "A soul that convinced of his rightness is always dangerous, but there is matter to Cable. He's not to be trusted with power, but what soul is? And he may point the way to exactly the kind of limits the office must have."

"The police always believe the law is not entirely for them. Same as the petty criminal."

"I think Cable is different from either. The law is his text and faith. I believe that he would never cross a limit that Parliament set on the bailiffs, not tolerate the bailiffs ignoring them. There are two problems with this: one is to get the Parliament to enact sensible rules, and the other is that there seems to be no room in the man's heart for human weakness. He can enforce the law to the uttermost, but justice is beyond him."

"Perhaps we could change the title of his office," Winterhill said, and was quiet. Then, "And what impression did you take of Heartsease?"

"That she makes an odd pair with Cable. That she probably does know the difference between people and steam-driven law-obeying machines. And that she is loyal to the Justiciar, but understands very well what he is."

"That's at least one thought too many for one spirit to hold."

They returned to their blanket. Varic poured some more tea; it was nearly cold. "I need your services in gathering information."

"They are available."

Varic explained the story Freshet had told, about the Archreader Shandrey.

Winterhill said, carefully, "You told Linnet there was no news."

"There is no news, yet. There is the possibility that someone will be allowed to examine Brook and the possibility that we will have an answer. That would be news. At the moment, I have not decided whether to agree to this at all. In that decision, I want your help. Shandrey has, as far as I know, been in Ferangard for some years, and I am not asking you to go there."

"I am pleased to hear that. It could be expensive for both of us."

"But it would seem likely that she left some tracks when she lived and worked here. Knowing anything would be useful."

"I will ask discreetly. But I wonder if you are missing a resource that is beyond my own reach."

"What?"

"The noise among the apprentices of the Sorcerers' Guild is that you made a very favorable impression on Guildmaster Whetstone, during a particular session of Parliament. It would be surprising if he did not know something about this Archreader. And—for Brook's sake—he might be willing to share it."

"That is an excellent thought," Varic said. "Remind me to buy you lunch sometime."

"You may be assured of it."

Varic picked up the map again. Winterhill had something he wanted to say and was not saying. Varic put the map down and folded his hands.

Winterhill gave a small nod and said, "I am about to put my neck in a noose, which my lord will be aware I do not do just every day."

"Then I shall not interfere."

"You're talking about this fair as you used to speak of the new Constitution. I am not suggesting that you have set that project aside—that would be noosing and throat-slitting—but it has been a little time since you have shown an eagerness for, well, anything."

"Has it?"

Winterhill counted on his fingers. "Noose, knife, leap from a precipice . . . At Equinoctials, you did show feelings toward your Coron."

"None of us are quite ourselves at the House."

"I'll count that as a touch, since you did not deny that she *is* 'your Coron.'"

"I have to deny it every time I enter Parliament House. Now it is only by omission. Do not be the cause of my having to make a public denial, or you can add 'walks in front of motive' to your list."

"I am paid for discretion, my lord," Winterhill said, and Varic could hear suppressed but real hurt and anger in it. He thought to apologize, but Winterhill went on:

"The point of a Coron's Fool," Winterhill said, his voice calm again but acute as a stylet dagger, "is to tell the truth when no one else will. We have an Ironway system, built and maintained at public expense for the benefit of all. My lord Varic can reach the Great Rogue Hills in eight to nine days. The end of the trip is a long ride, but the Palion Silvern would never allow my lord to ride it alone. My lord might also wish to break his journey at Strange House."

"You forget Brook."

"I do not. Take him to the House. If a sleeper won't serve, arrange a special coach—a special train. I know a Palion's conseil who can smooth the rails. Take the nurse with you, and by all means take Clarity; she can show Strange's people how to care for Brook, and they can give her a few hours' rest from doing it."

"And Trevan Dain?"

"He is a loyal soldier and will go where he is commanded. But he can make sure Brook's house is occupied—and I do not think it would be wise, and certainly not kind, to leave Linnet alone."

"You watch people very carefully."

"It's a survival trait." Winterhill took off his hat and waved it like a jester's taddelix, making a clicking noise in his throat.

For the first time today, Varic's head had ceased to ache. "Dr. Soonest did not train any fools."

"I beg to differ, my lord Coron. Capsanjangle is as we speak entertaining the crowned heads of Alinsea, and living better than a Duke doing it. The doctor had many gifts, but perhaps his finest was to see what each of his children could do, and to gentle their way toward it regardless of fashions or frowning souls. Even unto the least of us."

"I would like to have known him."

"You have paid for his work to go on. But I have another question, which may be even more suicidal than the last."

"We can only die once."

"I have reason to believe otherwise, but let it pass. What, exactly, is it about Corons and the one thing people do that is older than killing? I mean, there are plenty of tales about choosing the wrong partner, but anyone old enough to feel the pull can figure out why you're not supposed to dip your lord's duckie without express prior consent from all concerned. And almost all the stories have an ending in which all is forgiven, even if a bit of this and that has been spilled on the way. And certainly storybook Corons fall in love, almost as often as strolling tinkers with hearts of solder fall for them. But not for two Corons. There it's death if you're lucky, and death, war, and ruin if you're not. Why should that be, my lord?"

"Do you want the reason, or the true reason?"

"May I have both? It's a cold, dark day."

"You may. Let's sit on the ground and pretend there's a fire." They crouched on the blanket, and Varic said, "Remember that, before Redlance, Corons thought of themselves as kings in their own countries, and in practice some of them were. If you had a strong army, and your neighbor Coron had a weak one, very soon you might have a larger Coronage and a dead neighbor. But doing it that way meant you had to fight, and that's a story that always has two endings. Even success would eventually inspire your surviving neighbors to join forces and redraw the map.

"But suppose there were two neighbor Corons and one heir between them? Or two heirs with different ideas of dividing the inheritance? Wanting and not having are alike good cause for war.

"That wasn't good enough, of course. Land and power are things everyone believes they know. So legends were made up about how supernatural vengeance would fall on Corons who joined their lands, and there were some actual wars, though none of them had ghosts or Demons fighting on either side."

Winterhill nodded. "And what is the real reason?"

"Let me see if I can put it briefly. You have two women before you, and you can't have both. We won't ask why that should be. Both make you very happy and are made happy in return. One is a Coron—or a Duchess, if you like—and the other grew up on the streets, a stone-corner rogue same as you, but now is just as wealthy as the Coron. Whom do you go with?"

"The Duchess was misfortunate," Winterhill said.

"It's a misfortunate world."

"What the story would have me say is, because my language and manners and general knowledge of the world are going to sit better with the street maiden, because we have the same instincts, and because if we were to fall in love at all, it would be because we were thrown together by matching circumstances, that I would, then, follow her."

"That is how stories seem to go," Varic said.

"Stories are about what we ought to be, not what we are. Stories never say that the ways of our kind lead to mistrust, that our lives require that we constantly be something other than we would wish to be, just to get from day until night and back again. I understand the tale now, brother, and you have brought me to my own understanding, just as Strange would. Should there be anything within that understanding you and my lady Longlight have need of, you would honor me to command it; and I trust you will not take it ill if I say a prayer for both your spirits."

"It can do us no harm." Varic rummaged in the lunch hamper, found the last of the apple cake, and broke it to share with Winterhill. "I do not think that anyone, Coron or citizen, would care in the slightest about what Longlight and I did, if they were absolutely certain that it would end in tears and death. It's the possibility of nothing happening—that all the stories mean nothing—that frightens people."

Winterhill said quietly, "I'm sorry I made you angry."

"I'm not angry with you."

"I know that."

The cab pulled up on the road, very loud in the still afternoon. They put the debris of lunch in the hamper. Varic looked around the stretch of bog again. "One of the first things we shall need here," he said, "is rubbish collection."

They boarded the cab. Winterhill got off at the docks, and Varic went home and gave the driver his gratuity.

He entered the house, hung his coat and hat, and went straight to the secretary desk, to draft a letter to Master Whetstone.

Midden had neatly stacked the day's post on the desk. There

was a large, thick, heavy envelope on the bottom of the pile. Varic moved the letters out of the way and smiled to see the printing there.

He wrote and sealed the Guildmaster's letter quickly; it was straightforward enough, and the forms came automatically to him. From time to time he glanced at the envelope and smiled again.

It would call for a letter as well, but that one would take some care in the writing.

❧

Parliament House was all but deserted on Shineday. Almost any lengths might be resorted to, to avoid weekend sessions. The various public offices—Records, Taxes, Licenses—kept small staffs in case of dire need, and there were usually a few nonresident Lords of all three branches using the visitants' offices as free hotel space.

Birch had pointed out to Varic the advantages of looking in on such guests. They were almost always strangers in the City, and quite lonely, and they might be poor Corons (or sorcerers or priests), but they had the same vote as anyone else. Taking a visitant to a pleasant dinner or a play might tip a decision or two.

Varic had asked Master Whetstone to meet him here on this day, because it would be official, but quiet.

The bell on Varic's office door rang at a few minimi past eleven. Whetstone bowed, and said, "Well met, milord," with a faint wheeze. "The floors here . . . are quite a distance apart."

"The building is sometimes described as 'a work of giants,'" Varic said. "The public lift doesn't run on weekends. There's a service lift, but it's tucked in the back. Will it please you come in? I can have the porter bring some things."

As he spoke, he heard Leyva's voice from down the hall. "My lord Coron," she said. "And my lord Guildmaster. Two of you. That's just what we need. Come with me, please."

Whetstone glanced at Varic, who shrugged. "Well, it is Shineday," Whetstone said, and they followed her down the stairs. Varic was careful of his steps, and Whetstone breathed hard again, though Leyva did not seem to feel any strain at all on the extremely grand staircase.

Leyva led the party to one of the conference rooms, where Westwind, the Coron Blooms, was waiting. He looked terribly nervous.

Leyva said, "Does this make your count?"

Westwind said, "It will do," bowed slightly to the other Coron and the Guildmaster, and gestured them inside.

The room was big enough to seat fifty, but there were only eleven present; seated at the front were two hall maids, a handyman with his toolbox, and a stable groom. At the front, a young man and woman were standing before Lady Spiritual Curtmantle. It was suddenly obvious what they had all been drafted for.

The couple were Westwind's nephew, who worked as a clerk in the Records Office, and the quite young Lady Maris, who had come into the Coronage of Malentaye only a few months earlier.

Whetstone looked around and said, "Four Lords from all three branches. If this isn't legal, I don't know what is." Then he rose, and went to Leyva. Politely, he said, "I was well acquainted with the lady's father. May I stand for him?" Leyva smiled and went to sit by Varic. Westwind stood with the young man. Curtmantle looked around the room and said, "As we now have sufficient witnesses under the laws of the groom's Coronage for this service, I shall be pleased to proceed."

The priest was not known for prolonged oratory. She kept a dignified pace, and the couple were wed after a quarter of an hour. Leyva gave a hand signal, and a butler and a tired-looking pastry cook brought in wine and a decorated cake.

Varic and Whetstone joined in the celebration and congratulated the couple, who seemed very happy and more than a little eager to be gone. Coron Westwind, now that the ceremony was over, seemed fretful at the prospect of filling his nephew's position and said something distracted about the new groom remaining in his office—"At a significant promotion, of course."

Lady Maris said, "He is going to be quite busy enough. But do not worry, Uncle. I have seen enough not to let the Seat go empty." She turned suddenly to Varic. "Thank you for your attendance, milord. And I would like to ask you as one well settled in the City: What would be your view of our staying here and appointing a voice at home?"

"It would be unreasonable for me to speak ill of the practice." Maris smiled, and Varic said, "From what I know of your country, I imagine you would be much happier at home. You are an overnight away by Ironway, and a few instanti by wire. Pardon me if I have forgotten—was not Sulien your father's earlier proxy, and is she not still at the court?"

"She is," Maris said, "and I will certainly ask her. I think she misses the City. Thank you, milord."

"My lady."

The party dispersed, and Varic and Whetstone followed Leyva through high-ceilinged corridors to the service lift. It was rather a long walk compared to the stairway, but it was horizontal. When they were back at Varic's office, Leyva brought out tea and cheese with biscuits—"Enough cake, I think"—and left them alone.

Whetstone said, "You said you wished to ask my advice on a professional matter. I hardly ever have it asked on anything else, but do go ahead."

Varic explained about the Archreader Shandrey and the possibility of her reading for Brook.

"I see," Whetstone said, quietly. "What we say here is, of course, private."

"Thank you, milord."

"The Archana are not all equal, though we don't usually put it that way. It's obvious to most people that, say, an Armiger or an Ironhand isn't the first choice for healing, any more than they would expect a Chirurgeon to make armor or forge metal. The creative Crafts are the most versatile—but of course, you are well acquainted with the Master Agate."

"That is so."

"At another time we must speak of her," Whetstone said. "But you are aware that her strength is her limitation. I can't say definitely that an Archreader could not contact a sleeping mind, but it sounds wrong to me. At best, I would have to think of it as divination, and the Lescorial Guilds do not even recognize that as an Archanum. Nor, I should add, do the Ferangarder Guilds."

"And the Institut Preuszen?"

"Is a justly famous center for medical study, not a sorcerous institution." He chuckled. "But if we don't look over walls sometimes, we see nothing." Then, more seriously, he said, "I am sure you are aware that, in such cases as my lord Brook's, an Archempathic is often called in?"

"So I have been told."

The Guildmaster said gently, "Let me see if I can reason it through. You don't want Brook's mind intruded upon."

"I am sure that seems quite foolish."

"No, it doesn't. The Archana are hard, but most of them have definable rules—an Armiger's reach, an Archpoet's metrics. Entering minds is as different as minds are, and sometimes the minds strike back at an intruder. People think of it as like the conseil, but they have the most rules and limits of all, not least that their particular sorcery is, with very little exception, unshared. I can quite easily understand not wanting to conduct such an experiment with a dear friend, in anything but the most extreme conditions."

Varic said, "Brook's condition is not yet at that point, though he cannot remain as he is forever. And there is always the possibility of a crisis."

Whetstone nodded. "We have both been in Parliament long enough to know that, about some things, we cannot continue to do nothing. Particularly when all of the choices are hard.

"I am not, of course, the National Guildmaster at this time. But the Lystourel Master, along with some others—Ascorel, naturally, Port Rose, Loftgarden, and so on—are kept informed of matters significant to the Craft. Just as some Corons have a wider reach than others."

Varic nodded.

"I am in possession of a report on Archreader Shandrey's work. Unfortunately, it does not have any solid conclusions about her rate of success. Now, that is not any kind of a secret; 'There's a sorcerer doing something, and nobody knows if it works' is said all the time. The fact that there is a formal report—and its sources—are another matter. I'm sure you follow."

"I do."

"You have more than a little understanding of sorcery, and you know that what we do is uncertain. Let me tell you a thing I believe you'll understand. From my information, some of the doctors at Preuszen are trying to develop an exact philosophy of sorcery. The Pandekts tried that for generations and gave up. The Quercians tried it, and some of their failures are still infamous. I believe that the Ferangarders are falling into the same error. Not that we all don't lean that way. We can build a steam boiler that, with a little care, will do just what it's supposed to—and when one does blow up, it's almost always because some human being mishandled it. Someday sorcery may be engineering rather than craft, but I don't think it will happen in my time." He laughed, without bitterness. "Of course, we all know that sorcerers all live forever."

"True enough," Varic said.

"Forgive me," Whetstone said at once. "I should have recalled that you are close to Strange. Can you tell me how he is keeping?"

"He has said he believes his time is ending. That, too, is in confidence."

"Of course. Remember me to him when you can. Many of us owe him a great deal."

Varic nodded.

"As I say, there is nothing very definite in our report on the Archreader. But guilds by their nature see things from a particular angle. I propose to send you a copy, without comments. Tell me what you see in it. Perhaps you'll find something useful about Brook's situation; if not, none of us has lost anything. Of course, things being what they are, your copy will not exist."

"Of course. I would appreciate that very much."

"Then I will say good afternoon, and thank you for the adventure. If I had spent a usual dozy Shineday, I should have missed the wedding."

Silvern rolled out of bed, took a moment to orient himself to the room, then walked to the bathroom, struck the gaslight, and prepared to shower. The water was more than tepid but less than hot; Longlight had apologized at least twice for that, but had finally understood that he had done far more bathing in streams and from icy buckets than under Strange House's worthy piping.

The window was still dark. They were going on a long ride, down the Western coast to collect the man who would make the lucives for Silvern's land survey.

He dressed in riding trousers and a wool shirt, pulled on his boots and followed the winding path through Longlight's complicated manor toward the dining room. Partway along he was distracted by a museum-grade crossbow, hanging near a breastplate in the Quercian style. After a few minimi of inspection, he saw that it actually was from the Empire, and he found the hole where an arrow had gone into the legionary's liver.

—*You are very predictable in the morning.*

"I suppose I am getting old," he said aloud to Edaire.

—*You are looking at a prize someone took off a dead soldier a thousand or more years ago, and you feel old.*

"Point and concetta," he said, and then silently, *Where are you?*

—*About an hour away from the City. If I can persuade them to come out, I want to give Varic and Brook's caregivers dinner at the Terminus dining room.*

—*Even Linnet?*

—*Especially Linnet. Their cooking may be no better than his, but he shouldn't have to do all the sweating.*

—*Who will stay with Brook?*

—*I made a plan with Winterhill the last time I was through. In secret, so no one could find an excuse. He'll watch Brook, and we'll bring him a late supper.*

—*I suppose Winterhill is used to late suppers.*

—*I think Winterhill has missed more meals than any five of the rest of us. But yes, I love you.*

—You make me mindful of others, and I love you.

—Give my best to Longlight. I'm nearly to the yards. Go and eat, and we will talk later.

He went on to the dining room. Longlight was alone there, in a side-buttoned blue shirt and black riding trousers, with a mutton chop and plenty of bacon and muffins. There was tea to the side, but she was drinking dark beer. As Silvern sat down, she said, "It's five hours each way, and we'll only have saddle-bags to dine from."

She pushed a sheet of paper toward him. He read the neat handwriting:

MIDNIGHT

STATION 028 TO STATION 002

FORECAST FOR NORTH COAST ROAD

DAWN TO MIDDAY: CLEAR

MIDDAY TO SUNSET: GATHERING CLOUDS, RAIN NOT LIKELY

AFTER SUNSET: SMALL CHANCE RAIN

ALECTI SHOULD DRESS WARM

Silvern said, "I take it there is more to this than the weather report."

"Ventry and my secretary have been a pair for a little more than two years now. It's no secret, but you shouldn't be surprised."

"Do they see one another often?"

"When they can. Ventry mostly lives at the weather station, so any company is welcome. The truth is that I can't spare Alecti very often, which rather makes me the villain. Nobody else will say that, of course."

"I appreciate being told."

"Five hours used to seem like a long separation to me. I suppose people learn better."

"I suppose people do," Silvern said, and heard *Walk lightly* inside his head.

⟨⟨⟨⟩⟩⟩

They went down to the stables, where their horses were already saddled. They were traveling light, with a little trail food and a change of clothes if the weather forced them to stay at the station overnight. There would be plenty of space for Ventry's camera and plates without stressing the horses.

Besides Longlight and himself, Alecti, and a spare horse for Ventry, two guardsmen were in the company. Alecti arrived in tan trousers and boots and a dark green hunter's coat, not unlike one Silvern owned, though hers was heavier and had fur at the cuffs and a broad collar that could be turned up high. Her red hair spilled over it to striking effect, and she had a small green cap with a brim tilted on top.

"Good morning, my lady," she said in a modest voice. "And good morning, Palion."

They greeted her in return, and the party set off. As they passed through the town—Silvern had learned its name was Fairport, which seemed reasonable enough given the coast around it—people paused to wave and nod, and Longlight returned the gestures.

They went down the hedge-lined passage they had entered through, and then turned to the right, onto the approach to the Great Coast Road.

It had been a highway for seven hundred years, since Queen Lucie of the Westrene decided to bring her realm together with roads. She had Alinsever ancestry, and the typically Alinsever idea of improving trade had not gone well with her inland Corons, but the coastal lands—which had long been without contact with each other, and overly dependent on their eastern neighbors—set to work. The job outlasted many monarchs, but the road finally reached from warm, green Azaphel in the Southwest to the plainly put Northpoint, farther north even than Corvaric, where the world stopped.

They went through a long notch that had clearly been hand-cut through the rock, and saw the sea.

It was a good fifty steps below them, and the road was climbing ahead. The drop was interrupted by stone outcrops and pinnacles. Longlight gestured to the left, and Silvern saw a light tower to warn ships. There was in fact no safe anchorage between Fairport and a pair of trading towns near the south edge of Longlight's land, though as always there were places where smugglers and pirates might hide. It was often an advantage for such places to be unreachable from landward.

The edge was comfortably far away, ten to twenty steps. He had been told that it came closer at a few points, but this wasn't the Perilous Coast Road of gluebacks and stage thrillers; it had been built understanding that it would be used, by day and dark, often by people in a hurry.

From this height, Silvern could actually see the north coast of the next Coronage down; it extended almost due west for perhaps ten milae.

"That would be Berowne?" he asked Longlight.

"Yes. The Coron there was a friend of my father's; I owe him a visit soon. If it were a clear night, you could see Rowney light out at the end of land."

"How much night travel is there on the road?"

"Are you beginning your survey?"

"No point in waiting."

"A fair amount up here and in the south. Between it's mainly mail and messengers. We patrol it, and there isn't much danger—a highwayman would have a long ride to any safety. On full-moon nights, it can be quite a beautiful trip."

She was suddenly quiet.

—*What do you think she is thinking of, o man? You thought of me, after all.*

—*And do you think—*

—*I know her no better than you. And you recall that the last time Varic met a woman at Strange House who engaged his mind and heart together, it did not end well. It is much too soon to know about this, and the difficulties are obvious even to us, but it is not wrong to hope. Now, my train is arriving at the Terminus, and I shall be busy. I will speak to you over dinner, if our plans go well. And you must tell me about the weatherman.*

By midday they had met a dozen small groups of travelers on horseback, two pairs of Coronal guardsmen on patrol, and three donkey carts loaded with goods. They passed signs indicating the way to several towns, and two small villages that were visible from the road; the sound of smithing and the smell of cooking food carried to them.

At last there was a point where the cliff thrust out, a half circle a hundred and fifty steps across. There was a cluster of black buildings, some with towers, one with a circular dome. Framework towers of wood and iron held wind gauges and other instruments. A few sheep were grazing around them.

An elderly man came out to meet them. He said his name was Archilaos—and he looked as if he could have been a Pandektine sage—and led them to the stable, which could have housed twenty mounts and a few carriages, but at present had one spare horse for a patrolman, one for a dispatch rider, and a dozy mule. The guardsmen stayed behind at an offer of lunch and beer, and Longlight, Silvern, and Alecti went through a covered passage into the next building.

They entered a room lined with weather and navigational instruments, cased in wood and brass and glass. There were wall maps, of the locality, the Coronage, the region, the Western coast, and the whole of Lescoray, covered with symbols that Silvern recognized but couldn't easily interpret without a chart. In the corner was a large, freestanding, high-precision clock with faces for times across Lescoray and in great cities abroad, moon phase, and several that he guessed were astronomical indicators.

Alecti said, "Hello!" loudly and clearly. It was the first word Silvern had heard her speak since they had left the town.

A man entered. He was nearly as tall as Silvern, but bony and thin. That was easy to see, since he was wearing a tan leather vest without a shirt beneath, along with loose leather trousers and soft, well-worn boots.

He bowed to Longlight. "My lady."

She said, "Ventry, please you meet Silvern, Palion and Armiger, and my guest for the season. Silvern, I would have you know Ventry, chief weathermaster for this Coronage and the five surrounding."

"Most pleased, Palion," Ventry said, in a clear and musical voice. His face was sharp-featured but pleasantly smiling; his long brown hair was tied in a queue that fell over his shoulder and nearly to his waist. There, tools and keys hung from a wide black belt.

"Well," Longlight said, "do go on."

Ventry spread his arms wide, and Alecti ran from the back of the room straight into them, to be embraced and picked quite off her feet. Ventry might be thin, but he was clearly not weak. Alecti kissed him, and then rested her head on his shoulder. Then he put her down, took her hand, and said, "My lady, there is a small but real chance of rain before sunset. It should be clear tomorrow. If you wish to wait the night."

Longlight said, "Silvern?"

"I am at my lady's service."

She nodded, apparently deep in thought, and then said, "I think we will risk the rain. Your hospitality is always appreciated, Ventry, but it can be rather basic."

Ventry laughed, said to Silvern, "My lady means that the bathwater here is colder than she has at home. Though there is a very good inn in the town just over the rise, and this trip my lady's party is small enough for them to accommodate. Does that change your mind?"

"If you are ready to go, we will go."

"A few plates still to pack. Alecti and I will be just a few minimi. Please, Palion, examine anything that interests you; I do ask that you not disturb the instruments."

"Of course. Thank you."

He followed the couple into the next room, where there were five brass-cornered wooden cases waiting. Two were still open, and Ventry and Alecti began placing paper envelopes and small vials of chemicals into them.

This room was a lucivitry studio, with equipment in racks and on tables. It was remarkably neat; Silvern had seen such places that looked like an accident in a glassblower's shop.

The walls were nearly covered with lucives, most a span or so square, but some enlarged to nearly a step across. The pride of place belonged to an astonishing picture, showing the coast of Berowne—the lighthouse visible at the right—illuminated by a stroke of lightning like a huge tree, trunked and many-branched.

Silvern hesitated, not wanting to interrupt, but finally said, "Did you make this?"

"Ah. Yes. Took a lot of glass to get that. We're trying to learn more about lightning, for reasons I'm sure are obvious. Haven't gotten very far, I'm afraid. We're sure it's electrical fluid, not that we know everything about that. People get hurt, and sometimes killed, trying to find out."

Alecti paused in her work.

"My very dear, when you first met me you knew I did not have the sense to come in from the rain. Hm, put that one there."

They went back to filling the cases, and Silvern looked over the lucives. There were more of lightning, and storms, complex cloud formations, waterspouts. Others showed off the scenery of the region, sharp but beautiful. One, also enlarged, was of Longlight's manor house, and somehow it managed to make it look like a storybook castle, and not a series of boxes tumbling down a slope. Silvern was quite sure he had the right associate for the task.

And he looked for a picture of Alecti, but there were none here. He supposed they would be elsewhere, and felt a little ashamed at the curiosity. He hoped Edaire's mind was busy.

The last box was closed. They were not much bigger than full saddlebags and had leather straps to be mounted on a saddle. Ventry explained that only one box held the camera, another carrying a folding support, spare lenses, and other accessories. Three were taken up with plates and chemicals.

"So they're glass?"

"Not these. We can get glass in Fairport or other large towns, or order it by express in a few days. These are colloidal plates, which are new; they're chemically made, and slightly flexible. Not as sharp an image as glass, so we'll certainly carry some of that, but they will do for the majority of landscape work. And they don't break. We'll make our prints at the manor or back here."

As they carried the boxes back through the instrument room, a woman in a black dress came hurrying in the back door. She carried a large and apparently heavy woven basket.

"I'm terribly sorry to be late," she said. "You haven't been waiting?"

"Not at all. And you know where everything is anyway. My lady, you will recall Marcayl?"

"Of course."

"Palion Silvern, this is Archwind Marcayl, my first assistant. She'll be running the station while I'm away."

The woman looked nervously at Silvern, and said, "Ventry speaks too well of me, honored. I am barely a novice of the Craft, and I'm afraid I have learned too much about weather to want to tamper with it. But I cannot help my Archanum."

"None of us can," Silvern said gently. Marcayl's eyes widened—Silvern felt power touch power—and then she nodded and turned. "Hello, Alecti."

"Hello, Marcayl." She put down her box and embraced the other woman. "You'll 'style Ventry every few days? I know he's not at all worried about you, but he'll be fretting for his barometers in half a day."

"I will, of course. And—" She indicated the basket. "I brought you some lunch from the inn. If you have the time."

Everyone in the room looked at Longlight, who said, "Perhaps I have been a bit single-minded. And it is going to be a long time to supper."

There was a large room with a broad table and a window looking south along the coast. Ventry brought in Archilaos and the guardsmen, and they dined on lamb pie, paper-thin fried potatoes, and Archilaos's beer, nearly black, and delicious. "It's not that strong," Archilaos said. "Most of our guests are travelers, so it's just strength for the journey."

Ventry disappeared for a moment after dinner and returned wearing a wide-brimmed hat, and a linen shirt under his vest. The shirt had an open drawstring collar and was obviously not for warmth.

They loaded the horses, Ventry gave a few final instructions to Marcayl, and the party started north. Longlight and Alecti rode in front, the guards between, and Silvern and Ventry at the rear.

"If I may ask," Silvern said, "do you just not feel the cold, or are you proof against it?"

"Despite what Alecti may tell you, I've never tested it to the limits. I'm made of water like all of us, so I suppose it could freeze. I'm hot in what most people consider a cool room. I do always go decently covered in my lady's house, but don't look for furs."

"Is this common in your family?"

"Not that I know of. D'you seil my name?"

"No."

"It's local. A ventry wind is a northern gale along this coast. I gather I was named when I was a few months along and kept kicking off the blankets. The word originally meant an open window. Westrene is a fascinating speech."

"You don't mind my asking."

"Of course not. I like knowing things, and I'm not comfortable with souls who don't. Let me ask you something: Do you know more people who don't mind the cold?"

"They're born from time to time in Bryna Kóly, and there it tends to run in families. They're called *melegem vani,* and they have a reputation for becoming great heroes. Except for the few who become great villains."

"Legends don't differ much, do they?"

"Not in our half of the world. Around the other side, I'm told, some things vary a great deal."

"I'd like to go see that. I've been told that in Shayon-Shi they have sea waves that can submerge an island, or wipe out a coastal city."

"You might not see anything else after that."

"It wouldn't matter, if they found my camera and plates. Don't tell Alecti I said that."

"Of course."

"She isn't easily frightened, you understand. I suspect if we were both there, watching the wave, she'd be preparing the next plate and slipping the last one into a waterproof bag, with the address of the Lescorial Weather Society on the outside and adequate postage." He paused, looked ahead at Alecti's back, and then said quietly, "Am I saying too much? I'm not all alone at the station—there's Archilaos, and Marcayl, and people from the town dropping in for a crop forecast and a cup of tea, and all manner of travelers—but there are long stretches with no one to talk to. Do you know that?"

"Yes," Silvern said, and raised his ring. "Though my companion and I are conseil. So most of the time there is someone to listen."

"How long?"

"Eight years. We were together for two years before."

Quite softly, Ventry said, "Alecti and I spoke of that. As you have seen, our work separates us."

"We are the same way." Silvern explained about Edaire's job.

"I should like to meet her. Though the rails will be a long time bringing her here."

"You must know that's one of the things you and I will be looking at."

"Of course. And all it would take is a few barrels of powder at Wander's Gate. But I would not say that loud in this country." He pointed ahead and to the right, where a weed-grown path branched from the road. "Blasting powder is a great shortener of ways. This road is nearly a fifth shorter than when it was first completed. And as for the Gate, the Quercians had very strong ideas about roads. I think that if Wander had lost, they would have straightened it. They would have used axes and wedges, but everyone knows they moved around a lot of stone."

"Some people say that if the Empire had had guns, they would still be here."

"Ah, but you are in the Northwest," Ventry said cheerfully. "If they had had guns, then the first time a soldier dozed at his post we would have had them."

CHAPTER 8

There were Coronages that banned dueling. His was not one of them, though the woodcutters and fishermen he formally ruled did not have much use for it. There was a vague pattern of Old Ways against New Ways, stasis opposed to change, but it was ultimately a Coron's choice, adjusted by whoever that Coron listened to. There were three formal Anti-Dueling Societies in Lystourel alone. The subject had of course come up in Constitutional discussions.

"There are areas," Brook had said, "in which one changes the law and hopes that society will follow. By granting the national government the explicit right to raise an army, we cannot suppose that the Coronal and Householder armed companies, with their splendid uniforms and idiosyncrasies of drill, will suddenly disband, but we may hope that they will become more ceremonial and less warlike, and in the end will resolve into local police, drinking societies, and groups of battleboard players.

"In other areas, however, it is necessary that the society should first decide it can do without a thing, and then cast it into illegality. Dueling is one of those things. As long as men and women believe honor compels them to fight, they will fight. As long as people consider that the winner of a duel has done a mildly noble thing by risking his life for an issue, the survivors—who are, after all, the only ones we can prosecute—will be acquitted. An unenforced law invites its breakage. An unenforceable law practically compels it. And since practically no one enters such an affair with the intent to lose, the best we could hope for is that the pool of combatants would, by the mathematics of population, control itself."

"And when will that change?" Varic had said, knowing the answer perfectly well but wanting to hear Brook state it.

"Either when honor has so much decayed that people find dying for it inappropriate or when it advances to the point that killing for it is seen as the bully's way of proving he is right after all. I don't look for either in my lifetime, but you may see the day."

There did not seem much chance of it.

⚮

"The stakes are high enough when one has to steal one's dinner," Winterhill said, entirely without inflection.

"That is of interest as well," Varic said. "Because people have had to steal their bread for as long as there has been bread to steal, no doubt the third loaf ever baked vanished when the baker turned away. It is a truth more important than any tablet of laws."

Editor's Note

Here the manuscript breaks off.

John M. Ford passed away suddenly on the night of September 24, 2006. He had delivered most of this text in finished form, but the fragment of chapter 8 had not been revised.

We do not know exactly how he intended to end this novel, or the series of books he planned to write to follow it. But we have a hint of where the characters are going, in the remaining sonnets written to be the epigraphs of the series.

III: Complex Gardens

Bright passion's petals make it hard to see
That all our individuated loves
Are single blooms in complex gardens. We
Are lost too easily in forests of
Fantastic beasts with topiary smiles,
Or flytraps sweet with promises and glue.
The dark beneath the greenery beguiles,
And sense is drowned in nectar, till bamboo,
With just a whisper of insidious shoot,
Has pricked into the heart. Perhaps we ought
Step back to see the pattern in the root,
Or think, and not be frightened at the thought,
That love may blossom (and as always, die)
To please some unseen Gardener's heart and eye.

SONNET 2

IV: WAR BY DREAMS

There is a sort of war by glances made,
In which the tender eyes are forged to knives,
Now sheathed a blink, now nakedly displayed,
To pierce the heart, or flay the nerves alive.
War made by touch begs skill in great degree,
For touch when grossly used can only kill;
To conquer dust is bitter victory:
It is the gentlest touch that breaks the will.
Of all war, that by dreams is cruelest,
For only those who trusts and secrets keep
Are armed to land upon the shores of rest,
And raze the helpless citadel of sleep.
No truce is possible, no peace shall come
When hearts that beat together bang the drum.

SONNET 3

V: THE PUZZLE AT THE HEART

The problems only hands know how to frame,
The questions that the skin alone has heard,
We cope with in converse—but never name;
We discourse with the tongue, but not the word.
Though I'm no longer sure of your replies,
Though moans are pressed beneath an unknown load,
Thick breaths run thin, and perspiration lies.
We have to walk as though we knew the road.
Perhaps there is no way out of the knot
That fingers tie (and tighten till they bleed)
Supposing that, what I need, you do not,
Pretending what we want is what we need;
Till careless hands may tear the flesh apart,
Unraveling the puzzle at the heart.

SONNET 4

VI: HOME FROM DEATH

I do not number Death among my friends
And am not by soft silences beguiled;
Speak not to me of necessary ends:
I will not to His care be reconciled.
When I have gone (as you have known me to)
I'll not be eased (as you know I can be);
I'll lie unquiet (as you've felt me do)
And rise (as you've pretended not to see).
I know you may desert me when I wake,
With face and features much too strange to kiss;
Hearts damp or dry are liable to break.
Attraction risks repulsion. Thus it is.
Stay then, or go, but ask not where I've been
When I come home from death, and stumble in.

SONNET 5

ALTERNATE VI, WRITTEN LATER [ED.]:

VI: DEATH AND HOMEWARD

When I no longer in my flesh do dwell
When every other hunger gnaws no more
Then I shall ask whatever Time will tell,
And know at last what the charade was for.
Yet not to overreach, if there's a why
To love, red roses, chocolate, or the moon,
Beyond themselves, I'll gladly pass it by:
I'll not run out of other questions soon.
I want to know why life should so disguise
Its purposes, and fear a friendly touch;
And why we grow just old, and never wise,
And why this meat and bone should mean so much.
All this there will at last be time to learn,
When I am done with death, and homeward turn.